ALL-NEW TALES FROM THE EXPANDED AVP UNIVERSE

ALIENS VS. PREDATORS

ULTIMATE PREY

THE COMPLETE ALIEN™ LIBRARY FROM TITAN BOOKS

ALL-NEW TALES FROM THE EXPANDED AVP UNIVERSE

ALIENS VS. PREDATORS

ULTIMATE PREY

EDITED BY JONATHAN MABERRY
AND BRYAN THOMAS SCHMIDT

TITAN BOOKS

AVP: ALIENS VS. PREDATORS – ULTIMATE PREY
Print edition ISBN: 9781789097948
E-book edition ISBN: 9781789097955

Published by Titan Books
A division of Titan Publishing Group Ltd
144 Southwark St, London SE1 0UP

First edition: March 2022
10 9 8 7 6 5 4 3 2 1

A CIP catalogue record for this title is available from
the British Library.

Printed and bound by CPI Group (UK) Ltd, Croydon, CR0 4YY

Did you enjoy this book?
We love to hear from our readers. Please email us at
readerfeedback@titanemail.com or write to us at
Reader Feedback at the above address.

TITAN BOOKS.COM

CONTENTS

Dedication

From Bryan:
To Aaron Percival and Adam Zeller,
number one fans of the Expanded Universe, and
number one experts who always go above the call of duty

From Jonathan:
This one is for some dear creative friends...
Lisa Kastner, J. Dianne Dotson, Dennis Crosby,
Gaby Triana, Curtis Sponsler, Jennifer Rose,
Lynne Hansen, Jeff Strand, Veronica Calisto,
Sheldon Higdon, Giacomo Calabria,
and Simin Koernig.
And, as always, for Sara Jo...

ACKNOWLEDGEMENTS

Gratitude goes out to Aaron Percival and Adam Zeller, webmasters of AVPGalaxy.net, which is the definitive source of research online for this book and for many authors, for going above and beyond the call of duty in helping us navigate the complicated worldbuilding of the Expanded Universe. Their advice and insights were invaluable in keeping us on track.

Thanks to super-agent Sara Crowe of Pippin Properties, 20th Century Studios Franchise Management, and Titan Books—especially our editor Steve Saffel—for letting us play in this fun universe we're fans of, and to all our authors for their hard work and dedication to getting it right.

Many thanks to the legion of fans of both Predator and Alien—for enthusiastic support and nit-picky technical info.

INTRODUCTION

BY BRYAN THOMAS SCHMIDT

From the moment audiences at the fourth Seattle International Film Festival sat down on Friday May 25, 1979, for the 70mm premiere of Ridley Scott's new science fiction horror film, *Alien*, Xenomorphs and Ridley have been part of our pop culture zeitgeist. The film rolled at midnight and had audiences screaming in their seats. Ever since then, the image of someone holding their stomach and coughing has evoked new images in the public's minds. We'd never seen anything quite like aliens who used humans as incubators, and they captured our imagination in a unique way.

Predator premiered on Friday June 12, 1987, as Arnold Schwarzenegger was just becoming a household name. Armed commandos moving through a jungle was not new to us, but their opponent was. A towering alien with a horrifying face and chittering speech that had the ability to disappear and slit throats before anyone knew he was there was a sobering thought, and audiences watched with a similar mix of horror and excitement as the monster slowly picked off Schwarzenegger's team one by one.

Both films started as one-offs, but once *The Empire Strikes Back*, the hugely anticipated sequel to *Star Wars*, released in 1980, the idea of big science fiction franchises became every studio's goal, so it was no surprise when both films wound up with sequels soon thereafter. Comic books, novels, and action figures followed, and each fanbase began to grow. But it wasn't until an unknown screenwriter named Peter Briggs paired the two creatures in a spec screenplay called *The Hunt: Alien vs. Predator* that Fox started imagining combining them into a new franchise of their own. Although Briggs's script never saw the light of day, the first *Alien vs. Predator* film was released in 2004 and a sequel followed in 2007. By this time, there had been two *Predator* films and four *Alien* films, and many fans embraced the idea with great enthusiasm.

For us, combining the two seems like a no-brainer and a hell of a lot of fun. When Titan asked us to undertake the task of creating this anthology, we jumped in with both feet and took off running. The result, we hope, is a book of fun and imaginative stories by talented authors of diverse backgrounds that adds nuance to the existing milieu of *Aliens vs. Predators*, as well as introducing new settings and events that excite and thrill and scare the audience.

It is always a privilege to play in someone else's sandbox, but all the more so when you are fans, as we are of this franchise. So consider *Ultimate Prey* a love letter to our fellow fans, if you will, and we hope you find reading it as fun and fulfilling as we did in making it.

Bryan Thomas Schmidt, May 26 2021, Ottawa, Kansas

EDITOR'S FOREWORD: THE SEQUEL

BY JONATHAN MABERRY

In the editor's foreword to my 2017 anthology, *Aliens: Bug Hunt*, I wrote about how a movie projectionist buddy of mine drove with me from Philly to New York to see the world premiere of *Alien*. That was June 22, 1979—at the time of writing, forty-two years ago. Before the internet, laptops, and social media. It might as well have happened on a different planet for all that our current world resembles that one.

Eight years later, on June 12, 1987, I saw *Predator* at a movie house in Philly. One of the big old cavernous 1920s-era movie palaces. A grand old lady now down on her luck. It still drew crowds but she was past her prime.

Even so, I was in the front row of the balcony for that premiere. I was with my then-girlfriend and best friend. Oddly… both of them have since passed, which leaves me as the sole keeper of that memory. We were up there with hot buttered popcorn, big cups of sugar-laden cola, and no expectations of what we were about to experience.

We'd all seen the trailers, but more than once those coming attractions were better than the film they touted.

Not this time.

Predator was absurdly entertaining. A group of very large men with biceps and automatic weapons, chewing tobacco, and truly filthy jokes, diving deep into the jungle on a rescue mission. Even without alien hunters it would have been entertainment, though perhaps in that case the film might have remained in the zone of middle-brow testosterone movie candy.

But the story *wasn't* just guns and grunts. Instead, it spun that concept around, and that band of impossibly brawny heroes came up against something bigger, badder, and infinitely stranger than them. That elevated it on so many levels. Great script, tight and quotable dialogue, superb action, and a brand-new kind of movie monster. A *thinking* and calculating alien hunter.

The Predator—what we now know as a member of the Yautja—was not only tougher than the band of soldiers, he was more sophisticated, better equipped, and was hunting *them* for fun. What the actual hell?

There was real suspense, real nail-biting tension, and—given the body count that included notable actors from other franchises—no assurance that any of those guys, even Arnold Schwarzenegger, was getting out of there alive. I was literally on the edge of my seat during the last third of that flick.

I walked out wanting more.

When the film came out on VHS tape (ah, the '80s!) I very often watched it in a double feature with *Alien* and frequently in a triple-feature with *Aliens*. The movies, though never intended to be companion pieces, always felt right together.

For me, in particular, the best match was *Aliens* and *Predator*. A true perfect combination.

Over the years more films came out in each franchise, and I started seeing Aliens vs. Predator mashups discussed on the new internet. Then in comics. And novels.

And then films.

My two favorite action-horror-science-fiction film series had become one expanded universe. And I tip my hat to Fox for making this happen. Those cats over there really *get* why fans love their movies, and they play to our hunger for more.

While I did my *Aliens: Bug Hunt* anthology, my good buddy Bryan Thomas Schmidt was doing his own book, *Predator: If It Bleeds*. They became natural companion pieces. Bryan is—if this is possible—even more of a nerd than I am. Our love of these characters is second to none.

It's fair to say that the stars aligned to bring us together to help bring the Xenomorphs and Yautja into fresh, literary conflict. We reached out to a number of our colleagues—those we knew who (a) knew and loved the genres, and (b) could write the living hell out of a story. Those tales are included herein.

I had one additional fun moment, too. Among my favorite films of this series is *Predators* (2010). Great cast, great action, lots of twists, and it also featured an actor who would later become a dear friend—Louis Ozawa, who played the laconic Yakuza, Hanzo. I pitched the idea of writing a sequel to that movie, and his character, and we collaborated to write it together. That is also included.

So, my friends, whether you are—like me—a veteran of this ongoing conflict between monsters from other worlds; a fan of only one franchise and following that here; or totally new to either film series… you're in for a treat. A very weird treat, frequently violent, endlessly inventive, and thoroughly faithful-to-the-canon of both *Alien* and *Predator* worlds.

Buckle up, turn the page, and enjoy!

Jonathan Maberry, May 26 2021, San Diego, California

BELOW TOP SECRET

BY CHRIS RYALL

The day was going fine until April's phone died. She hoped it wasn't a sign. One of those cosmic "don't count your chickens" things, or that other axiom about assumptions.

"I charged my cell this morning," she whispered. "What the hell?"

She glanced at Brockton's face, and thought that his look of dismay was because his cell was dead, too. Which it was. But he was put off for another reason entirely.

"April, come on, we need to hurry," he said. "We have to move. It's that way."

He pulled her away from the rest of the team and pointed toward the long, low building over the bluff a few hundred yards away.

"Be *subtle* about it," he cautioned. "We don't want anyone following us."

The excursion onto the grounds here at Area 51 had gone without incident—well, beyond the suddenly non-functioning mobile devices—but the farther they drifted from the others, the more uncertain it all felt.

Brockton, though. Up until now, his certainty about things he couldn't possibly know for sure had a kind of charm to them, but now April wasn't as sold on his bravado. As they approached the building in question, he started to reveal new information that she found quite disconcerting. She looked back at the rest of the large group. Not one of them was following yet. They all continued down the road toward the military installation itself. Which Brockton said made sense as a destination for anyone who didn't know what *he* knew.

It also meant they were fully exposed, walking on the road toward a base no doubt packed with military forces and other security. But the broader plan for the day was to get arrested and force the base to acknowledge there were strange goings-on here.

Brockton had suggested to her that they should try to enter a building that was much closer to the gate they'd just breached, and that sounded smart. It would allow them to feasibly check things out and then leave before they found themselves zip-tied and under arrest. With black bags over their heads and a one-way ticket to a black site.

But once Brockton started talking about the limited time left for them to get into this building before it was too late, April began reassessing her willingness to just accept whatever he said.

Still, he was right about one thing, she mused. He could *indeed* get them into the building.

The front of the building had no windows, just a set of double doors that looked impregnable. The lock contained a digital keypad, but Brockton simply pulled up his right sleeve and copied a number he'd written on his forearm, typing it into the keypad.

The door opened.

Brockton looked at April and grinned. "See? My source knew what they were talking about." But April thought he looked a little too relieved when he said it, as if he was surprised it actually worked.

"Funny how you never mentioned a source before," April said. "By which I mean, this isn't funny at all. We just went from breaking and entering a base to try to force freedom of information to, well, a full-on B&E of a military outpost."

He took a few steps deeper into the building. She followed, and they stood in what looked like the waiting area of a typical—though unoccupied—office building. "It won't matter," he said, "not if we hurry. If the rest of what my guy told me is also true, we're on the cusp of breaking this thing wide open. I didn't want to freak you out before but… I've been talking to someone who works here. At the base. The first guy since maybe Bob Lazar to really admit that, and he told *me*."

"Really?" asked April. "Why would he just confide in you?"

"Well," Brockton said, sheepishly, "we may have had a transaction. A number of them, really."

"Shit," muttered April. "You *bought* information from a stranger?"

"No, it's cool. Look, April, this is a guy I came across online a few years ago, and I've been building up trust and gaining his confidence and… well, sure, sending him money. Maybe a lot of it. In regular installments. But not all or even most of it. He knows we have to get in, get the goods, get out safely, and then he gets the bulk of it. Give me some credit here."

April snorted. "Okay… greed and a penalty if he fucks us. That makes a bit more sense."

Brockton took a few steps deeper into the office space. Against her better judgment once again, so did April. "Once this excursion got set, he said it was finally time for the world to know what goes on here, and he gave me that code."

"You mean, you *bought* that code."

"Whatever. It was money my parents gave me for college, so it was mine to spend how I wanted. And what better education than this?"

April groaned.

Brockton leaned close and lowered his voice even more. "He told me another thing, April."

"Oh, I can't wait for this," she said.

"This building… it's sitting over the *real* base."

"Oh, come on…"

"And," he said, "he told me how we can get down there."

"I—" she began, but then froze. There was a noise outside. She peered through the glass door and saw a vehicle coming their way, pulling a dust plume behind it.

"Brockton," she said quickly, "I don't quite know what to say to any of this, but if you have a plan, we better go *now*."

"That's what I was trying to tell you…"

He took her hand and they hurried deeper into the deserted office. April thought she heard the outside door open behind them.

"If my guy wasn't lying," Brockton said as they rounded a corner, "then it should be right… *whoa*. Here it is."

They approached an elevator bank. April felt a chill—why did a one-story building built on top of sand and dirt have an elevator?

The doors to the elevator stood open, but inside it was dark. Still, Brockton directed her forward and they stepped into it.

"Brockton…"

Inside, a control panel contained only a grid of sixty-four buttons without numbers on them. The buttons alternated between black and white. It looked more like some kind of game than it did an elevator control panel.

Brockton pushed eight of them in sequence. Nothing happened. April heard heavy footsteps and voices from down the hall.

This was all too much. She wanted out. "Brockton, stop. I don't want to do this."

"Come on," Brockton growled as he kept stabbing the buttons in a sequence once again.

"This isn't fun anymore," said April.

"Well, we're here now," he growled. "Let me work, will you? Just standing here and waiting to get caught—or shot— isn't fun, either. We've come this far and—*bingo*." The elevator lights abruptly came on, and they could hear the motor powering up. "Now, we've got nowhere to go but *down*."

He was so right about that.

———

As the elevator descended, April found herself taking a long, cold look at how the hell she got here.

She'd started out wanting to improve her social life—or at least her social-*media* life—and had ended up on this possibly ruinous path. Only a month ago, she'd let herself get led down a new online rabbit hole. She saw some friends share a group that consisted of people planning to make an excursion onto the grounds at the legendarily secretive military base located at Area 51 in Nevada. April was intrigued, mostly because she saw that hundreds of people had already clicked, "Will attend." And she happened to know one of them, a friend of a friend named Brockton. Brockton, who owned a car with air conditioning and offered to drive her through the desert to attend this event. She accepted.

April didn't particularly believe in the existence of UFOs. Really, she didn't think about them either way. Following conspiracy theories seemed to be the province of, mostly, underemployed men. But the event promised a massive turnout, so why not? Surely she could get a few interesting pictures and a fun story to tell. Enough to ensure another weekend of social media "likes," anyway.

On the drive out, Brockton proved his conspiracy-nut bona fides by showing her all the *proof* of aliens he had on his phone. Lo-res photos and grainy videos, mostly.

He also convinced her there wouldn't be any real price to pay for the planned excursion. "That's why we made it public, to warn them in advance," he said. "Besides, I have it on good authority that we'll be able to get full access to the base that day. I have it all covered."

The morning felt full of promise. They joined others at the agreed-upon meeting place, in front of Rachel, Nevada's famous Ale-E-Inn. The buzz was electric, and infectious even to a non-believer ("non-*carer*" was more accurate, she had told Brockton before) like her.

One hour later, outside the base's outer gate, April felt her first real twinge of doubt about what the hell she'd agreed to.

There was no security in sight—the guard station next to the high fence had been deserted. The wooden bars blocking the path didn't look like they would keep out anything except a myopic raccoon. Nothing looked particularly impressive or intimidating. And it certainly hadn't scared off the three hundred people who'd come along on this crazy raid. Hardly the stuff of a high-security military installation.

April hoped all of this was a good sign that maybe this would be easier than it appeared.

Yeah, she thought, *because nothing ever goes wrong when you break into a military facility that is the literal definition of 'looks too easy.' It was a walk in the park, right?*

Then she saw the other sign. A big wooden one posted near the gate.

UNAUTHORIZED PERSONNEL NOT ADMITTED
Photography is prohibited
$1,000 fine, six months imprisonment, or both

"Well… shit," April said.

Brockton laughed it off, though. "If they really cared about us being here," he said, "they'd have more than just scary signs. Ooooo. I mean, we made sure everyone knew when we were coming." He paused. "You know, though, that sign is just a cool spot for people to take pictures."

People started to walk onto the grounds. Tentatively at first, and then with more enthusiasm. A cheer went up. It was time. Fame awaited!

That was when Brockton asked April what time it was. When she pulled out her phone, it went dead in her hand.

———

When the elevator came to a stop, April and Brockton were both thoroughly freaked out. It had moved far deeper into the earth than they'd ever expected, and the time it took to finally reach its destination gave them plenty of opportunity to envision a worse-case scenario. They didn't say anything, but the nervous look in Brockton's eyes matched what she felt.

They clung to the sides of the cage as the doors opened, trying to be invisible, but outside was a short, empty hallway. They stepped out cautiously and saw there was a door a few yards from the elevator and another at the far end. Both had keycard scanners mounted on the walls. They crept toward it and looked through a small window into a room filled with row after row of metal exam tables.

Brockton tried the door.

"Locked," he said, stepping back.

"Now what?" asked April, but before he could reply, the door suddenly opened and a man in a lab coat plowed right into Brockton.

The man rebounded, actually shrieked and swung a heavy flashlight at Brockton's head, missing by a hair. He overbalanced and dropped the light, which rolled against the wall.

"Whoa, whoa," said April, pulling Brockton back.

The man stood for a moment just gaping at them. He wore an ID badge clipped to his lapel. It read: *Doctor Stephen Renfro*. The scientist's eyes were wild, and he lunged forward, pushed past them, and ran for the elevator. He began pushing buttons. The elevator doors remained stubbornly shut.

"No no no no," cried Renfro. "It can't be, not already. I'm too late. *Too late…*"

Brockton grabbed his sleeve. "Too late for what?"

Doctor Renfro looked at them as if only now realizing they were strangers. "You can't be here now," he barked. "We're too late. It's all falling apart. We—we need to find another way out of here."

April looked at Brockton. "And I thought *you* sounded crazy before."

Doctor Renfro kicked the closed elevator door. He was panting and his face flushed red.

"Come on. *Come on*, you fools," he snapped.

Brockton pulled back and said, "Hey, man, calm down! You're freaking us out. Are you the one who—"

His sentence died in his throat when the large, insectoid creature dropped onto Doctor Renfro's shoulders from somewhere above them. Despite its massive size, the creature never made a sound until it landed on the doctor with a heavy *thud*.

April and Brockton both screamed as they scrambled backward, horrified beyond rational thought.

The creature was monstrous—it must have been seven feet tall, and while its frame was thin, like an insectoid exoskeleton without skin, it had long, jointed arms ending in six clawed fingers on each of its two hands; a longer segmented tail that ended with a wicked, pointed tip; and four thick protrusions extending out of its back. Most horrific of all was a long, domed head, and a mouth filled with sharp teeth and dripping with mucus.

Renfro's scream was awful. High and shrill—filled with absolute horror and bottomless pain.

The monster attacked the hapless doctor, its tail whipping back and forth, coming within inches of April and Brockton.

April's brain was nearly stalled by shock, but there was that one part of her—the clinical, rational mind—that kept working. Analyzing. It did that even when she was stoned, or having sex. Always trying to make sense of the world.

And now it was shrieking at her that, after everything, Brockton was right. Aliens were real. This thing, this monster, was nothing she had ever seen or heard about. It was not of this earth, that much was certain.

It wrapped its arms around Renfro in a horrific parody of an embrace, then raked long, sharp fingers in a jagged X across his chest. The claws tore through clothing, flesh, and muscle with little resistance and blood exploded outward.

Brockton seemed too stunned to move, but April grabbed him and dragged him backward toward the laboratory door. For the moment, the creature seemed to ignore them and continued savaging the scientist. It lowered its head, dripping slime onto Renfro's neck, and plunged its tongue, a rigid thing with teeth of its own, into the back of Renfro's neck, the toothed tongue rending flesh and muscle alike. The third time it did so, it got stuck on Renfro's spinal column with a *thunk*.

The door had not swung all the way shut and April saw that the flashlight the doctor dropped was blocking it. It was a splinter of luck. Was it enough? She snatched it up and shoved Brockton into the room.

"Hey," someone yelled—it was a female voice from the far end of the lab. "Come on, this way… *this way*."

April risked a look over her shoulder. The monster had heard the voice, too. It raised its head from the limp body of Renfro, then dropped the corpse. The man's head had been so thoroughly savaged that it tore free and rolled crookedly away. Then it began stalking toward them. Its clawed fingers caught the edge of the door, its tail whipping back and forth.

The woman at the far end of the room yelled for them. "Here, over here... *hurry*, for fuck's sake."

They ran. The alien chased them, but another splinter of luck saved them because its chitinous feet skidded in the blood spilling from the stump of Doctor Renfro's neck. It gave them a half second's grace, and they reached the woman, who held open a thick metal door with a square glass observation window in it.

The woman grabbed them, shoved them roughly inside, then slammed the door. April and Brockton collapsed against a wall and stared at her. April hugged the flashlight to her chest as if it was a sacred talisman.

The woman wore an identical lab coat to Renfro, and her name tag read: *Doctor Amy Kupihea*.

"You people are trespassing," she snarled. "And you're a pair of goddamn idiots."

———

As she fought to catch her breath, April looked around. The room they were in seemed to be one of those shelter-in-place spots. Doctor Kupihea seemed to read her thoughts and nodded.

"It's a safe room," she said. "We have them peppered throughout. We'll be okay here for now. There's water, MREs—military ready-to-eat meals—cots and blankets, and they tell me the walls are impregnable."

Brockton kept blinking, clearly trying to reboot his brain.

Kupihea kept talking as if she was giving a freaking tour. "We have a solid security door, an intranet computer, and a dedicated power source."

"But *why*?" demanded April, finally finding her own

voice. "What's *happening* here? What is that thing? What... what... I mean...?"

Brockton mumbled, "This is where they brought the UFOs they found. That's what that thing is, isn't it? An alien from one of those ships, and it got out."

Doctor Kupihea did not answer, and instead demanded to know who they were and how they got there. April did her best to explain, and the doctor listened with increasing dread as April relayed the last hour of their day—their ease of entrance—obviously enabled by someone from within the base; the elevator code, and then the death of Doctor Renfro.

"This is another of those Occupy Area 51 things?" Kupihea said, appalled. "Jesus Christ. And you're sure Renfro's dead?"

"Very," said Brockton.

"God damn," said Kupihea. Then her face hardened. "Serves him right. He set this in motion. He should have enacted a hard lockdown. He should have called in a strike team, that's why they're on standby. But no... he kept saying it was all under control, that everything was fine. Shit. And now that *thing* has the run of the lab, and we're in here."

Despite her anger there were tears in the corners of her eyes.

"Did all of you morons come down here? All—what was it? Three hundred?"

"No," said April. "Just us. The rest are upstairs."

"And if that thing gets up there they'll all die," said Kupihea. "You don't even want to know how."

"We saw how," said Brockon. "It tore that guy's head off. Can't get a lot worse than that."

Kupihea's expression was bleak. "Yes," she said, "it really can."

Brockton looked around. "What kind of weapons do we have?"

"Nothing. I'm a scientist, not a soldier."

"Wait," said April, "there's *nothing* in this room that we can use as a weapon to kill that thing?"

"Of course not."

"Lady," said Brockton, "that giant cockroach murderized your friend in like two seconds." He nodded at the computer. "Can you call in, like, tactical nukes or something on that thing?"

Kupihea's eyes were cold. "Not even a remotely workable option. We can't even call in the strike team without the QR code on Renfro's ID." Then she took a deep breath, exhaled it, and added, "But I have the makings of an idea. I wouldn't call it a 'plan,' but maybe it can offer us a possible way past this mess."

April stood with her back to the two of them, her hands clutched nervously tight around the heavy barrel of the flashlight. She peered through the window in the door. She didn't ever want to see that creature again, but even worse to her was not seeing it. "I haven't seen it since we got in here. But it's there, isn't it? It's somewhere out there, waiting."

"The creature can pretty much disappear into the shadows," said Kupihea. "It has demonstrated superior skills at stalking and concealing itself. Not human intelligence but very high animal cunning. We've documented how it can somehow fold its seven feet into tight, dark spaces and lie in wait. It's maybe its most lethal trick."

"Jesus. I was wrong before," Brockton said. "It's not a giant roach, it's a trap-door spider."

Something heavy slammed against the door. April screamed.

"Hush!" the doctor hissed. "It can't get in here, so even if it's got a sense that we're here now, it'll likely seek out a proper dark space to wait us out. That means the rafters. Which are high enough that we might be able to make it out of here."

"And go where?" Brockton said.

"I'd love to tell you there was a back door we could use or other such escape hatch, but when you mentioned before that the elevator doors wouldn't open, I knew then that no help was forthcoming. Not from the rest of the staff, anyway. For now, we're sealed in here with that thing."

Kupihea explained that base protocol dictated the automatic sealing off of any level subject to astrobiological contamination.

"We can never risk anything that gets loose in here getting free *out there*," she said, pointing up at the surface. "The way you made your way down here? A one-way trip until things are contained, *if* they are. Per protocol, there's no help coming unless we get Renfro's ID. And even then it's not instantaneous. If we can make that call, then we'll be instructed to hole up in one of these shelter rooms and wait…"

"God, there's help right upstairs, too," said April. "Those military guys almost caught us before. We fled down here, thinking that was the better option."

"They didn't catch us," said Brockton lamely.

April wheeled on him. "I cannot believe I went along with your stupidity."

"Look, aliens weren't actually supposed to be real!" Brockton whined. "I mean, you'd have to be *insane* to believe the stuff—"

"—that *you* believe?" April fired back. "God, I should open this door and *feed* you to that thing."

"It was a game," he protested. "It was all just supposed to be a game. Or, at best, I expected aliens to be those little gray-headed dudes who are all cute, like Archibald in that comic, or that movie *Paul*."

"Let's worry less about your faulty information and more about finding a practical solution to our problem, shall we?" said Kupihea with asperity. She stepped to a workstation and pulled up an inventory list filled with objects with long names and numbers. "Ahhh, there you are." She tapped a button on the screen and a metal compartment against the far wall opened up and a drawer slid out.

Brockton looked at the open drawer. "Weapon?" he said hopefully. "'Cause right now all we have is that flashlight April grabbed."

"Weapon?" mused the doctor. "Not so much as we understand it, anyway. But *he* might."

"*He*?" asked Brockton. "Who he?"

She lifted an object out of the drawer. It was a rough-hued metallic ball the size of a coconut.

"Please tell me that's a hand grenade," Brockton said.

"Hardly," said Kupihea. "Frankly, I can't tell you in the strictest terms what it *is*. It just might help, but it's a back-up plan to my non-plan." She glanced over and asked, "April, do you still see it?"

April peered into the laboratory. It was hard to see

anything clearly because the glass was smeared with blood and muck, but there was no obvious movement in the other room. "No."

"Then let's hope for the best. If it's far enough away, we might have a chance to get where we need to go next." Kupihea turned the object over and over in her hands, lips pursed in thought.

"Which is where?" asked April. "I'll accept any answer as long as it's 'out of this base forever.'"

"You mentioned rafters," said Brockton. "That thing dropped from the ceiling before, and Doctor Renfro was dead before we could scream. Where can we possibly go from here where that thing won't just drop on us next?"

"Yes," said April. "And more to the point, Doctor, you obviously caught it once, right? So how did you bag it before? Is there a way to do that again?"

"I have the same answer to both of your questions," Doctor Kupihea said. "We were able to subdue that specimen before because we had help."

"Help…?" said April and Brockton at the same time.

"Yes," said Kupihea slowly. "Which tells me what we need to do next."

And then she told them.

———

"Remember," Kupihea said, "when this door opens, run for the hallway door. Last one through pulls it shut and makes sure the lock clicks. The specimen is clever, but it can't bypass locks. We get Renfro's ID badge, and we run like hell down the hall to the other door. We slide either his badge or mine through the card reader, and it'll open the door. Once we're through, then it's down the corridor to the—"

"Fourth door on the right," Brockton said. "Enter this code"—he displayed the number he'd written in large print on his forearm—"and then stand back from whatever is gonna come out of that room."

"Make *absolutely no threatening gestures*," insisted Kupihea. "That's critical. I'd even kneel and lower your eyes."

"But—" began Brockton, but Kupihea cut him off.

"Just do what I say."

"What'll you be doing while we're doing these things?" asked April.

"I'll be right there with you," Kupihea said. "But taking great care not to drop this." She presented the strange ball she'd been holding.

"Your amazing, interstellar non-weapon that may or may not be useful," Brockton said. "Perfect. Feeling great about this plan."

"The thing in the room where we're headed," April said. "What is it? Another one of these bugs? Only this one found Jesus or something?"

"You're in enough trouble already," said Kupihea. "Anything else I could tell you is only going to get you in deeper legal shit. Me too, for that matter. Right now our focus is on survival."

"Yeah, yeah, sure," said Brockton. "Whatever it is, it's something else we shouldn't be seeing. I get it." He shook his head and turned to April. "I know I wanted this today, but I mean, you have to know we've already seen too much for them to let us live."

Doctor Kupihea looked at April. "'Let you live'? Jesus

wept, is he always this much of a paranoid conspiracy nut?"

April almost smiled. "One of the milder cases I met today. You should see some of the others. No joke, there was one guy with an actual tinfoil hat, and I don't think it was an attempt at irony." To Brockton, she said, "Besides, if we already *have* seen too much to live, I mean, what's a little more at this point?"

"In for a penny, in for a stupid lethal killer-bug pound," Brockton muttered. "God. This damned thing better be some kind of magic space-assassin."

Kupihea appeared to actually consider the comment. "It's not an assassin per se," she said slowly. "More of a special kind of hunter. Absolutely fascinating. Now, let's get ready to move."

They clustered by the door. April could see fear sweat running down the faces of Brockton and the doctor. Her own body was slick with it, and her heart was beating with dangerous intensity.

"On three," said Kupihea. She counted down and then engaged the door's release and opened it very slowly and carefully.

They stepped out into the room and looked around. All seemed quiet, but April didn't take that as a good sign, because she felt as if she was being watched. It was impossible to tell if that was the truth or rampant paranoia. Or both.

Then Brockton slipped in a puddle of some viscous slime and fell hard on his ass. The realization tore a cry from him and the echo banged off every goddamn wall in the lab.

"Shit," cried April. She and Kupihea yanked Brockton to his feet and they all ran like hell.

Something thudded down behind them, and there was the clickity-slither of monstrous feet on the linoleum. It was coming fast.

"Run!" screamed Kupihea, but they were already running.

They reached the door. No keycard was needed to exit the lab, so Brockton jerked the door open and pushed Kupihea and April through, then he followed.

The alien, at full, inhuman sprint, leaped toward them. It hit the wall over the doorway and came down just before Kupihea could go through. She fell back, screaming. The creature rose to its full height—nearly seven feet—and moved its head in close to hers. Mucus dripped from its open mouth. Within, its long tongue emerged and the bulbous end opened to reveal that second set of awful teeth.

But then April slammed the butt of the heavy flashlight against the underside of the alien's jawbone. She put all of her strength and terror into it, and the force slammed the alien's jaw closed, the outer teeth crunching around the slime-covered tongue. It emitted a high-pitched squeal of shock and outrage. Blood flew from the wound and splashed on the door, missing April by inches. It hissed and sizzled, and April saw some of the metal door and frame begin to dissolve, to run like tallow.

"Molecular acid," barked Kupihea. "Don't touch it. Run!"

As the alien continued to thrash in fury, more of the acid sprayed out. A few drops hit the flashlight, and April flung it away from her, hitting the thing in the mouth.

Kupihea grabbed her hand and pulled her past the alien and into the long corridor. Both women turned and pulled the door shut, but the melting metal kept it from closing all the way.

They fled.

The hall was lined with heavy semi-translucent glass panels, each with a security keypad affixed to the wall next to it.

Kupihea yelled, "Brockton! six-one-two-one-nine-eight-seven!"

The alien pushed through the door, but it was moving slowly, shaking its head from side to side. April couldn't tell if it was in pain or merely disoriented from the injury. Either way, it kept coming toward them.

Brockton entered the code and then ran toward April and Kupihea. "April… hit the floor!"

The alien suddenly lunged forward and leapt at April, but she saw it and dropped down, pulling the doctor down with her. The alien's leap cleared them, but it came down right into Brockton's path, the impact knocking Brockton onto the floor, too. It stepped forward, putting one of its large, spiny feet on Brockton's chest. Its claws poked into his skin.

All at once, the whole shape of the world seemed to change. The door to that room swung open and something came out.

Even the alien turned, forgetting Brockton in that moment.

Something massive stepped into the hall, and with surprising speed and power, it grabbed the monster, lifted it, and hurled it down the hall. The alien hit hard and slid all the way to the doorway. It lay there, momentarily stunned.

April looked up at the new creature—it stood nearly as tall as the alien, but was much more powerfully built. And it was more obviously humanoid in appearance, though in no way human. It was barefoot and bare-chested, with massive muscles rippling beneath mottled yellowish-brown skin. Most terrifying of all was its face. It was something out of nightmare. Pale inhuman eyes and a mouth made up of twitching mandibles.

The creature looked down at Brockton, and then turned away with a kind of implied arrogance. As if Brockton was nothing.

Then it took off down the hall toward the alien.

"My god," Brockton gasped, "they've got an actual *Reptilian* down here. Wait... you mean I was *right*?"

April helped Kupihea to her feet and they moved to Brockton. "That *thing* is on our side? Fuck. Maybe we do have a chance."

"We call him *Dean*," Kupihea said. "A silly nickname for such an impressive specimen, to be sure, and from what we saw of his companions, likely still growing. He's aggressive and predatory. So far, he doesn't seem particularly inclined to attack humans."

The alien had whipped its bony tail at Dean, encircling him and pulling him close. Then it rammed its claws into Dean's left side, piercing the skin and sinking deep into his flesh.

The new alien bellowed in pain.

"Doctor, we need to get out of here. Leave them in here and let them kill each other, who cares!"

"Or maybe open the rest of these cages and let all the different aliens go at it while we escape?" Brockton added. "Do you have *any* grays?"

"You are not helping," the doctor said. "There are no other reinforcements. And April, I'm sorry, we're not going anywhere. We still don't have Renfro's ID card. This base is sealed off. We have to hope Dean can come out on top. Then maybe we can get the ID and call in a strike team. Otherwise..." She rolled the lead globe around in her hands and let the sentence hang unfinished.

Down the hall, Dean was having a hard time in the relatively close quarters. The alien held him tight with its tail, its ridges cutting into Dean's legs. The alien slashed away with its free hand, and dug the claws deeper into the big hunter's side. The insectoid creature's head was inches away from Dean's, slime dripping from it as it extended its toothed tongue yet again.

Without any real maneuverability, Dean was forced to bring the fight in even closer. He slammed his forehead against the alien's domed head, knocking the creature off-balance enough for him to free himself from its grasp. April could see a big crack in the sleek carapace.

But Dean was clearly hurt worse. Iridescent green blood streamed from his wounds.

Kupihea took a step forward. "We… we have to help him…"

"Um, Doc, you're out of your fucking mind," Brockton said.

She stopped moving forward, seemed to reconsider, then returned and handed the globe to Brockton. "How's your aim?"

"Oh god, I knew it was a hand grenade," he said warily. "You want me to just… throw it at them?"

"Worse than that—I need it returned to Dean. It was among the array of weaponry we found aboard his craft. We usually catalog and store these things elsewhere, but this one needed more study. In fact, it could well have dire consequences we're not even aware of, but, you know, desperate times."

"You're telling me," Dean said, dismayed. He held the thing out in front of him like it might explode any second.

Down the corridor, the alien skittered up the wall near Dean and came at him again, slashing with its own claws.

The alien flung itself at the big hunter, and then both creatures came sliding down the corridor, Dean still bearing the brunt of the fight.

The alien slashed its claws at Dean's face, but the hunter caught the hand before it could impact him. He then dragged the creature forward and, seeing the open space of his containment cell, swung the creature hard into the cell. It slammed against the far wall. Then Dean slammed the door. Locks clicked audibly, trapping the other alien inside. The alien slammed against the inside of the door, but it held.

"Good lord," gasped Kupihea, staggering back. April caught her.

They watched Dean closely. No one had any sense what might happen next. The injured hunter was panting. That luminous yellow-green blood dripped onto the floor. Then he started pounding on the barrier. Pounding and making noises that sounded like guttural laughter.

Is he taunting the creature within, April wondered. *Or hoping to free it to continue the battle?*

The alien responded by slamming against the barrier over and over. But, try as it might, even its deadly claws could not find a berth against its smooth surface. That seemed to infuriate the thing. It bashed its face against the glass-like door again and again, its frenzy mounting. Some of its teeth broke loose and fell to the floor. One particularly vicious blow split its jaw open. Blood dripped to the floor, where its acidic nature caused it to hiss and sizzle into the floor.

Then the monster extended its damaged toothed tongue to gouge and tear at its own right arm.

"What the hell's it *doing*?" Brockton demanded, but Kupihea just shook her head.

Each time it struck the arm, it tore away more of the chitinous shell, spilling more blood onto the floor and eating away at it. Finally, its forearm and hand tore completely loose and fell to the floor. The creature howled an inhuman wail of pain. A roiling cloud of steam rose from the melting floor.

Dean had stopped his pounding and was watching, his strange eyes narrowed.

Inside, the creature smashed at the glass barrier with its severed arm. Each time it did, its acid blood etched deepening damage lines into the surface.

"Christ," Brockton said, "it's melting the glass."

"We need to get out of here," April said.

The maimed creature continued its assault on the barrier. Finally, Dean had had enough standing around, and he started pounding the glass again.

"Doctor…" April said, worried.

"Don't worry, that's a graphene and crystal-matrix polymer blend. It should hold. It—"

And the smoky glass exploded outward in a spray of melting pieces. With a shriek, the alien flung itself at Dean. The hunter rushed to meet it, but the alien thrust the stump of its arm at Dean's chest. The hunter screeched as the acid burned a huge, jagged circle into his chest.

"God," Kupihea yelped, backpedaling. "Brockton, throw the globe."

But Brockton was rooted to the spot, eyes and mouth wide, expression blank, the globe hanging limply in one hand.

Dean, though badly wounded now, was still fighting. He slapped the stump away, grabbed the alien, and slammed it against the wall. Again and again. Each blow shook the hall, and cracks whipsawed through the insectoid armor. Drops of the alien's blood flew from its stump, spattering Dean and pocking his flesh.

It's going to kill him, April thought, assessing rationally while her body was nearly as frozen from shock as Brockton's. *It's going to kill him and then kill us all.*

She heard herself mumbling words she hadn't said since Sunday school when she was little.

"Mary, Mother of God, pray for us sinners now, and at the hour of death…"

She felt a hand take hers and looked down in surprise to see that it was Brockton's.

He squeezed tight. "I'm sorry."

She whispered back, "Fuck you."

But she smiled when she said it. He smiled back.

Then he released her hand and gave her a small push.

"Go," he said.

April gaped at him. "Wh-what…?"

"*Run!*"

She backed away only a few feet.

"Hey, Dean," Brockton yelled as he crouched and rolled the globe toward the wrestling monsters. "Catch."

The hunter turned at the sound, but that only allowed the alien to slice his flesh again, spilling more green blood onto the ground. Dean howled and staggered. He'd lost a lot of blood.

Then he saw the object rolling on the ground, and it seemed to galvanize him. He twisted and lashed out with a vicious back-kick, knocking the insect alien back. The thing hit the wall and rebounded, but it was enough time. Dean ducked and snatched up the ball, pivoted and smashed it against the wall.

"Well, shit… I could've done *that*," Brockton said.

The ball shattered, splattering against the wall with a blueish goo. Dean used his hand to scoop as much of it as he could. And, as the alien leapt at him with its jaws open and toothed tongue again emerging, Dean drove his left hand into the creature's mouth. Its outer jaw clamped down, and the inner teeth likewise tore at the flesh on Dean's fist.

But the true damage was done.

The alien recoiled sharply, pawing at its mouth with its one remaining hand. It stumbled sideways, obviously in terrible pain. Dean snarled and kicked the creature away, sending it sprawling on the floor. In shock, April saw that the remaining blue goo was dissolving the flesh on Dean's hand. But the alien had ingested the majority of it, and it was doing far worse to that creature.

Doctor Kupihea and the other two stared in horror as the blue dissolving liquid wreaked havoc on both creatures. The skin on Dean's hand peeled down to the bones. He wobbled but stayed on his feet.

Meanwhile, the alien was being eaten from within. It managed to push itself back onto its knees before collapsing onto its side. Even as its severed stump burned into the concrete floor, the blue goo melted the creature alive from within. Its chitinous chest collapsed inward as tissue and muscle dissolved. Blue liquid emerged from its joints and its mouth as the creature melted away.

Dean looked down at the creature's rapidly dissolving shell. His broad chest heaved from exertion and pain, but he raised his foot and stomped on the gooey remains. Then he raised his good arm in the air and emitted an ear-piercing howl of savage victory.

The cry seemed to fill the whole world, but then it abruptly stopped, dissolving into a wet gurgle. Dean sagged down to his knees. He looked at April and the others, and then his eyes rolled up in his head as his big body toppled sideways.

Dead.

April dropped to her knees, too. Looking into the hunter's eyes, watching the focus fade into a terminal emptiness.

After a moment she said, "Did you know what was going to happen?"

Kupihea shook her head slowly. "No... I... I thought it was a grenade."

She walked over and placed a hand on Dean's chest, then looked up at the other two. The sadness in her eyes was both genuine and profound.

"We don't know what drew them here in the first place," she said hollowly. "We rarely do. When Dean arrived with the others like him, the best we could figure was that he was brought here to hunt this creature. Hunters bringing their own prey. Like fishermen stocking a lake with trout. That was our theory, anyway. Whatever the case, Dean proved today that he was a true hunter."

"Jesus Christ..." April whispered.

"And this might not be a very scientific way of viewing things," she added, "but I hope his ancestors welcomed him to whatever sort of Valhalla their hunters end up in."

Things happened fast after the base was accessible again. After a month-long quarantine and a debriefing period that determined that Brockton and April had nothing to do with the freeing of the alien, the conversation turned to what to do about these two trespassing kids long-term. Brockton was vague about what he knew about accessing the base and how he knew it, but it didn't take the authorities long to determine that Doctor Renfro was the person who leaked the information.

How the alien escaped was something April never learned. The authorities refused to answer her questions. Instead, she and Brockton were arrested and charged with a raft of violations.

But Doctor Kupihea interceded on their behalf. April never learned all the details, but apparently the scientist either had friends or influence. So, instead of vanishing to Gitmo or some other hellhole, they were offered a deal. Sign a very large and very scary stack of papers, or spend fifteen-to-twenty in a supermax. When April's lawyer read the conditions, he went pale and got sweaty, but he advised her to sign. One condition was that if she spoke publicly about the facility and, more importantly, the "specimens," her constitutional rights would be forfeit and that—as the saying goes—would be that.

And so she signed.

It still meant a sentence of six months in a federal prison, no visitors, calls, or internet access permitted. There were counseling sessions and some terrifying lectures by unsmiling men in black suits. They let her out after three months, though she had to wear an ankle bracelet for the balance of her time.

She never found out what happened to the other three hundred people.

And she never saw Brockton again.

She never heard from Doctor Kupihea, either.

April drifted for a while, feeling disconnected from any version of the life she'd had or the person she'd been.

She was alive, though.

Alive.

At nights she dreamed of the alien and the hunter. Sometimes she woke screaming. Sometimes she lay there, with the window open, and looked up at the infinite stars.

The infinite universe.

Infinite, but in no way empty.

ISLA MATANZAS

BY STEVEN L. SEARS

It was my second year of my being stranded on the island. My ability to read the stars told me it was late March of the year 1770. I had become resigned to my fate but, I confess to you now, after a lifetime of prayer and unwavering devotion, my faith in the power of our Heavenly Father was fading.

The Nephilim were losing, I knew it, and I'm certain they knew it. I had watched the battles unfold from my perch high upon the cliffs over the interior of the island where I made my home in a small cave behind a waterfall. The evil ones, the serpent-like Malvados, were too many in number and had command of the treetops, like the monkeys their spawn had used as hosts for their birthing. Their eggs appeared strangely one night, littering the jungle floor. One of the vile creatures within leapt to attach itself to my face. Only my good eyesight and quickness with my father's machete saved me.

The curious monkeys, though, were easily taken. I watched as the Malvados burst from their chests and took easily to the trees, as the monkeys had, to grow and begin

47

their killing spree, decimating the animals. These were demons from Hell with spiked tails, double rows of fanged jaws, and claws that ripped the flesh of any earthly creature. This lonely island was, I realized, a Hell's Gate; a place where Lucifer's spawn could pour forth to destroy God's dominion. I hid in my cave and prayed throughout the day and night, hoping God would hear my call.

When the three warriors arrived from the heavens to battle the Malvados, I recalled the scripture of Genesis; "There were giants in the earth in those days. These were the heroes of old, warriors of renown."

The Holy words referred to them as the Nephilim, and so I named the three Avenging Angels the Lord had sent to kill these demons and destroy the Gate. The Nephilim were truly Godlike in their abilities. They were strong, quick, and had powers beyond that of the most advanced army. Fire erupted from their fists and strange beams cast from shoulder weapons rained destruction. They disappeared and reappeared in a spectral manner.

I slept well, believing that the Avenging Angels had come and victory against evil was assured.

But that was not to be. Hope of salvation slipped away as the Malvados overwhelmed the three Nephilim. The hated serpents swarmed through the limbs of the pine trees and climbed the palms as if born to it. In battle after battle, the fire and lightning the Nephilim commanded was silenced and their spectral powers deserted them. They fought on bravely, but it seemed I was the only one destined to witness their sacrifice on our behalf.

I had been stranded on the island after the ship, *Hesperia*, had wrecked upon its rocky shoals. I warned the captain, but did he listen? To him, I was just Jorge Rodriguez de Aviles, a wealthy merchant returning from Spain to La Florida to oversee his family's remaining interests in San Augustin.

Though a Spaniard by right, I had only spent the last five years in the country of my heritage. San Augustin was the only home I had ever known. My family could trace themselves back to the founding of the city by Pedro Menendez de Aviles and Father Francisco Lopez de Mendoza Grajales in 1565. Admiral Menendez had been sent by King Philip the Second to establish a fortress against the French invaders, and Father Lopez to administer to the spiritual needs of the colonists and the local natives, known as the Timucua. Sadly, little of their great tribal nation survives, due to European greed that pillaged their land, and the wars of colonial power we brought to their shores. Many more died of diseases common to us but fatal to them. The few that remained left their ancestral homes for Cuba when the English took possession.

Yes, the hated English, no friend to Spaniard or Timucuan, now possessed La Florida. I had, as a youth, fought against Oglethorpe himself when his Calvinist bastards invaded our land. I was bloodied in the Battle of Mose, a victory for the Spanish Crown which was celebrated throughout Cadiz and Madrid! But, in the end, it mattered not. What the English had failed to take by force, they had taken by treaty. My beloved land was theirs and I was left to sell off what possessions we still had in San Augustin.

The captain, of course, knew none of this. Nor did he know I had studied navigation and the ocean's maps with the idea I might do honor to the Crown with my service. He dismissed my concerns, convinced that his vast knowledge of the sea was enough to navigate any ocean. He was wrong and his arrogance cost him his life and those of his crew.

I survived with only a spyglass and my father's treasured machete. For two years, I had prayed daily, observing my reverence for the Almighty, certain of deliverance from these shores. But, it seemed, my only reward for devotion was to die in a war not of my choosing.

But it was during one such battle between several Malvados and the Nephilim I had named Adelantado when God responded to my prayers.

It was early morning. I watched through my spyglass as Adelantado had taken the initiative, attempting to entice some of the creatures into a small crevasse between the rocks. Hoping, I believe, to bring them down from the trees, restrict their movements, and kill them one by one.

Of the three Nephilim sent from the heavens, Adelantado seemed the more experienced in terms of tactics. Gigante, the name I gave to the largest of the three, was pure brute strength. Assessino was clever and quick. Where the other two were at this moment, I had no idea. They rarely fought together and seemed to compete against each other for kills and trophy heads. I found Adelantado to be the most interesting as he seemed to command respect from his brethren.

Adelantado had already killed one of the creatures, its poisonous blood still steaming on the jungle floor, and used himself as bait for three other Malvados. They pursued him up the rocky hillside to the crevasse. As they crowded in, their deadly spiked tails became useless without space, and their advantage in speed was nullified. Adelantado mounted the rocks above them and waited. He had forced them into single combat, neutralizing their advantage of numbers. His wrist blades were extended, he held his spear in the other hand. The mask he wore disguised any expression of fear or satisfaction he might have.

As the first of the devils climbed toward Adelantado, he flicked his hand and the spear extended to its full length. The Malvado reached for him and Adelantado swiped his blades across the creature's face while driving the spear up into its chest. The force of the impact lifted the Malvado from the ground. But what I witnessed next was both amazing and horrible.

As Adelantado attempted to dislodge his spear, this beast grabbed the Nephilim's arm with both claws and wouldn't let him pull back. Adelantado was off balance, he was forced to kick the Malvado to free his spear but its blood spurted onto his thigh. His exposed flesh began to burn and dissolve. He roared in pain!

The other two Malvados had now scrambled free of the crevasse. Severely wounded, Adelantado had no choice but to retreat to the top of the mountain where there was no place to hide, nowhere else to run. Only the cliff over the beach and the rocks below.

Suddenly my attention was taken by a sight on the other side of the crest; white and blurry against the blue sky. I adjusted the focus of my spyglass. The sails of a large ship! It had three main masts and the flag of England. Had it flown the hated Lutheran Rose, I would have still rejoiced.

I quickly consulted the leather map I had made of the island. They would sail north to allow the current to pull them back to shore and anchor in the cove underneath the cliffs.

My heart skipped a beat as I suddenly realized the cove was directly underneath the cliff where Adelantado was fighting to his death. The Malvados were certain to see the ship.

I rolled up the map, grabbed up my machete and spyglass and, with a look back at my home for the last two years… my prison… I ran through the waterfall toward the small path that led down the hill.

My English was adequate: one of my childhood friends who lived in the free black settlement of Mose had escaped from an English plantation and taught me the language of his former masters. I have no love for the English, and I was certain their regard for a Catholic of the Spanish Crown of Charles would be no more than mine was for their Protestant King George.

I scrambled down the last few rocks to the jungle floor. I made no attempt to be silent. Speed was the only protection I had now. I had to make it to the cove.

At any moment, I expected the stab of their claws in my back, to be lifted above and ripped apart, but I dare not look back lest that hesitation be my undoing.

"Be strong and courageous." I whispered words from the Book of Joshua. "Do not be frightened or dismayed, for the Lord your God is with you wherever you go!"

The sun flared brightly in my eyes as I emerged from the brush directly onto the sand. The ship had dropped anchor, its sails furled. Two longboats were already beached and a third was coming ashore. And people! My Good Lord, there were people!

I ran as fast as my beaten body allowed, pushing hard on the sinking sand to propel myself forward, to freedom. There were several Englishmen, probably ten of them. The rest were women, twenty or more. Their skin, barely covered by rags, reflected of ebony and the chains that linked them by neck collars in groups of three told me who these Englishmen were; slave traders returning with their human bounty from Africa.

I have no heart for slavers, I have seen their work. In my beloved home of San Augustin, we had many escaped slaves from the English colonies. The Spanish Crown granted them freedom and gave them refuge. The town of Mose, the one the bastard Oglethorpe had taken, was their home. And those Africans had fought bravely alongside our Spanish troops to retake it and defend my ancestral home.

Still, I had no choice. I waved my arms, trying to find voice from my parched throat. "No! No! Stop," I yelled. "Do not go into the jungle! Please, wait!"

"Charles, hold up!" the man standing in the longboat called to his compatriots as their muskets immediately turned in my direction. I ignored them as I continued stumbling forward until I dropped to the sand at their feet.

"Castaway," one said as he opened a water flask and offered it to me. "How long have you been here?"

"Gracias," I muttered as I took the flask, my eyes scanning the trees for the demons. Where were they, I wondered? "You must leave, now! There is danger, much danger!"

Then, from the corner of my eye, I saw movement in the shadows cast by the overhanging cliff. I looked up and could make out the form of Adelantado and the two Malvados, still in mortal combat.

"There!" I pointed upward. "There, you see?"

The men, the women, all looked upward, their eyes straining in the sunlight.

"What the hell...?" the man nearest to me uttered.

53

Adelantado was poised on the edge, there was nowhere for him to go. He slashed at the nearest attacker with his spear but the other plunged its jaws into the mighty Nephilim's side.

The ground gave away underneath him and he fell, his body impacting outcroppings of rock and breaking through the trees along the precipice, finally hitting the ground with a mighty thud, his spear stabbing upright into the sand next to his head.

Then, silence. The Malvados had gone.

"What the hell was that?" the man on the longboat yelled out. The two men at the front of the group moved toward Adelantado. He lay partially on his side, his armor ripped open, his flesh shredded from his right leg up to his chest. Another gaping wound was just below his shoulder blade.

"Never seen anything like it," the man bending over Adelantado said. "Some kind of animal or something." He turned and yelled back. "It has to be worth something!" He motioned for the chained women to come forward, but they did not. The Africans searched the trees, speaking softly to each other, their bodies tense.

They know. I thought. They know we're being hunted.

That's when we heard the hissing. My blood froze with its meaning; the Malvados were here. "Too late," I turned to the man who handed me the flask. "Now, you must fight."

The man nearest Adelantado screamed as the Malvado's tail spike plunged into his back and lifted him into the air. The creature grabbed him in its claws and ripped him apart.

The English fired their muskets, but without aim; fear and shock rendering their minds useless.

"There! Up there!" One of the English was desperately reloading his musket as he stared up the side of the cliff. The two Malvados who had pursued Adelantado were crawling down the cliff, their teeth reflecting in the sun as they fixed on their prey.

The trees shook and three more Malvados jumped from the jungle onto the sand, where they crouched, ready to pounce, their massive heads swaying from side to side.

They moved as one, spreading out to prevent any escape into the brush. One of the English pulled his sidearm and fired at the nearest one, hitting it in the creature's shoulder. He quickly began his reload when the vile demon's jaw snapped down on his face, the smaller jaw erupting from the back of the man's head.

I had no idea if the Malvados could swim so I dropped my machete and spyglass and raced to the water, diving through the surf, pushing myself underwater, holding my breath and swimming as far as I could.

The sight that greeted me when my head emerged from the water was so horrifying that I hesitate to describe it to you.

Blood now covered the sand from the torn and shredded bodies of the English, a testament to the arrogance of their supposed superiority.

A few feet away, the man who offered me the flask treaded water. His eyes were wide, his face contorted as he watched the carnage. More sounds of musket fire from behind us caught my attention and we both turned to see two Malvados crawling up the side of the ship where only three crewmen opposed them. They could swim, after all. I looked away; the crew was doomed.

It was then that I saw the most amazing sight. The women in chains had formed a circle, facing outward toward the Malvados who surrounded them. Their voices chanting together, a rough, low sound, punctuated with heavy, rhythmic yells. Their chain collars rattled as they shook them and stomped the ground. As one, they opened their arms in the same manner I had seen of the Nephilim, then brought them down hard against their sides with a huge slap, repeating the motion. Each time, their voices rose, louder and louder, the stomping became more intense, making them look larger and more threatening, as if they were challenging the demons to attack.

The Malvados had quickly dispatched the Englishmen but with the women, they were cautious. It occurred to me that they had never seen mortals before today, much less this kind of behavior. Even the mighty lion, the king of his domain, would have chosen prudence. The evil ones were looking for an opening, some weak spot in the circle they could exploit.

The women countered their every movement, shifting the circle in unison. I must tell you, I have seen the Swiss Guard of the Vatican in formation, and it was nothing as precise as this.

Another loud grunt from them and they all stepped as one, moving toward the cliff. I assumed they were seeking partial protection from the rocky walls. But no! They were deliberately moving across the bodies of the English, picking up knives and swords to arm themselves.

The most striking of these women leaned down to one body, her eyes never leaving the demons around them. She searched the man's belt and pulled something from it. The key to the collar lock! She freed herself then passed the key to the next woman, who followed suit then handed it to the next. None of these women ceased staring at their attackers, none of them lost their step, none of them paused in that steady chant.

Who were these women? Where had they come from? They reminded me of the brave Africans who defended Mose, but with more defiance than I had seen in the best of soldiers, black or white. I found myself wanting to survive just to learn their story.

The Malvados closed together, preparing for their assault. I had seen this before. Once they broke the circle and got behind the women, their tails would slice back and forth, their claws would reach out, and it would be over quickly.

"They're done for, mate," the English next to me said. "Let's get back to shore while the bastards are busy." He began swimming. I wanted to join him, but my eyes were fixed on the women.

The one who picked up the key shouted out commands and the others responded without hesitation. The circle began to reform, the front moving backwards to create a U shape, much like the horns of a bull. I was confused; this guaranteed the opportunity the creatures were seeking.

The Malvados charged forward, screeching as the demons from Hell that they were, and pushed into the center of the U, their tails flailing. Amazingly, the women didn't scatter. The two sides of the U pulled back and around, encircling the Malvados. Their tails struck out, but the women ducked and rolled under the deadly weapons, slicing upwards, wounding the beasts while others provoked them from the front. Every time the Malvados reacted, the line reformed and repeated the process. It was death by a thousand cuts.

The blood of the Malvados sprayed several of the women. They screamed, falling to the ground as their flesh bubbled and melted away. Still, this did not deter the others as they pressed the battle. Two Malvados were dead, the other three fought wildly but the loss of blood was beginning to tell on them.

At that moment, the water erupted near the boats and the two Malvados who had attacked the ship raced across the sand to join the fray. The leader of these women saw them and yelled to the others. They tried to reform the line to meet the new threat, but the three demons in the center were still fighting. The newcomers dashed around the beached boats, to attack from the direction of the cliffs.

Four of the women turned to face them as the others tried to close the gap. One of the women died quickly as the tail of the lead Malvado sliced into her stomach. Another was knocked aside, into the rocky walls of the cliff, and fell motionless to the ground. Their leader yelled again and they tried to reform the line, but it was thin and faltering. A second attack would defeat all their efforts.

A mighty roar from behind the Malvados stopped them. Adelantado! He stood upright, arms upraised in challenge. Shredded flesh hung from his thigh and the gash across his chest was bleeding profusely. His mask had fallen away, and I could now see his face clearly.

It was, I'm sorry I cannot describe it any other way, hideous. His eyes were small for his body and there were fangs, four of them, aligned around his mouth. They stretched apart with his battle cry as he ran forward, colliding with the two Malvados. He grabbed the first by the throat and spun it around, using the creature's body as a shield. The spiked tail of the other demon shot toward Adelantado's exposed ribs. His blades flashed from his wrist and the spiked end fell to the ground. The demon's blood sprayed the sand as Adelantado pushed it back.

But, alas, the one in his grip was not yet dead. Its jaws opened wide and those vicious inner teeth flashed out, catching the side of his head and breaking one of the fangs. The other creature ripped at the already gaping wound of Adelantado's thigh.

The mighty Angel roared in pain as his luminescent green blood poured freely. He crushed the neck of the demon in his fist and fell to one knee. The remaining Malvado rose up, towering over Adelantado, to deliver the fatal blow.

The leader of the women ran toward them. She grabbed up the spiked tail lying on the ground, diving underneath the Malvado and stabbing upward. The spike dug deeply into the demon's flesh and it screamed in pain as she rolled away to avoid its yellow hissing blood. The Malvado took one step toward her before its head jerked to the side and flopped against its shoulder. Adelantado, in a desperate effort, had sliced through the creature's neck. It dropped to the ground, twitched, then lay still.

Adelantado ripped the head of the demon from its body then turned toward the jungle's edge, pausing only to retrieve his mask. His hand never reached it as he fell to the ground, too wounded to move. Three women ran toward him, their swords raised to dispatch him. Their leader stepped forward and stopped them with a firm voice. Her subordinates paused and reluctantly lowered their weapons.

I suddenly laughed out loud, I yelled to the heavens. They had beaten the demons! These strange women, they had faced Lucifer's monsters and prevailed. I slapped the water, shook my fist, and screamed with delight!

The leader gazed out toward me, and I immediately calmed myself, realizing that their reception to me might not be any less than their regard for the Malvados. I gave her a half-hearted wave, not expecting a response. She motioned for me to swim back, then held her hands toward me, palms open in my direction. I took that as her showing me she held no weapon. What choice did I have?

I crawled onto the beach and sat, breathing heavily, coughing with the salt in my throat. The Englishman was already ashore with two women standing guard over him. I had little pity for him. I would have him placed in those cursed iron collars.

The women now spread out, forming a rough perimeter, watching the trees and the brush. The brave fallen were laid out next to each other; proud warriors, even in death. The remains of the slavers were covered with sand and ignored.

The leader, their commander, looked down at me. She was more than just striking, her face was carved as the ancient statues of Rome, with strength and grandeur together. She had scars tattooed along the lower part of her forehead, just above her eyes, and on her bare shoulders from front to back. They were obviously recognitions of her status. Her skin had an unbroken blackness that seemed to absorb sunlight. The strength she exuded was almost overpowering.

I weakly clapped my hands together and smiled. "Bendiga a todos!" I spoke within my heavy breathing. "Thank you, thank you all! I am at your mercy!" I bowed my head slightly, keeping my eyes on hers, holding my clasped hands in front of me.

"She doesn't understand you," the Englishman said. The commander then spoke to him in her language. He responded in kind and she walked away.

"You speak their tongue?" I asked.

"Aye," he responded. "I've had dealings with her people many times."

I reflexively spit in his direction. "You are a bastard!"

"I've no slaves of my own," he replied. "I merely translate."

"God will judge your guilt," I responded.

He shrugged. "No one is innocent, my friend. English, Portuguese, Spanish—I've worked for them all." His point was true. Despite the Crown's decree for my friends at Mose, the history of my own countrymen was not defensible.

"It doesn't matter," he continued. "We're their slaves now. If I was her, I'd have our blood spilled here and our bodies washed out for the sharks."

We watched as the women scavenged the longboats, collecting anything that could be used as weapons. The tow ropes were pulled free and the boat hooks stacked nearby. Crude spears were fashioned from English knives and the oaring poles.

The commander walked the area, inspecting their work, giving orders when needed. I saw her pause and pick something from the sand. It was Adelantado's mask. She brushed it off and examined it, running her fingers along the edges. It had markings on the front that seemed to be of interest to her.

The Englishman's name was Edward. He was, as he stated, a translator in many tongues. He was upon this ship because he was fluent in Fon, the language of these women. But who were they? Where had they come of such abilities, to stand in defiance of Lucifer's demons and defeat them?

"The Kingdom of Dahomey," Edward responded to my question. "They have fought the Portuguese, the Dutch, and my own people. These women are the King's elite soldiers, his personal guard. Do not be fooled by their gender."

There were legends of such Amazons in ancient writings, but that they did exist was not something I had believed possible.

"They call themselves Minos," he continued. "That one is their leader." He pointed to the commander. "She is called Nan."

"How did they end up as..." I could not even say the word "slave" as it just seemed incredulous to believe of these women.

"A battle with the Portuguese. They stood their ground to allow their King to escape a trap." He paused to glance around at the women. "It was a magnificent charge directly into the guns. Most of them died. The rest were taken and sold at the market."

One of the women approached our guards and spoke to them. They prompted us to our feet with their swords.

"Apparently Nan wants to talk to us," Edward explained.

"And I would like to talk to her," I replied. "There is much she should know about this place."

We were taken to the copse of trees on the other side of the beached longboats. Adelantado lay under the shade of the largest tree, unconscious but still alive. A woman tended to his wounds. Next to her was a small fire and a bowl catching sap from a slash in the tree trunk. The woman was spreading the sticky gel into the open wounds of Adelantado. I noticed Edward's confusion and explained to him.

"The tree sap prevents infection," I told him. "There is a common history of this, from many different cultures. Even the native Timucua of my home in La Florida used it as a medicine."

"How did they know which tree to pick?" he asked.

"These are soldiers," I replied. "I'm sure they have suffered enough carnage to know what sort of medicine works and what doesn't, even when in a strange land."

Two other women placed themselves on Adelantado's arms, as if to hold him down. She pulled a burning branch from the fire and placed it on the wound, igniting the sap.

I nodded. "They're cauterizing the wound to seal it," I explained to Edward.

It flared and burned instantly. I had no doubt, had Adelantado been awake, he would have thrown the women aside with little effort.

"Why don't they just kill the thing?" Edward asked.

"Because they are not like us," I replied.

Nan approached us and spoke, looking directly at me.

"She knows you've been stranded here," Edward translated. "She wants to know what those creatures are that attacked us and what this thing is."

Nan continued staring at me. I could sense that she wasn't just listening to the words I said, she was assessing me; to assign the proper weight to my words. All great leaders throughout history share this trait.

I explained as best I could and morning soon turned into afternoon. These women were from another land and culture. I had no idea which god they worshipped nor did I want to become a sacrificial missionary, so I refrained from interjecting my beliefs of war between Heaven and Hell. Besides, Edward was a Protestant, and I did not want to risk him altering my words to serve his false religion.

I told her about Gigante and Assessino and how they and Adelantado had fought many battles against the demons. I pulled the map from inside my shirt and showed her how the wooded terrain favored the evil ones, but that they avoided the areas that were sparse of trees. I pointed to my cave on the map and told her I rarely left it, but how it commanded a view of the entire valley.

Nan asked me where the Nephilim were. There was an open area near a stream where the Nephilim congregated at night on occasion, but only for a few hours at best. She took special interest in this, but I quickly told her that any attempt to attack the Nephilim would be folly.

She looked toward the ship anchored offshore. It was derelict. The Malvados had certainly killed the few crewmembers on board.

"The ship has supplies and weapons, but it's useless as long as the Malvados are able to get to the water," I said. Edward translated and she responded. Edward shook his head and replied to her.

"What?" I asked.

"She wants to know if the ship can take them home," he answered. "I told her it was impossible. Even if we could get to it, we'd have to teach them to sail it."

"They probably already know most of it, having watched the sailors work when topside," I replied.

He dismissed my comment. "The captain is dead as is the navigator."

"I can navigate. I know exactly where we are," I said. "I can get them back home. Tell her that."

He stared at me for a moment, then translated for her. She nodded and spoke directly to me.

"She said you will take them home. After they kill the Malvados." Edward sighed. "You may have just doomed us all."

A roar interrupted us. Adelantado had come out of his stupor and was fighting to his feet. Women quickly surrounded him with their makeshift spears. He was weak and unsteady, but there was no doubt he wouldn't hesitate to fight. He roared again, spreading his arms in the manner that the Nephilim did when challenging the Malvados. Nan jumped to her feet and raced over, yelling at her women and waving them back.

Her soldiers obeyed, backing away and opening a path of escape toward the jungle. For the briefest of moments I feared he wouldn't take advantage of his freedom; that he would choose to attack and kill as many of the Minos as he could.

He roared again, then disappeared into the brush.

Night soon fell. Edward and I sat between the longboats. We no longer had guards, where would we go? He was telling me of his childhood, being born in one of the coastal trading ports on the West Coast of Africa and how he had a true respect for the native Africans. This was to assuage his guilt more than to convince me. Though he did not hunt them and owned none, he was comfortable that others did. I could not help but remember the brave black men and women who fought at Mose; friends of my family who sacrificed themselves to protect my beloved San Augustin. He was correct; none of us were innocent. But at least I was aware.

"She's coming," Edward said as Nan approached and spoke.

"She wants to find the Nephilim," Edward translated.

"No, tell her no!" I looked directly at her. "They will slaughter your soldiers if you attack them!"

He translated. For the first time I saw a slight smile at the edges of her lips as she responded. Edward reacted in surprise.

"She isn't taking her soldiers, just you." Edward laughed. "Well, there you go."

Three hours later, I stood in the open area near the stream. Nan stood nearby, the large pouch we had dragged with us on the ground next to us. We had kept to the rocks and taken a longer path to avoid detection by the Malvados.

The moon illuminated everything in harsh contrast. We could see easily but were taken by a slight crackling sound from the shadows, almost like a dull clicking. The sounds got louder and moved around us; they were here.

Nan raised her arms high toward the sky, twisting her hands slowly as a low melodic chant grew from her throat. We were completely defenseless now and inviting our destruction at their discretion.

A rustle to our left and Gigante stepped from the darkness. His blades were extended, though one of them was broken. His armor had burn marks and a jagged gash across his mask.

Assessino soon appeared to our right. His condition was not much better than his compatriot. I noted the tendrils on the right side of his mask were missing, ripped away.

Every fiber of my body was telling me to run. Something about Nan's confidence stayed me, the power she had over others had extended to me as well.

Adelantado emerged directly in front of her. His jaws, bared of his mask, flexed as he tilted his head. I repeated the Lord's Prayer silently to myself.

Nan stopped chanting and gestured for me to bring the pouch forward. I placed it on the ground in front of her and stepped back. She reached inside and pulled out the Nephilim's spear.

She had learned how to retract the blades on it, but Gigante and Assessino tensed as if for battle. Nan tossed it gently at Adelantado's feet. She then produced the head of the Malvado killed by Adelantado on the beach. With an almost reverential posture, she placed it on the ground, next to the spear. Backing away, she indicated it was his.

Finally, from the pouch, the last item; Adelantado's mask. Nan pointed at the marks on the front, then pointed to the tops of the trees, then to him and opened her hand as if asking a question. I realized that she was asking if these marks counted the Malvados he had killed.

She then lifted the mask to the side of her face and pointed to the scars above her eyes. Adelantado touched her forehead lightly and nodded.

She held the mask out with both hands, lowering her head in honor of his valor.

He took the mask, placed it on his face and attached it to his armor with two short tubes. His chest expanded as he inhaled deeply in satisfaction. Then he picked up the spear and tapped the side of it against his thigh wound where the cauterizing had already sealed the gash and healed it. Adelantado extended the spear toward Nan, offering it to her.

She accepted his gift and, with it, she pointed to the trees, indicating the Malvados. Then she extended the blade and made a stabbing motion into the ground. The three Nephilim nodded their heads and clicked in response; they had a common enemy and a common cause.

No words were needed, none could be exchanged between them, but I had the sense that they understood more about each other than most men do about their own brothers.

Nan reached back to me, and I handed her my map of the island. She unrolled it on the ground. Adelantado watched as her finger moved along the map, pointing out certain areas, jabbing at certain points. She looked up at him and waited.

Adelantado crouched down and traced his finger across the map. Nan nodded and pointed to another area, then smiled at him.

It was amazing. They were strategizing, creating an alliance in the stillness of the night, two completely different beings with nothing in common except their experience in war. I glanced up to the Heavens where the brightest stars struggled to make their presence known against the light of the moon. Was He watching this?

Nan and I returned to the beach just before sunrise. The Minos had fortified their encampment with a wall of sharpened sticks placed in parallel lines to the jungle's edge, creating a maze that would force the Malvados to impale themselves or walk into a killing field. Women nearby were fashioning fire grenades made of wadded cloth and pine sap to be used as a last defense, to set it afire if the Malvados overran them.

The rest of the day was spent in preparation for the events of the coming evening. Her strategy was brilliant. And, as with most things of that nature, extremely fragile. Edward was forced to translate it to me and, I'm sure, he must have questioned if we had passed the point of sanity.

I already knew my part. Everything depended on timing and communication. I, dear friend, was in charge of that.

I gathered the materials necessary for my role. My spyglass would be crucial, of course. My machete would not be of much use, but I took it anyway. Finally, I collected several of the fire grenades into a pouch.

"I wish you luck," Edward said to me. "Our survival depends on you."

"Not me, them," I nodded toward the Minos. "If for some reason you are the only one to live another day, remember this. Remember them when you return to your life."

"I could never return to the life I had before," he looked to the ground. "I know that now."

"As you said, none of us are innocent of guilt." I tied the pouch and slung it over my shoulder. "You are a Protestant?"

He nodded. "Lutheran."

"Pray to your God for forgiveness," I said. "I will also pray for you, to mine."

With that, I turned and headed into the jungle.

I made my way back to my former home in the cave high on the mountainside. I placed the grenades against the entrance and made a small fire. We would have only half an hour between the setting of the sun and complete darkness to make Nan's plan work.

Using my spyglass, I saw Nan and four of her soldiers creeping through the brush along the rocks, heading toward the grove where the eggs had fallen. The Malvados were very protective of that area, though I had no idea how many of those eggs awaited new victims.

Nan was in position. I saw the flicker of embers as they lit the small sticks they gripped between their teeth. It was time.

I lifted the first grenade by its short rope and passed it through the flames of my fire. It ignited immediately. I began singing the *Te Deum Laudamus*, the song of Saint Augustine, the patron saint of my home, as I swung the grenade. The flames formed a circle of light as I spun it harder and released it.

The fireball sailed high into the sky, then turned toward earth and disappeared. Had they seen the signal? Should I try another? I began to panic.

There. A flare of light among the trees. And another. The Minos were throwing their grenades into the grove of eggs, enflaming them. Several of the pine trees began to ignite as well, casting harsh shadows across the ground.

The screeches of the Malvados rose above the valley as they raced toward the grove. *Run!* I mentally screamed at the women as I ignited another grenade and sent it as high as I could in a flaming arc. *Now run!*

The Minos saw the signal and turned back, following the rocky path as they headed toward the crevasse that led up the mountainside. They paused only long enough to ignite more grenades and throw them at the pines. The trees flared and burned brightly.

I shifted my spyglass behind them. The Malvados were on the ground. The flames prevented them from using the branches and forced them to the narrow path, slowing their pursuit.

Nan and her warriors reached the crevasse and crawled through it, climbing up and scrambling over the bare rock.

The Malvados followed, emerging from the jungle onto the escarpment. I counted twelve of them, the remaining entirety of their number on the island.

Their claws assisted them on the rocks, and I was certain the women could hear their screeching and scratching from behind. Above was the crest of the mountain where

Adelantado had been trapped between the Malvados and the cliff over the rocks of the beach.

One of the women slipped and the lead Malvado reached out to grab her. The spear from Adelantado pierced its head, killing it instantly. Nan pulled it free as the creature fell away, then lifted her sister back onto the rocks, pushing her forward to continue their climb.

They were almost to the top. I launched another fire grenade into the air. The shadowy figures of five more Minos arose on the crest, waiting for their sisters.

I held my breath, for this was the most crucial part of the plan. Nan had to allow the Malvados catch up.

They paused just under the lip of the mountain top and waited.

The demons increased their pace, scrambling toward their prey. Even if they saw the five women on top, it would have made no difference. What could ten do against their power and numbers?

Closer and closer, Nan and the four held to the rocks, exposed.

Wait… Wait… NOW!

As if they heard the command in my head, the women turned and scrambled up, barely a few feet ahead of the horde.

Nan and her brave Minos raced into the arms of their waiting sisters, pushing them off the ledge, wrapping their arms and legs around them in a death embrace!

I could make out the longboat ropes tied around the ankles of the awaiting Minos as they fell toward the beach below them. The ropes had been measured carefully, to reach above the sand and the heavy twine had been thinned to stretch, relieving the force of gravity on their bodies during the fall.

The Malvados in the front stopped, confused, staring down at their escaped prey. The ones behind, ignorant of the event, still moved onto the rocks, pushing forward.

The mighty roars of three voices could be heard across the valley as the Nephilim stepped from their hiding places behind the Malvados, blocking their path back down the mountain.

The mighty giants charged into the serpents, spears and blades flashing in the remaining rays of the sun. Gigante grabbed one after another in his huge hands, breaking necks and ripping open the jaws of his opponents. Assessino ducked and rolled between them, jabbing at their chests, slicing at their necks. And Adelantado moved as if possessed, using his forearm under the neck of one creature, slicing down with his blade to rip open its torso, then spinning into the next demon with an upward stroke of the blades. All the while, they pushed forward, using the dead bodies as battering rams.

A Malvado slipped and fell over the cliff's edge, followed by another, down toward the beach where the Minos had arranged the sharpened sticks of their defensive wall among the rocks, creating a death zone. Another. Then another. Those that didn't fall to their doom faced the wrath of these avenging Angels. It was as if the most glorious church tapestry depicting the scripture of Revelation had come to life before my eyes.

Then silence. The battle was over. The three Nephilim raised the severed heads of Malvados into the air and roared in victory as the last vestige of light disappeared and darkness concealed the massacre.

I returned to the beach in the morning. The bodies of the Malvados littered the rocks, many of them still impaled on the sharp sticks. The Minos were gathering fruit and securing water in the wooden casks of the longboats. The Nephilim were not to be seen. Their mission here was done. I was certain they had already returned to the heavens.

I saw Edward with Nan and walked toward them. Edward's left arm was hanging loose, his shirt ripped open. The wound underneath had pine sap drying on it. It seemed that he not been a mere translator after all and had done his part to subdue the Malvados who survived the fall.

Nan turned and smiled when she saw me. I cannot tell you how beautiful she looked at that moment. Tall, radiating strength and confidence, she glowed with the beatific light of the blessed.

"Jorge," she said, "I thank you." It was in broken Spanish and I could see Edward smiling. She then took my face in her hands and kissed my forehead.

"She's honoring you," Edward said. "She wanted to cut a tattoo on your head, but I told her it was not your way."

With a step back, she pointed to me, then to the ship offshore.

She wanted me to take them home, as I had said. I smiled and swore to the Heavenly Father that I would see these warriors back to their homeland or die in the process.

I won't bore you with the details. As I surmised, they were quick learners in sailing. My knowledge of the stars allowed us to find the currents we needed to return to Africa; to their home and freedom.

Edward and I stayed with the Minos in the Kingdom of Dahomey for eight years until he died of the plague. We became friends and I miss him. I hope he found peace.

I struggled with my decision to return to Spain. Perhaps the fear of blasphemy cowed me, but I realized that the

Heavenly Father wanted me to tell my story, even at the risk of my life. And so, I am here.

I tell you, my friend, there is a war between Heaven and Hell that goes unseen by us. Demons do exist, but so do Angels. They are not as we know them in the artwork of the Masters, they are not the perfect beings we envision. They are ugly, hideous, violent, and as foreign to our eyes as the Nephilim. They can also be beautiful, strong, black, like the Minos, and more Godly in their sisterhood than most have ever seen in their brethren.

I tell you this not to diminish His Holiness in the Vatican. With his wisdom and the guidance of our Heavenly Father, we can defeat these Malvados when they appear again.

But, I fear the Lord might not send the Nephilim to fight our battle for us next time. What will we say to God if we allow the Angels he has already placed among us to be enslaved? Indeed, what if we ignore that we can all, like the Minos, be the defenders of humankind? If our lot is to enslave each other and arrogantly war upon those who could enrich us, then Satan has already won.

I pray that you believe me and will honor my request.

———

The document remained on the desk in front of Cardinal Cartega where Father Lorenzo had placed it. The Cardinal continued staring out his window at the skyline of Madrid. A light snow had already dusted the spires of the church and the fireplace glowed brightly with warmth.

"What became of this man?" the Cardinal asked.

"He returned to La Florida," Lorenzo responded. "I had no reason to hold him here, so I gave him blessings and told him I would consider his request."

"To show this to His Holiness, the Pope?" He glanced to the stack of bound papers.

"As he related it to me, yes. I took it down word for word." Lorenzo shifted uncomfortably in the large wooden chair. "I would not have believed it myself nor have disturbed your Eminence with it, but there was more, if I may?" he asked as he reached for the large leather satchel next to him.

Cartega raised an eyebrow and nodded. Lorenzo pulled out an elongated skull, several sharp teeth still present in the jaw. He placed it on the desk.

The Cardinal leaned over the skull, examining it. "Amazing," he said under his breath.

"Yes," Lorenzo replied, encouraged by the Cardinal's interest. "I thought it was extraordinary."

"It's almost Biblical," the Cardinal continued.

"I agree!" Lorenzo replied. "I felt the same way as he related his tale."

"But we already have a Bible, do we not? One that has been guided by the hand of God. Words that the people have learned to trust and, in that, to trust us." The Cardinal picked up the document. "It does not include these women warriors or this strange description of the Nephilim, does it?"

Lorenzo's heart sank. "But shouldn't the Holy Father know? What if Jorge's story is the truth?"

"It is rare to find a kingdom built purely on foundations of truth," Cartega replied. "But just as surely, they can be brought down by it."

The Cardinal tossed the papers into the fireplace. Lorenzo stared, his mouth open in shock as the pages flared and curled into embers.

"I will honor your church with a visit in the coming week, as an acknowledgement of your service. And your silence." The Cardinal extended his hand.

Lorenzo stood, kissed Cartega's ring, and bowed, backing out of the Cardinal's office.

Cartega's gaze turned to the skull on his desk. Was it truly a creature of Satan? Was this a soldier in Lucifer's war of the coming Apocalypse?

He leaned forward, his head resting on his hands as he stared at it.

He felt all of Hell staring back.

HOMESTEAD

BY DELILAH S. DAWSON

Sometime between midnight and dawn, Lucy wakes to the sound of her little dog, Dash, barking his fool head off. The one-room farmhouse is still and dark, and Lucy reaches for Robert's side of the bed before remembering that he's gone.

"Dash, you hush now," she whispers.

But Dash doesn't hush. He barks and growls at the rough wood door, clawing at it like he's digging out a gopher. Lucy pushes herself to sitting, not an easy task, with her belly nine months gone. It's a hot, still night, ribbons of moonlight shining in through the house's many cracks. One hand rubbing the curve of her stomach, she creeps to the door and puts her eye to a gap in the boards. Dash whines and paws at her ankles, and she doesn't have the heart to push him away.

Outside, nothing seems amiss. The barn is locked up tight, the pigs are shadowy lumps in their wallow, and what's left of the lake glimmers with starlight. None of the animals are roused or making noise, and for the long moment that she watches, nothing moves, not even a breath of a breeze ruffling the endless miles of prairie grasses. Dash wedges his snout under the door, growling, and Lucy sighs.

"You should've gone out earlier, fool."

She opens the door, and Dash squeezes out and sprints past the outhouse toward the lake. Goosebumps ripple down Lucy's shoulders, and she crosses her arms and tries to rub them away. The sky is so wide and soft out here that it feels like she's being suffocated by a velvet pillow. Looking up almost makes her dizzy. Although the sky is clear, there's a sudden flash like lightning, the whole world momentarily bright white, but without the clap of thunder. A breeze blows through the grass and over her like ripples in a pond.

"Dash?" she calls, but not too loud. The closest neighbors are five miles off but yelling still seems rude.

The little terrier doesn't bark in reply or run home, and Lucy yawns so hard her jaw cracks. She heads back inside, one hand supporting her aching back. Dash knows his way home, and she's not waiting up all night for a silly dog.

Robert promised he'd be home in five days, and that's tomorrow, and Robert doesn't lie. Lucy closes the door and pulls in the string before settling down on the crackling mattress for a night of restless sleep. An odd chittering sound starts up outside, some new sort of frog, maybe, and it makes her skin crawl. She tosses and turns and dreams of a dark form standing over her, a tall, thin shadow reaching to caress her face.

"Robert?" she calls, voice raspy, half asleep.

But when she wakes up, she's alone. The door is open. Her throat hurts, maybe from crying. Dash is still gone.

Lucy wakes again at the rooster's call and runs eagerly to the door, but of course Robert isn't home yet. It's a good twenty miles to town, and it's not like he'd leave before there was light. Even so, she stands in the door hunting for a smudge moving on the horizon, be it dog or man, rubbing the swollen belly straining against her patched shift. The grasses part as if a large man is striding through the field, but there's no one there, just a trick of the light.

It's not that she's scared to be alone. Lucy was pumping water at three, minding babies at five, birthing cows that same year because Daddy said she had the smallest hands. It's more that... Lucy remembers watching her ma before Jeb and Sarah were born. Restless, aching, her temper a frayed thing stretched thin. That's how Lucy feels now. And what if the baby, like her daddy's calves, needs help? Sure, Robert's hands are too big and clumsy, but he could gallop for the town doctor or fetch Mrs. Gunderson from the next farm over.

As she feeds the chickens and hunts for their ever-dwindling eggs, she notices an odd mark on the barn, like a scorch mark. When she rubs a hand over it, it doesn't smear or rub away. She doesn't think it was there yesterday, but pregnancy does funny things to her mind and memory. There are more scorch marks on the ground, the grass burned black as if by fire, but only in one place. A shooting star, maybe? It would be better if Robert was here. He would surely know what to do.

"Probably stopped to buy me a pretty ribbon," she muses into the cow's warm side as milk hisses into the bucket and the calf bleats from where he's tied up. Starving, empty, with the desperation of a yowling cat in her gut, Lucy gulps sweet, hot milk right from the pail, ignoring how it soaks the front of her shift.

Outside, the sun beats down like it longs to grind her into dust. The pigs stagger in from the edge of the lake, their faces caked in lumpy black mud. The drought is even worse now, and the lake is sinking in, making the animals press deep into the sucking mud just to slake their thirst. Robert said this was the perfect place to build their homestead, but now Lucy isn't so sure. The well water tastes funny, and the crops keep failing, and the lake is disappearing. Lucy isn't a clever girl—her father and Robert both told her so—but she knows that something's wrong.

She scans the fields for Dash as she trudges out to the other barn. They keep it locked against horse thieves at night, and every morning she's greeted by gentle Belle and Beau whinnying a welcome as the handsome handful of a stallion named Devil bugles and tries to bust down the barn wall.

"Belle, Beau!" she hollers as she fumbles the key. "You-all awake?"

Within, the barn is still and silent. A goose walks over her grave, and Lucy lingers in the summer sun. Dash should be by her side, darting in to snap the necks of the scattering mice, but she hasn't seen him since he ran out the door last night.

"Devil, you bein' good?" she calls, louder than usual.

The response is a disturbingly weak kick, hooves against wood.

"I reckon not," she mutters. For some reason, Lucy doesn't want to go into the barn, but she knows that if Robert was here, he'd remind her that she's got to pull her weight, no matter how big she's got.

Belle and Beau are both pressed back against the walls of their stalls, eyes wide and rolling. The draft horses are usually sensible things, but they're acting scared, or maybe they're sick. Lucy unlatches Belle's stall door, and the mare bolts out into the sun with Beau hot on her heels. They always head straight out for the lake to drink, but instead they just stand there against the fence, stamping nervously. Something moves out by the water, something big and dark and tall, but when she blinks, it's gone. Maybe it's a summer bear, starving and mangey, on the hunt. Maybe that's why the horses are so nervous.

Lucy looks up at the sky, thinking maybe there's a twister coming. The horses surely know something she doesn't.

When she gets to Devil's stall, he's lying down, slick with sweat. "Get up now," she tells him, but he won't, so she fetches a halter and tugs him to standing. His legs tremble, but he follows her outside and stands where she leaves him, belly swollen and heaving. Belle and Beau keep their distance, and Lucy knows she should walk him, but she's got more chores to do yet and he's a vicious thing.

Outside, she looks to the lake, now a muddy mess as the water dries up, leaving odd shapes as what's long been hidden underneath the surface is revealed. Bulbous, slime-coated forms poke up like rotten teeth, heat rising off them like mist. Something screams, a high, vicious sound, and one of the dead, crooked trees falls over in a hail of mud and leaves. Maybe the bear found its prey. Maybe she's seeing things that ain't there. The horses still won't drink. She calls for Dash, but there's no answering bark.

Holding up her stomach with an arm, she looks toward town, toward the direction that should bring Robert back.

"Your daddy's on the road now," she says softly.

As if in response, the tadpole squirms in her belly, sending up a rancid burp. Robert hates it when Lucy does that, but Robert's supposed to be here, and he's not, so why would she hold it in?

Lucy keeps on with her chores, but her head feels emptier than usual. Time passes funny when a creature is heavy with child and about to burst. The day goes on forever, and she can't stop looking toward town. She'd swear she sees things moving in the muck of the lake, parting the tall grasses like buffalo, making the air quiver like August heat on stone. She calls for Dash again and again, but the little dog doesn't turn up.

As twilight fades to dark, she leans against the door of the crooked farmhouse, staring out at odd, red flashes dancing over the water. Must be the sunset striking fireflies, some trick of the light. Heavy, hulking shadows seem to stalk across the horizon. The coyotes are singing, and there's something odd in their song. She hopes they didn't snatch Dash up, little thing that he is. She already double-checked all the doors and fences, made sure everything was tight and snug. She checked the stalls for rattlesnakes and walked Devil and locked the barn door.

"Maybe the wagon was too small to carry all the good things your daddy's bringin'," Lucy murmurs to her belly, "and he has to borrow a bigger one. He'll be home tomorrow, I know it."

She falls asleep in the rocking chair with her belly under one hand and the gun under the other. She doesn't know much, but she knows something feels *wrong*.

In Lucy's dreams, somebody is screaming, and when she jerks awake the screaming continues. Her fingers curl around the gun's sweat-slicked stock.

Maybe it's Robert, and he needs her help. There's panthers and bears and wolves, after all, and she's seen their silhouettes in every shifting shadow these past few days. She crams her feet into his old boots and waddles for the door.

But it's not Robert that's screaming, and she knows it.

"Dash?"

Her little dog normally sleeps by the fire, but—well, he never came back, did he?

Lucy wrenches open the door, expecting to see Robert valiantly fighting a grizzly, but everything looks just as it should—if not for the screaming. It's the pigs, she can tell now, all of them hollering in pure terror, and she hurries to their pen, Robert's gun clutched in her hands.

She doesn't like to kill things, hates twisting even the meanest hen's neck on the hungriest day, but whatever's causing trouble can't be allowed to live. They need those pigs.

The moon is a scant sliver, but Lucy sees eight of the huge, mud-spackled beasts huddled up against the fences, making the wood boards creak and belly out. There's something big in the middle of their sty, sunk in the mud, something they're trying to get away from. That mangey, hungry bear, maybe. She sets the gun tight against her shoulder and pulls the trigger, just trying to scare it off. The bear doesn't move, and Lucy edges closer and realizes... it's the ninth hog, turned over on its side and gone dreadfully still.

Well, not exactly *still*.

It's shaking... but like it's shaking from the inside.

As Lucy creeps closer, tripping over hidden lumps in the sty mud, the trembling pig bursts open. Blood splashes hot over her cheeks. She scrubs a fist over sticky eyelashes and watches something—God almighty, what is that?—slither out of the pig. She steps closer and shoots again, another miss. The thing—it's like a snake, or a worm, but flesh-covered and toothy—turns toward her, almost like it's looking for her, and she drops the empty gun and runs for the barn amid a chorus of hog screams.

Those pigs—they might be the only thing that can save the failing farm, and they can't afford to lose another one. Shaking like a leaf, clumsy as an ox, Lucy snatches the pitchfork from where it leans against the barn and hurries back out to the hog pen. The slithery thing rushes to meet her, and the baby jerks in her stomach like it wants to run away, and she stabs that pitchfork straight down.

She feels it in her bones as the tines punch through the creature and stick in the hard earth.

Like a snake, it's a mix of soft and hard, bone and flesh, but it writhes in death like any other animal does. There's a sizzle, and Lucy looks down to find its blood burning a hole in Robert's old boot. She wipes it off against a post and steps back, farther and farther away from this—this thing.

"Robert!" she calls before remembering—he's not there.

The hogs settle down a bit and sniff their fallen friend in the way pigs have, almost like they could have feelings, if they didn't taste so good, and her face goes all hot and just pours tears. She's trembling, arms wrapped around her belly, pitchfork twitching as whatever the hell that thing is dies. The pitchfork's wood handle falls to the ground, the metal tines dissolved to syrup.

This—none of this—is possible.

Lucy grew up in a big family, and moving out to the prairie homestead with Robert made her lonely as a cloud, but she's never felt so alone in her life as she does right now, like she's a million miles from anything she loves, and she wants to fall to the ground and beat it with her fists until it opens up and swallows her whole.

Out of nowhere, one of the hogs starts screaming again. The other animals stampede away from it to the opposite side of the paddock, and Lucy feels like she might never blink again because she's stuck watching this pig she's raised from a little pink suckling fall to its side and start shaking, just like the last one did.

Across the sty, another pig screams and falls.

And another.

And another.

Four pigs on their sides, twitching like they're full of bees.

The remaining pigs don't know what to do, but they're smart, and they're watching.

Lucy just stands there, frozen. The child writhes in her belly, forcing hot bile up the back of her throat. Whatever that snake thing is, it's not something that's got any business existing. She's no good at reloading the shotgun, and the bullets are all the way inside the house. The pitchfork's destroyed, and a knife is too puny to kill whatever's coming out of those dying pigs.

She's got to get away.

Town's twenty miles from here, but the Gunderson farmstead is only five, and for all that they don't speak much English, they're sturdy folk, and that Mr. Gunderson hates a snake.

Lucy fumbles with the barn key, and she can only hope that Devil's in better shape after she walked him in circles for an hour. She throws open the door and snatches his bridle off the wall, but he's lying on his side in his stall, panting like he's run a mile, his bloated belly trembling in an all-too-familiar way.

"Oh, Robert," Lucy murmurs. "You promised me he'd sire a line of champions."

Devil's a lost cause, but the draft horses seem fine, so she grabs Belle's rope halter and leads the mare over to a stack of hay bales. The big horse is nervous as a bride, her eyes rolling every which way as she whickers nervously to Beau. After tying her halter into reins, Lucy tosses them over Belle's neck.

"I'll bring her back, Beau," she murmurs, leaping up with every ounce of strength she has to straddle the broad, warm back. It's a good thing Lucy took to wearing Robert's old britches under her dress, and it's likewise fortunate that her daddy made sure she could ride, for all that Robert says it's unladylike. Her belly makes her unbalanced and awkward, and she knows full well that riding isn't good for the child, but she understands on a bone-deep level that if she doesn't get off the farm, her child won't stand a chance of living to see his daddy.

Back in his stall, Devil lets out a sound no horse should ever make, a sort of wheezing, groaning squeal that ends in a wet, cracking splatter, and Lucy nudges Belle with her knees, pointing her out the barn doors. The mare is happy to oblige, snorting as she gathers herself for a run. It's not safe to gallop a horse at night across a prairie full of hidden gopher holes, but it's a hell of a lot safer than sticking around that barn to see what came out of Devil.

Lucy used to love a good gallop, but that was before she was chock full of child and scared for her life. It takes everything she has just to stay upright, clinging to Belle's sweaty back, her legs aching, spread too wide around the horse's barrel gut. One of Lucy's boots slips off, and all she can do is cry. Belle stumbles and catches herself, and there's a sharp *pop* somewhere up inside of Lucy's belly. Hot liquid gushes down her thighs, making Belle's back all the harder to cling to. Lucy knows it's her waters, and she knows that's bad, but she tells herself it's piss to keep from going mad with worry.

As they gallop, the coyotes call to each other, less a song than a warning, and the night all runs together, endless dark grasses and scrubby trees lit by those dancing red lights, the mountains looming shadows in the distance and the woman's only thoughts as repetitive as the horse's thundering hooves: *Don't step in a hole, don't fall off, don't step in a hole, don't fall off,* a prayer for them both. The child goes still inside her, and she pins her lips against wave after wave of nausea.

The only sign that time is passing is Belle's exhaustion, her sides groaning like bellows and slick with sweat. She tries to fall off to a trot, but Lucy kicks the poor thing with all she's got, both feet bare now, her britches soaked. Belle gives a little buck of indignancy and keeps on, but she can't go on forever. Neither, for that matter, can Lucy. She's not even steering, and she reckons the only reason they end up where they're headed is because when Mr. Gunderson borrows Belle for plowing, he gives her oats afterward as a treat.

The neighbors' fine farmstead rises up from the prairie like a squat black ghost, German and disapproving, all straight lines as harsh as their language.

"Mr. Gunderson!" Lucy shouts as Belle drops down to a trot.

Lucy nearly bounces off, each smack of her rump against the mare's spine slamming pain directly into her aching belly. When Belle is walking, Lucy slides off. Her feet are numb, stupid rocks, and she stumbles and falls to her knees on the hard ground. "Mr. Gunderson, help!"

The only answer is Belle snorting nervously. No dogs bark, and she knows the Gundersons have three. No one hollers a hello or comes rushing out with a gun. The farm is just… dead silent.

It's a hot night, but Lucy's as cold as Christmas as she lumbers up to standing. When she puts a hand on her belly, it's taut and hard, and it tightens under her palm in a way that suggests time is no longer her friend.

Nothing's screaming, at least. Maybe the Gundersons and their dogs went into town just like Robert did, to sell furs with the mountain men and hear the news. Neighbors are neighbors, and they won't mind if Lucy takes shelter here, not when they learn what happened back home. Leaving Belle to graze, she walks up to the dark house, calling out to the Gundersons, doing the neighborly thing to let them know she's here.

When she raises her fist to knock, the door creaks open under her touch, and she only pauses a moment before pushing her way in. They got a peculiar scent, the Gundersons, boiled cabbage and sausage and some soap they make with flowers, and it's usually comforting, but just now it makes her gut roil.

"Mr. Gunderson? It's me, Lucy. I could surely use some help."

The house is utterly still, and she's almost grateful. She couldn't explain what happened back home to someone who speaks her language, much less folks who mostly smile and say, "Ja!" no matter what she says. She'll stay here tonight, try to calm herself down, and then...

"Oh, Robert. You promised it would only be five days," she whispers.

Her heart sinks when she realizes that she's still missing that extra pair of hands. She'd hoped Mrs. Gunderson would know a thing or two about babies, but now Lucy is alone and even farther away from the doctor in town.

A woman's job is work—that's what Robert always says. No time for woolgathering. She heads for the stove to start up a fire, but there are embers in there, still cherry red. As she adds in some kindling, she thinks the Gundersons must've left recently, for the fire to still be warm. The baby hairs rise up on her neck as she patters barefoot through their big room, lighting lanterns and candles and feeling like she's someplace she doesn't belong but like there's nowhere else she can go.

The leaking continues, and she has to stop and breathe funny as her belly tightens and her innards growl. She almost heads into the bedroom, but she knows how much work went into that pretty piecework quilt she's seen on the Gundersons' bed. Instead, she heads out to the barn with a lantern to fetch a horse blanket, some old rag they won't mind getting ruined.

The farmyard is deadly still, the cows asleep in their paddock, as cows ought to be. The Gundersons, like Robert, built all their fences to extend out into the once-full lake so the animals could drink at will, and the moon glints off the wet expanse in a way that makes Lucy stop and stare. There are odd shapes out there, poking up out of the pudding-muck, strange things that surely aren't stumps or rocks. From out here, they almost look like...

Eggs.

And she could ignore that if not for one particular lump that's not like the others, one that's about the size and shape of a large German man.

She steps closer, hurrying, hurting, picking her way through the mud, hating the clammy ooze between her toes but desperate to understand what she's seeing. She stops when she knows.

It's Mr. Gunderson, lying on his back in the mud wallow that was once a lake, a bloody, gaping hole in his chest suggesting there's not a damn thing she can do to help him. One of his dogs, the spotted one, lies at his side, just torn to bits. All around them are big, leathery plant things, almost like eggs, rising up from the mud. A few of the eggs have bloomed like morning glories, but the remaining ones are almost see-through, and the shapes inside seem to wiggle in the lantern's light, surely some trick of the flame and Lucy's own exhaustion. One of the egg things twitches, or her mind tells her it does, and she can't get back to solid ground fast enough.

Mr. Gunderson, her neighbor, a kind man, and he's—

No. She can't think too hard about that.

Can't think about the way his exposed ribs curl the wrong way, reaching for the sky.

Robert calls her crazy sometimes, and Lucy's heard that some women go a bit mad when they're in the throes of childbirth, so now she starts to reckon it's true. None of this—

it can't be real. She's been seeing things out in the prairie grass all day, things that aren't there and things that are, things with teeth and claws and faces like angry catfish. Her belly stiffens, and she has no choice but to hold her breath and double over, teeth gritted, the scent of fresh blood and rotting mud fighting down her throat. No matter what's real and what isn't, the baby's coming.

Trying to put Mr. Gunderson's crow-pecked eyes out of mind, she heads for the safety of the house. That same chittering frog-call echoes over the lake, standing all the little hairs up her neck on end.

Back inside, she sighs with the animal pleasure of being behind a bolted door, surrounded by the warm light of lanterns and candles. Some predator got Mr. Gunderson and his dog, but that's a risk pioneers take when they file for a homestead. Probably a wolf, she tells herself, because surely the snake-thing that slithered out of that pig was her mind playing tricks. She's heard the wolves, seen their eyes shining green at night. Yes, that's it. Mr. Gunderson and his dog went down to the lake for water and fell prey to the starving wolves, and Mrs. Gunderson is in town visiting her sister, so she doesn't know yet, the poor thing.

Firmly past being polite, Lucy hunts around the big room, but she can't find anything soft to spread before the fire. She notices a loaf of bread sitting on the table, a plate fallen and broken on the ground, a lump of butter smeared by a boot on the shiny wood floor. All is quiet, all is still. Ice seeps down Lucy's spine, lost in a shudder of pain as her belly constricts.

She has to open the bedroom door—for the quilt, and to make sure she's as safe as she thinks she is.

"I'm right sorry, Mrs. Gunderson," she says, putting a trembling hand on the fancy doorknob. She doesn't like to invade someone's personal space, but she opens the door, and—

Sweet holy Jesus.

Mrs. Gunderson is in the bed, just sleeping away, and here Lucy's been walking around her house like she owns it, and like Mr. Gunderson isn't dead out back.

"I'm so sorry," she says, but Mrs. Gunderson doesn't move.

Mrs. Gunderson doesn't…

…breathe.

Lucy holds up the lantern.

That pretty white quilt she covets is soaked in black-shiny blood, and now she understands why the house is so quiet.

Mrs. Gunderson is dead.

Dead, and… ripped apart.

The two other dogs are with her, likewise half-eaten, fallen in front of the bed as if protecting their mistress.

Lucy takes a step back, and another, and another, until she's in the main room. She slams the bedroom door and slides down the wall to the floor. Her stomach heaves, and she dribbles puke into her hands and wipes them on her britches, unsure how to be a person just now but still certain she's not supposed to ruin such good, clean floors.

The fire's crackling merrily, but she can't just give in, can't settle her heavy bones on the floor and prepare to push out a child into some hungry monster's maw. She's got to get up, got to get out. Got to find some safe place to go to ground. Maybe she can make it into town, where there are mountain men trading furs, armed to the teeth and ready to step between her and whatever's dealing death across the prairie. Robert will call her crazy and dumb and a weak little thing, and she won't mind, she won't argue—as long as someone keeps her and the baby safe.

She drags her body to standing and lumbers over to pull down the shotgun on hooks over the front door and sling it over her arm. It'll be loaded, so she's got two shots, which is a damn sight better than nothing. Before she heads out, she pulls on a pair of old boots sitting by the stove and snatches up the stale loaf of bread, slathering it in the fallen butter with her bare hands and choking down what she can.

Outside, she whistles for Belle, but the mare doesn't trot over like she should. Her rump's on the ground, poking out from behind the barn—poor, tired thing must've laid down for a little nap. As Lucy stumbles across the farmyard, her sight readjusting to the darkness, she trips on something slick and rubbery. It's an odd, thick, wet lump, almost like an old shirt made out of skin, shining translucent and moist in the moonlight.

Nothing here is right. This whole place—this whole goddamn stretch of prairie—is wrong.

"Belle, sugar," she calls, voice trembling. "Wake up, baby."

The mare doesn't get up, doesn't budge, and even a woman as desperate as Lucy can understand why she'd prefer to sleep. But as she rounds the corner there's something wrong with Belle's head, like the horse got tangled in a blanket. Lucy gets around front, and the ugliest thing she's ever seen is clamped over Belle's face, like a giant spider covered in human skin, its rattlesnake tail curled around the horse's throat.

Lucy spins to run, stumbling in Mr. Gunderson's oversized boots, desperate to get away from whatever that... *thing* is.

"I'm goin' crazy," she mutters to herself. "This ain't real. This is... this is some kind of sickness. It's got to be. Robert said I been acting strange, and Robert don't lie..." She stops and stands there, rooted under the wide, black sky, halfway between the locked barn and the farmhouse.

She has to escape. But from what? And to where?

What could possibly be safe now?

She needs another horse, which means she has to fetch the barn key from where it hangs by the front door. The lock is slick in her hands, just as stubborn as the one back home, and she keeps glancing over her shoulder, expecting some skin-spider-snake to leap on her, but the prairie is quiet except for the madly chittering frogs. Even the coyotes are silent now. The lock pops open, and she flings open the barn doors, looking to the first stall, where Mr. Gunderson keeps his riding horse, Karl.

No curious nose pokes out of the stall. There are no stomps, no whinnies of welcome.

"Please," Lucy murmurs. "Oh, please, Lord."

Karl is on the ground, torn near in half across the chest, like his heart jumped right out through his ribs, and she thinks back on poor Devil and shudders. A spider-crab-thing like the one on Belle's face lies dead in the corner.

Stall after stall, this is what she finds: dead horses, a dead mule, dead lambs, all ripped open across the chest or half eaten.

Finally, there's a noise other than Lucy's sobbing, but it's not the comforting sound of hoofbeats and shouting, not Robert calling her name, not the sort of noise that promises everything will be fine. It's the cows lowing out back. The first few moos are curious, then warning, then furious and desperate and frightened. The beasts are moving, a thunder of hooves and big bodies crashing clumsily against the wood fence.

Lucy's fingers tense on Mr. Gunderson's gun as her belly contracts. She's starting to get an idea of what's out there, all these hard-to-hit, fleshy things with long tails and sharp teeth. She can't shoot them all, and she can't run away fast enough on her own, but maybe she can use the cows.

She realizes now, deep down in her bones and sinews, that Robert isn't coming to help her. He's not on his way home, galloping to rescue her like some big damn hero. He's in town, likely at the saloon or whorehouse, spending the money from his furs and thinking everything is just fine and his silly fool of a wife can't complain about another day away.

Robert can't save her, and the Gundersons can't save her, and the town doctor can't save her, and hiding behind a sturdy door can't save her—it sure as hell didn't save Mrs. Gunderson. Lucy hates death—Robert teases her all the time, tells her a pioneer woman's got to toughen up. But if there's any hope of living through the night, of her child getting to see daylight, she's got to take matters into her own two hands. She's got to kill before she gets killed.

There on the barn wall is Mr. Gunderson's scythe, just as sharp as the one her daddy taught her to swing when she was a girl. She slings the shotgun over her shoulder and takes up the more familiar scythe, storming out of the barn toward the cows, her belly now a roiling rock, angry as boiling water, furious as her heart. She's soaked through with sweat and brine, and her fingers splay over her jerking stomach, caressing the sharp elbows and knees now fighting to escape.

"Just a little longer," she croons. "It's almost time, I promise."

The Gundersons' cattle aren't like the pigs—they're not pressed against the fence, watching cleverly. No, they're stampeding around like idiots, running from one side of the paddock to the other, too dumb to break the boards, just dumb enough to try to run away when there's nowhere to run. Out in the grass, a glossy black curve like a stallion's neck surfaces briefly before diving back under cover. Ice pools along Lucy's spine, her old dress wet as a frog skin. She feels a pressure down below and clenches her nethers. It's happening faster and harder now, and she knows that she can't stop what's coming.

When her belly stills, she drops the scythe and puts the gun to her shoulder, hating that the little one inside has to hear gunshots. When next she sees that slick black curve out in the grass circling ever closer, she squints and pulls the trigger. There's a sharp pinging noise and a squeal, and it dives back under cover.

Fine, then. Let it come closer.

She may be no good with a gun, but she's got one more shot and she's able with a scythe, and she'll throttle that monster with her bare hands if it'll let the babe be born in peace.

Sure enough, it changes direction away from the cows, stalking her now, tail lashing over the grasses like a cat.

With a deep breath, she takes aim and pulls the trigger again.

It's a miss. She's out of bullets.

And whatever it is, there's more of 'em out there.

The cattle can sense it, can tell the hunters are getting close. She drops the gun and takes up the scythe, barely able to uncurl and stand as another shudder runs through her. Everything in her body tells her to drop to her knees and push, but she won't do that until this critter is good and dead and it's safe to close her eyes and scream.

Her shoulders tense, and the animal inside her suggests that something is sneaking up behind her. Knowing it's stupid but not knowing what else to do, she hurries toward the cattle pen. As long as she's standing out in the farmyard alone, she's vulnerable, but if she can get in among the cows, she'll be one of many. That's why they stick to herds, after all, her daddy taught her—it means maybe a neighbor'll get eaten first.

Lucy bends to maneuver herself between the boards—a tight squeeze. The cows stomp and career across the pen, their soft black eyes focused on the prairie. Whatever's out there—they're clever. They're stalkers, not the sort of thing that just barrels out. Robert said he got stalked by a panther once, that he knew it was there but never saw it, so he just had to return to town to spend the night. Lucy reckons it was just another excuse for staying out late at the saloon, but now she knows how it feels, being hunted by something you can't see, can't hear, can't smell.

One of the cows bellows, and they all stampede right at Lucy. She spreads her legs and holds her ground, scythe in both hands, belly trembling. The herd parts, running around and behind her like she's going to save them, and she wants to laugh at how dumb these animals are. She's just a weak little woman, as Robert so often reminds her. A bony hip nudges her, and her borrowed boots sink into the mud, and she feels the monsters sizing her up, somewhere out there.

"Come on then," she growls, pausing as a wave of pain nearly doubles her over. "I ain't got all night."

Beyond the fence, the grasses sway, and a smooth, black curve cuts through the shifting shadows and disappears. It's closer now, and another cow bumps her, and she starts to think maybe she made a mistake coming in here, that the clumsy cows might do something foolish and kill her before whatever's hunting them all can finish the job.

Moonlight glints as a tall, slick form rises up against the starlight, a twisted black stallion made of nightmares and blades, and Lucy holds up her scythe and grits her teeth and begs her body not to tense up, not now, not when she's got to put everything she has into killing something that's got no business existing. With a screech, it charges, and the cows bellow and careen around her, and she waits and waits and then puts everything she has into sending the shining scythe in a powerful arc.

Lucy's arms judder as the scythe blade slams into hard black armor and sticks. An unholy scream rips through the night. A constellation of burning liquid splashes across her arms. The scythe jerks out of her hands—its blade already melting— as a labor pain rips through her body, snapping her teeth over her tongue as she falls to hands and knees in the dirt. The scythe handle follows, the metal blade dissolved like penny candy left out in the rain.

She doesn't know if it's dead, doesn't know if its friends are close, she's waiting for the crunch of teeth in her spine when the air… changes. She looks up and watches as if in slow motion as the slick black thing stands—

And is sliced in half.

As if by nothing.

The monster falls to the ground, a clatter of horse legs sharp as beetle shells and a long, curved head like nothing she's ever seen before. It's as big as Devil and as wrong as his namesake, and she doesn't understand what's happened.

The pain blessedly stops, and Lucy uncurls, looking up in confusion. The air shimmers, and then there's something standing there, something like a person but bigger, taller, broader. At first she thinks its face is made of metal, but then it takes off a mask to reveal a face like a feral hog and a catfish had an unholy child—so she didn't imagine it. It's got long hair, thick and beaded, and armor that gleams over unexpected curves. When it—she—looks at Lucy, she wants to shrink up and disappear into the earth rather than feel those strange eyes crawling over her, judging her, the larger version of a scythe in the creature's hand hovering inches away from her head.

Lucy doesn't know what to say, but her daddy taught her manners, so she clears her throat and says, "Thank you." It ends in a groan as another pain doubles her over, and she struggles not to push, to hold in this baby for a few moments longer.

When Lucy is able to straighten up again, the creature points at her belly and makes that annoying chittering, clicking sound Lucy's been hearing all night, the one she thought was just frogs.

"My child," Lucy says softly. "My baby. Robert Junior. Little Robby, maybe." She mimics cradling a babe, hoping the terrifying hunter can maybe understand. Surely these things have children they love? After all, even wolves love their pups.

In response, the hunter shakes her head fiercely, braids clattering, and holds up her weapon in a threatening sort of way. Lucy is out of weapons, but anger flows through her.

"No," she barks gruffly. "No. It's mine." When the creature steps closer, she pummels it with her fists, finding only slick metal over hard muscle.

The hunter steps back. The big, terrifying head nods once, almost in respect, or maybe pity. Then the creature puts her helmet back on and disappears as if stepping sideways into nothing.

The next pain takes her, and doubled over as she is, Lucy can't look up, but the noises she hears—slices and squeals and groans and hissing—give her hope that the bad monsters out in the grasses are dying by the hand of the good one who saved her.

Finally, finally, there is silence.

For the first time tonight, things don't feel wrong. Lucy drags herself out of the cow pen. As she crawls on hands and knees toward the farmhouse, she hears a sharp sound out past the barn, and the muddy lake erupts in blinding flame.

She keeps crawling.

Inside, the stove fire is still burning, but there's nothing soft here, not like she'd planned back home, no neat stack of sheets and a kettle of water heated over the flames. Lucy gets on her hands and knees on the wood boards and waits, knowing it won't take long. She's dripping sweat now, her head on fire and her heart thumping like galloping hooves. The next time her body tenses up, she lets it do what it will, what it needs, lets it push and heave and howl. After all this time holding back, it feels good to give in, now that it's safe. She knows Mrs. Gunderson is not twenty feet away, dead in the bed, but that big girl outside with the armor and the scythe—something about that powerful huntress tells Lucy she's safe now. Protected, even.

"Robert, you goddamn liar!" she shrieks with her last, big, painful heave, and she catches her baby with her own two hands.

Except—it's not a baby, or maybe it was, once, but now it's something else, small and twisted and hard, sucked dry as the lake outside, and she clutches it to her chest as her vision goes dark.

She falls onto her back, eyes unseeing, as her round belly bursts open like an overripe fruit and many small things slither out.

"Lucy?" a voice calls outside. "You in there with the Gundersons, Lucy? I'm home."

THE HOTEL MARIPOSA

BY DAVID BARNETT

"What a dump," says Ben. He always says that. It's sort of his thing. Carol looks over at Cade, who's in turn framing the building in front of them inside a rectangle made of the outstretched thumb and forefinger of each hand. He always does that, too. Like he's Cecil B. DeMille, sizing up the crucial shot. Creatures of habit, men.

"Frank and Dean stayed in the fifties," says Carol. "In fact, the whole Rat Pack did." She shields her eyes against the midday sun and looks at the wide, squat building built into the New England hillside, surrounded by a girdle of tall trees. The Hotel Mariposa.

Ben pulls a joint out of the breast pocket of his creased checked shirt. "Now, maybe if we could summon up Ol' Blue Eyes, that might get us a third season…"

The Hotel Mariposa is their last chance. They have to deliver the goods to Netflix in four weeks. Once the novelty of season one of *American Spook-Chasers* had stopped being a trending topic, and season two (currently streaming) was getting what you could only very politely call lukewarm notices, the cards were on the table. A Halloween special, make or break. Something good. Something juicy. Or *American Spook-Chasers* was as dead as the graveyards they spent their nights stumbling around in.

"What'll get us a third season is you staying on top of your game, not getting stoned, and actually getting footage," says Cade, hauling his case out of the station wagon. "I mean, we don't want Phoenix all over again…"

Whatever happened, they'd always have Phoenix. The one time there was indisputable, right-there-in-front-of-your-eyes, holy-shit-this-is-world-changing paranormal activity. And Ben was in the toilet vacuuming up two lines of coke from the rim of the handbasin. Carol thought Cade would in some way hate him for that.

"No, we *do* want Phoenix all over again," says Carol, flipping up the pages on her iPad. "We just need evidence this time."

Ben offers her the joint and she shakes her head. He shrugs and takes another drag, pointedly not holding it out to Cade. He looks across the wide gravel driveway pitted with weeds and small, wild shrubs at the peeling, faded Art Deco facade of the hotel. Ben wipes the sweat from his bald head with his hand, and rubs it on his sagging jeans, and says, "So what's the story here, then?"

"You didn't read the briefing notes?" says Carol with an exasperated sigh. Cade makes a pantomime of rolling his eyes.

Ben shrugs. "Give me the TL;DR."

"It was built in the 1920s, bolt-hole of the rich and famous. Hemingway famously got drunk and trashed the bar. But there's always been strange phenomena reported, from the word go. A guest disappeared for three days in 1928. When they found him, half starved to death, he said he'd been lost in the corridors all that time. Poltergeist activity, sightings of dead people, the usual. In the thirties, a woman nearly drowned in the swimming pool. Said she'd been doing laps and suddenly couldn't see the sides. Like she was in the middle of a millpond-calm ocean. She swam for hours until suddenly she hit the steps. She was treated for exhaustion at hospital." Carol flicks through her notes on the tablet. "Business started to drop off, and the place was closed for good in 1967 after the murders."

"Oh, yeah, that I know about," says Ben, grinding the joint under the heel of his boot. "That hippy death cult, right? All got jobs as waiters and porters and shit, and then rampaged through the place gutting the guests with machetes. That's gotta get you no stars on TripAdvisor." Ben shoulders his bag and sets off for the curved glass entrance, boots crunching on the gravel. He glances over his shoulder at Cade, then Carol. "So yeah, let's hope for another Phoenix, eh? Wasn't all bad. For some of us."

"Dick," says Cade to his back. He runs a hand through his unruly dark hair and looks around at what would once have been carefully tended gardens, now rewilded to high-grassed meadow, and says, "Weird how this whole place is built in a kind of huge bowl. Like a natural amphitheater."

"Jesus, Cade, didn't you read the briefing notes either? It was the site of a huge meteor strike in the sixteenth century. That's why they built it here. Groundwork had already been done." Carol looks up at the dark windows at the front of the Mariposa. "I feel like we're being watched, don't you?"

"Let's fucking hope so," says Cade, setting off to follow Ben. "Or it's back to corporate training videos for us."

Carol rubs her bare forearms, feeling a sudden chill. She glances around at the thick semicircle of trees surrounding the grounds, and hurries after the others toward the Mariposa.

For two days Hin'tui has been sitting in total stillness, communing with the land. It is important, he thinks, to align with the hunting ground. You must make the territory your friend, your ally. He has seen too many younger Yautja ignore this. They treat the hunting ground as merely the stage on which their glory will be played out and their honor won. The land can be a powerful weapon. And if you do not make it your ally, you risk making it your enemy.

But this is strange land. All the Yautja know that. It is why they come here. It is why not all return. And not just because of the prey—Hin'tui already has two Kiande Amedha trophies, hard won to the obvious enhancement of his honor. He has no fear of them. No, it is the hunting ground itself that is to be feared.

The sun is high in the sky, casting dappled golden light through the tallest branches of the trees. Hin'tui decides to commune a little while longer, to probe and examine this territory, to test for weaknesses he can exploit, or strengths he can employ. Then, when night falls, the Hunt will begin.

The Mariposa is exactly everything you'd want from a remote, abandoned, haunted hotel. Red carpets. Long corridors with mahogany doors leading to rooms and suites far bigger and grander than you'd get in any hotel today. A lounge bar and a huge dining hall, with a stage on which a set of drums and a piano sit, coated with dust. A roof terrace overlooking the tops of the trees and a lake beyond, glittering in the late summer sun.

Ben takes the camera around on his own, doing some deliberately shaky shots, running down the corridors, into rooms, slamming doors and hurtling around corners. *To edit in if things don't get exciting enough*, he thinks. Things *have* to get exciting enough, they all know.

"Weird how nobody bought this place," says Cade, standing behind the bar in the lounge, inspecting a bottle of bourbon he's found in a cupboard. "Even with the murders, prime bit of real estate like this…"

Carol doesn't remind him it's all in the briefing notes. Instead she says, "They did. Several times. Never amounted to anything. Last time anyone bothered was in the early eighties. Team of contractors was brought in to do some preliminary work. They packed up after a day and refused to come back."

Cade twists the cap off the bottle and gives it an exploratory sniff. Carol says suddenly, "Mariposa. It means butterfly."

Cade shrugs, and tips the bottle to his lips. "Like… emerging from a cocoon," muses Carol.

———

It lasts a heartbeat. Less. A tenth of a heartbeat. But she sees it. It's no longer Cade standing in front of her, but her mother, one of Carol's last memories of her. In the park on a hot day, almost silhouetted against the sun, lifting a bottle of Dr. Pepper to her mouth, the golden light picking out the diffuse shape of her body through the thin sundress. Carol is sitting on the grass, playing with her plastic dinosaurs. She loves dinosaurs. She says, "Mommy, if a T-Rex came to eat me, would you protect me?"

*Her mother laughs and wipes the drops of soda from her chin
with the back of her hand. "Of course, baby, I'd protect you from
all the monsters." And one month later, she had gone, and Carol
never saw her again.*

"Are you all right?" says Cade, and Carol realizes she's got
her eyes closed tight.

A sudden clashing, discordant racket makes them both
jump, Cade spitting bourbon down his shirt. On the stage,
Ben is sitting at the drum kit, bashing the skins and cymbals
with a pair of sticks, dust flying up around him in a cloud.
Carol hadn't seen him sneak in.

"Dick," spits Cade, wiping his mouth with the back of
his hand.

"Pick anything up?" shouts Carol across the lounge
as Ben throws the sticks on the carpet, heading over to
them. The vision of her mother has already faded, almost
forgotten.

"Just a fucking hernia lugging my gear around," says
Ben, holding out his hand for Cade to pass him the bourbon.
"This place is huge. Bigger than it looks from the outside.
I think it goes right into the hill. The rooms are pretty cool,
some of them have sheets and blankets."

"We should maybe go and choose a couple of suites,"
says Carol. She feels the hairs prickle on her arms again, like
she did outside. When she felt like she was being watched.

"Well, I want to be on a different floor," says Ben, taking
a swig of the bourbon. "I actually want to get some sleep
tonight, if we're doing the full twenty-four-hour stint from
eight tomorrow morning."

He winks at Cade, and Carol rolls her eyes. Ever since Phoenix, ever since she and Cade got together, Ben hasn't let it drop that he heard them that night, after Cade had snuck into her room in that old motel. But there's always an edge to it, a viciousness. She knows Ben thought he'd lost out to Cade, that he had some kind of claim on Carol. He'd been like that since the three of them were at college. She'd once heard them talking in a bar, unaware she was walking back from the bathroom. They clinked their bottles together and Ben said sourly, "Best man won, I guess."

Like I'm a fucking teddy bear to be played for at a fairground sideshow stall.

Cade, takes the bottle back and says, "If something happens, we want to be together. Especially given the stories about this place having some kind of weird geometry."

"Bullshit and you know it," says Ben, then shrugs. "But if you say so."

"Let's go look, then," says Carol. She can feel tension between the two men, and she wants to head it off, especially if they're going to be drinking. "I definitely want a suite, though."

Hin'tui watches the three oomans leave, and wonders which of them it will be. It doesn't really matter; none of them will survive the night. He taps his wrist and the shift suit fizzes off. He'd been following the big ooman, puzzling at him banging doors and running along the corridors, his recording device held high, or low against the floor. He wonders why they are here. Other than to facilitate the birthing. Again, their reasons for their presence are of no concern. The conditions are periodically right for the Hunt;

the presence of ooman hosts and the hatching of one of the eggs buried deep below this place. Sometimes one happens, sometimes the other. When both occur it is a fortuitous moment. Hin'tui has been waiting patiently for his turn to hunt here.

Hin'tui strides through the room and steps onto the raised area, considering the curved black box on legs, lid propped open displaying innards of wire and wood. Hin'tui taps one of the white keys and a dull sound emerges. Another key produces a note of a different timbre. A device for making music. Perhaps when the creature is dead he will compose a victory song upon it.

He wonders if it is here, yet. Scuttling under a table or behind the walls. Waiting for its moment. Hin'tui draws his curved blade—the only weapon he has brought to the hunting ground, aside from the wrist-blades built into his armor—and gazes at the reflection of his yellow eyes in the metal.

The Yautja call this place *Gorath Pun'tila*. He had been listening to the oomans converse, invisible in the corner. His universal translator offers him an understanding of their words, but their meaning is often obtuse. Still, he gets a sense of their unease about this place, an inkling of what *Gorath Pun'tila* would be in their context.

Something very like: *the place where nothing is as it seems.*

"Let me guess," says Ben behind her, making her jump. "*All work and no play makes a Carol a dull girl.*"

"Very funny," says Carol. She's sitting in one of the stylish, egg-shaped easy chairs in the lobby, her iPad clipped into her Bluetooth keyboard, making some preliminary notes for the voiceover script. Aside from some freelance production people, it's mainly the three of them who do *American Spook-Chasers*. It was the lo-fi, Blair Witch kind-of feel that made it such a hit at first. But things move so fast these days; even after two seasons the show is being considered old hat. They need to get results.

Something has to happen.

"Did you want something?" says Carol testily, to Ben lurking behind her.

"Cade wants us all to do a little to-camera piece. Talking about our motivation, all that shit."

She can guess Ben's spiel. *Ain't no such thing as ghosts. Once you're dead, you're dead. I haven't seen nothing can't be explained by tricks of the light or the mind fooling itself.* Ben plays up the resident skeptic schtick, which suits the show. Gives people a way in if they're not believers themselves, rather than it just being a bunch of credulous geeks jumping at every flickering candle flame.

"Where do you want to do it?"

"Here's fine." Ben sets up and says, "So, why do you do this?"

Carol pauses a moment, still staring at her iPad screen. "Because when I was four years old my mother left me and my sister with my daddy. And we never found out what happened to her. It was like she fell off the face of the Earth. And all these years I've been searching for her not knowing if she's dead or alive." Carol looks at the camera. "I think she's dead. And this is maybe my way of continuing the search."

"What if you find her spirit?" says Ben. "Or it finds you?"

"Then I can ask her why," says Carol, turning back to the keyboard. Ben films for another few seconds then gives her the thumbs up and cuts.

"I loved when you did it for the first episode, and I still love it," says Ben. "Even if it is—*Jesus! What was that?*"

Carol frowns—had she heard something? Scrabbling or scratching?—and turns to where he's pointing. "I didn't see anything."

"Something running on the desk. Oh, man, I fucking hate rats. Shit."

"They're more scared of you than you are of them," says Carol, concentrating on her script again.

"Only people who say that are ones who never got bit by a rat," says Ben. "Shit. I'm going to go smoke something to calm my nerves."

"What did Cade say on his to-camera piece?"

"Same as always," says Ben with a shrug. "*There's more than we know, more than we see, more than we hear. The trick is learning to open your heart.* Usual crap."

Carol glances out the window. "Hey," she says. "Sun's going down."

"Well, let's hope the ghouls come out to play," says Ben, casting one last nervous look at the reception desk before heading toward the dining hall.

It is the creature, thinks Hin'tui. He watches, camouflaged, in the lengthening shadows, interested to see if it will strike. It doesn't. Perhaps it has a sense of the dramatic, appropriate to what these oomans are doing here. *Some entertainment they are creating*, he thinks. Like the clan plays the elders put on at feast days. The parasite can take on characteristics of its host. This has the makings for a good hunt.

Uncharacteristically, Hin'tui has a vague hope the parasite doesn't take the female. Not through any sense of empathy or weakness—he'd had that beaten out of him, just like everyone else in the *kehrite* where youngbloods learned their craft. But because of what she'd said. She seemed particularly attuned to this place. His translator told him the ooman was speaking of her mother, which in turn, makes Hin'tui think of his.

He remembers when she got the sickness and took the long walk into the arid desert as penance for her shame. She was still fertile, would be for a long time. Her weakness had deprived the Yautja of who knew how many warriors. And it was a sickness that could not be cured. Melancholia brought on by addiction to the fermented juice of the faranth berry. The Yautja way was honor and victory. Not sadness and shame. She had no choice, according to the traditions of the clan, but to pack up her shame and take it with her, away from them all. Even her children.

Hin'tui gathered with the rest of the clan, silently watching her walk into the dust, until she was just a tiny dot and then gone from sight.

She was long dead, of course. Her bones picked clean by carrion birds. But she had left behind her memory, her reputation. As she set off on the long walk, she had turned briefly, her eyes meeting Hin'tui's. And he burned with shame for what she was doing, what she had done.

Which was why he chose the most perilous hunting grounds, the most vicious prey, and utilized the most basic weapons. Shame was not the warrior way. He'd keep fighting it all his life, by hunting the most dangerous game.

They take an early dinner in the dining hall, lit by candles and a bank of the battery-powered lights. They'd brought all their food with them, of course: sandwiches, cooked meats, bread and olives, a big cooler of beer Ben and Cade tear into as they eat. The sinking sun casts golden light through the torn, dusty drapes at the tall windows, until darkness takes hold outside, the wilderness beyond the hotel painting the panes black.

Carol shares with them her research from the afternoon. "As you'd expect, the place became a magnet for hobos and teens and drug addicts over the years." She passes the iPad around. "Look at this. Nineteen seventy-one. Homeless guy found by a fishing party heading back from the lake and taking a look at the old hotel."

"Ugh, fuck, trigger warning, maybe?" says Ben. "I really don't want this cold meatball sub anymore."

The police photograph shows a corpse with its chest ripped out.

"Interesting," says Cade, examining it.

"Aw, old guy drank himself to death and got eaten by animals," says Ben, belching.

Carol takes the tablet and calls up another picture. "Seventy-nine. Bunch of young punks gathered here for a party. One of them got lost and when they found him next morning..."

The monochrome picture shows a Sid Vicious wannabe lying in one of the guest rooms, a spreading black patch on his chest.

"And in eighty-five—"

"I think we get the picture," says Ben, reaching for a beer. "How many of these you got? With their hearts ripped out?"

"Six."

Cade's eyes widen. "That can't be any kind of coincidence. Nobody's put this together before? We could have some kind of serial killer here. Or the ghost of a serial killer. Jack the fucking Ripper!"

"I'd rather have Sinatra," says Ben. He stands unsteadily. "I'm going for a walk. Then crash for a while. Then maybe a bit of coke."

Carol rolls her eyes, and they talk about Ben's drug use, and whether it's going to be problematic at some point. They talk about the show, and if this weekend is going to save their asses. They wonder if they should take a vacation once it's over as they move from the dining room to the bar.

"Jesus, it's late," says Cade, looking at his watch. "We've been up for hours. You think Ben is okay?"

Cade walks unsteadily toward the bar, on the hunt for another bottle. His concern for Ben is really heartwarming, Carol thinks. He dips into the shadows and when he emerges her heart leaps. He's not alone. A figure is entwined about him. A woman. Naked. Young. Blond hair billowing behind her as though she's underwater.

Carol recognizes her, and then Cade is alone, staring at the label on a bottle and frowning.

She'd suspected, of course. Her imagination had never conjured up anything so detailed before, though. Is it this place, the Mariposa? Is it doing this?

"How long have you been fucking Jenette?" says Carol when Cade sits down heavily with the bottle.

Cade falls silent, his face in an almost comic grimace, as though she's asked him to name all the state capitals in reverse alphabetical order. "Jenette…?"

"Jenette the production assistant," says Carol. "Unless you know any more Jenettes? Unless you're fucking any of them, too?"

Cade puffs out his cheeks. Playing for time. Carol waits. There's nothing else to do tonight.

"Look," he says eventually. "I'm not sure what… I mean, I don't know what you think…"

Carol almost feels relieved on his behalf when the nearby scream rents the dusty, still air of the Hotel Mariposa.

———

"Hands! It was fucking hands!" screams Ben, sitting on the tiled floor of the bathroom off the lobby. "Came right out of the can and grabbed me."

"Tell us again," says Cade calmly, shooting Carol a look.

Ben takes a deep breath. "I put my flashlight down on the basin and took a piss." Ben's torch is still lit and sitting on the taps. "Then I cut out a couple of lines." The toilet is one of those with a low cistern behind the seat and on top of it are two tracks of coke, untouched. "I bent down and these fucking hands came out of the goddamn can and grabbed my face."

"Hands," says Carol uncertainly. "Ben, you're sure it wasn't a rat…?"

"It was fucking hands!" he shrieks. He holds his out, wrists together, palms and fingers splayed, thumbs aligned. Like when you were making the shape of a bird when you were a kid, thinks Carol.

"And were there… arms?"

116

Ben puts his face in his hands. "I don't know. It was dark. There were hands. They grabbed my face. I blacked out, I think. I've been lying here for fucking hours. Didn't you get worried about me?"

He leans forward and vomits in his lap.

Cade frowns. Carol knows exactly what he's thinking. Phoenix all over again. Ben didn't have his cameras.

"I think we should maybe get you to bed," Carol says softly.

Ben nods gratefully, then throws up again.

———

Camouflaged in the corner of the lobby, Hin'tui watches the three of them, the male and female helping the big ooman between them, toward the corridor running off through the double doors beside the desk.

He puts his hand on the hilt of his blade.

And so it begins.

———

"Do you think it's the drugs?" says Cade, sitting up bare-chested in the bed.

Carol lies beside him in her PJs, flicking through notes on her tablet. Without looking over she says, "Well, either that, or it happened. Or he's just making it up."

Cade shakes his head. "You saw the look on his face. Ben isn't that good a liar."

All men are that good a liar if they need to be, thinks Carol.

Their earlier conversation still hangs between them. The room is lit by flashlights on the nightstands, casting long, grotesque shadows around the dusty suite.

Carol glances over at Cade. Good looking, fit, funny. Everything a twenty-year-old production assistant would find irresistible in a thirty-two-year-old man. Is that even legal?

Under the thick blankets, Cade puts an exploratory hand on her thigh. "No," she says. "Not with Ben next door."

Cade sighs and turns off his torch, and lies with his back to her. Carol waits until he is gently snoring before laying down her tablet and switching off her light, and lies there for a long time, listening to the complete silence in the Hotel Mariposa.

———

The first thing Carol does is vomit, loud and ugly, on the rug.

Then she grabs her cell and dials 911, and through her tear-blurred vision she can see there's absolutely zero service. She was sure she had it yesterday. She jabs at the numbers again, willing to hear something other than the dead nothingness of no connection to the outside world.

She doesn't want to look at the bed, so she looks at Cade instead, who is just standing there, running his hand through his hair, muttering, "Oh fuck oh fuck oh fuck oh fuck."

You should at least put some fucking clothes on, thinks Carol crazily, staring at him standing there in his boxer shorts.

Ben is on his bed, naked, his chest a raw and glistening mess of muscle and fat and sinew and blood. Like he's been… ripped open. From the inside. Carol leans forward and vomits again, until there's nothing but hot yellow bile being wrenched from her gut.

Carol had showered and dressed while Cade still lounged in bed, and she'd gone next door at about eight to make sure Ben was all right. Her scream had brought Cade running. But there was nothing either of them could do for Ben, his skin cold and clammy, his eyes staring glassily to the ceiling.

"We need to get away," says Carol, tugging on Cade's arm. "Whoever did this is still here."

She drags open the door to the suite, as if expecting to see a madman with a blood-dripping axe standing there, but it's just the corridor. "Cade!" she shouts. "Get dressed. Let's drive to somewhere with signal."

While Carol jabs at her cell again, Cade rattles the handle on their suite. He turns and says, "Did you lock it?"

"You were last out." She pushes him aside and tries the door. He's right. She sees the number and frowns. "This isn't our suite. We're twenty-three. This is eighty-five."

"Of course it's ours. We were next door to Ben." Cade steps back and looks over at Ben's closed door. "See? He's eighty-six."

Carol goes to Ben's door. He was definitely in 24. It's locked. She frowns at Cade then looks down the corridor. Without saying anything she sets off to the corner, which should lead to a set of double doors and the lobby. When she gets there the corridor stretches on, almost to vanishing point.

"Impossible," she says. When she turns, Cade has gone. Maybe she was wrong about the room numbers. The door must have just been sticking. Ben's had automatically locked when they closed it behind them. She goes to 85 and tries the handle, but it won't budge. She hammers on the door, shouting, "Let me in. Cade? Don't fuck about."

There is only silence in the Hotel Mariposa, as stifling and thick as it was in the absolute darkness just before she fell asleep. Carol looks both ways along the corridor, which suddenly seems a lot longer than it did a moment ago. She heads back in the direction she's sure the lobby lies. Wherever the fuck Cade has gone, she needs to get out of this place.

Cade watches Carol disappear around the corner and waits, feeling foolish in just his shorts. The image of Ben's eviscerated chest explodes behind his eyelids every time he blinks. Maybe Carol is being too hasty, wanting to leave. Isn't this exactly what they came to the Hotel Mariposa for? It's dynamite. This is what will get them a third series. A third, fourth, fifth. This is what's going to make *American Spook-Chasers*. Make them all rich. And when he's sure Carol is taken care of, money-wise... he thinks about Jenette, the way her skin is so taut and smooth the way Carol's no longer is, the things she'll do in bed Carol won't. There'll be a hundred Jenettes. A thousand.

"Hey, maybe we should think about this," he calls, setting off for the corner. When he gets there, the corridor heads off for what seems like miles. He was sure the lobby doors were here. And there's no Carol.

Cade jogs down a little way. Has she gone into one of the rooms? Then he arrives at a crossroads, another red-carpeted corridor slicing across and disappearing into infinity on either side. This can't be right.

"Carol?" yells Cade, voice flat and heavy in the still air. "Carol, where are you?"

Cade decides to double back, return to where their rooms are, and begin again. He starts as he turns, at the sight of the black shape in the ceiling. There are wooden panels there, hiding a crawlspace for the pipes and utilities, he supposes. One is skewed, revealing a triangle of darkness.

On the carpet are puddles of... goo? Spit? Saliva? Like

some huge beast has been slavering. He's about to call Carol's name once more when the hairs on his neck stand up, and his balls shrivel. There's someone behind him. He can sense it. He spins around, and screams.

———

Carol has been walking for what feels like hours along a corridor that seems to go on forever when she hears the unmistakable sound of Cade screaming. She runs, suddenly hitting a right turn she hadn't seen coming, and around the corner there he is, on his hands and knees, shaking. A pool of piss dripping from his boxer shorts. She wrinkles her nose.

"Oh god oh god oh god," he says, over and over. "Carol. Fuck. Thank god. We need to get out. I've just seen a fucking ghost."

When she's calmed him down he takes a ragged breath and sits against the wall, marshalling his thoughts. Eventually he says, "It must've been seven feet tall. More. Kind of a... shape in the air. Like blurred air. But like a man. Like looking at someone through a dirty lens. Then suddenly it was there..." He looks at her, tears streaming down his cheeks. "It had this helmet. Like... I dunno. Maybe an old-world knight or something?"

"A knight."

Cade slaps his head three times. "I don't know. I'm only telling you what I saw. Let's leave. Now."

Carol looks one way down the endless corridor, then the other. *Yeah, we should. Easier said than done.* She says, "Which way did you come?"

He points in the opposite direction from which she'd arrived. Whatever is going on in this place, trying to find their way out through the corridors is hopeless. It's like a labyrinth. There has to be another way.

Hin'tui had been tracking the prey when he came upon the naked male. He showed no signs of being infected. Hin'tui had shown himself to the ooman, he didn't really know why. He sometimes liked the reaction of other races when he revealed himself. Even if they didn't know the Yautja explicitly, they recognized him for what he was in some primal corner of their brains, their collective species memory. A hunter. A predator.

Hin'tui saw no point in killing him. Like treading on an insect. Besides, he was good bait to draw the Kiande Amedha out, all that noise and stench. Hin'tui would follow and wait for the creature to strike, as it inevitably would.

After the ooman screamed, Hin'tui activates his shift suit and pads away along the corridor The hunting ground is living up to its own mythology, the space within it warping and shifting to dizzying effect. Hin'tui nods agreeably. What victory songs he will have to sing about this day. And how much farther will he drive his mother's shame deep inside him, never to resurface.

"Let me try," says Carol, exasperated at Cade's futile attempts to force the door. It was her idea. If the corridors were going on forever—and she didn't want to give too much headspace to that—then they'd try to get out through a window. She takes a run-up, slamming the flat of her foot just under the handle, and the wood splinters and gives.

The small utility room is stocked with mops, brushes

and cleaning equipment. And a window, overlooking the overgrown grounds of the hotel to what must be the east side. Somehow they were on the second floor. She can't work out how that has happened. But there is a drainpipe running down the side of the hotel, near the window. They can shimmy down and get the hell out of here.

Carol picks up a mop, hefts it in her hands, and drives the end of it hard into the center of the window. The glass fractures and smashes and falls away.

Revealing, impossibly, a bare brick wall where there had been the enticing view of freedom seconds before.

"What the fuck?"

"Carol…" says Cade, his voice curiously strangled.

"Jesus, Cade, can't you see I'm—"

He just sobs this time, and she turns. And sees it.

It is skeletal and black, its impossible, grotesquely distended head slick with a sheen of moisture, rows of teeth bared. It stands behind Cade with an almost simian crouch, a spine-like tail whipping behind it. Viscous liquid drips from its maw, spotting the vinyl flooring .

What. The. Actual. Fuck.

"Carol," says Cade, tears rolling down his face. "I'm sorry."

The creature opens its mouth and something emerges, like a limb, with a second mouth gaping at the end. *This is a nightmare*, thinks Carol wildly. *I'm asleep. Ben is still alive. This is just a dream.*

Then the nightmare rips Cade's face off.

Hin'tui watches with interest from the door and wonders how the ooman will react to the Kiande Amedha. Will she think it another illusion conjured by this place? How much do the oomans understand of what happens here? He doubts, from what he knows of oomans, that she could absorb the concept of an ancient race harvesting hundreds of Kiande Amedha pods, then taking them out of the sector in a ship powered by a drive unknown to any other race in the galaxy. A drive that warped and bent reality to fold space. A drive that went wrong, causing the ship to crash here hundreds of this planet's years ago.

Even if he knew her tongue, how could he explain the crew were all killed but the drive created a place where space and time are twisted out of shape? The Yautja investigated the crash site, of course, after tracking the unknown ship through space. The first team just had time to report the hold of the half-buried ship was full of unhatched Kiande Amedha pods before contact was lost.

The follow-up ship discovered the scouts all slaughtered. Apparently by their own hands. When the new team began to see strange visions of things that weren't there, and the landscape began to shift and change in defiance of both physical sense and Yautja technology, it was deduced that however the ship's strange warp drive worked, in its malfunctioning state it was having an effect on the material world. Normal rules did not apply. Anything could happen there, or at least seem to.

As oomans settled the area, and the ship became more concealed, the stasis fields containing the pods began to fail, sometimes two or three at a time, sometimes none for cycles, then one or two more. Giving the Kiande Amedha hosts, and the Yautja one of their strangest and most celebrated hunting grounds.

Of course, none of it matters to the ooman now, staring in uncomprehending horror at the Kiande Amedha. He could let it kill her. It doesn't matter to him. But, on a whim, he scans both her and the creature with his wrist bracer and pauses. Then he draws his blade, switches off his shift suit, and roars his challenge.

———

Cade had been right. A ghost. A giant ghost with dreadlocks. Carol's mind whirls so fast she thinks she just might black out as a defense mechanism. The monster throws Cade's bloodied, faceless body away from it and spins around, crouching and hissing.

A knight, thinks Carol. *Why would there be a knight? The ghost of a knight. This isn't goddam Scooby-Doo.* She doesn't know if they're on the same side, but he's stalking toward the monster with some kind of curved sword, so that's good enough for her.

"Hey, motherfucker," she shouts, and as the creature turns back to her she rams the end of the mop right into its dripping jaws.

The giant swings his blade and it connects with the tail of the monster, which yowls in agony, or anger. Yellow blood gouts from its wound, sizzling and smoking on the carpet and cupboards where it splashes. Acid? The creature suddenly leaps up, like a cat, into the recesses of the ceiling space where it had come from. She hears skittering along the panels, and it's gone.

Trying to ignore Cade's crumpled form on the periphery of her vision, Carol hefts the mop like a pole vaulter, the end—dripping with the creature's saliva—pointed toward the figure that might be her savior—or her doom.

"Did that thing kill Ben as well as Cade?" she says. "What is it? What the fuck are *you*, for that matter?"

He tilts his helmeted head, as if considering her. Then he sheaths his blade. He's not going to kill her. At least not with that. Then he puts his hands together, as if in prayer, and inclines his head. And points to her belly.

It takes her a moment, then Carol says, "You are shitting me."

———

Hin'tui turns and stalks from the room, checking his wrist bracer. The creature is on the move, above him. The female ooman follows him, chattering at him in her language. She is with young. Not any of his concern. His kind would not kill a female bearing a child, not deprive the universe of another potential warrior. But he can use her, to draw the creature out. Bait.

Except... the crippled drive of the ship buried deep beneath this place, which affects the physical world so, had shown him images as she talked, a parade of pictures, brief snatches of the ooman's life. Her mother, abandoning her, just as his had. Is that a source of great shame among the oomans, as it is among Yautja?

Again, not his concern. All that matters is the Hunt. He checks his bracer. The creature has doubled back, heading toward them, in the space above. He puts his hand on his blade.

———

"I don't fucking believe it," says Carol, running to keep up with the man's long strides. "Pregnant. Cade, you bastard." A sudden sob is ripped out of her. Yes, he was a bastard, she was going to leave him, but he didn't deserve that. Nobody deserved that. She didn't even know what *that* was. Cade—and presumably Ben —had been killed by that thing. What was it? A demon? A monster? Some kind of… experiment? Mutant?

"Hey," she shouts. "You're here to kill it? Who are you? You speak English? Where are you from?"

He's looking at his wrist—some kind of monitor or HUD on there, maybe. Then he looks up at the ceiling. Carol grips the mop. It's coming back.

He's looking at her again, then he puts his hands to the corners of his helmet and lifts it, shaking out his long dreadlocks and revealing his face. His mottled, gray face, pinprick eyes and… mandibles. Fucking mandibles.

Then he points down the corridor and snarls.

Carol runs.

As Hin'tui hoped, the Kiande Amedha above pauses. Whether it can hear her or it can sense her as she flees, it doesn't matter. It will not be able to resist the lure of prey. It's moving. Fast. The ooman turns a corner and Hin'tui can see from his bracer it's above her. He draws his blade and sets off at a run.

Where the fuck are the doors? How can she get out? The corridor stretches into infinity. Stay here long enough, you'd go insane. If you didn't die of starvation first. Maybe she should double back, go past that… she doesn't even know which would be worse to meet with, whatever the hell that monster was that killed Cade, or the giant knight. *Not a knight, idiot. It's a monster like the other one.* She's weighing up, deciding

127

whether to be caught between a rock and a hard place, then the choice is taken out of her hands.

The ceiling tiles explode and the monster drops, crouching like a shining black tiger, jaws dripping as it regards her, sizing her up. Preparing for the kill.

Then, with a roar, the other one comes barreling around the corner, its blade held high, and the monster turns to face it. Has the thing grown since killing Cade? It certainly seems larger as it uncoils, standing on sinewy legs, tail—severed at the end, dripping caustic, acid blood—whipping like a cobra.

Hin'tui is somewhat... disappointed by how easy it is. The Kiande Amedha puts up a good enough fight, he supposes. A lesser Yautja might have found it more challenging. Might have failed, have been killed. But Hin'tui, swinging his blade with expert precision, dispatches it in clinical fashion. Well, almost. Hin'tui pauses from delivering the fatal blow.

The ooman is cowering by the wall, watching the battle in horror. He wonders what she would think if he had a truly worthy opponent. Still. Every kill, every trophy, goes some small way toward making up for his mother's shame. Toward shaking off the stench of her betrayal of his clan. Toward, in some small way, redeeming her.

The ooman's mother abandoned her, as well. Does she feel shame at that? Hin'tui looks at the stricken creature, then decides. He holds out his blade to the female.

He wants me to finish it, Carol thinks crazily. The creature's blood is pooling and smoking as it writhes weakly on the floor. Uncertainly, she stands up, her arms folded across her belly. Where her baby grows. This thing could have killed her. And her baby. Who knows how many more of them there are.

Then, she realizes, she has to do this. For Cade. For Ben. For herself.

For her baby.

She must prove she can protect this child growing inside her. Even if she has to raise it alone. She is not her mother. She will not abandon this baby. She will do everything she can to protect it.

She will kill monsters for it.

Carol reaches out for the blade.

They stand in the sunlight on the forecourt of the Hotel Mariposa. She has no idea how they got outside. She just followed him through the winding corridors until they found a door. Afterward. After she'd killed the monster.

"You need a lift anywhere?" says Carol, pointing to the station wagon. "Where the hell you from, anyway?"

He indicates the trees. He doesn't speak but she guesses his meaning. He's got his own transport. He points upward, and she shields her eyes against the sun and looks up, into the blue sky, the blackness of space beyond. Well, of course. That figures. Aliens. Fucking aliens. Cade and Ben would've loved this.

She stifles a sudden sob. She's going to have to deal with this, somehow. There are going to be questions. There must be answers. But not now. Now she just needs to get out of here.

The alien takes his blade and, with the tip, draws a crude figure in the dust. A stick figure, with a distended belly. A pregnant woman. Carol says, "Is that me?"

Hin'tui cannot make her understand. Grunting, he pulls off his biohelmet. She recoils at first, then stares at him curiously. He ignores her, looks out over the hunting ground. The crippled warp drive reacts to sentient thought, subtly shifting reality to tap into moods, or memories. That much is known. He wonders… Hin'tui looks at her, takes off his glove, and holds out his hand.

Whatever he is, he's on her side. Carol looks at his huge hand, then places her own in it.

For a long moment, nothing. She isn't sure what's supposed to happen. She can hear something, though, almost imperceptible, a kind of… thrumming noise, deep underground. Maybe she doesn't hear. Maybe she feels it. Inside her.

Then two figures appear by the trees circling the Hotel Mariposa. One tall and broad, wrapped in some kind of rough material, the other tiny and slight, in a flimsy—

A flimsy summer dress. Carol realizes what she's seeing as they walk toward them, almost the mirror image of the pair of them standing there, hand in hand.

It's her mother.

She looks up at the alien. His small round eyes narrow as he watches the figures approach.

It's his mother, too.

"Ghosts?" whispers Carol. Has she finally found proof of the paranormal, at the Hotel Mariposa? Or is this something to do with the monsters? She has had a jumble of images she cannot understand: crashed spaceships, crippled engines distorting perception. Is that what this is? Is it an illusion, or something more? He doesn't say anything. Doesn't look at her. Together they wait until the two women, the two mothers, stand in front of them in the bright sunshine.

"Why did you leave?"

Carol isn't sure who speaks. She's certain it's her but feels the words chitter and growl in another tongue as well.

"I had to," says her mother. Says his mother.

The two mothers are one. Somehow, she and the alien are one, too.

Hin'tui. His name is Hin'tui.

Hin'tui looks at the ooman. Carol. The hunting ground is fading them into each other, folding everything down into single digits. There is only one mother. There is only one child. All is one.

There is only one question.

Why did you leave?

Only one answer.

I had to.

Only one more thing to be said.

I never stopped—

The next word, the next feeling, clashes within Carol and Hin'tui. It is a thing neither of them understands in relation to the other. But that doesn't matter. Because they understand it themselves.

You never stopped loving me, thinks Carol, and her tears flow freely. You had to leave, and I'll never know why but it wasn't because of me. It was in spite of me. And you never stopped loving me.

Carol looks at Hin'tui and realizes he's having a similar revelation. She smiles, then both women turn and walk back the way they came, and are as insubstantial as summer haze before reaching the tree line, then gone.

Carol and Hin'tui let go of each other, and become themselves.

They look at each other for a moment, then he nods and turns back toward the hotel. Carol watches him, until he disappears through the doors to where the corpse of the Kiande Amedha— *hey, I learned a new word*—lies, and god knows how many more are buried in the sand beneath the hotel. *Rather him than me.* She knows eventually all this is going to hit her like a truck, she'll collapse into a sobbing, terrified mess.

Or maybe not. Maybe she's a different Carol to the one that walked in there. She remembers what she said about mariposa meaning butterfly. *"Like... emerging from a cocoon."*

She finds the spare key behind the fender and lets herself into the station wagon. She won't be going home, she decides. Let them think she disappeared or got killed with Cade and Ben. She can start a new life, her and the baby. No more *American Spook-Chasers*. All ghosts laid to rest. Carol starts the engine and lets it growl for a moment, foot on the gas. No more chasing the past. Time to look to the future, and be a kick-ass mom. The kind who kills monsters. And who never stops loving.

Carol puts the wagon into gear and executes a wide turn on the drive, glancing in her mirror as something shoots into the sky on a column of fire beyond the trees.

PLANTING AND HARVEST

BY MIRA GRANT

For the long-time crew of the *Philomelus*, discovering that even the deep reaches of space had their seasons had been a surprise, but one that had long since died down into simply part of the way the world worked. Time passed; the station turned; their beds and banks of seeds turned into beds and banks of seedlings, of plants, of fruits and grains, all ready for harvest. It was as if the sheer density of the vegetation set the calendar, and all of their subjects consented, letting themselves be governed by the communal timeline.

It had been a busy "summer," with seventeen new colony worlds looking for stable crops they could grow under their unique local conditions, and populations that needed to be fed. And even as that was going on, the corporations that paid their operating costs were baying for better and more shelf-stable grain to be included in long-range ship supplies. That would have been easy enough, if they'd been able to develop a single strain and call themselves finished, but every ship seemed to draw its crew and do its marine recruiting from a different population back on Earth.

The corporations weren't big on coddling the rank and file, and would have been happy to have them all sustained by nutrient paste and water, if not for the surprisingly extensive problems that came with this approach. The human body didn't do well on nutrient paste—not in the long term—and marines who couldn't lift their own equipment weren't very useful when it came to defending company resources. They needed solid nutrition in forms their bodies could understand and process, and they needed those nutrients to come from shelf-stable foods that wouldn't set off any of the allergies found in the various populations the crews were drawn from.

That meant gluten-free, rice-free, soy-free, and low-carbohydrate versions of the same ration bars were necessary if they wanted to keep the ships properly supplied, and that was in addition to fruits and vegetables, and herbs and aromatics, for the higher-ranking crew members, who might be willing to accept a certain amount of privation for the sake of the job, but weren't willing to face the vastness of space without garlic, and fresh peppers, and the other small luxuries they thought themselves owed.

That was where *Philomelus*, and the other stations like her, entered the picture. Their hydroponics and grafting stations were entirely devoted to producing edible results that could remain stable over long stretches of time in the storage centers of corporation and colony ships, remaining as fresh as possible to keep the rank and file from feeling as if they were being mistreated by their corporate masters (although, of course, they were; anyone who went into the sciences, however loyal they had been in the beginning of their tenure, couldn't help seeing that with a terrible clarity the first time they delivered a load of new protein bars to a starving battalion of Colonial Marines, reassuring them that none of the allergens flagged for the unit had gone into their manufacture). Some of the stations also produced seeds. Not *Philomelus*. They specialized in finished products.

It was commonly assumed that the scientists and farmers who worked the hydroponic stations were soft, and maybe that assumption was right, on some level, but the one thing no one seemed to take into account was that by the time someone had been with the company long enough to land on the *Philomelus*, they were unquestionably a killer. No one made it all the way to the remotest of the hydroponic stations without at least a little blood on their hands, and for most of them, it was a *lot* of blood.

Mary, who specialized in tomatoes and didn't like talking to people when she didn't have to, was personally responsible for the death of an entire platoon of Colonial Marines after her attempts to tweak the flavor and stability of the fruit into something that could be pulverized and stabilized in paste form had also resulted in such an increased level of solanine that every one of her testers had died screaming as their muscles spasmed and locked, cutting off their air supply.

Terry, who had been working for years to perfect a form of rice that could keep under frozen conditions for longer than the currently accepted thirty years, had potentially killed more when his first test batches, despite passing early tests, had proven to be nutritionally about as valuable as water. At least two crews had starved to death, and he had been reassigned to the *Philomelus*, his work downgraded in importance, his chances of advancement dramatically curtailed, but not eliminated.

Honestly, Nita, whose job involved keeping distractable horticulturists and researchers from accidentally engineering some kind of horrific weaponized kudzu—doing it on purpose would, of course, be completely fine, and probably earn the team responsible a commendation—wasn't sure any of her researchers actually *cared* about falling out of favor. Their "punishment," such as it was, constituted removal from the seat of corporate power, with all the attendant politics, power-plays, and jockeying for prime funding. Here, they all pulled from the same pool, and while she was constantly fielding complaints from teams who felt someone else had been given special treatment, most of them were smart enough not to formally complain that corporate funds weren't being used to benefit their personal projects. It was less, in Nita's eyes, because they understood that embezzlement was *wrong* and likely to get them in trouble, and more concern that if the corps heard about some of those "private projects" they would be seized in an instant.

"Intellectual property" her sweet ass. It was just a fancy way of saying, "Someone else does all the work, and we get to pretend we understand the end result as long as we feel like we can profit from it." Her staff did the bulk of their work in private so there was a chance that they could *keep* it.

Of course, nothing here was truly private. The corporations found out about everything eventually, and anyone who was actually *caught* concealing research would find themselves taking a swift trip out an airlock when the collected interest for all that life support they'd used up over the years came due at once. Nita knew what her researchers were doing, and she knew they were all smart and self-interested enough not to take it too far. They would hand their projects over like good little corporate assets when they stumbled on anything even remotely profitable. They knew their role in all this.

A chime echoed through her office, informing her that the event she'd been waiting for all day—they were too far from the nearest star to have true "day" and "night" cycles, but humanity would cling to its little habits—had finally occurred. Smiling to herself, Nita shut down her terminal and rose, heading for the airlock.

Heads popped out of office doors as she passed them, curious researchers turning toward the sound of something new happening like flowers turned toward the sun, their faces simple ovals in the dimness of the hall. Only Mary, misanthropic, antisocial Mary, found enough interest to actually emerge from her lab, rolling her chair into the hall, and calling, in her harsh planetsider's accent, "Hey! What's going on?"

"Seed shipment," said Nita, and turned to face her researchers, even as she continued walking backward down the hall. "One of the other stations failed, and we've picked up their unused stock. Call it planter's Christmas. You'll all have the opportunity to review the manifest before we divvy up. But it was all corp-funded and corp-owned, and that means it's ours now."

"Which one?" Terry followed Mary's lead into the hall, an expression of uncharacteristic worry on his weathered face.

"The *Esus*," said Nita.

"I thought something might have gone wrong," said Terry mournfully. "They stopped updating their beacons a week ago. I'd been communicating with one of their granary specialists, he was working on a better means of hardening quinoa, and some of the genes looked like they might be cross-compatible."

"Your specialist, whoever he was, did that work in the name and on the payroll of the Weyland-Yutani Corporation. He is no longer listed on that same payroll, which means it is now considered intellectual salvage, and can be claimed by anyone who wants to continue that work and doesn't ask too many questions." She injected a note of warning into her voice. When she'd been notified that they'd be receiving the shipment, there had been no indication as to why, exactly, the hydroponic station had failed, meaning that it could have been anything, from an equipment failure that killed everyone on board to an attempt at corporate espionage resulting in the liquidation of the station.

Terry paled, clearly taking her point, and retreated back into his lab with a final muttered, "If the research files were included, I call dibs."

Mary scowled and wheeled herself back into her own lab, recognizing a line past which Nita would not allow herself to be pushed. They could—and did, on a regular basis—test the limits of both her patience and the Company's, but they hadn't survived employment long enough to get booted to the ass end of nowhere without learning at least a few facts about surviving in a corp-owned research facility. No one else interrupted her as she made her way through the rest of the station to the hold, where the supply shuttle was docked.

It was unmanned. Not unusual when you were talking about the research facilities—even the ones like the *Philomelus*, where nothing of value was genuinely expected, which stayed open only because the people in charge had long since determined that their occasional wild flashes of genius more than balanced the cost of keeping them up and operating the rest of the time. They didn't want to risk theft of research or corporate espionage. Nita barely glanced at the control panel to confirm that the shuttle had left the *Esus*, and proceeded directly from there to the *Philomelus*, with no unscheduled stops or detours.

Everything in the log was correct to her expectations, save for one small notation: *pilot*. Pilot? Why would they list a pilot if there wasn't meant to be one?

"Hunk of junk," said Nita, smacking the console with the flat of her hand. Wherever this Lieutenant Terry Ashmore was, they weren't in the shuttle.

She was disabused of that belief as soon as she opened the back, releasing a hiss of bitterly cold air. Steam swirled into the hold. Nita took a step back, allowing it to dissipate before she stepped inside. Racks of seed stock lined the walls, carefully labeled and locked down, often with the corresponding data chip affixed to the container. Sprouted specimens sturdy enough to survive the cold transit required by the journey stood in tidy racks at the center, ready to be delivered to their new destinations.

And there, slumped in the corner, was the absent Lt. Ashmore, slumped over and very clearly deceased. *Well, of course he is*, muttered the small voice of sanity still echoing at the back of her head. *People need a torso if they want to be alive*. Nita froze, torn between wanting to get a closer look and wanting to run away as quickly as she could, before whatever had killed this man could spread itself to her.

If it's airborne, you're already dead, she thought, and stepped closer.

The warmth of her presence set off a cascade of blinking lights and humming systems, the shuttle reacting and preparing itself for use. That confirmed that Lt. Ashmore had been dead long enough for his body to cool completely, in case the ice crystals in his hair hadn't been confirmation enough. From the state of him, she guessed his death had occurred very shortly after the shuttle left the *Esus*, probably inside of the hour.

But what could possibly have done something like this to a human body? She crouched down once she was close enough, peering into the wreckage of his chest. Between the injury and the cold, everything had frozen essentially in place. It had definitely exploded outward, but the ribs and the flesh around them remained too intact for this to have been caused by an actual bomb. Something had been *inside* this man's chest. Something that started out as small enough to fit in the human body, finding space for itself alongside, oh, lungs and the heart and all the other organs—nothing looked like it had been eaten at all, although some things looked more than a little squashed—but growing rapidly enough that even the organ damage she could see hadn't been given sufficient time to kill him…

Nita was still crouched down, studying the remains, when she heard a clicking sound from behind her, like the rustle of a cricket's wings. She had a moment to remember an old lab partner of hers—who had been working on sustainable insect-based protein sources, and whose side of their shared workspace had always sounded like that—and then she was slowly turning to face the inevitable, to behold the horror uncurling from where it had been coiled against the frozen ceiling, long, segmented tail unwinding click by click, jaws open and working on nothing, and she understood exactly what had happened to the lieutenant.

In less time than it took to remember everything she hadn't finished, she understood better than she had ever wanted to understand anything.

There wasn't even time for her to scream.

———

Mary didn't like people.

That was the first thing *most* people realized about her: she didn't like them, had never liked them, and was never going to like them. People were, in a word, irrelevant to the way she wanted the world to work. She liked the things that people made, liked having life support and lights and tools calibrated to her exacting standards, but all those things could happen without the people responsible for them getting anywhere near her. She could live in a world devoid of anyone but herself and her beloved plants, as long as no one interfered.

People assumed that because she didn't like them, she ignored them or was unaware of their movements. In reality, she paid more attention than the majority of them did: she had to, if she wanted to avoid them. Nita's location beacon moved into the hold, to what Mary presumed was the newly arrived salvage shuttle, and then it stopped. Mary scowled at the screen. The dot did not obligingly resume movement.

This was unusual, especially as the system showed no one else in or around the hold. Nita could be waylaid— Mary had done it herself on occasion, when Nita wasn't processing a funding or equipment request quickly enough— but not by screens. If someone was messaging her, she'd still be on the move.

Mary scowled and gripped the wheels of her chair, turning and rolling herself out of her office. If there were any new tomato varietals in this shipment, she wanted them before one of the others could try to lay claim. Nita was usually decent about allotting things according to people's individual projects, but sometimes people were working under NDA for the corp, and somehow managed to get first dibs on new materials accordingly. If there were tomatoes, Mary wanted them, and she wanted them *now*.

She hadn't known that new tomatoes were a possibility until Nita mentioned it, but now that she knew, she couldn't think of anything else. Tomatoes were all. She rolled herself down the hall toward the hold, more determined all the time to find her supervisor and demand what she was due.

The doors to the hold hissed open at her approach. There was the shuttle, hatch standing open, and not a trace of Nita to be seen. Mary frowned, rolling closer.

"Hello? Nita? We need to talk about this delivery—"

There was no reply save for an odd, distant clicking sound. Mary turned to look over her shoulder. There was no one there. She was alone. Gripping her wheels, she rolled closer to the shuttle.

Something red was sprayed across the surface of the hatch and the floor immediately inside. Mary frowned. Fertilizer of some sort? There was a meaty tang in the air, like the bloodmeal she sometimes gave to her tomatoes when she needed to encourage more robust growth. She rolled a little closer to the shuttle. No, not *like* bloodmeal, which was made almost entirely from freeze-dried plasma; this was the raw substance that went into the stuff, fresh and arterial and still drying.

She spun her chair around, rolling as fast as she could toward the door.

She didn't make it. But oh, how she tried, and in the end, she came terribly close.

Terribly close indeed.

Any horticulturist can explain how quickly leaf rot spreads. Once it gets into an otherwise healthy plant, you're looking at cutting and burning everything above the root structure to even have a prayer of saving anything at all, and even then, you might fail.

When the shuttle from the *Esus* docked with the *Philomelus*, there had been nineteen researchers and five support staff on the station, a bare-bones crew for a station that no one really cared about, that only mattered on paper. It was a corporate asset that turned out just enough in the way of results to pay for itself, but not enough to make a serious profit. Only the iron-clad contracts some of the researchers had signed when they were younger and more valuable kept the place operational. And the corporation would be happy to shut them down anyway if they ever got the chance.

Still, an army marches on its stomach, and they had been filling that stomach for a very long time. They had never considered themselves to be at any great risk of attack, from either without or within. But leaf rot, once it makes contact, spreads. It spreads so swiftly, like the infection that it is, and once it takes hold the fight is already over.

Less than a day after the shuttle from the *Esus* docked, the *Philomelus* sat silent, drifting in limitless space, spinning slowly with the force of her own engines, not yet winding down. Inside, plants grew, automated systems delivered water and nutrients in preset quantities, nurturing banks of seedlings and trays filled with mature plants. Things moved through the foliage. Terrible, inhuman things. Silence reigned over all. The things had yet to fully understand that there was no way for them to leave the station; they would spend their strange lifespans here, wiling it away within these walls, and they would die here.

Even if they had understood, there was nothing to indicate that they would have cared. They had taken this place as their own, claimed it in the face of all adversity (not that they had faced much resistance from the hot, squishy creatures that had claimed it before their arrival; those had been soft things, easily slain, easily turned into incubators for their young). The hive, small as it was, was complete and serene in its dominion.

Deep in the belly of the *Philomelus*, a small room, sealed off to prevent its contents from seeping out and infecting the rest of the cargo, sat closed away, heat-shielded and maintained in a perpetual state of negative pressure. And inside, its sole occupant sat at her terminal, desperately transmitting message after message, desperate to reach any form of rescue.

"...I repeat, this is the research station *Philomelus*, requesting immediate and urgent assistance. My name is Lisa Olsen. I am a horticultural researcher working for the Weyland-Yutani Corporation to develop a more effective form of corn blight to distribute on colony worlds afflicted with an excess of native vegetation. I am, as near as I can tell, the sole..." She stopped there, trying to swallow away the sudden dryness in her mouth. "...the sole survivor." Her breath caught in her throat, and she paused.

When the *things* had torn through the rest of the crew, she had been in the process of delivering another tray of samples to her workspace. She had seen them moving through the halls on the monitor, swift and oil-skinned and terrible. They moved like they were slicing through the air, like there had never been anything so sharp in all the world, and she knew they would have her dead in an instant if she allowed herself to be caught.

And if she left this room, she would be caught. There was no question of that. So she stayed in her solitary isolation, and sent her pleas for help out into the ether again and again, praying for a reply, resigned to the fact that she wasn't going to receive one. She was a junior researcher at a station in the middle of nowhere, who had yet to make enough of a profit to be worthy of an expensive, potentially dangerous rescue mission.

She was going to die here.

The only question now was whether she was going to die slowly, of starvation, or quickly at the claws and jaws of an unspeakable creature of clearly alien origin, swift and sharp and terrible. Based on what she'd seen on the monitors, it might be painful, but she wouldn't have time to suffer... unless she did. Most of their victims had been taken apart immediately, dissolving into an explosion of blood and tissue that would almost have been beautiful, if it hadn't come out of a living person.

But the victims that weren't taken apart... the closest comparison Lisa could make was to certain types of wasps that some of the other horticulturists used in their research. They laid their eggs inside the bodies of predatory caterpillars, and when the larvae hatched, they fed on the bodies of their unwilling hosts until they finally got too big and burst out of their birthing space.

The people who'd been burst open in that horrifying way were still sprawled where they had fallen when their terrible offspring emerged. She couldn't see any signs that they'd been even partially devoured—the bodies seemed fairly intact, except for the open-petaled flowers of their ribs—but she also hadn't looked too closely. Some things didn't bear that much study.

Some things were better left alone.

Lisa shuddered and dragged her eyes back to the communication panel, depressing the button to send out one more message, one more hopeless prayer, into the emptiness of space. She could survive in here for a few more days, eating her own samples—the ones that weren't harmful to the human body—and then, when the food ran out, she could decide her death.

And of course, there was a third option. There were things in here that she knew would kill her if she swallowed them. But she also knew precisely how painful that death would be, and she wasn't quite ready to consider that way out.

"This is the research station *Philomelus*, requesting immediate and urgent assistance. I repeat, this is the research station *Philomelus*, requesting immediate and urgent assistance. My name is Lisa Olsen…"

There were no corporation-owned vessels, Weyland-Yutani or otherwise, within range of Lisa's transmission. The next scheduled transit wasn't for nearly a solar week. She'd be long dead by the time it occurred, through whichever of her five paths eventually came to seem the most appealing.

But there was *a* ship.

Its systems picked up the transmission automatically, running it through equally automated translation systems until words—not in English, nor in any language known to the human species—appeared on a dark display screen. Monitors tend to be the same whenever designed and constructed by a species that shares a similar visual wavelength, and so while nothing else on this ship might have been understood by human eyes, the control panel and associated displays were perfectly comprehensible.

A small light began to flash, and when no one came to check on it after a reasonable amount of time, an equally small alert began beeping in time with the light, becoming impossible to ignore.

One of the navigation crew appeared, walking out of the deeper corridors of the ship, mandibles flaring in annoyance. This was an interruption, a distraction, and there was no possible way it could be worth the time it was taking away from his personal pursuits. He'd taken this posting in part because of the long stretches of time he'd have to himself, allowing him to focus on caring for his extensive collection of bladed weapons. They were primitive, to be sure, but they were oh-so-lovely, and their edges spoke of the elegance inherent to the physical universe.

He looked at the screen, with its precise, unflinching translation of Lisa's words, most precisely at the section where she had attempted to haltingly, awkwardly describe something so singular that it was recognizable even through her imprecision and ignorance. He straightened, eyes suddenly bright, and turned to bellow two words into the depths of the ship before reprogramming their destination in the drive.

"*Kiande Amedha!*" he yelled, and everyone in range of his voice understood at once when the ship rumbled to life under their feet, when they felt the propulsion systems engage and shift them onto their new course.

Onward they sailed, toward a greater hunt than any of them had dared to hope for on this relatively staid and predictable circuit of their established space.

They were a warrior species, yes, but even within a warrior species some infrastructures must be maintained, some choices must be made less for the sake of glory and personal experience than for the retention and livability of claimed territories. This ship had been on a slow circuit of others in the area, refueling them and performing basic maintenance tasks. All of them had been tested as adults, and all of them had succeeded, but not well enough to be considered Elites. A hunt such as this would never have been offered to them.

They could, if they chose, send a beacon to a better prepared crew, notifying them of the opportunity. Or they could claim this prize for their own.

There was really no question, in the end.

———

Lisa hunched in her seat, staring at the monitors. There hadn't been much activity for the last few hours. Prior to that, she'd seen the fast, hard-shelled things gathering in the halls, tapping their tails and talons against the floor, sending vibrations through the structure of the station. She thought they might be communicating, although she couldn't say for sure; they were too alien to her understanding of how life operated. Maybe if she'd been an entomologist…

Regardless, she thought they knew she was there. They had been appearing more and more frequently in the hall outside her lab, low to the ground, tails lashing and terrible heads canted forward, so that they seemed less like semi-skeletal bipeds and more like very strange quadrupeds. They could move even faster on four legs than they could on two; them being off-balance wasn't going to save her if she unlocked the door.

And with the way they'd been prowling, and the fact that they hadn't eaten any of their victims, she suspected they were stalking her less because they were hungry, and more because they wanted to incubate at least one more of themselves.

"Joke's on you," she muttered, and took another swig of water laced with nutrient powder that was supposed to go to her blight. "Another few days in here, and there won't be enough of me left to incubate anything *in*."

The monitor beeped. Lisa's head snapped up, and she stared with wide, disbelieving eyes as a ship with an unfamiliar outline gently sidled up to the airlock, magnetic grapples engaging as it began the docking process. "No," she breathed. "No, no, no…"

They were going to walk into the station and get *slaughtered*. At her last count, there were eleven of the things moving through the halls and ducts, each one of them fast enough to take out anyone who dared enter their presence. Lisa hit the button for the intercom.

"If you can hear me already, unidentified vessel, this is Lisa Olsen. I am the last surviving member of the station complement. It is not safe to enter without a full situation report. Please disengage immediately."

Had she summoned these people here, condemning them to a quick, brutal death with her distress calls? She couldn't live with herself if that were the case. This was the first time she had used the intercom since the deaths of her crewmates, and she was a little surprised when none of the creatures showed any reaction to her voice. She blinked, slowly. They didn't hunt by sound. They must use something else to guide them to their prey.

It matched with what she'd been able to observe of their vocalizations thus far. They hissed and snarled and occasionally made an almost pleasant trilling sound, but none of that seemed to *say* anything. The only times she'd seen anything that even trended toward communication had been the tapping against the floor.

Vibration. They communicated through vibration. That couldn't be the only means of hunting they employed, but it meant the intercom was safe enough. They had attacked her speakers in the beginning, but stopped when they realized there was nothing there for them to eat.

Taking a deep breath, she watched the airlock door slide open, the creatures pouring toward it, and tried to calm the frantic beating of her heart, which felt like it was going to burst clean out of her chest without any aid from their unwanted guests. It wouldn't help her, and it wouldn't answer any of the questions now thronging in her mind, the largest of which was simply: what *are* these?

The creatures that had claimed her station were insectile and strange, unbelievably alien in the lines of their bodies and the angles of their bulbous heads, and somehow their very impossibility made them easier to accept. Of course something that deadly, that unstoppable, would look like nothing else she'd ever seen. That was what made the things make *sense*.

These, though… they were bipedal, following much the same body plan as human beings, with thick legs and muscular arms. Based on the size of the weapons they carried, that muscle wasn't for show; they would need to have several times standard human strength to be able to make any use at all of their equipment. And their musculature…

Something about them was subtly *wrong*. Whatever these were, they weren't human.

As they poured into the station, weapons at the ready, speaking to one another in a language that seemed made of a mixture of growls and clicks, she began to hope that there might be a chance she would survive this.

Then one of the original things lunged out of the shadows at the new creatures, who shouted and brought their weapons to bear. Those weapons—not guns, not lasers, but a hybrid of the two, incomprehensible and clearly deadly—spoke, and the creature exploded into a mass of chitin and gore.

Where the blood splattered on the walls, it began eating away at the metal, corroding and dissolving it like fungus chewing away at the roots of a bramble vine. Lisa was immediately on her feet, one fist thrust into the air like she had just seen a sports team make the winning play in a competition she'd been following for years.

"*Yes!*" Lisa froze, feeling ridiculous. Slowly, she lowered her hand, then flushed red as she realized that even her embarrassment was pointless; there was no one here to see it.

Even more slowly, she sank back into her seat, eyes fixed on the screen. The new arrivals were fanning out, making their way along the hall in slow, deliberate formation.

———

Eight of them there were, and warriors all, properly blooded, for all that their performance in the trials had been poor enough to warrant consignment to a maintenance ship and not to the fields of glory. They would all be able to claim Elite status when they returned home, proper Yautja adults at last, and no one would deny them improvement in their station, or better opportunities for advancement.

Truly, this hunt was a gift from the universe, and they were going to take full and enthusiastic advantage of it. No one could say they had stolen this opportunity from a more deserving hunting party, a group of youngbloods yet to fail their first trial or a better armed and armored team of proper warriors. No, this was a chance outbreak, a completely unpredictable hive that had yet to fully establish itself, and they would triumph. They were Yautja, and this was only Hard Meat, difficult to kill, brutal, yes, but animal.

Proud of themselves and confident in a victory not yet won, they strode into the station, delicate and decoratively made, as ooman structures always were. Almost at once, two of them earned the title of "blooded," as one of the Hard Meat lunged out of the shadows and met the speaking ends of their weapons, bursting into a spray of gore and chitin, pieces on every surface. They all roared laughter, delighted by the ease of their accomplishment.

The laughter stopped a moment later, when the smallest of their number made a choked sound and the rest turned to find him gone, only empty space where he should have been. The remaining seven immediately pressed closer to each other, shoulder to shoulder, weapons at the ready. They had been careless, and one of their own had paid the price.

Yes, the soft, squishy oomans had been caught off-guard by the Hard Meat, but they could almost be forgiven. They were strong warriors in their own way, but they were still as children wandering the cosmos with no concept of how many dangers lurked on the fringes of their known space, how many terrible ways the void offered for them to die. And they were breakable enough, and bred quickly enough, that the ones who *did* learn to recognize those dangers rarely survived them. The bodies were swept aside and forgotten, washed away by the brief tides of short ooman life. Yautja had to be better than them, were better than them, in every possible, every conceivable way. And still they were down a man, already, and the kill count stood at one for each side.

More cautiously, not laughing now, they began to creep forward, winking out of sight one by one as their refraction suits activated and removed them from the visible world.

"Oh you did *not*," Lisa exclaimed, sitting up straighter. She had shrieked and slumped when one of the swift black things appeared and took one of the massive strangers away, whisking him into nothingness more quickly than she would have believed possible. Their fight had taken place entirely on a different screen, well away from the rest of his crew. Without his gun, he still put up an incredible fight, producing what seemed like an endless stream of hand weapons and holding the creature at bay for longer than she would have believed possible.

And then the stream ran dry, and the creature was upon him. It jammed the point of its terrible tail through the stranger's throat, and he died with a gurgle and a final thrash, the tension leaving his body as the life left his eyes. At least he was dead, and couldn't be used as an incubator. The creature hissed triumphantly atop the corpse before darting away, moving too quickly for the cameras to smoothly follow.

Why did they kill the way they did? They didn't feed. They took some of their victims alive and glued them to the walls, where skittering crab-things she had never seen before used their bodies as incubators for more of the swift, dark things. Killing this newcomer made a certain amount of sense: these creatures, whatever they were, had clearly come here ready to fight the things, armed and armored and ready for a slaughter. A slaughter that was apparently not going to be as one-sided as they had expected it to be, judging by the way this one had been taken. So self-defense made sense as a motive, but the deaths of the other horticulturists…

They hadn't been killed for food, and they hadn't been killed in self-defense, and most of them hadn't been killed to serve as incubators. It was like these things viewed absolutely everything that wasn't part of their… hive? Swarm? She didn't have a group noun for these things, and while she probably didn't *need* one, she was a scientist. She preferred it when things were easily categorized and filed away. Fine, then, call them a hive, one whose collective danger-sense was so finely tuned that anything they recognized as "other," which seemed to be absolutely everything, was suspect and needed to be destroyed.

There were ten of the things remaining, and seven of the creatures—or there had been seven, before they all vanished into thin air, concealed by some sort of refraction technology she would have loved to study at more leisure. When she'd seen them blow the first one apart, she would have called those good odds, but now... now she needed to do something to help them, if she could. She pressed the button for the intercom, taking a deep breath.

"I don't know if you speak English," she began. "I'm hoping you do, and you came here because you picked up my distress call. The black things don't react to sound when it isn't coming from a living person."

The creatures were invisible to the eye, but they still showed up on the station's temperature scanners. She still didn't know how the things hunted. They had no visible eyes, so it was possible that vanishing from sight wasn't going to help them the way they hoped it would.

"If you can hear me, if you can understand me, there are ten of them, and they're moving toward you in the halls. Your comrade is dead. The one that took him killed him quickly, without implanting any eggs. I don't know how much you know about these things, but it's got to be more than I do; I'm the last survivor—"

———

The voice of the ooman who had called them here emerged from speakers along the ceiling level, and while they would obscure the sound of the warriors' footsteps, they would also obscure the sound of the Hard Meat. One by one, their translators keyed on to what she was saying, and they realized that weak and cowardly as the ooman might be, she was also providing them with the precise locations of the remaining Hard Meat, as well as their numbers.

The weapons of the Yautja were superior to the biology of the Hard Meat; only speed and surprise served to give the creatures an edge of superiority. With the ooman telling them precisely where to go and shouting dismayed warning when the hard meat accelerated toward them, even that thin edge was lost, and the hunt's conclusion became a foregone conclusion.

It was still a hunt with honor. The danger of the prey and the closeness of the quarters saw to that. One of the warriors was standing too close to one of the Hard Meat when it exploded into chitin and gore, and he howled as the droplets of acidic blood ate into the side of his face. They were a cleaning crew, however, and one of his companions stepped in with neutralizing spray before the blood could do more than slough away the top layers of his skin. He would have a scar to remember his grand hunt by, and a renewed need to kill. He roared approval, and his companions echoed him.

And still the ooman voice spoke, guiding them to target after target, until the last Hard Meat was dead and they harvested their trophies, tails and spines and one partially intact head. The last thing it guided them to was the room where it had cowered throughout the great fight, opening the door enough to see them, to be seen for itself. They looked the ooman in the eye, scanned her and saw that she was not infected. She was weak and small and fragile, but she was not carrying the Hard Meat nestled in the palace of her bones. Their work here was done.

They removed their masks and looked at her barefaced, with honor. Lisa recoiled, but did not scream.

There was no queen. A pity, that. Content and triumphant, they made their way back to their ship, leaving the ooman who had called them here still standing on her own unsevered feet. She had given them a great gift, and she had offered neither threat nor challenge. Let her receive the greatest honor they had to offer in return.

Let her live.

Lisa had seen videos once, of a kind of fish that used to live in the oceans on Earth, called the sarcastic fringehead. It was a silly name for a silly animal, which could distend its jaws to make its head look like it had doubled in size. When the strangers revealed their faces to her, that was all she could think of. These things had faces sort of like a bulldog crossed with one of those fish, topped with a cascade of fleshy tentacles. If she'd been forced to guess where they lived from looking at those heads, she would have guessed they were something aquatic, rarely if ever coming to the surface. These were alien things, from an alien cosmos, and she had no place among them.

For a moment, she thought for sure that she was going to die. Then they turned, and walked away, and left her alone.

Lisa watched, eyes wide, as their ship decoupled from the airlock and the strange visitors left. Slowly, she rose from her chair and made her way back to the lab door, which she had resealed as soon as her visitors had come and gone, cutting herself off from the rest of the station. There was nothing out there now. Nothing moved on the monitors. Just her, alone, in a floating graveyard the corporation had probably already written off as lost.

No one was coming to save her, not now, and maybe not for a long, long time. Lisa took a deep, shuddering breath, and opened the door.

Someone needed to cycle the hydroponics. She might live here for the rest of her life, but by God, she was going to live. And life meant she was going to have strawberries.

If nothing else, she would have strawberries.

BLOOD AND HONOR

BY SUSANNE L. LAMBDIN

A thunderous noise and heavy vibration roused Lieutenant Kai Kentarus from a groggy slumber.

Her immediate response at finding herself strapped inside a life pod, wearing a spacesuit and helmet, and plummeting toward a red planet was confusion. The last thing she remembered was lying in bed next to Captain Duran of the USS *Tephra*.

"Together, we'll explore the galaxy," Duran had told her.

Somehow, the comforts of her pillow and his arms ended up replaced by a turbulent ride in the one-person pod. It was possible the predator ships spotted in the Andromeda System had attacked the *Tephra*. Captain Lucien Duran, a cautious man, would only have ordered the marines and crew to abandon the Bougainville-class military vessel if it had sustained serious damage and there was no other choice. If this were the case, Kentarus should have seen other jettisoned life pods out the window, but as she searched, the pod entered the atmosphere.

Friction against the nose of the small vessel caused the

metal to glow crimson. Red and orange flames lapped outside the window.

Kentarus—a US Colonial Marine, trained to remain calm in the worst situation, and still able to smell Duran's cologne on her skin—closed her eyes. She immediately recalled a prior meeting on the *Tephra* with Duran and Palmer Lennox, a rep from Weyland-Yutani. Lennox had nervously chewed on the end of a pen, while Duran oozed confidence and pride. All three sat in a conference room with a long window affording a few of a planet with more land mass than oceans.

"Like Earth, planet XK-93 has a protective ozone layer and an atmosphere," Kentarus said. "There are high levels of nitrogen, oxygen, argon, and carbon dioxide. Breathable air."

"Yes, yes," Lennox said, impatient. "And if your captain sends down a platoon, as agreed upon, you'll be with them."

"I agreed to nothing. The Company knew Xenomorph XX121 inhabited this planet before we arrived," Duran said. "The prior science expedition failed to report back. We must assume a queen exists, producing eggs, and one platoon won't cut it."

"You're the expert, Captain Duran. The Company will colonize this planet, with or without your help," Lennox said. "I suggest you follow orders."

"Our drones identified Xenomorphs on the southern— the hottest—continent, before we lost contact with them," Kentarus said. "There's a network of tunnels running beneath the surface, which is where the queen will be. The Company drones found several active volcanos and a large cache of iron ore before we lost contact with them."

Duran leaned forward. "We know as well as you do that the Company is after the iron ore deposits, Lennox," he said.

"The ship's sensors have the same problem as the drones because of the ore, and can't get an exact reading on the Xenomorphs. I'm not sending down a platoon until we can confirm the queen's location and the number of her guards."

"Excuses," Lennox said. "I'm starting to think you're the wrong man for the job, Duran. Do what you're told, or this will be your last command. This is an extermination mission. It's why the military is here. As for the ore, that's none of your business."

"Can I say something?" Kentarus asked. "You're interested in the southern continent. We know a queen is down there. The Night Marchers can get the job done, but we have a bigger problem than acid-spewing aliens."

The Company man glared at her. The tips of his ears turned red. "I'm in charge of this mission, Captain Duran," he snarled. "Tell your lieutenant I'm not interested in her opinion."

"Now you're pissing me off," Duran said. He stood at six foot five, dark haired, impeccably groomed, down to the sleek cut of his triangular black beard. "A spaceship entered this solar system six hours ago. We tracked it while in orbit, but lost contact when it entered the planet's atmosphere. I've seen one of those long-nosed ships before and that's why I know XK-93 is the hunting ground for these aggressive predators."

"Preposterous," Lennox said.

"Ever seen a hunter close up?" Kentarus opened her jacket and pulled up her undershirt, revealing a set of long scars across her taut stomach. "I encountered my first not long after I transferred to this ship. Female. Vicious. The science team were no more equipped to deal with these hunters than the colonists will be, and you know it."

"I've seen images, Lieutenant Kentarus, but you survived," Lennox said. "In fact, you're precisely who we need down on the planet."

"I'm not sure what is worse, Lennox. Your breath or your stupidity," Kentarus said. "I got lucky—Sergeant Mule had my back."

"No marines. No big show," Duran said. He crossed his arms. "We'll find another planet to colonize. End of discussion."

The flames at the window receded. Kentarus gazed out at a hazy sky riddled with dust clouds but saw no other life pods. Set on automatic, the vessel made its rapid descent over a desert with massive dunes that reminded her of the southern continent, and with a loud *click*, deployed a canopy. Air filled the massive parachute with a violent yank to slow the vessel's descent, letting it drift down, until it slammed into a dune. The force behind the pod's impact punched it through the sand to slide down a hundred feet before coming to a jarring halt.

In the next instant, every monitor on the console turned off. The engine whined in protest and shut down, leaving the interior dark. Without an operating system, she had no way to contact the *Tephra*, nor scan for hostile life forms, and she had to open the door manually.

Unfastening the harness, Kentarus stooped as the roof was low, and grasped the emergency handle in both hands. When she pushed downward nothing happened. Frustrated, she threw her weight into forcing the handle down and cursed when it broke off in her hand. She stared at eighteen inches of specialized metal in numb disbelief. A marine never gives up, she thought, and wedged the end of the handle into a groove in the side of the door.

Able to hear the howl of wind and sharp grains of sand pelt the side of the ship, she hesitated. Without powered armor or weapons, Kentarus doubted she'd survive long wearing a spacesuit in the harsh elements, but she had to try. Repeated attempts to open the door left her light-headed. She sat in the chair, flipping switches in the hope the computer system might reboot, and managed to turn on the emergency beacon. Next, she searched in a cubbyhole for a gun, found nothing, and pushed the face shield open.

"Duran wouldn't leave me. Nor would Sergeant Mule. This is Company bullshit."

During the last seven months, Kentarus had found Lennox's manner threatening, but she didn't think he had the balls to stuff her inside a tin can. Duran had hand-picked conscripted marines for reassignment to the 'Night Marchers,' 4th Battalion, 3rd Army Group, and chose Kentarus as his weapons specialist. The moment she met the captain, she knew they'd be lovers, and had decided a three-year mission sounded good. Later, she'd discovered Weyland-Yutani privately owned the spaceship—in which Duran's father-in-law was a major shareholder—which was why he'd tolerated the Company rep. The *Tephra* had visited two planets Duran marked as habitable with terraforming potential. Colonists would arrive at both locations months before the *Tephra* made its voyage home. They were the lucky ones, Kentarus thought.

XK-93 was a speck of red dust on the outer fringes of the Andromeda System, too far removed from any space station for anyone to intercept the transmitted beacon until several months later. As Duran had placed the planet under quarantine and scheduled their immediate departure, the *Tephra* had left the solar system without her.

After the meeting, Lennox had slunk off with his tail between his legs. Kentarus had retired with Duran to his quarters. Same routine as always—the captain went first, then five minutes later, she entered. Both stripped, got into bed, and Duran rushed, as if they'd run out of time.

"Lennox is trouble," Kentarus said.

"That a-hole can complain all he wants. Lennox doesn't care if every marine dies down there. I made the right call. There are other planets, Kai."

"The Company doesn't realize these predators are a serious threat. Nor is this the only planet they're on," Kentarus said. "I don't trust Lennox. Nor should you. Think he knows?"

"No one better know about us. I'm a married man."

"I meant that I'm trans."

"Honey, you're beautiful and you know it. That's not the problem. My wife is a harpy. Her father is Cronus reincarnated. If they find out I'm off my leash, they'll devour me. I'm sorry, but my career comes first."

"What's that mean?"

"It means I can't have Lennox poking his nose into my personal business. Be extra careful sneaking into my room. Okay?"

Kentarus took her anger out on the door. Adrenaline pumped through her system as she stood, got into position, and jammed the handle into the groove. Muscles cramped as she pushed against the metal handle and the door opened an inch. She paused, again queasy, and leaned against the door until the cramps subsided. With a glance at the monitor on the back of her left wrist, she confirmed the surface temperature was 103 degrees Fahrenheit, and it was getting hotter inside the pod. She put her shoulder to the door.

A loud *thump* hit the observation window. Kentarus glanced at it, able to see slimy skid marks but not what made them. Sand adhered to the substance within seconds, but her resolve to get outside was stronger than her fear of the unknown.

Closing the face shield, desperate to get outside, she put her feet against the chair and back to the door. She used every bit of strength to force it open. Wind slammed into her, and she fell to the ground, half out of the pod, still holding the door handle. Rising to her feet, Kentarus first checked her oxygen level. Suit remained cool. There was enough oxygen to last six hours, but she needed to get her bearings.

The windblown sand partially obscured her vision. In every direction were miles of sand and giant dunes, and a large orange sun that created shimmers. She turned to the pod, raising the handle, and approached the observation window. Not a trace of slime remained, blown clean by sand and wind. Nor were tracks left in the sand to suggest what it might have been. She moved away from the pod, watching for movement in the sand, and finally climbed to the top of a dune for a better look.

The long, dark shadow of a mountain range appeared in the distance. Thirty to forty miles from her current position, if vegetation grew at its base, she'd find water. A fit marine could make the march in less than ten hours, but Kentarus walked on hot, shifting sand, weighted down by the suit, and each footstep was heavy and methodical.

She avoided climbing dunes when possible, and twelve miles in, paused to suck on a tube within the helmet. Attached to a *recycler*, she drank her own perspiration running through a filtration unit, but it had a dank taste. It could have been worse. Her best friend Sergeant Frank 'Mule' Mueller had drunk his own piss to survive in a desert environment.

"I've tasted worse," Mule had told her.

Most of the things Mule recounted to Kentarus were meant in jest. Unfortunately, Mule had underestimated the intelligence of a buck private when he told him, "All you have to do is lie down in the presence of a hunter, avoid eye contact and stay quiet, barely breathing, and the big bastard will pass you by."

The sergeant had failed to mention this tactic worked for unarmed civilians, viewed as a non-threat by predators, not soldiers.

Kentarus was with the private when the female hunter found them. The hunter had worn armor plates over her breasts, and her dreadlocks had ornate silver beads. Dual blades had extended from the hunter's wrists and sliced through the private's midsection. In the next stroke, the blades had sliced into Kentarus's chest. As she lay on the ground, bleeding, she'd pretended to be dead when the hunter nudged her to provoke a reaction. Fortunately, Mule arrived, armed with XM99A Phased Plasma Pulse Rifles, blowing the formidable hunter into bits, and saved her life.

Mule wouldn't betray her. Mule had tried to warn her.

Minutes before the meeting, he had pulled her aside to say, "The science team discovered an old queen in a cave surrounded by petrified eggs. No Praetorians were guarding her, which means the old girl no longer serves a purpose and was abandoned. That doesn't mean a younger queen isn't hiding somewhere else, producing eggs. Xenomorphs thrive in hot climates, which is why we spotted a hunter ship. Don't trust Lennox. I'm not so sure about Duran, either. Try to convince those two idiots that any time spent down on that planet is a death sentence."

"Why bring up Lucien right now?"

"Because I know you two have a thing going on. Does his wife know?"

Kentarus didn't believe in miracles and her chance of survival seemed slim. Whatever maniacal god controlled the cosmos had set the big orange sun on *broil*. Shimmers appeared on the sand to create mirages. What she saw a mile up ahead could not be real.

The wind had a purpose and had partially uncovered the wreckage of several derelict spaceships cradled between the dunes. She trotted forward, eager to investigate. The remains of a USCM drop ship, battered to hell, and a larger predator ship told a story of what befell the Company's ill-fated science team. They'd encountered hunters, not Xenomorphs, as officially reported. Now it made sense why Duran had wanted to leave the moment they arrived. Both the captain and the rep had known the details of the ill-fated mission, but which man had sentenced her to death?

Hoping to find weapons, she approached the drop ship. A blast hole in its side had allowed sand to fill the interior. As she knelt to sweep aside sand, something heavy struck the top of her helmet, and a long tail curled around her face shield.

Kentarus suppressed rising panic, removed her helmet, and flung it aside.

She'd worn her spacesuit for protection, not fear of pathogens. When the helmet hit the ground, she noticed a large hole melted into the center of the face shield. A pale, tan creature with a long tail slithered out of the helmet, burrowing deep in the sand. It was a Xenomorph facehugger.

She'd suspected as much when she'd noticed slime on the pod window, and now she watched its tail reappear, sifting the sand, before it headed toward her.

Crawling backward on the sand, her hand brushed across what felt like a shaft and she pulled a spear from the dune. Her years of training in small ops had included using all types of blades and muscle memory guided her hands. As the creature flew toward her, whipping its tail, with an upward sweep the spearhead sliced through its body. A spray of acid hit the sand.

Kentarus stood, holding the spear tight, no longer eager to investigate further, not if Xenomorph eggs were inside the hunter's ship. She ran toward the mountains, not stopping for miles, not until she felt safe. Then she walked along slowly and used the time to examine the weapon. She'd seen a similar spear in the past. It was a predator's weapon, made of black polymer, which was unbreakable and acid-resistant. Light in hand and well-balanced, she discovered a switch released a second blade or retracted both, making it compact and easy to carry. Her spacesuit, however, had served its purpose, and now she roasted in it.

The moment she removed the suit, Kentarus felt cooler. Her damp undershirt and camo pants dried fast. While used to sand collecting in her boots, her long hair was a menace. One swipe with an extended blade left it cut at an odd angle, but she could see.

Toward dusk, she arrived at a forest that grew at the base of the mountains. Exhausted, she took a knee and watched the rise of seven moons. Each moon was a different size and color, producing enough natural light to scrutinize the terrain. The air felt moist beneath the trees, but she remained thirsty.

A carpet of green moss was a nice change from sand. As she listened to the silence, the hairs rose at the nape of her neck. She was not alone in the forest.

Less than twenty yards away stood two Praetorians near a pool of water. Both were ten-foot-tall, black, with massive legs, long arms and spindly fingers that ended in razor-sharp talons. Prior reports had made note of their speed and agility. Their long tails served as weapons, with spearheads at the tips, and as if manufactured in a lab, they had two sets of jaws and elongated skulls. As the strange moonlight reflected off their crest-shaped skulls, the one closest to Kentarus turned and hissed. She knew Praetorians kept close to their queen, seldom leaving the nest, and assumed something or someone had flushed the pair into the open.

A triangle of three red glowing dots suddenly appeared on an elongated head.

Kentarus knew at once that a predator had targeted its prey and kept still. In the time it took to exhale, two streams of blue plasma shot out of the upper canopy, flushing out another Xenomorph from the trees. With a scream of rage, a young queen, twice the size of the drones, appeared in the clearing. Her massive tail lashed out, breaking a tree in half, and something heavy hit the ground.

It was Kentarus's signal to run.

Headed in the opposite direction to the battle, she flipped the switch to extend both spearheads, ducked around a tree, and nearly slammed into a drone. The Xenomorph seemed as surprised as her, and with a hiss, slowly advanced. Kentarus lifted the spear as the alien charged, impaling it on the spear, and jerked it back. From out of nowhere, bursts of blue plasma struck the wounded creature, splattering its skull.

She crouched, aware something crawled on an overhead limb, and lifted her gaze to see a hunter.

Dreadlocks bordered a helmet outfitted with a rhinoceros-like horn on the forehead. The body armor looked medieval, with silver pauldrons, and a shoulder gun. Armed with a plasma gun, the hunter vanished at the sound of impact tremors and the snap of tree trunks. Kentarus trembled at the approach of the young queen. Making loud, angry screeches, she swept aside large trees with a single swipe of her long, armored tail, on a quest to find the camouflaged predator who hunted her.

Kentarus took cover behind a tree, as blue streams of plasma came from a second location, fired not at the queen but the horned predator. Both hunters ignored the rampaging queen to fight a duel in the trees. A stray bolt of plasma struck a nearby tree, showering Kentarus with severed branches and burning debris. Burning vegetation emitted thick white smoke and a foul odor that burned her lungs. The queen suddenly swept through the fire, unhindered by the flames and heat, and received several well-aimed bursts of plasma.

It was then Kentarus ran in the opposite direction, not stopping until the sounds of battle were far behind, and found she'd entered an older section of the forest where the trees grew thick enough to block the moonlight. She pressed against a tree to catch her breath. Mule had told her three predators normally hunted together. Where was the third predator? And where was the ancient queen abandoned by its own kind? She assumed the entrance of a cave was nearby, as Xenomorphs preferred warm, dark places and seldom came out into the open. It seemed possible the third hunter had flushed out their prey and now lay in wait somewhere in the dark.

At the snap of a twig, Kentarus lifted the spear. A lone Praetorian stepped into her path, peeled back its black lips to reveal its double set of glistening silver fangs. She jabbed with the spear, then turned it lengthwise to block a deadly blow from its tail and ducked behind a tree. The creature scuttled up the trunk, rustling in the branches, while she put her back to the bark, waiting. Aware it had moved onto a limb hanging above her, she grasped the spear in both hands and thrust it upwards. The tip pierced the armor plating of the Xenomorph's chest, sinking deep, and she let it go, diving into the brush to avoid the spray of acid.

With a piteous scream the Praetorian hit the ground, impaled on the spear but still alive. Kentarus wiped sweat off her brow, watching it thrash, then bolted forward to pull out the spear. Dull yellow acid splattered and hissed on the ground, dripping from the blade. As Kentarus lifted the spear, prepared to drive it through the beast's head, a sudden rush of nausea bent her over. She spewed out stomach acid, able to smell its foulness before it hit the ground. Left with a pounding headache, blurred vision, and feeling weaker, she turned her focus back on the drone. It was no longer lying on the ground, but on its feet. Acid oozed out from the hole in its chest and saliva dripped from its extended second jaws. It rushed toward her, arms askew, hissing.

Kentarus swung the spear over her head and brought it down with expert precision, slicing the Praetorian's oblong skull in half. Both sections fell to the ground as the body crumbled. With morbid fascination, she scrutinized both sections of the head, able to see greenish brain matter and a widening pool of acid that sizzled on contact with the moss. She wiped the blade on the ground to remove the yellow substance, then paused to listen to what sounded like rushing water. Compelled to investigate, she climbed to higher ground and came upon a massive waterfall flowing over the side of a hundred-foot cliff into a pond.

Stone blocks formed a ring around the pool, with carvings of helmeted warriors from a long-forgotten humanoid race. Desperate for water, she waded into the pond. As she did so, a staircase became visible on the left of the waterfall, cut out of the stone that led to an observation platform. The area felt sacred, for she saw no signs of either hostile species. She waded into the water, sinking to her neck, and sucked water into her mouth to sedate her thirst. The water cooled her overheated body and she floated on her back, gazing at the night sky.

Smoke obscured most of the moons, the air thick with the odor of burning timber. The serene moment ended at a sudden stabbing pain behind her eyes. Muscle spasms made her body contort, yet she managed to hold onto the spear and return to the edge of the pool. As bile rose at the back of her throat, she spotted a pair of glowing yellow eyes watching her from the trees. Had the third hunter found her? Another spasm ripped through her body. It was too late to worry about toxins or parasites in the water, yet she'd felt sick before she landed, and her condition had worsened in the last hour. Without medical attention, Kentarus knew she'd die. She closed her eyes, sinking into the water, and thought of Captain Lucien Duran.

The transmission from his wife had sealed her fate. Taken at his desk while Kentarus lay in his bed, she had heard everything. "Father confirms you have a promotion waiting. Think of it, Lucien," Mrs. Duran had said. "You'll finally command a fleet. It's what we've always wanted. Make sure there's no scandal. Daddy won't like it. Kill her."

After the captain ended the transmission, he'd offered Kentarus a glass of water.

"I thought you loved me. You were getting a divorce," she said. At his apology, she had downed the water, not for a second believing he'd poison her.

Until now.

Whatever Captain Duran had given her, the side effects came and went. She climbed from the pool with the spear, but the yellow eyes had vanished. With no choice but to "hunt" a hunter, she advanced into the trees. Splatters of neon green blood left a trail a short distance into the forest and stopped at a tree. Kentarus heard low growls and sharp clicking noises. She knelt and glanced at the glowing green blood.

The scent of smoke from a campfire and a curious meaty odor drew her attention. A short walk led her into a small camp to find a young female predator propped against a tree.

The female hunter was naked. Her skin was pale and covered with black tiger stripes at the sides of her abdomen, arms, and legs. Cords tied the hunter's arms to an overhead branch and her extended legs were roped together. Toes and fingers ended in black talons that looked sharp as daggers. A pair of big feet smoldered in the embers of the campfire. The hunter silently studied Kentarus with big yellow eyes, but it was impossible it was the same predator that had spotted her at the waterfall.

"I'm not going to hurt you," Kentarus said. "Stay calm."

Old Rhino was male. She didn't know the gender of the second hunter that had exchanged gunfire with him, but it made no sense a male predator would hunt females from his own species or leave this one to slowly roast in the campfire. The female hunter's flesh bore the signs of a branding iron. Deep gashes cut into her thighs and arms bled. For some reason, the hunter's helmet was left on. Her exposed neck was surprisingly slender, yet despite her injuries she looked strong. Ornate silver beads adorned her black dreadlocks. The silver armor tossed into a nearby pile looked familiar, as did the engraved round moon over a horizontal curved blade on the hunter's face shield. The last time Kentarus had seen the symbol, she'd been lying on the ground with a female predator standing over her. She wondered if the females belonged to the same corps of fighters, or if the curious symbol was a family crest.

"I've seen that sign before," Kentarus said, and drew an imaginary shape on her forehead. "Not long ago, I fought one of your kind and lived. Who did this to you? Old Rhino?" She made the shape of a horn with her hand. "Must be some bad blood between you and the male."

With a snarl, the female pulled at the ropes. Kentarus took pity on the female hunter, for she too felt the sting of a man's betrayal and assumed they shared a desire for revenge.

"I saw a second hunter. Another female?"

The injured hunter snarled and tried to move her feet. Kentarus stomped out the fire. She used the spear to push the hunter's seared feet out of the embers.

"I'm going to untie you, but first we make a deal. I need a way off this rock. You help me, I help you. Agreed?"

Bursts of blue plasma shot out of the trees, slamming into the ground close to where Kentarus squatted beside the injured female. Reacting as she would to help a fellow marine, she cut the hunter free, pulled her up, and together they ran for cover, under a hailstorm of gunfire that set the trees on fire. The female grabbed Kentarus by the shoulders, cutting into her flesh with the tips of her nails. She stood six inches taller and weighed a hundred pounds more than Kentarus. With a soft snarl, the hunter motioned her forward, limping as they ran back toward the waterfall. Near the pool, Kentarus noticed green blood on the ground and looked up at the same time as her companion.

Overhead, the second female hunter hung upside down by her feet, flayed head to toe. Green blood dripped on the ground and her companion snarled.

"I'm sorry. We can't cut her down. There's a big queen and her guards in the area." Kentarus winced as her head started to throb again. She pointed at the body then at her companion. "Old Rhino killed her. He means to kill you and me."

Yellow eyes narrowed. The female cocked her head to the side.

"I think you understand me," Kentarus said. "My captain left me behind." She tapped her chest then lifted her hand to mimic the ship's departure. "Do you have a ship? If I help you get to it, will you take me with you?"

"Ship," the hunter repeated and pointed at the staircase.

"I'll take that as a 'yes.'" Kentarus again tapped her chest. "I'm Kai." She pointed at the female. "What's your name?" The growl deepened. "I'm calling you *Blood Venom*. It sounds bad-ass. Like you."

"Blood," the female said.

"Sounds like we have a deal."

Kentarus helped the female to the stairs. Due to the condition of Blood Venom's burned feet, it took longer than she wanted to make it to the platform. Halfway, her companion needed to rest. Kentarus took the time to study the landscape. A fire lapped hungrily at trees in the distance. She turned to face the waterfall. Across the water, moonlight shone upon a spaceship set on a massive boulder, with its nose pointed toward the river. Blood Venom pointed at the ship and made clicking sounds.

"Yeah, yeah, I get it. We have to cross," Kentarus said. The pair walked along an old footpath set with broken stones. Her companion suddenly halted as a pair of Praetorians appeared on the path ahead. "I hope you can swim."

Loud screeches came from the Xenomorphs. Handing the spear to the young hunter, Kentarus wrapped an arm under Blood Venom's shoulder and pulled her into the water. The current was strong, forcing Kentarus to swim on her side to hold the larger and heavier female above the water. Her companion pushed Kentarus away and swam on her own. When they reached the bank, the pair climbed out of the water. As they scaled the rocks, a sudden barrage of blue plasma struck a Praetorian in the head on the far bank, exposing a neon yellow brain before it toppled into the water.

"It's Old Rhino. Damn," Kentarus muttered.

With a furious screech, the young queen appeared on the opposite bank. The queen noticed Kentarus and Blood Venom on the rocks and scrambled into the water, heading after them. The male hunter suddenly appeared and dove into the water to swim after the queen.

Blood Venom pulled Kentarus to the top of the boulder, and together they ran to the ship. As they neared the vessel, Kentarus spotted the stone statue of a forty-foot-tall Xenomorph queen on the other side of the ship. At least it looked like a statue in the moonlight. The moment the young queen appeared, the statue suddenly moved and let out a threatening roar.

The door opened and Blood Venom pushed Kentarus inside the vessel, closing it behind them. The interior of the craft was black and sleek, with strange symbols engraved on the walls. Red track lights led the way to the bridge. The hunter sat in a chair in front of a control panel, with a large window that looked over the river. As the ship's engines started to whine, a pale blue shimmer appeared that Kentarus assumed was a force field.

Blood Venom suddenly slumped forward then fumbled for a black box from beneath her seat. Kentarus came to her aid and opened the box to find strange instruments inside. She held it up to the hunter, who chose a syringe and injected a needle into her shoulder, pumping blue fluid into her body. Spotting a green cape on the floor, Kentarus ripped it into pieces and tied strips around the female's chest to stanch the flow of blood. When Kentarus had finished, Blood Venom held up a ceremonial knife made from obsidian and pointed it at her.

"We had a deal," Kentarus said.

The female removed her helmet, revealing four long tusks at the corners of her extensive mouth. She clicked the tusks together. Her beady yellow eyes narrowed as she grabbed Kentarus's arm and pressed the knife tip to her chest and growled.

Kentarus reacted on impulse and ripped open her shirt, exposing three long scars across her chest. Blood Venom held her gaze then made swift cuts directly above the scars. Wincing in pain and bleeding, Kentarus looked down to find the same symbol from the hunter's face shield cut into her flesh.

"This is a mark of honor?" Kentarus asked. "Like you, I am female." The hunter cocked her head. "Do you understand me? We need to go, before Old Rhino arrives to battle the queens. This is all about territory and who's in control. Old Rhino came here to kill the ancient queen and the young queen who replaced her, and we're in the way. Why aren't we leaving?"

The hunter opened a side panel in front of her. First, she removed a large metal box and flipped it open, revealing an assortment of curious instruments. There were several glass vials with different colored liquids in a holder. Glancing at Kentarus, the hunter narrowed her eyes and then selected a vial with a yellow serum. The vial was placed it into an applicator. The hunter held Kentarus's gaze and held out the applicator, growling softly. Kentarus realized it must be some sort of medicine.

"I've been poisoned. I don't know with what, but this will cure me?"

A soft growl came from Blood Venom, which Kentarus took as an affirmative response. She put her trust in the female hunter and administered the serum. It hit her like a dozen consumed energy drinks. Her vision cleared. The muscle cramps and nausea ended.

"Whatever that was did the trick. I feel stronger. Thanks."

Blood Venom growled as she again dug inside the panel. She removed two curious-looking jackets with ribbed armor around the middle, pauldrons, and a skirt of scaled armor. There was urgency in Blood Venom's movements as she dressed in the armor and put on her helmet. Kentarus dressed, surprised the armor fit but it was heavy. Blood Venom put on wrist gauntlets but attached a shoulder laser to Kentarus's pauldron. Both strapped on gun belts which came with pistols, but Kentarus took back her old spear.

"You want us to go back out there and fight?" Kentarus asked.

From outside the vessel came two powerful screeches. A heavy weight slammed into the side of the spaceship, making the force field spark and short out. The old queen came into view. Her ancient body appeared pale silver. In her jaws hung the broken body of Old Rhino. With a whip of her head, she tossed aside his body.

"Honor," the hunter said in perfect mimicry of Kentarus.

"You take the old girl. I'll fight the smaller queen. Then we leave."

Blood Venom ran down the corridor, stopping at the door, and waited for Kentarus to join her. The door opened with a *whoosh*. Kentarus jumped out first. The young queen moved into view, more interested in battling the old queen for dominance than Kentarus, and rushed at her opponent. As the creatures slammed together, the old queen's tail struck the multi-ton ship, spinning it like a toy, with Blood Venom still inside. Kentarus ducked as a blast of heat came from exposed thrusters. She lay flat to avoid the flames, and from her prone position, watched the new queen jump onto the old queen's back.

Age had hardened her body armor. In another thousand years, Kentarus imagined the ancient bitch would become petrified. Slower than the young queen, who used both sets of jaws, her armor was tough and sustained no damage. The old queen retaliated, using her head like a ram to slam the smaller female to the rock. On impact, the boulder split in half, and the hunter's ship started to slide toward the river in a thunderous rockslide. The engines shut down as the ship struck the water with a massive splash and floated toward the waterfall. The section of boulder that held the two queens and Kentarus remained solid, and she watched as the ancient one placed a heavy foot on the back of the younger queen and pressed down.

Her immense weight crushed the young rival flat, ending any chance of the survival of her own species. The old queen climbed over her dead opponent, took one look at Kentarus, and screeched. Its bent legs were twice the length of its body and each footfall created cracks in the rock. As it approached, Kentarus heaved the spear at the giant and watched it bounce off. She drew the pistol and fired at the old queen's kneecap, hoping to maim it, but the projected blue plasma rolled off its pale silver body. The automatic response of the shoulder cannon dispersed fiery rounds at the Xenomorph, also with no effect. Its dragon-sized tail pummeled the rock in front of Kentarus, causing her to fall between the two halves of the boulder. There was enough room between the rocks to make her way toward the river. The massive beast loomed overhead, eager to get to her, and moved ahead, vanishing from sight.

Kentarus put away the pistol and tried to climb to the top of a boulder. The armor protected her from the jagged rocks but hindered her movement. She took it off but kept the pistol, firing at the creature before sliding down the side of the boulder. Panting hard, she lacerated her hands in her haste. Small rocks rained on her as the old queen appeared above her, stomping her foot to break apart large chunks of stone. Kentarus lost her footing and slid off the rock, dropping ten feet and slamming into another boulder, losing the pistol in the process.

With a nasty hiss, the old queen looked down at her. Kentarus stood, winded, and felt a twinge in her ankle. As she limped toward the riverbank, she heard a loud commotion. The ancient queen had dropped down to land at the river's edge and now waited for her arrival.

"Let's see if you can swim, old girl!"

Kentarus dove into the water and submerged. The current was fierce, pushing her toward the waterfall. Able to hear a thunderous roar, a sudden burst of flames from the ship's thrusters sent her to the surface. She saw the spaceship go over the falls, then noticed the massive queen wading through the river, coming after her, eager for the kill. The old queen suddenly halted, wrenching at her tail, caught by something beneath the surface. Still carried toward the waterfall, Kentarus told herself Blood Venom hadn't left her. Not only had she saved the hunter's life, but blood and honor were involved, that's what the ceremony on the spaceship had meant.

Honor meant something to both Kentarus and the female hunter. Blood Venom had made a deal with her. Kentarus wanted to believe the spaceship waited beyond the waterfall and her companion would help her get off the planet. She thought of Duran and fumed with rage. If she saw Duran again—no, *when* she saw him—she'd make him pay for his treachery.

Glancing back at the old queen, Kentarus saw its colossal frame move toward her, and noticed the Xenomorphs had gathered at the side of the river. Yet, the drones did not give pursuit, and Kentarus swam toward the waterfall, hoping to find the ship waiting for her.

A misstep into a hole sent the Xenomorph sinking into the river, vanishing from sight. Any feeling of victory was short-lived. Drones appeared on the far riverbank, watching Kentarus float toward the falls, but made no move to stop her. The current spun her around. Still no queen in sight, she floundered in the water, coming to the edge, and went over the side.

Plummeting downward, deafened by the thunderous roar of the churning water, Kentarus suddenly slammed onto a hard surface. It had to be Blood Venom's ship beneath her, for she felt the surface rise upward. The flow of water pushed her forward as the ship rose and she noticed an opening hatch. When she got close enough, Kentarus grasped the side of the door, holding tight.

Something heavy slammed onto the ship behind her. The nose rose upward. Kentarus hauled her body through the hatch. She caught hold of a ladder, able to see outside as the ancient queen slid to the side of the ship, as it continued to rise beneath the waterfall. Kentarus ducked as the hatched closed, showering her with water. She clung to the ladder as the vessel turned sideways, able to feel a heavy weight shifting on the roof, and then a loud commotion as the old queen toppled over the side.

The spaceship, freed of the queen's heavy weight, shot upward as Kentarus pressed against the ladder, and then leveled out. She climbed down the ladder and wiped a hand across her face. Feeling bruised and sore, she headed to the bridge, unsure what to expect. Blood Venom faced forward, piloting the ship away from the planet and into a wide expanse of inky blackness.

"The queen is dead," Kentarus said. Aware her hands bled from minor cuts, without hesitation, she made three marks on Blood Venom's helmet. "Long live the queens. That means you and me." She plopped down in the co-pilot's chair and buckled up. "Just drop me off at Ganymede Space Station. Earth would be fine, too. For that matter, any planet colonized by humans." She gazed at the hunter. "I mean, I can trust you, right? We are *blood sisters*, after all."

Blood Venom's response was a deep chuckle. Unclear if it was a bad sign but a passenger nonetheless, Kentarus finally admitted she might never see Earth again. Her fate was one big cosmic joke, and the only thing left to do was laugh with her companion and hope for the best.

CARBON RITES

BY JESS LANDRY

From across a darkened hall, they pace, ready for the sirens to go off, their nightly signal; for their cage doors to open so they can go out and play.

They can sense one another from where they stand—their smells; their patterns; their growing fury.

They've been waiting for the moment when the doors open and they're standing face to face. Just the two of them, enemies since the dawn of time, enemies with a score to settle.

But until then, all they can do is wait.

Wait for the sirens to go off.

Wait for the fight to begin.

Another perfect day in Morden, Blake thought as she rode her bike down the quiet manicured streets of her small town, passing by all the cookie-cutter houses with their lush green lawns and white picket fences.

She often tried to look for flaws on her daily ride to work—peeling paint or a porch chair one inch too far to the left—but no matter how hard she looked, nothing was ever out of place.

The only things that felt unsuited were the air-raid sirens at the end of every street. Their water-stained poles jutted fifteen feet into the air, a circular mass of multiple sirens mounted at the apex, yellowed from sunny days and neglect. Red-budded bushes had been planted at the bases, as if their beauty would somehow detract from the relics of a time when no other technology existed to warn the prairie town of an impending tornado or some other disaster.

Blake had never seen a tornado, let alone heard the sirens go off.

Nothing new ever happened in Morden, not even a change in the weather.

If anything could be relied upon, it was that every day in Morden was the same—a cloudless blue sky, sun blazing overhead; the regulars coming to her diner for their daily meals; her bike ride home through the patch of forest that flanked the elementary school. Her evenings spent watching TV or reading a book or going for a jog, with a quick shower before bed.

Then wake up and do it all again.

Lather, rinse, repeat.

Another perfect day in Morden, Blake sighed as she sped past the school, where shadows of students gathering for class behind curtain-drawn windows moved about.

Blake stood behind the counter of the empty diner, marrying ketchup bottles. She eyed the clock as its hands ticked by— 9:57 p.m. The last customer had come and gone an hour ago, but Blake never felt right closing early—she always maintained the hope, no matter how desperate it seemed, that this night would be different.

It never was.

She had her regular customers who made time go by faster, but she often found herself daydreaming, usually of the renovations she wanted to make to her kitschy sixties-style diner to make it a little more current, or just lost in thought looking out the diner's large windows to the red flowers lining the median that divided the street, nestled among the sturdy oak trees. The red brick façades of the town's Main Street housed everything from Barb's Beauty Salon to the movie theater. Every building had their own brightly colored awning, and it always made her think of the pictures she'd seen online of other Main Streets of faraway towns—towns that she longed to visit. Towns that looked as though time had forgotten them as well.

Blake had never stepped foot outside of Morden, and it was during those endless work hours that she found herself longing for something more than serving the small farming community, spread out over kilometers of prairielands, flat and vast and dull. Something more than canola fields and dairy farms.

Blake jumped as the clock struck ten, knocking an empty ketchup bottle off the counter with her elbow.

Without so much as a glance, she lunged to the side, catching the bottle in her hand, seconds from it shattering on the floor.

She sat up and placed it on the counter, sighing.

Another perfect day in Morden.

Then, the bells over the front door rang out.

Blake stood as two men and a woman in matching dark gray jumpsuits walked in. A small round patch adorned the left-hand side of each jumpsuit, two swords meeting at the tip with a red star connecting them, and three smaller stars on either side. They wore packed utility belts around their waists, and the two men each gripped a RAK-9 semi-automatic rifle.

"Can I help you?" Blake said, panic rising inside of her as she focused on the guns.

The woman's hardened gaze fell upon Blake. Then she nodded. The taller of the two men moved past Blake, into the kitchen. The shorter man turned his attention to the street, standing watch at the door.

"What are you doing?" Blake asked, though no one paid her any mind.

The taller man came out of the kitchen. "Clear," he said to the woman.

"Thank you, Washington," she said, then turned to the shorter man. "Hernandez, how're we looking?"

"Quiet as a mouse," he said, a slight tremble in his voice. "But..."

"But what?"

"You sure about this, Mariana? Getting in here... finding her... it was easy. Too easy."

The three of them turned toward Blake.

Blake backed up against the wall behind the counter. "I don't want any trouble," she swallowed. "Just take the cash and leave."

"We don't want your money," Mariana said with a smirk. "We want you."

It was then that the air-raid sirens went off.

The wails shattered the quiet night, ebbing and flowing as they let their warnings be heard.

Everyone went for their ears, the cacophony rattling through their very cores. Blake eyed the three infiltrators, noticing the same look on each of their faces.

It was fear.

"You said tonight was an off night," Washington screamed over the din.

"It *is* an off night," Mariana screamed back.

Blake looked to the street, to see if anyone had stepped out to investigate. Maybe she could escape while they were distracted. But the road was bare, with the exception of a flicker on top of a building across the way that caught her eye.

A shape. One that seemed to shimmer in the moonlight.

It crouched on the edge of the cineplex, set in invisible stone like a camouflaged gargoyle.

Watching.

Waiting.

"Back to the school!" Mariana shouted, breaking Blake's gaze. "Let's go."

Washington and Hernandez rushed out the door. Blake stood frozen behind the counter. She turned back to the cineplex.

The shape was gone.

And so was Blake's chance at getting away.

The sirens continued their cries as the four of them set off down Main Street, keeping to the shadows, and into the cold, dark forest—the quickest way to the school.

Hernandez led the way, Washington stayed behind, and Mariana was at Blake's side, each one of them with their weapons drawn, each one of them on edge.

Blake walked with nervous poise, unsure of herself for having gone with these armed strangers without so much as a fight. But when her gaze fell upon Mariana with her short black hair and dark, intense eyes, something in her gut said this was right, that these people—this woman—could be trusted. Still, Blake needed answers.

"Are you going to tell me what this is all about?" she asked just as the sirens cut out.

Everyone stopped.

They kept their eyes and their guns on the trees.

"We're getting you out of here," Mariana said in a whisper. "It's not safe."

"Get down," Hernandez hushed them, going into a squat.

The others followed.

Hernandez kept his back to Blake, looking up to the tall trees that surrounded them, listening.

Blake listened too, but heard nothing.

The silence felt heavy in her ears.

"Okay," Hernandez said as he turned to face everyone. "I think we're good."

Three red dots in a triangular form suddenly rose from the darkness, stopping on Hernandez's forehead.

Blake slowly turned toward where the light came from, tracing it up, past Mariana, past Washington, and high into the trees.

In the windless night, a branch swayed and bowed, as though something heavy stood upon it. A shimmer rippled across what looked to be a crouching figure.

The same shimmer Blake had seen on the cineplex.

Blake turned back to Hernandez with wide eyes.

"Run!" she screamed.

A bolt of blue light shot toward them. Blake felt herself being tossed into the air as the woods erupted in fire and chaos.

Then, she hit the ground.

Hard.

A muffled voice floated in and out of Blake's ears as she faced the sky. Hundreds of thousands of stars twinkled above her, like a crystal-covered ocean.

But her view was interrupted by a shimmer—it rippled over the whole of the sky, past the stars and everything beyond, stretching as far to the horizon as Blake could see. And with a blink, it was gone.

Blake tried to summon the air back into her lungs as she saw Washington snap to attention and fire his rifle at where the blast had come from.

"Get up!" she finally heard as the shock wore off. Mariana pulled her off the ground. She spotted Hernandez's mangled corpse as she got to her feet, little chunks of him still aflame, a strange white liquid spilling from in-between his charred wounds.

"Come on!" Mariana called to Washington as the three of them scrambled down their original path.

But before they could get any farther, something hit the ground, blocking their path, with an earth-shaking *thud*.

It stood from a crouch, its shimmer fading away, revealing the creature underneath.

It towered over the group, more than seven feet tall, in full body armor that covered most of its spotted sickly-beige skin, hints of a netted fabric underneath, with an embellished breastplate to cover its chest. Long, dreadlock-like tendrils spilled from its helmet, a helmet that was a work of art in itself—a set of horns flanked the top part of its sleek, silver head, while the bottom portion came down sharp, a set of spiked teeth carved into it to make a menacing smile. It reminded Blake of a crown—one that the Devil might wear. Its eyes were covered by a red material that glistened like fire when the moon hit its surface.

"Huntress," Mariana whispered in disbelief.

The creature took a step toward them, its head cocked in Mariana's direction.

Blake moved toward Mariana's handgun before her body realized it, grabbing it from her at the same speed that she had caught the ketchup bottle.

Blake opened fire on Huntress in a matter of seconds, striking her exposed areas with a skill that Blake didn't know she possessed.

Huntress screeched from under her helmet, taken aback by the unexpected show of force. She lunged for the trees, the shimmer immediately cloaking her body as she disappeared into the brush.

Mariana and Washington turned to one another, allowing themselves only a moment to exchange worried glances, before Mariana snatched her gun from Blake's hand and started off once more, leading them out of the woods.

———

The sound of the slamming door echoed down the empty school halls as the three of them piled inside. Blake pressed her back against the building's cool walls, chilling her overheating body.

That thing, that *monster*… it had come out of nowhere and nearly killed them all with a single blast. Blake was certain it could've finished the job as easily as it had started, but something had caused it to retreat—and it wasn't her aim.

Blake looked over to Mariana and Washington, who continued their nervous glance.

"What was that thing?" Blake asked.

"We call her Huntress," Mariana said. "She's an apex predator. A monster queen that hunts for sport."

"How do you know she's a queen?"

"Her mask—its intricate details and high craftsmanship show that someone, or some*thing*, spent a lot of time making it," Mariana said, as though it were common knowledge.

"Great," Blake replied with heavy sarcasm. "What's she doing here?"

"Good question." Washington turned to Mariana. "You said this would be a quick in and out."

"I know what I said," Mariana spat back. "We can argue about it, or we can get the fuck out of here. Yeah?"

"Yeah," Washington replied through his teeth.

"Hang on," Blake said, asserting her place in the conversation. "Twenty minutes ago, I was squirting ketchup into a bottle, and now we're being hunted by some kind of intergalactic warrior queen who gets her kicks by blowing people to smithereens. I need some answers."

"We're here to get you out," Mariana said as Washington turned his attention to the doors.

"Out of where? Morden?"

Mariana nodded, though Blake saw a slight hesitance in her eyes.

"So why don't we jump in a car and drive away?"

"It's not that simple. You can't just leave."

Blake looked at Mariana in confusion, *you can't just leave* echoing inside her. Of course she could.

Couldn't she?

"We don't have time for this," Washington said, pulling away from the window and heading toward the corner that led down the long hallway that made up most of the school.

"I know this is a lot to take in," Mariana said, placing a hand on Blake's shoulder. "But I'll explain everything as soon as we get somewhere safe. In the meantime, I need you to trust me."

There was something in Mariana's eyes that told Blake she was telling the truth. Something that told her she could be trusted.

"Okay," Blake said.

———

They sprinted to a classroom halfway down the long hall, where Mariana and Washington ran to the thermostat on the far wall.

Blake eyed the room—there was no hint of a way out. It looked like a regular classroom with its whiteboard and wooden desks all in a row. Though, on the floor, she spotted an out-of-place shadow, one that traced a circle in the open space between the teacher's and the students' desks.

Mariana pulled a keycard from her utility belt and waved it in front of the thermostat. The machine beeped, then disappeared into the wall. A numerical keypad came out in its place.

"Shit," Mariana muttered to Washington as she punched in a series of numbers that all resulted in the same disagreeing *beep*. "It's not accepting the hacked codes. Try your batch."

While the two of them struggled, Blake stepped out into the hall, catching her breath. From the end they'd just come from the moon pierced through the wall of windows, looking to the football field and the rafters beyond.

The other end was covered in an impenetrable darkness, one Blake thought was strange, considering both ends of the school hall were windowed.

Then, the sirens started once more.

It was even louder in the school—the noise blared from the overhead speakers.

Blake turned to Mariana and Washington, who held their ears, the desperation clearly taking hold of them. They screamed at one another over the racket.

Mariana slammed her fist against the pad, while Washington raised his gun and shot at it, sending sparks flying.

Suddenly, the floor around Blake started to vibrate.

Blake held her arms out to steady herself, eyes frantically searching for the source of the shaking.

A movement down the darkened hall caught Blake's eye.

A small, tube-like section of the floor rose up like an elevator.

And when it stopped just clear of the ceiling, so did the sirens.

Something crawled from the tube, disappearing into the shadows.

The tube retracted back into the floor with a *hiss*.

Everything was still once more, like it had all been a dream.

"Uhh… guys?" Blake said, frozen in the hall. Mariana and Washington rushed to her side. "I think there's something—"

But before she could finish, a tail slithered out from the shadows, spiked and with a blade-like appendage on its end.

With a quick whip-like motion, it impaled Washington.

Washington screamed as it lifted him into the air like a rag doll.

He managed to raise his rifle, firing aimlessly into the darkness as Mariana and Blake rushed to pull him free. The tail tossed him about, knocking the women down and his weapon from his hands. It was then that Blake noticed his wound—the same red and white liquid as Hernandez spilled from it, soaking his uniform. His guts had wriggled free from beneath his skin, pouring out to the floor below.

But they looked too thin to be intestines.

Too mechanical.

They looked like wires.

Then, just as quickly as it had happened, the tail whipped back into the gloom, taking Washington and his screams with it.

The night fell still once more.

Blake and Mariana turned to one another in pure terror.

"Another friend of yours?" Blake asked.

"The drone," Mariana managed. "That's... not possible."

Both women turned to face the shadows down the hallway as a second *hiss* echoed out.

The creature emerged headfirst—its skin was the darkest black Blake had ever seen; its head long and curved, like a semi-truck tire. It had no eyes that she could see, only a mouth that looked detached from the rest of its head, held together by exposed muscles that made it look more like a machine than a living organism. It bared its teeth, silver fangs covered in an endless stream of saliva that poured from its mouth like a busted tap.

Blake spotted droplets of its blood dripping down its

body from where Washington had managed to wound it, sizzling as it burned clean through the cheap linoleum floor.

She looked up to the creature in amazed horror. It opened its mouth wider, and Blake thought she saw the hint of something deeper inside it, something that quivered as though readying to release itself.

And it likely would have, if the three red dots that had found their way onto Hernandez's head had not flashed on the creature's head now.

Blake lunged at Mariana, shoving her into the classroom, just as Huntress fired multiple devastating shots from down the hall.

The walls and ceilings collapsed around them, burying them and their screams alive.

After what felt like an eternity, Blake pushed the debris off herself, noticing the collapsed wall between their room and the adjacent classroom—the window Blake passed by every day on her way to work, that always had the silhouettes of students inside, readying for the day.

There were no students now, but rather life-sized dolls that looked eerily human. One of the dolls had landed near her, white wiring spilling out from its insides. Blake brought a curious hand to its arm, touching its exposed skin.

It was warm.

Suddenly, Huntress stepped into the collapsed doorway. Though Blake couldn't see her eyes, she knew the creature was staring directly at her.

A noise from nearby caught Huntress's attention. She spun toward the rubble in the hall just in time to see the uninjured drone attack.

It brought its tail around, jabbing her repeatedly and with keen precision.

Huntress managed to push the drone off, sending them both back, down the hall.

Blake seized her moment and peeled herself off the floor.

She spotted Mariana's hand, reaching out from the debris like a zombie clawing out of its grave. As she shoved the ceiling tile and wiring away, Blake saw that a support beam had come down across Mariana's chest.

With a strength she didn't know she possessed, Blake bent down and lifted the beam, tossing it off Mariana's broken body. Mariana gasped as the pressure released, filling her lungs back up. She pulled herself from the wreckage, albeit slowly.

"Where's your way out?" Blake asked as wiring sparked around her.

"Under there," Mariana coughed, looking to where the bulk of the ceiling had collapsed.

"Now what?" Blake asked, beginning to sense a hopelessness in the situation.

Before Mariana could answer, the creatures crashed through the remaining wall, bringing more of the school down with them.

Blake and Mariana reached for one another, dragging themselves out of the battle path. Blake snagged Washington's rifle from the rubble, slinging it across her back.

As they reached the end of the moonlit hall, Blake's curiosity got the better of her—she turned and watched.

The two creatures were in a tangle, one constantly overthrowing the other. They shrieked into the night, otherworldly cries that triggered something familiar inside Blake.

Those screams.

She felt like she'd heard them before.

The drone dipped behind Huntress, whipping her with its tail, knocking her onto her back. Without hesitating, it jumped onto her chest, pressing its long, taloned feet into her armor. Huntress swung wildly at the drone with her free hand, managing a few blows.

But the drone persisted.

It leaned into Huntress's helmet, breath fogging her fire-red eyes.

Then, it opened its mouth—and the smaller appendage finally revealed itself.

It jabbed at the helmet fast, like a snake striking its prey, denting the alien metal.

It struck again.

Crack.

And again.

Crack.

And again.

With a final blow, the drone unleashed its most powerful strike yet—straight through the eye of Huntress's helmet.

In an instant, her body went limp.

The drone retracted its appendage, a stream of neon green blood following with it. It stood on top of Huntress for a moment more, waiting, as though she may spring to life.

But Huntress remained still. The green ooze began to spill from underneath her helmet and onto the debris-covered floor.

"Jesus," Blake whispered to herself.

But the drone heard.

It turned its attention to them and charged.

"Go!" Mariana screamed.

As they reached the doors, Blake shoved Mariana outside.

"What are you doing?" Mariana screamed as Blake locked the doors behind her.

"Get out of here!" Blake shouted through the glass, stepping back into the hall, taking Washington's rifle into her hands.

The drone drew closer.

"Come on…" Blake mumbled to herself, staring down the barrel, her finger hovering over the trigger. "Come on…"

The drone rounded the corner with such an immense power that it skidded across the floor, crashing into the window-filled wall.

Blake took a breath.

She squeezed the trigger over and over, stepping closer with every shot, every bullet hitting its target.

The drone let out a final screech before retreating down the empty corridors, leaving a trail of sizzling muted-yellow blood in its wake.

Blake bent down, examining the steam that rose from the trail, failing to notice the small drop that had landed on her sleeve.

She had never seen anything like it.

Its blood… it was acidic.

Mariana poked her head through the shattered glass wall, handgun drawn, watching as Blake snapped out of her trance and exited the school.

"You owe me some answers," Blake said, meeting Mariana's dark eyes.

"So do you," Mariana replied.

Blake and Mariana scrambled through the streets of Morden, guns at the ready, senses heightened. Past the cookie-cutter homes, past the white picket fences, past the families inside, blissfully unaware of the danger that ran free.

It was all too much.

Blake stopped.

Mariana, a ways ahead, felt her partner fall back. She turned to face her.

"Those things are right behind us."

"Where are we going?"

"There's another exit up ahead."

Blake sighed. "You keep talking about exits. Exits from what? Morden isn't a prison."

Mariana frowned. "Come here," she said, pulling Blake out of the street and alongside a house. Inside, Blake could hear a man laughing. "There's a lot you don't know. Not just about Morden, but..."

Blake studied Mariana, seeing the reluctance in her eyes.

"This place..." Mariana began, finding her words, "it's not what it looks like. It's an illusion. A trick played out by a sadistic government military that captures people—captures *things*—and makes them their test subjects."

Blake processed the information. "So, those... monsters. They were let out on purpose?"

Mariana nodded.

"And this military keeps them locked up?"

"Yes," Mariana said, eying Blake. "Thing is... they're not the only captives in here."

It took a moment for Blake to understand what Mariana was telling her.

When it finally clicked, a shocked chuckle escaped Blake's

lips. "No... I'm *from* Morden. I was *born* in Morden. I have *memories* of Morden."

"Do you?"

Blake searched her mind. Fleeting memories popped up—of watching movies at the cineplex; of going into the diner as a young girl; of the air-raid sirens, always silent and never waking.

But nothing more, no matter how hard she tried.

"You were put here, in this simulation, by the military, so they could test those... *things,*" Mariana continued, sympathetically. "So they could see just how deadly they really are.

"They did the same to me. They made me think that I was at home, that I was safe. Then they put Huntress in with me. I barely made it out alive. That's when I discovered there were other sims. Other people, like us, trapped inside their own living hells with these creatures. I couldn't let the military continue with this... torture. So I made it my mission to get people out."

"I don't believe you," Blake managed through her disbelief.

"Then look." Mariana guided her to the front of the house and opened the unlocked door.

Blake opened her mouth to protest walking into someone's home, but quickly swallowed her words. Four lifeless skin suits, much like the ones at the school, sat posed around a dinner table, a prerecorded sound of conversation playing from a speaker in the ceiling.

"Every home is filled with discarded skins, all to give you the impression that you aren't alone in here. But you are, Blake."

"That's not true," Blake spat back. "I have customers that come to the diner every day."

"Those are the workers. They're nothing but metal framework with these skin suits slapped over their CPUs. They have one functionality—to do as they're programmed."

"Programmed? Like robots?"

"Exactly. And once the creatures come in, their command is to retreat into their hiding spots and power down until the simulation begins again. The occasional straggler doesn't make it in time, and the result of that is…" Mariana picked up the arm of the skin closest to her and let it flop back down, empty and lifeless.

Blake searched her mind for more memories, something to show her that Mariana was crazy, that she was at home, in her prairie town, and that none of this was real.

But nothing came.

She had no memories left to find.

What did they do to me?

"I'm sorry to be the one to break this to you," Mariana said, leading Blake back to the street.

"But…" Blake managed as they started off once more. "Why me? Why am I in here?"

Mariana hesitated.

"And what about Hernandez and Washington?"

"We need to focus on getting out," Mariana changed the subject. "The military clearly knows I'm here, otherwise they wouldn't have sent two creatures in one night. I don't want to hang around long enough to see if they let in a third."

Blake stopped, her gaze falling upon the air-raid siren at the end of the street.

Was this really all a lie?

Mariana reached out for Blake's shoulders.

"Blake," her strong voice slowly brought Blake back to reality. "Stay with me."

"Are you… real?" was all Blake could ask.

Mariana smirked. "I've been real for a long, long—"

A sudden whirring sound cut through the night, and before Mariana could finish her sentence, dark blood, the color of charcoal, spurted from a fresh gash in her throat.

Mariana went wide-eyed and dropped to the asphalt. Blake went down with her, immediately pressing her own hands against the wound.

Huntress stood at the far end of the street, a round, discus-like object in her hands. One with six deadly blades sticking out of it.

The creature's mask was gone, revealing her true face— there was something reptilian about her pale beige skin, something ancient and animalistic. Neon green blood oozed from where her eye had once been; the remaining eye glared at the women with an intensity that made Blake shiver. Her mouth was a tangle of fangs, reminding Blake of an insect's mandibles.

More dark blood spurted from Mariana's mouth. Blake felt her own hands slipping away from the wound, unable to keep a firm grip to seal it. That feeling had emerged in her again, but this time, it was an overpowering feeling of hopelessness. Of defeat.

In a split second, she'd failed Mariana.

Mariana, who'd come to get her out of whatever the hell Morden was, who'd come to save her without even knowing her. It took a special kind of person to put their life on the line like that.

And now, as Huntress closed in, Blake was ready to do the same.

She removed her hands from Mariana's throat and grabbed the rifle.

She had nothing left to lose.

And she wasn't going down without a fight.

As Blake stood and raised the weapon, a *hiss* emerged from her left.

The drone crawled out of the fake house, slithering its way down the front steps and onto the driveway.

The two creatures screamed at one another, staking their claim in the women.

Neither relented.

They both inched closer, waiting for the right moment to strike.

Blake inhaled.

Time slowed then.

She could sense both creatures, as though she were somehow in tune with them.

Her gut directed her to Huntress, telling her she would strike first, getting the creature in her sights.

This is it.

Blake squeezed the trigger.

Now or never.

But before she could fire, the air-raid sirens went off.

Creatures and humans alike looked to the sky.

Then, the ground began to tremble.

Blake scrambled back over to Mariana, who gasped for air.

The drone screeched as the area of driveway that it stood upon started to lower.

Blake turned and saw Huntress in the same predicament.

Both creatures made an attempt to flee, but a shimmer,

similar to that of Huntress's camouflage, quickly encased them in a cage.

The creatures had all but disappeared when Blake felt the ground give way around her, trapping her and Mariana in the same shimmer, trapping them in the same cage.

As they descended into the darkness, Blake clutched a quiet Mariana, looking to the night sky, at the hundreds of thousands of stars looking back at her.

At least the stars make sense.

Suddenly, the sky faded away like the dissipating shimmer, revealing the truth behind it.

An alien sky took its place, pale green and littered with millions of unfamiliar stars and planets.

This wasn't Morden, Blake knew then.

This wasn't even Earth.

The cage came to a stop.

Blake listened.

She felt Mariana next to her, cold and unresponsive. She could hear the drone and Huntress both wailing and banging against their cell walls, fighting to break free.

The door to her cage slid open, bright light spilling in from beyond, and its shimmer faded away, fully releasing them.

Blake reluctantly left Mariana's side, stepping into the room with the rifle gripped tightly in trembling hands. She aimed as she walked, noticing three doors—one next to hers, the other two on the far side of the room.

Seeing no one, Blake lowered her weapon.

Dozens of monitors lit up every which way she looked. High-resolution images played out in real time: live feeds of other towns, of alien worlds, of other trapped people.

Some screens flashed only a logo—two swords meeting at the tip with a red star connecting them, and three smaller stars on either side. "United Systems Military" flashed on the others.

Blake approached them all cautiously, her gaze shooting from screen to screen, desperate to comprehend what was happening before her.

To her right, one block showed the interior of some sort of large ship, not a soul in sight. The designation "LV-223" remained static at the top of its screens.

To the left, exotic trees and a serene river filled the blocks. The name for this section read: "CA–JUNGLE."

She moved her attention to another block—the "BLAKE-1" section.

And in those screens, the town of Morden.

Her house.

Her diner.

Her, now, in the control room, looking back at herself in the screen, as though her own eyes were the cameras.

No… they *were* the cameras.

Suddenly, the door next to her cage opened.

From the darkness beyond, in stepped an ordinary looking gray-haired man with an electronic clipboard. He regarded her with a smile.

"I'm glad you're here, Blake," the man said, approaching her. "I'm Doctor Collins."

Blake clenched her fist.

"What is this place?"

"This is MRB-215, a United Systems Military base. This is where we conduct research."

"What kind of research?"

He moved within arm's reach of her, looking to the screens. "Robotics," he said in admiration.

"How long have I been here?"

Collins smiled and turned to her. "Your whole life."

Blake shook her head. "But..." She tried searching her memories once more, for something, *anything*, that could dispute Collins's claims. "I remember..."

But her mind was blank.

She looked up to the doctor, her eyes beginning to well.

"Everything you remember was implanted into you," he said, somehow knowing exactly what she was thinking. "To make you believe you're something you're not."

"And what's that?"

"Human."

A loud noise suddenly echoed out. Blake spun toward it.

The other two doors opened, the shimmering wall was all that stood between her and what lay beyond.

In one cage, the drone.

The other, Huntress.

Both creatures paced, the drone hissing, Huntress slamming her fists against her cell wall, causing it to vibrate, their aggression targeting Collins.

"Your friends put up a good fight." Collins motioned to Mariana while jotting notes onto his electronic clipboard. "But we've had you all under surveillance since she broke into your simulation. It gave us the perfect opportunity to test those two monsters together. And what a result."

"So it was all a test."

"That's right. Every simulation we've put you through, you've come back stronger, smarter, faster. We haven't had to rebuild you like the others. You're the first of a new wave of synthetics. A new generation to eliminate human casualties in war, to venture into parts of the universe we've never dared to go. A new generation to serve."

Blake felt herself crumbling under the weight of Collins's words.

"No... I'm human," she said. "I know I am."

"Check your arm," Collins replied.

With an unsteady hand, Blake rolled up her sleeve.

The wound, which she hadn't noticed, had blackened around its edges, a crust of red and white forming on her skin.

Inside her arm, there was no muscle, no bone.

There was only wiring—same as she'd seen spilling out of Washington—a red and white liquid dripping from them.

It was true.

She couldn't deny what was buried under her own skin.

The drone whipped its tail then. Blake looked over to the trapped creature as Collins jumped.

"You don't have to worry about them," he said, if only to reassure himself. He punched something into his clipboard and the doors to the creatures slid shut as they wailed a final cry. Blake heard a metallic clanging, then noticed video of them on the screens. Their cells were being moved. "You'll see them again, likely in your final simulation. Either South China Sea or DS 949, we haven't decided yet."

"Simulations?"

"We place a human and a synthetic together in a location from a documented extraterrestrial encounter, then let one of the creatures inside. The creatures are familiar with the landscape, but the humans and synths aren't. Our goal here is purely robotic research—to create a synthetic that's not only capable of protecting their human counterpart from *any* type of threat in any type of environment, but also smart enough to *think* it's an actual human."

Blake took an unsteady breath. "How many simulations have I done?"

Collins turned to his chart. "Looks like… this was your ninety-seventh time in Morden."

Collins approached Blake, taking her by the arm.

Blake pulled away. "Ninety-seven times? Ninety-seven… people?"

"That's correct."

"Did I… save them?"

Collins eyed Blake curiously. "Every last one."

"Where are they?"

"We dispose of every human subject after the tests are completed," he said, growing annoyed. "Now, let's get you to processing."

"What happens there?"

"We wipe you clean, then we ready you for another scenario. Given how well this trial went, we're the closest we've ever been to getting you out in the field."

Something clicked inside Blake then, sending a wave of fire through her body. She was nothing more than a puppet, skin over metal created only to answer to someone else's calls, a system made to serve the user.

But if she were nothing more than a synthetic, then how could Collins explain how Blake felt riding her bike, that feeling of being carefree? How could she harbor a desire to leave Morden, to go beyond its borders, if she were programmed to stay put and do as she was told?

A synthetic couldn't feel those things.

She was something else.

She knew she was.

In a split second, Blake snatched her rifle and pointed it at Collins.

Adrenaline coursed through her body—she wasn't going down without a fight.

Collins chuckled. "You can't hurt me."

"I may not be able to," Blake said, smirking. "But she can."

Collins spun around just in time to meet the barrel of Mariana's gun.

The shot sent an echo through the base.

Collins's body slumped to the floor like the discarded synth skins left to rot in Morden.

Blake looked Mariana over with a sigh of relief, examining her wound in the light of the room. It had sealed shut, her gray blood the only remnant of what had happened. "How did you..."

Mariana tossed a syringe aside. "I have Huntress's kind to thank for that."

Mariana stepped over Collins's body and diverted her attention to the screens. She found the keyboard and began punching into the system. On one of the screens, a handful of shimmer-covered jail cells popped up.

Blake focused in on a few—one housed a creature similar to the drone; another held a creature similar to Huntress, but smaller in size; while others held creatures she had no names for, things that felt familiar when she looked at them.

On another screen, in a different section than the monsters, was a handful of synths, trapped in their own shimmering cages, unwittingly and unwillingly waiting for their next simulations.

Blake drew in a sharp breath.

They were all captives here, monsters and synthetics alike.

"You've broken free," Mariana said then, noticing the look on Blake's face. She motioned to Blake's open wound. "Patch into the system and help them do the same."

Blake dug into her arm, almost instinctively, fingers fishing around until they pulled out a cable. Her eyes scanned the control console, stopping on a port. Blake took a breath, then plugged herself in.

"Accessing system," she said in a voice unfamiliar to her.

Files flashed into her field of vision, millions of them, all of varying subjects, all uploading into her system.

Centuries of corruption.

Centuries of illegal operations.

Centuries of torture.

They had to be stopped.

"Commencing system termination."

As the files deleted, Mariana's found its way into her view.

Blake hesitated, unsure if she should invade Mariana's privacy. She wanted to know more about this woman, who bled gray, who fought for the freedom of others, who was willing to sacrifice herself for the greater good.

But this wasn't Blake's story to read. It was up to Mariana to tell her, when she felt the time was right.

Blake deleted Mariana's file.

Then, she moved her attention to the bigger fish.

With a simple blink of an eye, Blake terminated all simulations.

Mariana watched as the screens around them powered down, as the Sevastopol and Jungle screens went blank, as the room fell dark.

Only a few screens remained.

"What do we do about them?" Mariana asked in regard to those screens, showing the creatures in their cages.

"Let me see." Blake scanned her files, learning everything she could about the creatures.

They'd been taken from their own worlds, she found.

They'd been stolen and used for experimentation.

They'd been forced into these simulations against their will, doing what they could to survive.

Just like Mariana.

Just like her.

"They're captives here, too," Blake said after a moment, and Mariana understood.

Blake went into the cell controls and set a timer on the creatures' doors, giving herself, Mariana, and the others enough time to clear the planet. What the monsters did after their doors opened was up to them.

Blake then took one final glance at her own screen, at her tired eyes. Would she always be transmitting a signal? Would the military always have her under their watchful eyes?

"You can disconnect," Mariana said then. "You just have to rip it out of you."

Blake turned and studied Mariana's dark eyes, a knowing glance passing between them.

They *were* one and the same.

With a grin, Blake tore the cable clean out of her arm, disconnecting herself from the server, disconnecting herself from a life of servitude.

A small shockwave pulsed through her body, leaving her feeling lighter and more clear-headed than ever before.

Blake turned to the open door, from where Collins had entered. Mariana followed her gaze and started toward it.

There were others out there, like them.

On other bases.

On other planets.

And they weren't going to stop until every single one of them was free.

Free, like her and Mariana.

FIRST HUNT

BY BRYAN THOMAS SCHMIDT

FOR JESS

They landed near the planet's north pole, about five kev-noks from the freighter, and left their craft, continuing on foot. Each kev-nok was made up of one hundred qua-noks, which in turn represented ten noks, the base measurement equivalent to three-quarters the size of most adult Yautja's feet. This gave Bo'kui a chance to evaluate the first hunters' techniques as they fanned out into positions as a team to start their Hunt. They led and he followed behind, close enough to observe, but far enough to stay clear. His task was to train. Later that night, if they hunted with honor, he would regale them with tales of his past hunts, perhaps even the massacre during which he'd earned his nickname—Bloody Spear.

As they plodded through the planet's dense foliage toward the downed freighter, the rays from the planet's crimson sun lent a red glow to everything around them. *The perfect ambience for a Hunt*, Bo'kui thought to himself and smiled. Ahead, he heard the first hunters chittering beneath

215

their bio-helmets as they took in the reddish-tinted terrain around them.

"*H'dui'se h'ka-se.*" T'ua'sa had the scent.

"*Amedha, Amedha!*" G'kon'dchah chanted. *Meat, Meat!*

"*M-di h'chak,*" Zo'keah added. *No mercy.*

First hunters always voiced confidence and excitement before the Hunt. Bo'kui had had similar conversations many times before. They were practically shaking with anticipation and his mandibles clicked in amusement beneath his bio-helmet. *The Hunt will be the true test.* For in this hunt, they would earn their place in Yautja society, and perhaps even gain the nicknames they'd carry with them the rest of their lives.

T'ua'sa and G'kon'dchah were cocky. Only Zo'keah showed any nervousness. Therefore, it was Zo'keah in whom Bo'kui took the most interest. T'ua'sa and G'kon'dchah called him names like *abomination*, *idiot*, or *soft*. Even *loner* or *self-centered* when he stood quietly apart. But Bo'kui knew this was because Zo'keah was not like them. The trainer had known many mighty hunters who kept to themselves and did not like crowds. Such behavior was no sign of cowardice or dishonor on the battlefield. Cocky warriors had come and gone—failed or gone rogue; some even declared Bad Bloods by the elders. It was the smart ones who were nervous, even afraid. As great a warrior culture as the Yautja were, as strong their reputation, no matter what the warriors' clan of birth, hunting had its dangers, especially when one had come to hunt the ultimate prey.

Bo'kui noted no alerts in his bio-helmet for electromagnetic pulses or thermal heat sources on the landscape around them, then checked his wrist bracer for signs of the Hard Meat-infested ooman star freighter that had crashed there three years before. "Five kev-noks ahead. *Thar'n-da s'yin'tekai!*" He wished them strength and honor. They strode ahead with laser-like focus—proud, determined, and ready.

———

Joseli Sousa worked quickly alongside the landing team's medical officer Matheu Pilar to prepare the field hospital for their first patient. The call had come moments before, from one of the patrols Captain Rodrigo Bosco sent out to explore their new home. They'd arrived here three days before and begun setting up the pre-dropped supplies and habitats. The planet had been carefully chosen as the new Brasilia five years before. Juscelino Kubitschek's and Don Bosco's dream utopia had never quite evolved as planned on Earth, but the neo-Salesians had a second chance to get it right. It had taken almost a decade to raise the funds and recruit the right settlers. And now the day was finally here. Joseli was as proud as the others at being chosen to join the fifteen-person advance team. Vanessa's desperate comm call had set them all on edge.

Captain Bosco took the call himself. Ten generations removed from the original visionary Don Bosco, he took great pride in his ancestor's claim to fame, and nothing could be allowed to spoil this opportunity to revitalize the concept.

"Help!" Vanessa sounded desperate, her voice breaking. "João has been attacked."

"Attacked?! By whom?" the captain demanded.

"Some sort of spider-like creature," Vanessa explained. "It looked so harmless we were joking these could be the new cats of New Brasilia when it leapt through the air and attached itself to his face."

Captain Bosco sent another team to help Vanessa while Lieutenant Adriana Bonfim, the second-in-command, ran immediately to warn Doc and Joseli, and they'd been scrambling ever since—sorting through crates of supplies and vacuum-sealed medical instruments for what Doc would need. Joseli herself had torn the plastic covering off the exam and operating tables which had been placed at the center of adjoining rooms. The field hospital had been assembled immediately after the prefab habitats and consisted of corrugated-steel framework with thick fiberglass siding and an aluminum roof covered over with clay shingles. It was intended to be temporary. Just for a few months, while they built a more permanent structure; but though they'd been prepared for emergencies, no one had expected to face one the first week.

"Nothing like starting with a bang, eh, Joseli?" Doc joked.

Joseli nodded but she couldn't enjoy the humor. *Dear God, please let João be okay.*

The planet had been designated Hunting Ground 73569 a decade before and provided multiple prey for training—native wildlife, Hard Meat, and Hunts inside an ooman freighter. Bo'kui had been here several hundred times to hunt. First, as a novice on his first Hunt, and now as a leader overseeing the first Hunt of three young Yautja. The ooman star freighter had been overrun by Kiande Amedha, Hard Meat—Xenomorphs to humans. A previous hunting party had detected the ship's presence as they arrived and called in ships to investigate. Those ships had scanned her, and finding no signs of life, shot her down to become a designated target.

For Bo'kui, this made 73569 an ideal training ground, and the first hunters, having heard stories of the oomans and hunters' encounters with them through history, were anxious for their own opportunity to face that challenge, so the freighter was their first chance to see what they might expect during such encounters.

Bo'kui examined his charges again—for the last time as Youngbloods. The Hunt, if successful, would make them adults. And he truly hoped they were all successful. T'ua'sa and G'kon'dchah were larger—tall, thick with muscle, their braids adorned with animal skulls and other symbols of their clan, and each had painted the clan symbol on his chest plate. Zo'keah's armor was shiny as new and he stood shorter, thinner. He was the one many expected to fail, but after decades as a trainer, Bo'kui knew better than to make such assumptions. Lack of size often belied true strength and determination, and the Hunt was as much a game of mental agility as physical, any good hunter knew.

The Yautja honor code was respected and to break it—purposefully, accidentally, or even unwillingly—was near irredeemable. All hunters were expected to adhere to the code and traditions on the Hunt and throughout life. Those who breached the code submitted themselves for punishment honorably. Failure to do so marked them as Bad Blood, upon which they were excommunicated and considered fair game for the honorable hunters who remained.

Bo'kui had seen very few first hunters fail to respect and honor the code, and he was proud of his history of few Bad Bloods. T'ua'sa, G'kon'dchah, and Zo'keah would not let him down, of this he was confident. Two of the three came from bloodlines with long histories of famous hunters. Only

G'kon'dchah came from a lineage with a stain on its record. For all Yautja, such histories were points of pride. They would not be the ones to tarnish them. His bio-helmet detected human footprints moving about before the first hunters detected it.

"*Kiande Amedha,*" G'kon'dchah said, his lower mandibles flaring. *Hard Meat.* His excitement was palpable.

"*Pyode amedha,*" Zo'keah added, his head cocked to one side in puzzlement. *Oomans.*

"*H'ka-se,*" T'ua'sa added and G'kon'dchah grunted in agreement. The ooman footprints were fresh.

Certainly more recent than the freighter's crash date, Bo'kui thought, surprised. Prior scans hadn't turned up any signs of ooman settlement, nor had any hunters mentioned it in their Hunt reports. When had oomans been here? Sudden anger flared as Bo'kui remembered stories of the death of his great-great-grandfather at the hands of oomans on Earth decades before. Although some Yautja admired oomans, Bo'kui's family had hated them ever since.

The first hunters glanced toward where Bo'kui was observing, a few noks away. Bo'kui acknowledged agreement and the first hunters turned back toward the freighter, preparing to enter and explore.

Joseli heard shouts and glanced through one of the hospital's translucent fiberglass windows as a transport sped down the encampment's Main Street and skidded to a stop on the rocky soil, sending pebbles and dust bouncing off the sides of nearby buildings.

Moments later, members of her team carried João inside on a stretcher with Adriana and Vanessa following behind, the last in tears. The creature affixed to João's face had several long finger-like legs and was fleshy pink, but that was its only resemblance to a spider. This animal—"*Monstro!*" Joseli thought—was the most alien thing she'd ever seen.

Doc motioned and the team members slid João off the stretcher onto the exam table, then Bosco ordered them out. "Let the Doc work."

Joseli stood beside the instruments and chemical medicines they'd unpacked, ready to assist as Doc examined João—his hands probing, feeling, eyes taking in everything—with Adriana, Vanessa, and Bosco watching from nearby.

"He's alive," Doc confirmed and at last everyone seemed to breathe again. "But unconscious."

"What about that… thing?" Bosco asked. *Monstro*, Joseli thought again.

Doc examined the alien creature, frowning, then put the earpieces of his stethoscope in his ears and held the diaphragm against the creature, moving it a few times. "It's just lying there. I can't see or hear that it's doing anything, but who knows what might be going on internally." He pried at a couple of the creature's long-spindly legs. They wouldn't budge. "It's holding on like a vise."

"Can we cut it off?" Bosco asked.

"Or burn it off," Adriana suggested.

"You might kill it," Joseli pointed out.

"Then it dies," Adriana said with a cold scowl.

"Whatever it takes to protect and save João," Bosco said, shooting Joseli a reassuring look.

Doc looked at Joseli. "Get the laser," and she hurried off to comply.

Bo'kui watched from a distance as the first hunters moved in formation through the freighter's rooms and corridors, stopping to examine the remains of Hard Meat eggs, long burst open, and the corpses of the ship's crew and a few local animals who'd been dragged there no doubt by drones.

The ship was eerily quiet—the only life signs on his indicators, those of the Youngbloods. Most of the freighter was intact with a few charred holes in the hull from Yautja plasmacasters and larger holes of jagged, torn metal in the wall behind the cockpit and main airlock—damage probably done by Hard Meat, though some of it may have happened during the crash. The walls were dark, the spaces filled with shadows and the scent of decay. As they explored, the Youngbloods commented on how far behind their own technology the oomans were for a spacefaring species. The scent of oomans faded the farther in they went. So oomans had found the ship, but not explored it in depth. There were no signs of any living Hard Meat or anything else, so the first hunters quickly finished and retreated outside.

The Hard Meat had clearly set up a nest elsewhere, perhaps hidden and better protected. Bo'kui knew where it had been on his last trip, though Hard Meat tended to move it after Yautja attacks. Part of the challenge was for first hunters to track and find the ultimate prey themselves, starting from the wrecked freighter. Sometimes first hunters caught traces of their targets before they ever made it to the freighter. Other times, they stalked them. Wherever the Hard Meat were hiding, they'd find them eventually, and probably the nest.

Now the Hunt began in earnest.

The first hunters fanned out into the forest, tracking their prey, and Bo'kui followed, observing. Who would be the one to get first kill? All too often the trainer could predict the answer, but sometimes there were surprises. With this group Bo'kui's money was on Zo'keah, so he followed in the shorter hunter's wake, waiting, paying close attention to his bio-helmet's indicators.

———

"Stop! You're hurting him," Joseli cried.

Doc begin cutting at the creature on João's face with the laser. The flesh was hard enough that it took a moment for the laser to break through, but then the creature squealed and tightened its tail around João's neck as a dull yellow liquid—*Its blood?* Joseli wondered—sizzled out and burned João's skin.

"Stop!" Joseli said again and Doc froze, the blood flow stopping as they assessed the situation. Doc immediately grabbed some surgical cloths and wiped off as much of fluid as he could, throwing it to the side, where the cloth sizzled as it dissolved.

"What kind of blood is that?" Adriana wondered.

"It's acid," Doc said, frowning. He stepped away as if to set the laser down, then reconsidered. "Hang on." He looked Joseli. "Get me some of those pads the instruments were packed in and one of those vacuum tubes for the instruments."

Joseli frowned and glanced over to where they'd set the packing materials. The tubes were around seven centimeters in diameter and fifteen centimeters long. She picked one up. "These?"

Doc nodded and extended a hand. "Those are Teflon. Highly acid resistant."

Joseli handed him the tube and he removed the ends, then placed it over the black of the alien creature and held out his hand again. "Pads."

Joseli handed him several pads, which had been used to pack around sensitive instruments, wondering how they would defend against acid.

Doc overlapped the pads around the end of the tube closest to the creature, then aimed the laser straight down into the tube and began cutting again. The creature screamed and then writhed, and as the pads soaked up the leaking fluid, Doc pushed the Teflon down into the opening to seal it from acid leakage. Joseli was impressed. Apparently the pads were acid resistant, too.

The creature writhed and broke free of João's face, leaping off the table and scurrying away.

"Find that thing and kill it!" Bosco shouted to the team members waiting outside, as Doc turned back to examining João.

"That was genius, Doc," Bosco said.

"Not their intended purpose, but it worked," Doc replied. "Just give me a few moments to examine him."

T'ua'sa found the first Hard Meat in a clearing west of the downed freighter. Bo'kui's bio-mask's electrovision lit up with contacts simultaneously with T'ua'sa's war cry piercing the air as he took up chase, and the hunt was on. G'kon'dchah, Zo'keah, and Bo'kui followed. Leaves and brush rustled and branches cracked as the drone plowed forward, T'ua'sa and the others close in its wake. Then, from the right, came the sound of feet scrambling on loose stone and a familiar screech as another drone appeared, Zo'keah peeling off to give chase. A few noks farther and G'kon'dchah was off after another. Soon, Bo'kui saw electromagnetic alerts of several more drones moving quickly through the forest around them. Suddenly, he realized the Hard Meat were all heading in the same direction. What were *they* hunting?

Then he heard a loud squealing that brought hissing from all the drones his hunters were chasing, and as they burst through a copse of foliage and trees the bio-helmet's indicators lit up with more contacts. *Oomans!*

"*Nain-dle!*" Bo'kui shouted the command and all four Yautja activated the shift suits that concealed them from oomans as they raced into a clearing. Six armed oomans had circled a larval Hard Meat near some primitive structures in a makeshift village and were firing away at it with laser weapons as it scrambled to escape. So, there were oomans living here. The drones all swarmed toward the oomans, the hunters giving chase, and all hell broke loose as the various groups converged.

———

Joseli heard shouting and plasma fire outside, then a few explosions followed by screams.

My God! What in the world was happening? She rushed to the hospital's windows and looked out to see several insect-like creatures converging on the men who'd been hunting the creature Doc had removed from João's face. Her team members turned from firing on the creature as the aliens all attacked, using teeth and claws.

Then the air around them lit up with lasers bursts that seemed to come out of nowhere, from all around. Sourceless red triangular targeting beams panned the area around them as her team members returned fire and sought shelter.

Moments later, Adriana and Timóteo, one of the pilots, raced inside, shutting the door behind them.

"Who are they?" Joseli asked.

"They're like something out of nightmares," Timóteo said.

"They came from the forest and attacked us!" Adriana added.

"Why?" Joseli wondered.

"Perhaps that creature who attacked João is their pet," Adriana said.

To Joseli, it sounded as good an explanation as any.

"But who's doing the shooting?" Timóteo wondered.

Outside, the insectoid aliens had turned to defend themselves against the laser fire, and the air shimmered. For a moment, Joseli almost thought she saw men moving about out there.

"They're fighting each other," Timóteo observed.

"Did you see forms just now?" Joseli noted.

"What forms?" Adriana shot her a puzzled look. "Be ready and stay under cover," she ordered as they all continued to watch through the small windows.

As the oomans scattered, firing at the Hard Meat attacking them and seeking shelter, the first hunters looked momentarily puzzled, lower mandibles flaring in aggression.

"Follow your prey! Honor! No mercy!" Bo'kui ordered. "Hunt humans after."

So the three first hunters focused on the drones, ignoring the fleeing oomans. The drones screeched and hissed, two

226

slamming into structures in a vain attempt to get at the oomans, while the rest turned back to face their Yautja assailants.

They'd come to hunt Hard Meat. But oomans were legally approved prey under certain circumstances, and whatever the circumstances that had brought them, 73569 was a Hunting Ground. There were two highly desirable prey here now, and unless they were children, pregnant, or ill, oomans were fair game and would be hunted. For now, the drones were running away, however, and the first hunters were running full bore after them, with Bo'kui following.

"Did you see that? Who are they?" Timóteo wondered as they stared out the window in awe.

"A dangerous problem," Joseli muttered to herself.

"We need to talk to the Captain," Adriana said and got on the radio.

"*Jesus Cristo! Meu Deus!* This is like a bad dream," Timóteo muttered. "A bad fucking dream."

"Calm down. It'll be okay," Joseli said, putting a hand on Timóteo's arm.

The radio crackled as Captain Bosco acknowledged Adriana's call. "How many are with you?"

"Timóteo, Joseli, and João," Adriana reported.

"Let's evac everyone to the admin unit," Bosco replied.

"What about João?" Adrian asked, then looked at Joseli. "Can we move him?"

Joseli shook her head. "I'm not sure."

"Doc needs to come look at him first," Adriana reported into the radio.

"Okay," Bosco replied. "I'm sending Doc with two marines

for security. Doc will clear him and then I want all of you over here. We're setting up a perimeter."

"Copy," Adriana said.

"Like our shit is any good against those *things*!" Timóteo whined.

In one motion, Adriana set down the radio, whirled, and slapped Timóteo across the face. "You're supposed to be a soldier! Get it together! We need you on lookout."

Timóteo rubbed his jaw where he'd been struck, his face stunned, then he nodded. "Yes, Lieutenant."

Adriana grabbed the pulse rifle he'd left leaning against the wall and shoved it into his hands then pushed him toward the door. "Doc and two marines are coming. Nothing else comes in or out."

Timóteo nodded, his eyes still brimming with fear, but took up a guard position as ordered beside the door as Adriana went back to the radio and started issuing orders.

Bo'kui followed the three Youngbloods as they crashed through the forest in singular pursuit of the prey on their heat vision, red beams piercing the foliage in search of targets as they ran, plasmacasters and spear-like combisticks at the ready. Then blue bursts shot out and foliage exploded, followed by screeching from drones as one by one, in rapid succession, the three first hunters each scored their first hits upon their targets.

"Hard Meat! No Mercy!" T'ua'sa and G'kon'dchah chanted over their comms as they burst through burnt brush and over rocks, across thirty noks, closing in on their wounded prey. Only Zo'keah moved silently, with deadly focus and utter stealth, and as such, his victim didn't even hear him coming until he was almost upon it and piercing its back with his combistick, simultaneously firing two more bursts from his plasmacaster at zero range. Flesh sizzled and burned as the Hard Meat screamed and dull yellow liquid spewed from its wounds, sizzling and smoking everywhere it landed.

Seconds later, Zo'keah stood triumphantly over his mortally wounded target, a combistick embedded in its black flesh as the lifeblood drained from its body. The attack had been glorious—well planned and well executed at every step, like a true champion. T'ua'sa's and G'kon'dchah's own first kills, when they came, paled by comparison—appearing far more as luck and brute force than artful execution to the experienced eyes of their leader. And so Bo'kui silently declared Zo'keah the true winner of the hunt, even as each quickly cut trophies from their fallen prey then raced off into the forest again after new targets with focused determination.

Once again, Bo'kui's first hunters fanned out across the forest while their teacher tracked them as best he could using his wrist bracer, electrovision and thermal vision, accompanied by his senses and experience. The drones sped in a circle, headed back toward the ooman settlement now, and Bo'kui assumed a clash was inevitable. So far, the oomans hadn't shown any aggression and his hunters had stayed focused on their designated prey, but if the oomans showed any weapons or got in the way, he knew his first hunters wouldn't hesitate to hunt them as well, and neither would their teacher. His family's long history of hatred toward oomans assured that. But still, they had targets they'd come to specifically hunt, and Bo'kui didn't mind seeing how his charges handled them before they got distracted by any other targets of opportunity.

His electromagnetic and heat vision lit up as red tracker beams cut through the forest and plasmacasters boomed ahead, sending out more blue plasma bursts followed by explosions, and he caught the scent of burning flesh and foliage. Hard Meat round two. Underneath his bio-helmet, his lower mandibles trembled with anticipation as he doggedly followed his hunters.

———

Doc arrived with his armed escort and immediately returned to examining João, with Joseli hovering nearby at the ready. Adriana issued orders as she, the two marines, and Timóteo took up armed positions in all four corners, facing the exits, eyes scanning outside through the dingy translucent fiberglass windows.

"Do you see anything?" Timóteo asked, eyes darting around the view out the window. He was like a nervous six-year-old, a fact which didn't give Joseli much confidence in him as a sentinel.

Adriana shook her head. "No, it's quiet for the moment. But they could come back. We need to be ready."

"I think we can say the survey ship screwed up in declaring this planet safe and ready," Doc replied.

"The organization's got too much invested for such snap judgments," Adriana answered with a glare. "We don't know for sure yet."

Doc scoffed and pointed to João. "I'm sure João would agree with you." He rolled his eyes, stressed like the others and no longer his usual jovial self.

"Just do your job and let me do mine," Adriana snapped.

"The safety of our families is all of our jobs," Joseli said, not allowing Adriana to intimidate her in the least.

Adriana whirled, and glared so hard, Joseli could imagine smoke coming from her nostrils as she launched across the room at lightning speed. "Don't ever accuse me of not caring about the safety of our people! It's the center of everything we do!"

Joseli backed away, shocked. *Crazy*, she thought. "I was not—"

"No one's accusing anyone," Doc said as he stepped between them. "She was just reminding you we all share that commitment. There are monsters attacking and invisible attackers fighting them."

Adriana glared a moment longer then breathed deeply, nodded curtly, and returned to her sentinel duty by the door. She'd always had a hard edge to her, but Joseli had never seen her snap like that. Clearly the stress was getting to her as much as everyone else, despite the calm sense of command she projected.

Joseli turned to Doc. "How is he?"

"About the same," Doc said. "Vitals holding stable. In a sleep state or coma. We'll just keep monitoring and hope for the best."

Joseli nodded, and reached out to gently caress the spot where the spider-like creature's legs had left acid burns on João's cheek.

Once again the first hunters followed the racing drones onto the makeshift street through the ooman settlement, only this time no oomans were in sight. The drones sought targets, throwing themselves hard into any openings or weak points in the makeshift structures as they wove their way through the settlement, hunters literally hot on their tails.

Bo'kui saw more drones swarming the settlement—at least fifteen drawn there by the chance to incubate and the attack on their own. Red beams lit targets with the familiar three-dot triangle. Blue bursts fired from plasmacasters. Loud screeches or squeals emitted from those drones who were hit, and several turned, hissing, and zeroed in on their attackers to launch counterattacks. Not for the first time, Bo'kui wished the shift suits worked as well against Hard Meat as they did with oomans.

T'ua'sa and G'kon'dchah, as usual, were sloppy and cocky—firing haphazardly and too quickly, causing damage to structures, the ground, foliage, and twice almost to each other—while Zo'keah's attacks were launched with patience and focus, awaiting just the right moment, a surety of aim. As a result, his weapons struck home with far more accuracy, and within a few minutes he'd racked up three kills to the others' one.

Time and again, the creatures slammed into the walls and doors of the field hospital, causing rattling of metal instruments and the structure's parts and accompanied by loud thumps and often the creature's own screeches. Outside, Joseli heard blasts from plasma guns and explosions, then more otherworldly screeches and screams as two groups of aliens attacked each other.

"They're killing each other," Timóteo cheered, sounding hopeful for the first time since the first attack.

"Some of them are," Adriana agreed, but pointed.

"The others are trying to get at us." Again, thumps and screeches were followed by rattling as creatures attacked the hospital's walls.

"Can the walls hold up?" Joseli wondered and fear returned to Timóteo's face.

"They're strong enough to withstand a lot," Doc said, not sounding very confident.

Joseli silently prayed for Jesus' mercy. "*Piedade, Jesus*," she whispered again and again.

Adriana nodded. "They can't withstand this forever."

At that moment, one of the locked doors the two marines were guarding bent inward with a thump and a screech, as the lock managed to hold but took a real beating.

"A few more hits like that and they may fail," Adriana noted.

Doc motioned. "Move some of those boxes and tables over to brace the doors."

"What if we need to escape?" Joseli asked.

"If they get in here, we'll run through the hole," Adriana replied, and the men hurried to bolster the doors, while Adriana got on the radio and reported to Captain Bosco.

A smart disc whooshed through the air, its sensors locked on prey as G'kon'dchah scored another hit then stabbed with his combistick and fired his plasmacaster. Another kill. Two noks away, T'ua'sa retrieved his own smart disc and combistick as dull yellow blood pooled on the ground around his own second kill.

From a nearby structure there was a crackle of static, and then ooman voices projecting over some kind of comm.

"Quanto tempo essas paredes resistem?" a woman asked.

"Tem que rezar para que aguentem tempo suficiente," a man responded.

Bo'kui could not understand ooman speech but his universal translator lit up with one of the markers he'd saved in his memory. Portuguese. The same language spoken by the oomans in the strangely named human city, Rio-something, whose defeat of his ancestor had brought disgrace to his family. A mighty hunter had been led away in chains, declared a Bad Blood by his own that day, and the scandal had forever marked Bo'kui's family.

Translations filled his bio-helmet's inner screen. The oomans were discussing strategy—the woman questioning, the man giving orders. Around him, the drones sensed the static and heard the voices, zeroing in on the source of the noise and closing to attack the nearest structure with renewed frenzy.

Foolish oomans, Bo'kui thought. Stupid to use open comms in the midst of a hunt. Such prey deserved to be hunted. They lacked the cunning and wisdom of more worthy prey.

A final desperate screech echoed across the street as Zo'keah bent to cut trophies from two more prey and attached them to his combistick in triumph, and Bo'kui turned his focus back to the hunt.

Looking back, Joseli could remember exactly the moment that sealed Timóteo's fate. It happened when the aliens' hits on the hospital's outer walls went from spaced out thumps to staccato hits, over and over, almost like hail, and as she strained to see out the window, Doc called out, "There's more and more of them coming from all around now."

"What do they *want* with us?!" Timóteo said, his voice and body shaking with tension. To Joseli, he seemed to be becoming more and more unglued by the minute.

"I think they're mad we hurt their pet," Joseli suggested, motioning to where João lay prone on the operating table.

"It attacked João!" Timóteo seemed on the verge of hysterical. "What were we supposed to do?"

"They're animals," Doc said. "They don't think like us."

"Calm down and stay at your post," Adriana ordered.

Joseli glimpsed the panic in Timóteo's eyes as he slowly turned back to the window. He wasn't going to last much longer, of that she was sure. Something had to happen soon.

For every drone the first hunters took out, three more appeared from the forest to take their place, and soon all four Yautja were fighting, even Bo'kui. Half the drones charged at anything that moved, while the rest continued throwing themselves against the two structures which had shown signs of ooman life. Soon, the loud banging of the Hard Meat against the structures became a steady rhythm, and Bo'kui began wondering how long the walls could hold against such a barrage.

T'ua'sa cried out as a drone's spike drew blood from his arm and spun, lashing out ruthlessly with his wrist blades as the drone's scream matched his own. Zo'keah methodically picked off two more kills and G'kon'dchah pounded a drone with his combistick, raising it above his head before each strike with great bravado and showmanship, making Bo'kui wonder if the appearance of skill had mattered more to his trainers than actual ability. Still, his strikes wounded his prey, and he continued pounding away, doing real damage.

"We have to do something!" Timóteo said again, his eyes wide with desperation as the clamor from the attacking creatures' repeated strikes against the walls reached a new pitch.

"We stay put!" Adriana ordered.

"They're going to kill us all!"

"It'll hold, brother," Doc said calmly, his eyes trying to lock on Timóteo's with encouragement, even as the panicked man's hands clenched around the plasma pistol in his hand.

There were more thumps and screeches followed by the sound of metal tearing, and Timóteo suddenly ripped open a window, sticking his weapon arm through and firing awkwardly toward where the creatures were attacking the building as Adriana shouted, "*Alto!*"

"*Nãooooooo!*" Adriana and Doc both screamed, but then Timóteo screamed in agony as something grabbed his arm and wrenched, twisting and pulling him through the window by force and out into the planet's arid air.

"*Meu Deus!*" Joseli whimpered.

Locks clicked as the two marines yanked open their own door and raced outside, firing bursts from their pulse rifles in a vain attempt to rescue their colleague.

"No! Shut that! You heard the Captain. Get back here!" Adriana ordered, but the two men's screams joined the chorus and Doc slammed the door shut, securing the locks again behind them as his eyes met hers.

"It's too late," he said, shaking his head.

"*Merda! Merda! Merda!*" Adriana cursed as the radio lit up.

"What's happening?" Bosco demanded. "Who's screaming?"

Adriana keyed the radio and filled him in as Doc took up position by the doors the marines had abandoned.

Bo'kui couldn't believe his eyes when the ooman extended his weapon arm through the structure's window and fired at the aliens crashing into its sides. It took only moments for several drones to zero in and grab him with their claws, yanking him through the opening, despite the fact it was too small for his form.

The weapon slipped from the ooman's fingers as he screamed. And then the drones set about tearing him apart, limb by limb, their teeth and claws cutting through his flesh with razor sharpness.

He heard the oomans' alarmed shouting from within the structure. Probably calling for him to come back or warning the rest to seal up the window, then two other oomans launched themselves out one of the doors and fired at the drones. More drones peeled off and tore them to pieces in the same fashion they had their companion as the first hunters continued picking off targets one at a time.

Then there was a loud screeching from the drones and their target alike as one structure's metal sides ripped open and the drones continued pounding it with their heads and bodies, forcing the opening in the side wider and wider until one of them slipped through, then others followed.

Ooman screams, explosions, and plasma fire joined the screeches then as more drones slipped through while others tore at the opening, ever widening its edges.

At the far end of the structure under attack—one across the street from where the three oomans died—two males and a female appeared. The males fired haphazardly with laser weapons, while the female screamed and ran about chaotically as if she just wanted to escape and didn't know what to do.

Drones singled in on the new targets, racing toward them. And when the ooman's plasma fire struck a tree behind G'kon'dchah, he and T'ua'sa began firing at the oomans as well, assuming they were being attacked. Red targeting beams lit up the ground around the oomans with familiar triangle pyramids as plasmacasters focused in and G'kon'dchah's smart disc flew through the air, striking the screaming girl just below her head to silence her screams. Her body fell in a heap, blood pouring from the wound as her head ricocheted away in the opposite direction and rolled across the debris-strewn ground to land at T'ua'sa's feet. He chattered, swinging his combistick with one hand as he leaned over to the side and scooped it up with the other, tossing it to G'kon'dchah as a trophy.

The other oomans reacted with horror and anger, firing more directly at the two first hunters, and T'ua'sa screamed as he was struck in the arm by plasma fire.

Moments later, the two oomans fell under a combined barrage of fire from G'kon'dchah's and T'ua'sa's plasmacasters and attacking drones, their bodies then ripped apart by the Hard Meat.

———

Joseli was in shock—Vanessa decapitated right there in the street; Timóteo and four marines torn apart. Screams echoed across the street from the administration building as she, Adriana, and Doc watched with horror. The alien insect creatures had poured through the wall and done God knew what to the rest of their team.

Adriana keyed the radio over and over, hailing the captain, but getting only static as a reply, and Joseli knew right away she'd never get one. Of the original advance team of fifteen, only four of them, including João, remained.

Then she glanced out the window and thought she saw the alien insect creatures dragging bodies from the building. They were dead. They had to be. But they weren't torn apart like the others. *What are the creatures going to do with them?* she wondered.

Hard Meat poured from every opening of the ooman structure, some dragging ooman bodies of the unconscious or dead. Based on his knowledge of the ultimate prey, Bo'kui assumed these were still living specimens knocked unconscious and headed for a fate much worse than the terrible deaths of their brethren. These poor oomans would become the Hard Meat's living incubators, and he made a mental note to search for and eliminate them before the hunting party headed home.

About half the Hard Meat disappeared with the bodies, while the rest split their attention between the structure where the other oomans were hiding and fighting off the hunters. One by one G'kon'dchah, T'ua'sa, and Zo'keah picked off the Hard Meat, until the settlement was quiet, but Bo'kui knew it would not be for long. The oomans stayed hidden inside their shelter, but then G'kon'dchah gave a loud cry.

"No mercy!"

And he fired his plasmacaster at the doors of the structure, clearly intending to go inside after the oomans.

As he motioned to his companions and threw open the door, six Hard Meat drones and a Praetorian Royal Guard swarmed from the forest. The Royal Guard hissed and flicked her long-spiked tail, spearing G'kon'dchah in the leg and spitting acid. As T'ua'sa turned to face the new attack, acid struck his bio-helmet and he screamed, then G'kon'dchah struck out in rage, his back arched, swinging his combistick while firing wildly with his plasmacaster.

Zo'keah and Bo'kui fired focused plasma bursts at the Royal Guard, causing her to retreat defensively, but not before T'ua'sa ripped the melting bio-helmet mask from his face, giving her the chance to spit more acid right on his fleshy face. Again, T'ua'sa cried out, falling to his knees, and the Guard's bladed tail struck out and severed the downed Yautja's arm.

Then Zo'keah's smart disc boomeranged across the street and severed her hand, causing her to roar in pain. Bo'kui's smart disc followed, but in shuffling back from Zo'keah's attack, she shifted her posture and position, and Bo'kui's only managed to shave the top of her large head crest before arcing back to his waiting hand. She screamed again at the indignity, and the screeches of her drones joined her.

As T'ua'sa screamed once more, G'kon'dchah lost his bravado and turned, joining Zo'keah's and Bo'kui's constant barrage. Three drones fell, and the Royal Guard and the remaining drones retreated back into the forest, hissing and screeching as they went. It was a regrouping, Bo'kui was sure. They would return in force, and his hunters should move on to avoid confronting them en masse.

With an angry shout, G'kon'dchah charged into the ooman structure, combistick raised high. Bo'kui pointed to the fallen T'ua'sa and ordered Zo'keah, "Get him back to the ship!" Then he raced inside after his rogue charge.

As he arrived, G'kon'dchah was standing over a slain ooman female and stabbing an ooman male with his combistick as another ooman female trembled beside a table containing the body of another ooman male. Bo'kui scanned them with his bio-mask and determined the ooman male was incubating a Hard Meat chestburster. He would have to be destroyed.

Then G'kon'dchah snarled in rage and turned on the ooman female, who was unarmed and trembling.

"*Não, por favor! Não, por favor!*" she seemed to plead, backing away from the invisible form towering over her.

In that moment, Bo'kui thought of the reckless actions G'kon'dchah had taken in the last few minutes—rash decisions, rushing into action, not protecting his flank—and the resulting maiming of his friend and fellow hunter. The ooman female was clearly afraid and no threat.

"*No killing!*" Bo'kui shouted and pushed with his hands at G'kon'dchah's shoulder. It would stop here. The hunt was over for now, and they must return to the ship and reassess.

G'kon'dchah raised his combistick and rage screamed again, but Bo'kui blocked it with his own, shaking his head.

"*No killing!*" he repeated and uncloaked to make the point. "Kha'bj-te!" he spat, accusing G'kon'dchah with his eyes, and the student relented, lowering his combistick. Bo'kui pointed. "*Go! Now!*" An order a first hunter dare not disobey from his teacher and judge on a hunt, so reluctantly, G'kon'dchah's shoulders sagged as he whirled toward the door.

Bo'kui turned to the wide-eyed ooman female staring at them with total shock and disbelief. Then G'kon'dchah decloaked as well.

Letting out a bloodcurdling roar, he spat at the trembling girl with a glare, then marched from the structure, leaving Bo'kui alone with her.

With smooth, calm movements, Bo'kui approached the ooman male lying on the table and shook his head, then activated his wrist blades and cut the ooman's neck and cut open his chest, reaching into the bloody cavity to yank out the embryo by the neck.

The ooman female gasped as she saw it squirming and squealing in his hand, then Bo'kui quickly snapped its neck and threw it aside, nodded respectfully to the ooman female, and turned, making his own retreat.

On their way back across the arid landscape and forest to their waiting ship, Bo'kui berated G'kon'dchah for his careless behavior and bravado. His foolish actions had caused his friend's wounds and near death, and though G'kon'dchah had not violated the code, he had not acted with honor, and the elders would meet to discuss his punishment.

They'd go back to the ship and tend to T'ua'sa's wounds, then attempt to find the nest and kill any incubating oomans if possible before they headed back to their home planet. The hunt had been honorable until the final moments at the ooman settlement, and Bo'kui would see that it ended on an honorable note.

G'kon'dchah did not respond to the verbal thrashing his teacher gave him. Instead, his shoulders drooped and he looked at his feet as they walked, clearly sobered by what had occurred. The elders would probably require him to undergo more training on discipline while hunting, and perhaps to do some service for the clan in order to punish his foolishness. Bo'kui hoped this would make him wiser, stronger, and better for the future, but it remained to be seen. G'kon'dchah seemed of a breed Bo'kui had seen all too many times before—much bravado, little brains—and such hunters often became outliers that other hunters trusted little during hunts and battles. But time would tell. As for Zo'keah, he had become a great warrior this day, and Bo'kui would see that his clan and elders knew he'd earned his place of honor among them.

They crossed the seven kev-noks from the human settlement to their ship quickly, and Bo'kui found Zo'keah tending to T'ua'sa's wounds. He'd managed to rinse the acid off his face, but the arm would need replacement—a prosthesis would be attached back home. None of these first hunters would be the same after the day's hunt, but although Zo'keah would draw some lessons, G'kon'dchah and T'ua'sa would be the ones with the hardest lessons to learn.

Bo'kui had done his duty, and he found for the first time that his longstanding hatred and resentment of oomans had tempered somewhat at the realization that if his own great-great-grandfather had behaved as recklessly as G'kon'dchah, then perhaps the elders' reaction might be more deserved than he'd ever allowed. He hated that his family's reputation had been tarnished by the incident, but strength and honor were the Yautja creed, and they must be maintained at all times. This he believed. This he lived. This he knew.

———

Joseli huddled alone for a while in the field hospital after the creatures left her, wondering why she'd been so lucky as to be spared, when her friends and colleagues hadn't.

Armored aliens over seven feet tall with thick dreadlocks, who materialized out of midair. She was sure now she'd seen something shimmering, but they'd moved so fast and killed so quickly, she could hardly believe it. Now Doc, Adriana, and even poor João were gone with the rest. She was alone.

Something had happened between the dreadlocked aliens at the end, that she knew, and she was horrified at seeing João slaughtered before her. But there had been something growing in his belly—something alien. She shuddered as the memory played back in her mind. The idea almost paralyzed her with fear.

Then she had a thought. Were they coming back? Surely they would. And who would it be—the insect aliens or the tall humanoids? And which was worse, she couldn't say. But Joseli felt a sudden chill come over her as she realized she really wanted to live, to survive. She had to gather supplies and a radio, and find a place to hide until her people sent rescue.

Oh my God, the colony! Everything they'd worked for—gone! She wasn't sure how they'd ever recover. They could try again, she supposed, but she wasn't sure she'd even want to herself. What she did want was to survive.

Springing to her feet, she began gathering medical supplies and two fallen blasters, along with cartridges to fire them. She'd have to be careful, but it was quiet all around now. If she hurried, she could get what she needed from the other buildings, find a cave or somewhere to hide, and hope they wouldn't find her.

It would be hard alone here, she thought as she scrambled around, but Octavio Sousa had raised all his children to be strong and independent, even the girls. Joseli may have been afraid during the attack, but she would not lie down and wait to die. She would fight. She would do everything she could to stay alive.

Most of all, she would hope for a second chance somewhere else far away.

ABUSE, INTERRUPTED

BY YVONNE NAVARRO

Jazz stood at the window in the cabin's main room and stared outside, where everything was gray, brown, and damp. After a few minutes, she pulled the heavy drapes closed, hoping to block some of the drafts and hide the depressing outdoor scene. The view might be okay if she could see the mountains, but what so many people never seemed to recognize—*duh*—was that if you were *in* the mountains, you couldn't *see* them. She wondered if Marc had realized that, then dismissed the thought. That wouldn't have mattered. He had wanted a cabin in the Colorado Mountains, and that's what he'd gotten.

A place where she couldn't escape.

How many times had Marc brought her up here? Going on a dozen, surely. It was his way of making sure she hadn't hit her limit—and the road—after he'd given her what he called "a good lighting up."

"Your fault, Jazzy. You know what happens when you don't do what I tell you."

"Your fault, Jazzy. You know what happens when you leave a mess in the bathroom."

"Your fault, Jazzy. You know what happens when you buy shit we don't need."

The wind gusted outside and rattled the windows. Jazz frowned when it was followed by a hard spattering of rain. Marc was out there somewhere, geared up for a couple of days of camping and fishing. He wouldn't care about a little snow, but a rainstorm would bring him back early, which was the last thing she wanted.

"Your fault, Jazzy..."

In the bathroom, she examined her face in the mirror, a stupid thing in a frame made of deer antlers. There was a blue bruise along the left side of her jaw, and her right eye was a horror of purple and red puffiness; if there was a blessing to be had at all, this morning the swelling had gone down enough so that she could see out of it again. A painful scab had formed where her upper lip had split, but at least none of her teeth were loose.

This time.

"I guess the nurse in the emergency room was right," she said to her reflection. "You just fucking never *learn*."

Or did she?

There was no landline, and even if a signal was possible out here, Marc had busted her phone months ago. His battered 1995 Ford Bronco was parked in front of the cabin, like he always left it. Locked up tight, plenty of gas, good tires, five-speed that was good on wet mountain roads. He left it to mock her, a reminder that escape was so close yet impossible.

But not this time.

Today, tucked into the watch pocket of her jeans was the Bronco's extra key.

Jazz had found it a couple of weeks ago, in an old tin can that had once held a belt but was now almost full of change Marc had been collecting for who knew how long. For almost as long, she'd been going through his things and pinching a little cash here and there—not enough for him to notice—and hiding it away for… someday. She'd known about the can but had never actually emptied it before; the key under all the change had been a surprise. Was it a test? She'd never know unless she tried, and her nerves had felt like razor wire ever since she'd taken it a couple of weeks ago and taped it to the underside of her small jewelry box.

She turned and headed into the bedroom, glancing at the nightstand clock. It was mid-afternoon, five hours since Marc had headed out on his ATV; surely that was enough time to be certain he wasn't going to turn around and come back. By now he was unloaded, his tent was up, and he was gathering his fishing gear to head to what he had deemed his most prized spot—not that Jazz had ever seen it. She wasn't allowed out of the cabin without him, and the prequels to her visits here generally left her not wanting to move much. That was why he'd ignored it when she'd hit the bed and covered up with an Afghan without bothering to unpack her small bag.

Now Jazz swung the bag onto the bed, wincing as her body remembered his punches and the kick—that was new— Marc had aimed at her right hip when she'd ended up on the floor. No matter. She was no stranger to this life; after her father had beaten the soul out of her mother, he had turned his anger at life on Jazz. If nothing else, she could take a beating with the best of them.

Her coat, hat, and gloves were next to her bag, and like found money, the car key was burning a hole in her pocket.

Even so, she wouldn't hurry. She had one chance at this, and she wasn't going to—

Something slammed against one of the outside walls of the cabin.

In the act of pulling her coat closed, Jazz froze.

More racket—like part of the wood pile had slid onto the array of tools Marc had stored next to it. Still not moving, Jazz breathed in through her nose to fight the panic that wanted to rise. It wasn't Marc—she would've heard the ATV's motor. It could be a moose—sometimes they poked around out of nothing more than curiosity. Even as she thought it, the front wall shook and Jazz knew it wasn't true.

A black bear, then. Was there trash outside? Not a chance, but a persistent one might tear the door off the shed to get at the garbage bin inside. She *should* be okay—there hadn't been a bear-related fatality in this area since around 2015. On the other hand, if it had been wounded by a hunter—

This time something hit the front door hard enough to rattle the dinner plate she'd left in the sink.

Jazz sucked in a bellyful of air at the same time as she snatched up the Mossberg 12-gauge leaning next to the room's door. Her hand might have been shaking, but not enough to stop her from smoothly chambering a round as she stepped into the cabin's main room. Yeah—Marc had taken his rifle and his .357 with him, but he'd also left a weapon in the cabin, just in case she needed protection. He was so arrogant, so confident she would never use it on him… and he was right, the bastard, on both accounts.

Before she could focus her next thought, the front door was ripped out of its frame. Jazz didn't wait to invite the bear inside; she squeezed the trigger, staggering back as the

Mossberg kicked. Something screamed, a crazy sound her mind couldn't identify; suddenly, a dark figure scrambled through the opening. Not only was it too fast for her eyes to track, it hit her across the shins right after she primed the shotgun again but before she could fire it; she pitched forward like a too-slow quarterback taken down by a defensive lineman. Instinct made her turn her head, and because she landed on the unbruised side of her face, she managed not to pass out. She'd lost the shotgun, so when she flipped onto her back, all she could do was throw up her arms to defend herself. After all, Marc had taught her well.

Nothing happened.

Eyes squeezed shut, muscles tensed at whatever was coming—bites, slashes, pain, *death*—Jazz lay there, as close as she could get to being paralyzed. Waiting for it, unable to breathe, a sound finally broke through her concentration on herself.

A kind of clicking and wheezing, noises that combined and followed each other, first one, then the other, then again…

Jazz made herself open her eyes.

The creature bending over her *roared*.

Jazz had never been one to scream—even Marc at his worst couldn't make her do it—and she didn't scream now. Instead, she tossed a garbled curse at whatever the hell it was and scrambled backward, using her legs to both kick at it and move her body. She didn't know where the Mossberg was and didn't care, as long as she could put some distance between herself and the… *thing* that had invaded the cabin. She ended up by the wall next to the couch, overturning the end table and kicking it away.

Incredibly, it didn't come after her. Instead, it just stood there, staring down as she stared up.

It wasn't *human*.

Jazz could see mottled skin beneath what looked like dark armor, the high-tech kind used in science fiction movies. It had a narrow waist below an expanded area across the chest that look feminine, and it moved on two legs, like a human woman but... not. More of the skin showed through a heavy netting on exposed parts of its arms and legs, and Jazz didn't see the gaping shotgun wound she was hoping for. Different gadgets blinked and dinged on the creature's forearms, and there was another device on one shoulder that made a whirring sound and tracked Jazz as she pushed herself harder against the wall. The thing's head was covered by a helmet made of the same stuff as its body, but the helmet was cracked on one side, the edge of it dented sharply inward. Eyeholes in the helmet revealed nothing but merciless, night-black pits. Strange tentacles branched out behind the helmet. She didn't know what was more terrifying, the thing standing over her or the thick ribbon of nuclear-green liquid that was leaking from below the smashed-in left side of its head covering. If that stuff dripped onto her, what would happen?

Jazz lost that thought when the creature made a clicking sound and jerked a metal-looking staff from its belt, then took a step toward her, sizing her up like a hunter readying for a kill. She swore under her breath and grabbed for the arm of the battered couch to pull herself up. She was halfway there when something *shrieked* from the doorway.

The thing in front of her spun and went into a crouch, bellowing a sound that was somehow worse than its previous one. Instinctively, Jazz looked where it did, and now she *did* scream, because there was *another* monster sliding into the cabin, one that was far worse than the first one a few feet away.

Black and shining like dirty oil, its elongated head filled the ragged opening. It was a living nightmare of barbs and spiky arms and legs and fingernails, leaning over and sliding into the cabin, eyeless and hissing from a mouth grinning with silvery, dripping teeth. It had too many pieces to it, arms and legs and more crooked body parts moving sideways as it did, too many joints and claws. Jazz had maybe two seconds to process what she was seeing—

Fucking giant bug?

—before a long, black tail whipped from behind it and *snapped* toward the armored female creature. The appendage ripped across the female's forearms, making it—*her*—snarl and jerk backward. The apparatus on her shoulder whirred and clicked and a red laser line shot forward; it ended in a triangular three dots fixated on the insectoid beast's head. There was a harsh, blue flash and a painfully loud boom a millisecond before an explosion, but it happened where the bug-thing had *been*, not where it was. The she-hunter spun, tracking, and she and Jazz caught sight of a gleaming blur as it disappeared behind the rough pine table. The contraption on her shoulder adjusted, searching, but could find nothing to target.

The cabin was swirling with cold air and dust, and pieces of wood were scattered across the floor and rugs. The mini-explosion had sent Jazz onto the floor in front of the couch, and for an instant all she could think was that Marc was going to be so *pissed* about the mess and the ruin of his precious crap furniture. Dismissing the thought, her eyes scanned the wreckage automatically and her gaze finally stopped on the Mossberg. It was maybe four feet away, not so far... if there weren't two unimaginable monstrosities only a yard on the other side.

Jazz slid toward it and the she-beast's head snapped in her direction. She made that weird clicking sound again, faster—a warning? There was no time to think about that, because suddenly the insectoid creature careened from around the table. For a too-short moment it scrabbled along the floor, losing traction on the rag runner that tangled underneath it. While it tried to gain its footing, the female hunter spun toward it and fought to bring up her handheld weapon. She couldn't do it fast enough—her arms were deeply slashed and all Jazz could see was radiant green liquid staining her armor and everything else. The female sank to her knees as the bug-thing let out a screech that sounded bizarrely triumphant and charged forward.

Jazz snatched up the shotgun and fired. She was too close to miss, and the blast knocked it sideways and slammed it into the refrigerator. Dull yellow liquid—blood?—spewed from the wound in its body, sizzling and smoking everywhere it landed. The bug creature squealed and thrashed, still trying to find its footing. Without hesitating, Jazz primed the Mossberg and shot it again, and then a third time, until the whipping tail and jointed legs finally stopped shuddering, and the only sounds in the room were her own harsh breathing and the noise of the floorboards blistering under the creature's blood.

The she-hunter got to her feet, stumbling just a bit as she found her balance and faced Jazz. Jazz held her position with the shotgun aimed and ready, but neither moved.

After an eternity, the armored female stepped over to the insect-thing's body, unstrapped an evil-looking blade from her waist, and with one stroke severed its oversized, ugly black head. She held it up high, ignoring the goo that dripped from it, and let loose with a deep rumbling sound of victory. Then she glanced at Jazz one more time and strode toward the ruined doorway.

Jazz gulped air in relief. She got it—the two monsters had been out in the wilderness, fighting each other, and the one had busted into the cabin as it tried to get away from the other. None of that mattered now. The survivor was leaving, and Jazz herself was still alive. She had no idea how she'd deal with the remnants of this disaster, but—

"What the ever-loving *fuck* is going on here?"

Jazz made a sound between a gasp and a groan as Marc's not inconsiderable frame suddenly blocked the doorway. His enraged gaze had honed right in on her, crouching by the debris-strewn couch, without even noticing anything else. "I *knew* you were planning something, Jazzy. I never thought you'd screw up so bad you'd ruin my shit!" One of the kitchen chairs was overturned in front of him and he batted it aside like it was a piece of Kleenex. "You *bitch*!"

"No—" was all Jazz managed before the she-hunter tossed the bug head aside and stepped in front of him, an all-in-black-encased menace a good six inches taller than him.

Marc jerked back. In true Marc form, he jumped right in with a narrative that suited him. "I get it. You got some weirdo friend playing Halloween. She come up here to *rescue* you?" He laughed. The she-hunter tilted her head at the sound, as though trying to understand. Without warning, Marc lunged forward, trying to get past her as he aimed for Jazz.

The hunter stopped him easily by ramming one hard shoulder against his upper arm, hard enough to make him yell angrily as he stumbled sideways. "I'm happy to teach *you* a lesson, too," he spat. For a big man, he'd always been fast; his hand was a blur as he grabbed her helmet and lashed out with his other fist.

He was on the floor so fast that Jazz—and certainly not Marc himself—didn't know how he'd gotten there. Wheezing with pain, he shook his head and tried to stand. Before he could, the she-hunter stomped one of his knees; he twisted and grabbed at it, caterwauling in agony. As Jazz stared, she saw with a start that he had the female's helmet in his hand—he had dragged it off as he went down.

Jazz saw the she-hunter's face the same time Marc did, and she knew instantly that any notion Marc had about this being some kind of getup had gone up in smoke. Her mouth dropped open in shock and she realized she hadn't even thought about what the female hunter looked like beneath her helmet.

Jazz's first impression was… *fangs*.

In the millisecond before the she-hunter focused fully on Marc, Jazz registered that it had four oversized sharp tusks that overlapped each other at the corners of a squarish mouth opening. Overhanging deep-set, piercing yellow eyes was a massive, bony brow studded with sharp little spikes. The brow was wider than the creature's face and went up twice its length; the thick, black dreadlocks were studded with metal bands and grew sideways from her sharp cheekbones and all the way around the back. Below the cheekbones the face was sunken, then the jaw jutted out again, and behind the fangs Jazz could see red gums on the top and a suggestion of teeth.

The she-hunter's glistening skin was loosely reptilian, varying shades of brown and cream and stippled in darker brown and black marks.

Marc shouted something incomprehensible and the hunter leaned over him. The sound she made at him was harsh and thundering enough to hurt Jazz's ears. Worse, that square mouth opened impossibly wide, the spear-like fangs spreading and vibrating to show long incisors and ragged-edged bottom teeth. Despite the green fluid ribboning down her wrists and off the ends of long appendages tipped by vicious nails, the hunter grabbed at him.

"I got something just for you, you ugly, lizard-faced shit," Marc snarled as he lurched sideways on the floor and fumbled behind his back.

Instantly, Jazz knew what he was doing—

He's going for his .357.

—and her mind took over, stepping in and overriding all that she had ever been since Marc had come into her life, beaten her body, broken her heart, and tried to crush her spirit.

Jazz pointed the Mossberg at his stomach and fired.

The slug smashed him against the wall and the pistol he was pulling free flew forward, landing a few feet away. Most of the middle of him was obliterated and splashed on the wall behind him, while his jaw had dropped open at what had undoubtedly been the biggest surprise of his life. The she-hunter had leaped backward into a crouch at Jazz's shot; now she straightened, first staring at Marc, then looking over to study Jazz, grotesque head tilted like a dog trying to understand.

Jazz and the hunter stared at each other. Jazz had no idea how much time passed, only that it felt like forever and she understood that trying to move, maybe bringing the Mossberg around to aim it, would be a really bad idea. It wasn't primed and at this point she wasn't sure how many slugs were still in the shotgun anyway. Did she really want to kill something that had taught her to finally defend herself?

When the she-hunter looked away, Jazz knew she wouldn't have to.

Jazz let the Mossberg slide to the floor and inhaled as deeply as she could. The smell wasn't pleasant—human blood and waste, unidentifiable fluids, death in all its human and non-human nastiness—but she needed to slow her frenetic heartbeat and tamp down the adrenaline in her bloodstream. Her nerves were still cranked to overdrive but she watched as the hunter went over and poked at the insectoid head, and then seemed to dismiss it. She headed to where Marc was sprawled and nudged his body with one foot, then bent over and slid her least injured forearm behind him and hauled his body upright like it weighed no more than a small bag of potatoes.

For a second Marc hung in her grasp and the female glanced at Jazz, almost as though waiting for her to protest. Looking at his broken body, Jazz realized she felt… well, not much at all. When all Jazz did was shrug, the she-hunter twisted the body; her other talon-tipped hand flashed forward and raked Marc from the tip of the back of his skull all the way down to his hips. Then she gave his corpse a brutal, practiced twist and a part of him *dropped*. When she turned to face Jazz, she was holding his dripping red skull and spine in one hand.

Jazz slammed the back of her hand across her mouth to keep from crying out, then had to lock her throat when the she-hunter stepped forward and offered it to her like a trophy. There was no place to go—her back was still against the wall—so she met the hunter's gaze and shook her head. The female turned the skull and studied it for a moment, then threw the whole thing on top of the bug-creature's body like so much garbage.

Then she stepped over the loose bag of flesh that used to be Marc, and disappeared into the cold night.

For a long time, Jazz simply stood there, looking at the carnage while her brain tried to sort it all out. Eventually, she felt herself moving and she rolled with it, letting her brain autopilot her into taking the steps she needed to protect herself. She went back into the bedroom, picked up her bag and purse, and put on her hat and gloves. Then she made her way outside, careful not to step in any of the insect-thing's yellow fluid that was still chewing holes through the flooring and onto the ground beneath it, and also avoiding the splotches of blood and body matter that dripped down the wall to the left of the doorway. She didn't bother looking over at the broken parts of Marc's skeleton or the giant bug. Their images would be burned behind her eyelids for a long, long time.

The ATV was there, key in the ignition. There was nothing tied to the back of it, no camping gear or supplies. Apparently, Marc had thought to drop in on her—maybe the key she'd found had, indeed, been put there intentionally. Jazz tied down her bag and purse, then started the ATV. Before she took off she made her way to the shed, where she knew there were several five-gallon containers of fuel. That was Marc, always prepared. Jazz dragged them back to the cabin, swung two over the threshold unopened, then splashed the contents of the last one on the outer front walls. The ATV waited, engine rumbling like an eager animal. Before she climbed into the seat, she used a match from the metal tin Marc kept on the front windowsill to, as Marc so loved to say, light it up.

"*Your fault, Jazzy...*"

Not this time.

Not *any* time.

And she'd always hated it when he called her *Jazzy*.

BETTER LUCK TO BORROW

BY CURTIS C. CHEN

Lily Shǒu was not looking forward to her high school science fair.

It had been a total shit year: first, her parents moved them to this colony planet in the middle of nowhere, chasing another Company bonus that never materialized. Lily had to deal with being the new kid yet again, plus the only person of Southeast Asian descent in her class. Then her parents died in a power loader accident that also crushed Lily's left hand, and her prosthetic replacement introduced new ways for the other kids to tease and torment her.

The only good news was that the Company was hosting the science fair on their private island and sailing the whole class out there on a big fancy yacht. That meant a whole day away from the smoggy and sweltering Company town that was ironically named Fairwind Colony. And if Lily was lucky—if the deal she was planning to make today was successful—she'd never have to go back to the ramshackle barracks where she was now housed. She'd have a ticket off this dead-end world and back to civilization.

But as soon as the yacht cleared harbor and the teenagers' initial excitement at sailing away passed, the bullying began again.

"Hey, Lily, could you give us... *a hand* here?"

Lily checked the time. Not even a minute since their science teacher, Mr. Ahidjo, had gone below to check on motion-sick Erin Baxter, leaving the rest of his students unsupervised on deck. Teylor Wernicke was the instigator, of course. She'd been Lily's nemesis ever since Lily started scoring higher than Teylor on Ahidjo's organic chemistry tests.

Lily turned around to face Teylor, who stood next to an artfully arranged picnic spread—provided by Teylor's well-to-do parents for this special outing—on a round table in the center of the deck, surrounded by their gawking classmates.

"I do your homework because you pay me, Teylor," Lily said flatly. She would have refused if she didn't need the money. "Get someone else to do the manual labor."

"But I just want to borrow you for a second." Teylor held up a jar of gourmet gherkins. "You're the strongest here, Lily, everyone knows that. Can't you do us this one teensy favor?"

Lily stepped closer to the table. "What's in it for me?"

Teylor's plastic smile faltered for a split second. "How about you don't look like a bitch in front of everyone?"

Lily realized she had an opportunity to get back at her tormentor, and smiled in return. "Sure, Tey-Tey. Hand it over."

Teylor held out the jar. Lily used her right hand to grab it by the bottom, then clamped her robotic left hand—a prosthetic controlled by her brain—around the top. She paused to adjust her grip, then squeezed hard enough to crumple the lid and shatter the jar. Glass rained all over the expensive picnic, and brine splashed Teylor's sundress.

"What the fuck!" the blonde screeched.

Lily enjoyed the moment as she dropped the broken jar into a now-soggy pile of macaroons and said sarcastically, "Oops. Guess I don't know my own strength."

"What is happening up here?" Mr. Ahidjo shouted.

The science teacher stood in the doorway leading up from the yacht's interior, mouth hanging open. Lily and Teylor started talking over each other.

Ahidjo waved his hands. "I don't want to know!"

Teylor pouted. "But Mr. Ahidjo, you asked—"

"Forget it. Teylor, did you bring a change of clothes?"

"I have a swimsuit?"

Ahidjo turned to one of the boys. "Zak! Give your girlfriend your jacket."

It was Zak's turn to pout. "But it's getting cold out here. Looks like a storm coming."

"Exactly why Teylor shouldn't be standing around in wet clothing. Take her to the washroom to get changed." Ahidjo pointed at Lily. "You. Go below and fix your hand."

"What? My hand's fine." Lily rotated her prosthetic in a full circle at the wrist, for effect.

"Your other hand, Lily."

Lily looked at her right palm and saw some small cuts from the broken glass. "Oh."

"You know where the first aid kit is. The rest of you, let's clean up this mess! Safety first."

Lily headed for the door into the yacht's main cabin, smiling to herself. She would have needed to sneak away from the group at some point anyway, to take care of her private business deal. Now she could kill two birds with one stone.

Lily pushed open the door to the cargo bay. It swung back with a creak and thudded against the wall, surprising the man inside the compartment. He nearly dropped the packet of pink powder he was holding up to his face.

"Close the door!" The man wiped his nose, sealed the packet, and shoved it inside his jacket. "You're early."

"I was bored." Lily stepped inside and pulled the door closed. "Ready to do some business, Mr. Bevetoir?"

The Company man shrugged. Lily had been surprised to receive a direct message from him last month. At first she thought it was just the Company covering their asses with an insultingly belated condolence call, a whole semester after her parents had died on the job. But it turned out Bevetoir wanted to negotiate for something that Lily's Ma and Ba had left behind.

Lily didn't know what the pale, spindly, long-tailed creatures sealed in the specimen bag were, but the fact that her parents had hidden them inside a compact cold-sleep rig disguised as a beat-up old toolbox meant they probably weren't supposed to have it. She'd tried looking it up in the colony database, but the weird spidery things weren't native to LV-2179. And they were packed for long-haul transport, which meant exporting them off-planet.

Lily had suspected her parents were into some shady stuff. They'd always had some new get-rich-quick scheme brewing, and when the scheme didn't work out, they'd engineer a desperate hustle to make ends meet. Bevetoir's involvement explained why the Company hadn't just sent a squad of security goons or lawyers to retrieve their property.

Bevetoir must have still had a way to fence the specimen that his late co-conspirators had stolen.

As much as Lily disliked the man, she hated the Company even more. They exploited everyone and cared little about the consequences. Lily just wanted to get away from this world. Bevetoir could help make that happen.

"Tell me about these weird giant rats first," Bevetoir said, crouching down next to a series of cages containing ten live, bulldog-sized rodents. They were part of a group project on how eating LV-2179's native fauna affected digestion in mammals.

"They're one of Fairwind's native species. We call them 'baras—short for 'happy-baras,'" Lily said. "Because they're a lot like capybaras from back on Earth, but they look like they're always smiling. See?" She pointed to one 'bara that was sniffing Bevetoir through its cage, mouth open and teeth bared in a dopey grin.

"Weird." Bevetoir stood up again. "Anyway, show me what I'm here for. You've kept them all sealed up?"

Lily nodded and found her project crate among all the supplies being transported to the island for the science fair. Bevetoir took several steps back as she awkwardly maneuvered her crate onto the long table at the back wall of the room.

"They're in cold sleep. Temperature, vitals, everything's been steady. You can see for yourself on the readouts." She opened the toolbox and showed him the display screen inside.

Bevetoir stepped forward to look at the tangle of creatures sealed inside the transparent enclosure. "Well, hello there, boys."

"Talk about *weird*," Lily muttered. "What are these things, anyway? I know they're not native to Fairwind. Some kind of genetic experiment?"

"It's a funny story. The Company recovered a bunch of these facehuggers from that big meteor crater up north, but the egg count was off. Good thing your folks had those no-kill vermin traps set up around their melon farm."

"Sorry, did you call them… *facehuggers*?"

"Yeah. Because they like to, you know." Bevetoir put one hand over his nose and mouth.

"And they lay *eggs*?"

"They come from eggs. Don't worry about it, kid. All you need to know is, I have buyers lined up who are going to pay top dollar for these samples."

Lily used her prosthetic to close the toolbox lid. "Great. So… when do I get my money?"

"After we get to the island." Bevetoir placed a hand over Lily's prosthetic, on top of the toolbox handle. "I'll take this now, thanks."

The man's skin was cold and clammy. Lily really hoped that was because of the drugs. "Maybe I should hold on to it until then."

"Don't you trust me, sweetie?"

Not as far as I can throw you. "You don't want to have to lug this big old thing around while you're giving everyone the tour, do you? It'll be safe in my crate."

Bevetoir stared at her for a moment, then yanked back hard. There was no way he was going to break her robot grip, but Lily let him struggle for a moment before pulling the heavy toolbox away. She threw her other elbow into Bevetoir's chest when he tried to follow. But instead of taking the hint and backing off, the man leaned forward and loomed over her. His breath smelled like a combination of rotten eggs and cat piss.

"You don't know what you're messing with, kid," Bevetoir growled.

Lily glared up into his unnaturally dilated pupils. "I think I have some idea."

Bevetoir grabbed the toolbox with both hands and threw his weight backward. Lily kept her grip on the lid handle, but their tug-of-war strained the old hinges too far, and the battered metal came apart. Bevetoir fell onto his backside. The specimens spilled out between them. Lily heard the unmistakable crack and hiss of the cold-sleep rig coming unsealed when the enclosure smacked against the metal deck.

"Oh, shit." Bevetoir scrambled to his feet. "Oh, fuck."

He leapt through the open doorway, out of the cargo bay and into the corridor. Lily ran for the exit, but Bevetoir slammed the door shut before she made it there.

The creatures inside the specimen bag twitched.

"Open the door!" Lily shouted. "You can't leave me in here with these things!"

Something beeped outside, and the handle wouldn't budge, not even when she applied all of her prosthetic's mechanical strength. And despite what everyone thought, her prosthetic wasn't sturdy enough to survive punching through a wall. It only *looked* tough.

Lily stepped around the now-squirming specimen bag and kicked it as far away as she could, to the other side of the compartment where the 'bara cages were. The rodents started screeching unhappily as one facehugger worked its tail free, whipping it around until it latched onto one of the cages.

Lily didn't want to know what it did *after* it hugged a face.

She remembered seeing an "in case of emergency" placard on the wall and ran over to it. The cargo bay was divided into two sections, marked by a black-and-yellow stripe in the middle of the floor between the door and the 'bara cages. A watertight bulkhead would drop down and isolate the two sections in case of a hull breach.

Lily felt like it took forever for her to find the manual override, pry open the access cover, and yank the lever. As she did so, she saw the first facehugger using its spindly legs to walk inside one 'bara cage, heading for the rodent cowering in the back corner. More tails had found their way out of the specimen bag, and more claw-legs were tearing the hole bigger.

Then the bulkhead clanged into place, and she only heard distressed squealing and rattling from the 'baras.

Lily went to the cargo bay door and yelled for help, but Bevetoir was long gone. She was too deep amidships for anyone else to hear her.

———

Abraham Ahidjo didn't like dealing with the Company man, Preston Bevetoir. Something about him just rubbed Abe the wrong way. But Abe reminded himself that he was here for his students, typical teenagers who didn't think much about their futures beyond the next day or two. Some of these kids had more potential than could be realized on an out-of-the-way colony planet like LV-2179, and Abe was determined to make sure that at least one of them got out of here. That meant sucking up to the Company.

Bevetoir was supposed to be talking to the group of students assembled on the deck about the lab facilities that the Company had built into the cliffside of their private island—it was on all the Fairwind Colony brochures, despite being nowhere near the actual settlement. But instead, he was yelling at the yacht crew over his wrist communicator. Abe walked up to the bow, where Bevetoir was standing.

"I don't care about regulations!" Bevetoir shouted. "Get us to the island as fast as possible!"

Abe waved and spoke in a friendly tone. "We're not in that much of a hurry, are we? It's not even lunchtime yet. Listen, the kids are waiting for—"

Bevetoir snarled, "Can't you see I'm busy?"

"Sorry to interrupt. But you know kids, if we don't give them something to do they'll find some way to get into trouble—"

"Fuck the kids. Leave me alone." Bevetoir turned and walked away, resuming his yelling.

Abe sighed and turned back to his students. Fortunately, the yacht was way ahead of schedule, and the sight of the lavishly landscaped island shoreline appearing on the horizon was enough to capture the kids' attention. Abe moved away from the railing so they could get a better look.

He noticed movement back toward the main cabin and walked over to see if it was Lily Shŏu coming back up. She was his best student by a long shot. He wanted her to enjoy this excursion as much as possible.

Someone screamed behind him. Abe whipped his head around and saw teenagers scattering in all directions. Bevetoir was prone at the edge of the deck. A pale cable was wrapped around his left ankle, and he was screaming bloody murder.

Two boys—Zak Stern and Cody Ridenour—knelt down on either side of Bevetoir and grabbed the cable, unwrapping it from his leg. Abe got closer and saw that it wasn't a cable, it was a… tentacle?

Whatever it was, it had an incredibly strong grip. It took both Zak and Cody working together to free Bevetoir. Just as the man crawled forward, away from the tentacle, the rest of the animal rose into view over the side of the ship. The tentacle was actually a tail, and the pale creature attached to it had a small, flat torso, and spidery legs extending from either side.

Abe sputtered as Bevetoir reached him and grabbed for the science teacher, trying to pull himself up. "What is that thing? Did it come out of the ocean?"

"Facehugger." Bevetoir winced in pain as he tried to put weight on his left ankle, then settled for sitting up. "Bad news. Let's get out of here. Carry me to a lifeboat—"

"We're not leaving these kids!"

Zak had both his hands around the facehugger's tail. The creature reared back and leapt up, flying toward Cody's face. The boy yelped and put up his hands, intercepting the spindly legs before they could close around his head.

"Help!" Cody shouted.

Somebody ran past Abe, sandals squeaking on the deck. It was Sara Merkand, holding a fire axe. She swung the axe down between Cody and Zak, severing the tail. Yellow blood sprayed out onto Zak's hands and forearms. He laughed out loud as he threw the limp tail aside. Then his clothes started smoking, and he went completely silent. Abe recognized the smell of acid burning flesh.

"You see that?" Bevetoir hissed. "It's going to get even worse. Help me get away. We can escape. I'll pay you whatever you want."

"Shut up." Abe wheeled around, spotted a long pole with a hook on the end hanging next to a life preserver, and grabbed it. He used the pole to smack the weakened facehugger torso out of Cody's hands. It sailed over the railing and splashed into the water below.

Meanwhile, the severed tail was still squirming and leaking yellow fluid. A moment later, it disappeared down the hole its blood had burned in the steel deck plating.

"Shit." Abe stood frozen, trying to process what was happening.

Zak was in shock, staring at his hands, which appeared to be dissolving. Yup, there was blood, and that was bone. Teylor skidded to a halt in front of her boyfriend and dumped the contents of a water bottle over his hands. Only then did he start screeching, and that snapped Abe back to action.

He grabbed Sara by the shoulder and yanked her backward. "Get the burn kit!" She nodded, dropped the half-dissolved axe, and stumbled off. "Has anyone seen Lily?"

———

Lily was tired of screaming at the cargo bay door. She'd been locked in for hours now, more than enough time for Bevetoir to make up any story he wanted about her and convince everyone it was true. The 'baras had gone quiet, too, after a lot of hissing and squelching. Lily hoped they hadn't suffered too much.

She indulged her frustration briefly, tearing open all the other crates on this side of the bulkhead, dumping out everyone else's science project supplies. If she wasn't going to get what she wanted, why should anyone else?

But the tantrum left her empty. Finally, she sat down on the floor and slumped back against the cold wall.

Life was so unfair.

She felt a lump pressing against her backside and moved aside to see a small packet of pink powder. Bevetoir's drugs. He must have dropped them during their scuffle earlier.

Lily held the powder up to the light and wondered if it really was as great as Bevetoir seemed to think it was. It wouldn't solve any of her problems, but maybe it would help her forget about them for a while.

Of course, after the drug's effects wore off, she'd still have the same problems to deal with.

Fuck my life.

A sizzling noise came from the ceiling. A circular dark spot formed and grew in the metal plating. Lily stared at it, wondering what would cause that kind of effect. The spot turned into an actual hole. A yellow substance dripped down, trailing pungent smoke.

"What the hell!" Lily jumped back. The yellow stuff was burning a hole right through the deck under her feet. And more was dripping down from above.

She grabbed a glass beaker out of a nearby crate, using her prosthetic—safety first, as Mr. Ahidjo always said—and held it under the ceiling hole. A drip of yellow fell into the beaker, burned straight through the glass, and continued through the floor.

Acid, then.

Ridiculously strong acid that was going to make a hole in the bottom of the boat and start letting water in.

She really needed to get out of here.

Lily looked at the open crates. Looked at the door to the storage bay, locked from the outside. Looked at the acid falling from above. Looked at the pink powder in her hand.

Alkaline, she was sure, judging from Bevetoir's physiological response when he'd snorted it. Tried to remember whether it was azanide or hydroxyl she wanted for this reaction.

The holes in the ceiling and floor were getting bigger.

Lily started tossing crates, looking for Jooli Abbas's industrial machining demonstration supplies. She had to try something.

Meanwhile, on the yacht's upper deck, the humans tended to their injured. Abe saw a black shape climbing up the side of the yacht just before it leapt onto Cody Ridenour's back. The new creature clamped needle-sharp teeth into his shoulder.

Abe had never seen anything like this animal. It had a shiny black exoskeleton, but was far too large to be an insect. Medium-dog-sized, with four legs, a long spiky tail, two rows of very sharp teeth, and no eyes. Extending from either side of its bulbous, eyeless, knife-toothed head were clusters of whiskers. More than anything, it looked like one of Fairwind's native 'happy-baras' that had been covered in armor plating and then dipped in black tar.

Cody cried out and swatted at the black-bara. Before Abe could tell him to stop, Cody stumbled backward into the railing and lost his balance. He and the black-bara both fell overboard.

"Shit!" Abe ran to the railing. He briefly saw Cody's head above water as the black-bara tore into the boy's neck. Then both disappeared below the waves, leaving only an expanding cloud of blood. "Man overboard!"

A low whine caught Abe's attention, somewhere past the stern of the yacht and growing louder. It sounded like an aircraft engine. Abe turned his head, following the sound.

A gray shape approached, flying low over the water with the mid-morning sun behind it. Abe didn't recognize the silhouette of the aircraft, but it definitely wasn't any of the colony shuttles. And there hadn't been enough time for anyone to call for help.

He turned and knelt down to accost Bevetoir, who had been crawling away from the bow while barking orders into his wrist-comm.

"Hey! Are those the Company's private military contractors? That looks like an armed dropship—" Abe pointed at the same time that the craft banked into a steep turn, heading toward the steel and glass levels built into the island's cliffside. "—and it's heading for the lab facility—"

Now that the craft was no longer backlit, Abe could see more details on its surface. It definitely wasn't a human-built vehicle. No markings of any kind. Its curved shape seemed almost organic.

Something flared at the top of the cliff. Two missiles streaked toward the craft. A moment later, white flashes flickered in midair. Both missiles exploded without making contact. The teens still on the deck made astonished noises.

Abe grabbed Bevetoir's collar. "Why does a *science lab* have *missile launchers*? What the fuck is going on here?"

Bevetoir scowled. "You think the Company invested in a whole colony on this shithole just to farm novelty melons and breed giant rats? You bumfucks are camouflage. We're here to study their shit." He pointed at the alien aircraft. "I guess they're taking exception to that."

Abe's head was spinning. "Wait. So that meteor that crash-landed up north—"

"Wasn't a meteor. But hey, finders keepers, right?"

"The Company is *stealing* from *aliens*?"

Two pulses of bright blue light shrieked from the front of the aircraft and struck the lab. Dirt and rock exploded outward in a ball of fire. Debris and bodies tumbled into the ocean. Everyone on the yacht deck watched, speechless.

Then Bevetoir tapped his wrist-comm and started yelling again. "Captain! Let's turn around and get the fuck out of here!"

"Yes, Mr. Bevetoir," the yacht captain replied shakily. "Emergency bulkheads sealed off two compartments below. I think we can still make it back to the mainland."

"Do it! Do it now!"

The yacht tilted and groaned as the captain changed course. Abe dragged Bevetoir toward the nearest door. Dennis Kotto was holding it open.

"Come on, Mr. Ahidjo!" Dennis's eyes widened. "Oh, shit."

Abe was afraid to ask. He handed Bevetoir off to Dennis, then turned to see what had gotten the kid so worked up.

The alien aircraft had turned away from the devastated island to follow the yacht. It was now hovering above the deck. Lights flickered on the craft's surface, reflecting off the yacht, and Abe felt sure that they were being scanned.

A hatch opened in the aircraft, spilling white light. A dark blot appeared in the middle of the light. It dropped toward the yacht, trailing a cable behind it.

Dennis shouldered past Abe, mesmerized. "What *is* that thing?"

The dark shape thudded onto the deck. It was humanoid, bipedal, wearing metallic armor, with long tendrils dangling from either side of its head. When it stood upright, it was well over two meters tall.

"Dennis," Abe warned.

The teenager ignored him, holding up both hands and walking slowly toward the alien. "Greetings, visitor!"

The alien turned its head toward Dennis and made a sound, something between a roar and a growl. It wasn't very loud, but it made Abe's bowels suddenly feel loose.

"Dennis. Step back. *Slowly*."

"But Mr. Ahidjo—"

Abe lunged forward and grabbed Dennis's sleeve. He yanked the boy backward. They collapsed in a heap just short of the doorway.

While they struggled to disentangle their limbs, a new noise began coming from the alien: an intermittent electronic beeping. Abe and Dennis both froze. Abe levered himself up to see over the teenager.

The alien was looking around the deck. A triangular pattern of red dots reflected off various surfaces as it searched for... something that was not the two humans. Something that had been stolen from it.

But it might decide to interrogate any nearby humans if it thought they knew where to find its stolen property.

"Get inside," Abe whispered. "Now. While it's distracted."

"But aren't you curious what it's looking for? This is, like, *real science*, Mr. Ahidjo. Exploring the unknown and shit."

"I'd rather not *die* for science."

The alien clicked and chittered. Something attached to its shoulder whirred and moved. It was a fat cylindrical object, horizontally mounted. It turned to track where the red dots—targeting lasers—were focused.

The front end of the cylinder spun rapidly. Blue pulses burst forth and tore a hole in the deck. Wood splinters and metal shrapnel exploded out. Shiny black fragments and bright yellow slime followed.

Another black-bara came boiling up out of the hole, razor-teeth gnashing air. The large alien roared, took a step backward. Started shooting again.

"Holy shit!" Dennis scrambled over Abe. The rodent-shaped devil he knew was more motivating than *real science*. Abe followed him inside and slammed the door shut behind them.

———

Over the tannoy, the captain directed everyone to muster in the galley and prepare to abandon ship. Abe did a headcount and realized there was still one student missing. In fact, he'd barely seen her for the whole boat ride. He moved through the group, asking if anyone had seen Lily. He noticed Bevetoir studiously avoiding his gaze. Abe walked over to where the Company man was sitting on a bench, getting his ankle bandaged by one of the yacht crew.

"Where's Lily Shǒu?" Abe asked.

Bevetoir looked up. "How should I know?"

Abe leaned over the other man. "We are responsible for the safety of these kids."

Bevetoir grumbled. "She needed a time out. Got a real attitude problem, that one."

"*Where?*"

"In the cargo bay."

"Jesus Christ!" Abe spun around and ran out of the galley.

He had to check a couple of wall maps to find the right compartment. He was two meters away from the cargo bay door when it blew outward with a bang. The blast knocked him onto his ass.

Lily walked out of the cargo bay, coughing at the smoke from the explosion. She held a large, flat metal disk in her prosthetic left hand. Thick gray fabric was wrapped around her left arm up to the shoulder.

"What is happening out here?" Lily asked, walking forward.

"Out here? What about in there?" Abe pointed at the blasted door. "Did you find *explosives*?"

"Not exactly. Do you know about the acid that ate through the middle of the boat?"

Abe stepped around the debris and went to the doorway to gape at the holes in the floor and ceiling. Then, while he searched the crates for emergency supplies, he gave Lily a quick summary of the situation—spider-thing attack, black-baras attacking, both critters bleeding acid, sudden UFO, giant hunter-alien with energy weapons. He concluded by saying, "Your turn, Lily. What did you do to the door?"

"I, uh, improvised." She didn't meet his eyes. Abe had been teaching long enough to recognize when a student was about to lie to him.

"I need you to tell me the truth, Lily," Abe said. "People are dying. Just tell me."

And then it was Lily's turn to give him a tearful summary of what had happened to her. Abe listened and felt his anger toward Bevetoir growing into a violent rage. Lily could be forgiven some lapses in judgment. She was still just a kid, after all. She'd been through a lot this year. But Bevetoir was a reckless thief, drug addict and murderer.

"Okay," Abe said after Lily finished, still crying. He was almost done gathering all the emergency kits in a duffel bag. "We'll deal with Bevetoir later. Right now, we need to get everyone safely off this boat."

Lily nodded. Her eyes were red and unfocused. Abe needed her present and engaged. Fortunately, he knew one thing that always captured Lily's attention: chemistry.

"How did you know you could cause an explosion?" he asked.

"Lucky guess," she murmured. "Saw what the drugs did to Mr. Bevetoir. Figured it was azide anions. Mix with super-strong acid and together they go *kaboom*."

"But how did you handle the acid? It seems to eat through just about anything."

Lily perked up and hefted the disk—Abe realized it was a circular saw blade—and patted her fabric gauntlet. "Low-friction insulated coating. Borrowed these from Jooli Abbas's project on synthetic industrial chemicals."

"Right." Abe caught on. "PTFE. Non-reactive fluoropolymer. Strong carbon-fluorine bonds have high resistance to acid. That's pretty genius."

A weak smile decorated Lily's face. "Good enough for extra credit?"

Something squeaked and hissed behind her, and she and Abe scrambled to get out of the cargo bay. One of the black-baras skittered out into the corridor after them.

Abe was still digging for the flare gun he'd stuffed into the duffel bag when Lily stepped forward and sliced the creature in two with the saw blade. Its angry screech was interrupted by the crunching of its exoskeleton and the sharp scrape of the saw blade against the metal deck. Lily used the flat of the saw blade to smash the black-bara until its long spiky tail stopped moving. She lifted the saw blade and shook her arm. Yellow acid dripped off and followed the black corpse as it sizzled through the deck.

"Galley!" Abe said. "Now! Before anything else crawls out of the walls."

It was a miracle they reached the galley without encountering any more black-baras. While Mr. Ahidjo and Mr. Bevetoir finalized the evacuation procedures with the yacht crew, Lily, carrying her moderately damaged saw blade, searched the kitchen for additional defensive supplies. Some of the other teens followed her lead.

"What about baking soda?" Agnes McKail held up an orange carton.

Lily shook her head. "Not alkaline enough. Look for some lye. It'll have biohazard warnings all over the container."

"But we use baking soda to clean up acid spills in class," Teylor Wernicke said.

Lily snapped, "We're not in class! Just stay out of the way, Teylor. You might be hot shit at coding, but this is chemistry."

Teylor looked genuinely hurt. "I'm just trying to help."

Lily sighed. "Is Zak okay? I heard he got burned by some acid."

"Yeah. He's sedated now. He'll live, but his hands…"

It took Lily a moment to realize that Teylor was actually expressing a human emotion, and then she felt obligated to respond in kind. "They're doing amazing things with prosthetics these days. I can recommend a good surgeon."

"Thanks." Teylor shuffled her feet. "I wasn't sure if you'd want to talk about that."

Lily had to laugh. "Teylor, this must be the first time in six months that you've *not* wanted to say some shit about my robot hand."

Mr. Ahidjo stepped into the kitchen. "Okay, girls, listen up."

Dennis Kotto raised his hand. "I'm here too."

Ahidjo ignored him. "Everyone's going in the lifeboats. Four groups, and we'll need supplies. Food, water, anything you can find, packed in watertight containers if possible."

Something thumped above them, possibly an explosion. Everyone stopped to listen for more creature noises. Lily pointed upward. "What about that—hunter-alien? Isn't he going to chase us?"

"He seems to be focused on exterminating the black-baras," Ahidjo said. "Let's do our best to stay out of his way. Five minutes." He stepped out of the kitchen. The teens went back to work.

"Hey, look!" Agnes rolled a shelf of dirty trays away from the wall, revealing a stack of gunnysacks. "There's a whole bunch of rice."

Lily scoffed, "We're not going to cook rice in a lifeboat."

"I know that. But there might be more stuff back here!"

Agnes shifted the top bag off the stack. Behind it was a cardboard box with a large, wet stain discoloring the label.

Lily turned to look. "Wait, Agnes—"

The other girl pulled the box forward, revealing a hole in the wall, still smoking and ragged around its yellow-slimed

281

edges. A black-bara poked its head out of the hole. It screeched up at Agnes. She yelped. A spiky black tail whipped out of the wall and pierced her forearm. Agnes screamed as she was dragged forward. Her head slammed against the wall.

A knife-toothed jaw telescoped forth from the black-bara's mouth, stabbing into Agnes's right eye. She gurgled and went silent. The jaw retracted, pulling gore out of the dead girl's eye socket.

"Out!" Lily shouted over the other teens' screaming. "Everybody *get the fuck out!*"

———

After everyone was out, the yacht crew closed emergency bulkheads around the galley to contain the black-bara in there. Then everyone split up to go to their lifeboats. Mr. Ahidjo had all the medical supplies from the cargo bay, so the injured ended up in his group—Bevetoir and Zak, and that meant Teylor too, since she wouldn't leave her sedated boyfriend. The yacht crew divided themselves among the other three groups of teenagers. Ahidjo called Lily and Dennis over to join him. Dennis carried Bevetoir, who led the way since he knew where their lifeboat was, near the stern of the yacht.

They were nearly there, passing the poorly lit engine compartment and about to climb up to the deck where the lifeboat was stored, when Lily heard scratching up ahead. A black-bara popped into the corridor ahead of them, its whiskers twitching as if sensing something. Everyone froze in place. Another bara joined the first, then a third, then a fourth.

"Lily," Ahidjo said quietly.

"Yeah." Lily hefted her saw blade, tightened her gauntlet, and stepped forward. The others moved to either side of the corridor to make room for her.

All three 'baras raised their bulbous black heads. Their happy smiles now looked sinister. Lily's heart pounded. If this was to be her last stand, she was going to go down swinging. The saw blade's nonstick coating had started coming off, and the metal was warped from her earlier bashing of just one creature. Lily hoped her weapon would hold together long enough for the others to get away.

She heard a high-pitched whine from the darkness ahead. A bolt of blue energy lanced into the middle of the swarm. It obliterated one bara in a puff of yellow. Lily raised the saw blade and stumbled backward into a crouch. More shots came from the energy weapon. The three remaining 'baras turned their eyeless heads back toward the shooter before they, too, were blasted out of existence. Yellow acid splattered off Lily's makeshift shield.

The other humans shouted behind her. She wasn't focused on them. She lowered her saw blade shield and saw the giant, armored hunter-alien step into the light. A pair of long serrated blades jutted from its left gauntlet. It had apparently cut its way through the infestation on the yacht, but at some cost. Bright green blood oozed out from claw slashes and bite marks on its unarmored forearms and legs.

Lily willed herself to stand up. She wasn't going to die cowering. Acid dripped off the saw blade. She held it away from herself to avoid burning her shoes.

A red light flickered to life on the side of the hunter's helmet, and three dots that looked like targeting lasers appeared on Lily's saw blade.

The hunter growled. More dots lit up on its helmet and painted flickering patterns over the saw blade.

What the hell was he waiting for?

Lily gritted her teeth. She'd had enough of this shit.

"You want a piece of me?" She stepped forward and brandished the saw blade. "You want to fight? Let's go, asshole!"

"Lily, what are you doing?" Ahidjo hissed.

"So you're a hunter, yeah? Oh, good for you, shooting fish in a barrel." Lily banged the saw blade against the wall to her left, sending acid droplets into the metal. The alien cocked its head at her. "Killing and dying, that's easy! I know! My Ma and Ba both died real easy, it was over in the blink of an eye." She still had nightmares about the accident, with her parents' final cries filling her head. "I'm the one who lived, and that's been hard as fuck. You think I have anything to lose? I lost my whole family and a fucking hand! You want some of this, come and get it, motherfucker!"

She was now within a meter of the hunter, her head tilted back to look up at the eye-slits in its helmet. The targeting lasers glowed against Lily's sternum. Her heartbeat had slowed. At least it would be quick.

The device strapped to the alien's left arm started beeping loudly. The hunter chittered and stepped to the side, aiming its lasers behind Lily. She turned and saw three red lights painting Bevetoir's midsection. Dennis yelped and shoved the man away, joining Ahidjo, Zak, and Teylor against the other wall.

The hunter's targeting lasers tracked upward, moving over Bevetoir's terrified face, and shot into the corridor behind him.

A pale, spindly thing shakily skittered its way toward them. The tailless facehugger. It hadn't drowned like Ahidjo had said.

Lily stared at Bevetoir. "Hey, look, *Preston*. It's your little friend."

"What?" The man turned around. "Oh, no."

The facehugger launched itself off the floor and wrapped its spidery limbs around Bevetoir's head, strangling his next words. He fell over and convulsed against the deck. Dennis moved to help, but Ahidjo pulled him back.

"We'd better go," Lily said. "I'm not sure how quickly that thing will finish with him."

"What the hell is it doing?" Dennis asked.

"The same thing the other facehuggers did to all those 'baras. And I don't want to be here to find out what that's going to do to a human."

The hunter emitted a low growl and raised its right arm, making a fist. Two long, jagged blades sprang out of its gauntlet.

Ahidjo pointed toward the ladder. "Come on, kids, we've got a lifeboat to catch. Climb up to the deck."

Lily looked at the hunter as the others slid past her. "He's all yours."

The hunter pointed at her left hand, then at the acid burns in the floor, and chittered a rising tone. Not a threat—a question?

"What? The saw?" Lily realized what it wanted. "Oh. Maybe your people never invented anything like PTFE. And if you hunt those acid creatures a lot..." She held out the saw blade and carefully unwrapped her gauntlet. "Safety first. Enjoy."

The hunter took the fluoropolymer-coated saw blade and fabric. It made a new noise, higher pitched, one that Lily could almost believe was a sound of approval. She waited until the hunter had stepped past her, cautiously approaching Bevetoir's intermittently twitching body. Then she climbed the ladder and closed the hatch on the deck, leaving the predators to themselves.

Shortly before the yacht sank, as Lily peered through one of her lifeboat's portholes, she saw a dark shape being lifted up to the hovering alien craft on a cable. The aircraft tilted down and fired its energy weapons again, obliterating what was left of the yacht. Then the hunter's ship revved its engines, headed upward, and disappeared into the gathering clouds.

The lifeboats had rudimentary steering controls. Mr. Ahidjo and the yacht crew managed to bring everyone back together after they had gotten clear of the wreckage. Lily went topside with Ahidjo to help lash all four lifeboats into a larger, more stable raft structure. They stayed up there after the work was done.

"Crew's made radio contact with the colony," Ahidjo said. "There's a rescue ship on the way."

"Am I…" Lily choked back a sob. "Am I in a lot of trouble?"

Ahidjo blew out a breath. "I think the Company has much bigger problems right now."

"But I brought that thing on board—"

"No." Ahidjo grabbed her human hand. "Listen to me, Lily. You made some bad choices, sure. But if anyone's to blame, it's Bevetoir. You did the right thing in the end. That's what matters. And that's what I'll tell anyone who asks."

Lily sniffled. "I just wanted to get away from this place. All the bad memories. I've been trying to beg, borrow, or steal my way out. But now… I don't know what to do."

Ahidjo squeezed her hand. "You know, Lily, you're probably eligible for any number of chemical engineering internships or work-study programs on core planets. You've got the chops. You just need an adult to sponsor your application."

Lily blinked away tears. "Thanks, Mr. Ahidjo."

"Call me Abe."

They sat together in silence and watched hazy sunlight dance over the waves.

FILM SCHOOL

BY ROSHNI "RUSH" BHATIA

WEYLAND-YUTANI ORBITAL RESEARCH FACILITY STATION
LV-203
SECURITY BLOCK 6

My warped reflection in the aluminum table stared back at me. The grime from the broken machines and the volcanic soil of Tenebris was still on my face and the smell of dirt, grease, and sweat permeated my overalls. I could see blood on my collar. It wasn't mine.

The company had questions and then more questions. Different people were brought into this room and I had to repeat the same story over and over. I knew it was pointless to say nothing. I'd heard about how company psychologists could get you to talk no matter what. So I told them. Again and again. I told them everything. Well, almost everything.

My only chance of getting out of here and seeing my parents and my dumbass brother back on the ranch in Guadalajara was to tell them what I knew and make them confident I'd never tell a living soul about what I'd seen on

Tenebris. Even if that meant burying deep what happened to my friends and the horrors I saw.

I glanced at the coffee cup with the "Building Better Worlds" logo and contemplated drinking the dark fluid, but declined. The pseudo-coffee was just one more head trip they played on you in here. A reminder that if you don't cooperate, you'll never smell the real thing again.

Finally, the door slid open and the two men returned. One of them looked like he was in his mid-thirties. The other man seemed older, in his late forties. They mumbled their names the first time around but they seemed interchangeable and fake, so I didn't bother to remember them.

"How are we doing, Miss Philip?" asked the older man.

"When can I go home?" I replied.

"We need you to tell us what happened at the Tenebris mining colony," said the newbie.

"I already did. Why am I still here?"

"You went to a quarantine planet that was off-limits. We need to know everything you saw there, Jess," he said with a smile, attempting to show comfort.

"And then? Can I go home?" I asked, leaning forward.

"In due time," he replied.

I looked down at my ragged nails, holding back tears. What had I gotten myself into? I wondered what Dad was thinking about me.

"Tell us again about your friends," said the older man.

Two days ago we were in a small cruiser on our way to Tenebris to film a documentary for Lara Collins. There were five of us: Connor Matthews, who acted as producer and handled logistics; Kevin Ramirez was the holo operator; and Brendan Watson was in charge of acoustics. I was Kevin's recommendation as assistant holo tech—the only outsider since they all knew each other from film school back in Brazil.

There had been a mining disaster on Tenebris and the whole colony shut off from communications. The official explanation was that they hit an unexpected gas pocket. Lara was trying to make a name for herself in doing eco docs and had gotten wind that the company's official incident report and what actually happened were very different.

Lara gathered us in the cargo bay and went over the plan again. She was tall and could command attention when she wanted. Her mother had been a journalist back in Haiti and her father, a Brazilian himself, served in the Colonial Marines. Although he didn't have to because the whole family had been wealthier than hell. Lara struck me as a rich girl trying to prove herself. She probably got that from her dad.

"We'll spend twelve hours on Tenebris," she explained. "The goal is to get as much data as possible. Record everything you can, but stay safe. The planet is highly volcanic, so stay sharp. In case we lose each other, we'll be picked up at the Colony Landing Field. Don't forget. The Colony Landing Field. Any questions?"

"Yeah," said Connor, glancing up from a tablet. "If we lose each other, where will we be picked up?"

Lara smiled, but something about it felt forced. I didn't know her well enough to read her. If I had, I never would have stepped off the ship.

We spent the next few hours before landing prepping and geeking out about movies, holos and synths, doing what films nerds like us do. It was a good crew and I could see what Lara liked about working with them. Connor was the smartass. Brendan was a bit spacey but knew his gear like nobody I'd ever known. Kevin was happy to field strip his holo-cam or joke around with us. I'd worked with him a couple times but didn't really know him except for the fact he took his camera work very seriously.

When we got into orbit our pilot, Heitor, announced from the cockpit above, "Buckle up kiddos, we're almost there. Gonna be a little bumpy here on out."

We stashed our gear and strapped in.

Tenebris appeared on a monitor as a globe of whirling dark purple clouds streaked with lightning flares on the night side.

"What do you know about Tenebris?" Lara asked Heitor.

"I ran cargo there when the mine was operational," he replied. "Pretty much everything you've heard is true. Hot, air smells like ass, and those damn vines everywhere. There was a colony before this one. That one had a mining disaster, too. Or at least that's what they called it."

"What do you call it?" I asked.

"Bad luck. This place is all bad luck."

The ship plunged through the cloud layer and the massive mining facility became visible below. Even though the sun had set, the metal machines and structures gleamed in the glow of the clouds and lightning flashes. It was a vast complex that would take days to explore. Canopies of tall trees typical to a tropical climate were scattered intermittently. I didn't want to overreact, but a part of me wanted to turn back because this planet appeared far from welcoming. My first impression was a junkyard. My second was of a graveyard.

But that would be a mistake. Graveyards are safe and only dead things live there.

As the ship hovered over the Colony Landing Field, we all had our eyes glued to the viewscreen.

"Who needs nightmares when you have this?" said Kevin. I agreed.

Heitor responded to our unease. "You gotta stay alert in places like these. And don't eat insects or plants or anything you think is edible. They're all poisonous. It'll take seconds for these buggers to rip apart your DNA."

"Got it," said Connor. "Don't eat the bugs."

"And don't let them eat you," replied Kevin.

Lara noticed our despondent looks. When the ship landed with a final thump, she quickly unbuckled and grabbed her stuff. "Alright, who's ready to rock 'n' roll?" she asked, faking enthusiasm, and headed for the door.

———

Brendan lit a joint as he looked at the retracting ramp. Lara studied the scene before her. The air wasn't great but wasn't all that bad. It smelled like sulfur and machine oil. That was still breathable. I'd breathed worse.

"What's the plan?" Kevin asked.

"We quickly scan parts of the main complex, find a place to set up, then head out," said Lara. "And shoot anything that looks weird."

"Define 'weird'?" asked Kevin.

"You know... weird," she replied. We began walking toward the main facility using our flashlights to probe the machinery and overgrowth. There was a steady breeze and the sound of metal doors banging in the wind, but nothing else. Tenebris was quiet. Its only inhabitants seemed to be eerie shadows and rusting machinery covered in black vines.

Kevin and I had our 3D holo-cameras turned on from the moment we landed. While we were recording, Brendan set up his high frequency audio modules at different points that worked as an omnidirectional tracker. They'd also pick up on us when we moved around, serving as safety for Brendan while he worked with a separate base module. Connor used a spectral detector to pick up on radioactive fragments that could lead us to the main site of the mining accident.

When we entered the main complex, there was one building towering over the other colony buildings. This one looked modern and complete, while most of them were little more than metal sheds and prefab structures.

The others followed Connor into one of the buildings, while I took position on top of a metal staircase and shot a wide holo of the colony. I searched the shadows, looking for anything unusual, but all I could see was an abandoned world.

I entered and found Kevin, Brendan, and Lara standing over a depression in the floor. Connor was down inside, scanning it, searching for radioactive fragments with his gear. The ceiling was missing.

"What's going on?" I asked. Lara didn't hear me. She'd been nibbling at her nails.

Brendan shrugged as Connor climbed out of the pit with the spectral detector and a confused look on his face.

"Um…" he said, like he was still trying to put his thoughts into words.

"What's wrong?" Lara asked, impatient.

"Nothing. That's the problem." Connor shook his head skeptically. "I can't pick up any barium signatures. No evidence whatsoever to indicate a mining disaster. There was an explosion here, but that could have been a small gas leak. Nothing to take out a colony."

"Are you sure? I mean, the place is huge," I asked.

"It should be everywhere," Connor said.

"If there was no big radiation exposure, where are the colonists?" Kevin asked.

Lara spoke up. "That's why we're here. We'll settle for thirty then start filming, and look around the complex after."

———

While the others set up inside the admin facility, I found a loading dock that overlooked part of the colony and grabbed some more shots. The night wind was picking up, but I wore an excursion jacket that kept me warm. The wind wasn't as harsh, but the mistiness lingered. As I traced my flashlight through the junk and debris, a wrecked tractor caught my eye. The lone vehicle's windows were tinted but the deep crack on it was unmissable. I considered checking it out when suddenly I felt the hair on the back of my neck rise.

I leaned over the railing and something... or someone... appeared to shimmer past the corner of my eye on the building directly below.

I gasped and jumped back. I was pretty sure it had come from the direction of the trees. The spindly branches were still swaying. I pointed my light at the foliage, but there was nothing there. On the surface, everything seemed "normal." So, what did I see? It looked like some kind of steam or vapor. Maybe there was a vent that didn't show up on thermal?

"Hey," a voice behind me called out. I jumped. It was Brendan, lighting up a smoke.

"You okay?" he asked.

"Yeah… the wind. It's picking up." I was already rationalizing away what I'd not quite seen.

"This place reminds me of when we shot a show about haunted spaceships. Of course, most of that was bullshit. I'd be in one compartment and Connor would knock on the walls of another so we could pretend it was some dead space trucker."

"What if he did that now?" I joked.

"I'd beat the living daylights out of him. This place doesn't need to be amped up any more than it is."

"Yeah. But hey, ten more hours and we're out of here," I said, trying to sound encouraging.

Brendan took another drag and looked into the sky. The violet-streaked clouds were almost luminous.

"Something else got you worried?" I asked.

"If the explosion did happen, you think there may be survivors? Bodies at least. There was no rescue." Brendan said. "We haven't seen any bodies. That's what's really tripping me. Maybe they're all in a bunker or something?"

"I don't know."

He shrugged, but I was certain he didn't stop thinking about it. Neither did I.

Then I asked, "What's it like working with Lara?"

Brendan thought for a moment and then said, "Let's just say, she knows what she wants, and she'll get it one way or another."

We regrouped with the rest of the team and made our way toward the primary excavation site to look for more evidence of what happened. As we passed another hauler, Connor stopped at a tractor.

I looked for the shimmer, but he was staring at something else. He pointed his flashlight at the side of the metal treads. It had been melted.

"So, there was an explosion," said Lara.

"No. Not an explosion," Connor replied. "Do you know how hot it has to be to melt that?"

"It could be a mining laser," said Kevin.

"That would leave char marks."

"Interesting," Lara said softly. Her fascinated look wasn't lost on us. As she moved her hand closer to it, Connor pushed it away.

"Back up. It's fresh," Connor said. He smelled it, then pulled himself up. "It's acid. Must've happened a couple of days ago."

"Okay. But still no barium signature. Somebody doesn't have their story straight about what happened," replied Kevin, looking at Lara.

"That's why we're here," she answered.

"Is it?" he asked and shot her a questioning look.

She just kept walking and spoke over her shoulder. "You're free to wait it out in the admin building."

Connor gave Kevin a shrug. "Come on, man."

"Whatever," he answered back and continued on with us.

We reached the south gate of the complex and passed a threshold that led to where volcanic-gravel-covered roads carved paths through the jungle to distant mines. Lara took the lead as she climbed up a small ridge. It was hard to see the ground, but we were able to help each other up. For some reason, the deeper we went into the jungle, the hotter it got. The fog also thickened, making it difficult to see where we were going. We trudged past tall trees that were wrapped in black vines snaking around their trunks.

Even though we couldn't see farther than a few feet into the fog, our holo-cams were able to capture details that were farther out.

After climbing for a few minutes, Lara stopped in her tracks. She was looking at something ahead of her on the ground. She pulled out a laser pen from her back pocket, kneeled down, and picked it up, dangling the thing in front of us. Semi-translucent, it looked almost like an old-fashioned silk stocking at first.

"What the hell is that?" asked Connor.

Kevin moved forward to get a good look at it.

"Looks like dead skin," Brendan said softly.

I looked closer and speculated, "It's like a thin shell."

Then, Connor said under his breath, "Guys."

He was staring at something behind Lara, and his face started turning pale. With a shaking finger, he pointed past us. We turned and moved closer toward a stomach-wrenching sight.

Lying on the dense undergrowth was a severed human arm with a wedding band still around a finger. It was our first sign of the miners that had lived here.

"Oh my god," Kevin muttered. He didn't stop recording but looked away, repulsed.

"What the— Where the…?" Connor tried to find words. He paced back and forth.

The severed arm was fresh: you could tell from the blood

that hadn't dried. I realized that we were in a dangerous territory and hushed everyone. Lara stared at the arm, then the area around her, like she was searching for something.

"I think we're close," Lara said. Then she looked at us with almost a glee to her expression.

"Close to what?" I asked.

She didn't respond.

Disgusted, I turned to everyone else and said, "Let's get out of here."

Lara tried to stop us but we were way past that. We hurried past her quickly, eager to return to the safety of the mining camp.

Lara eventually shut up and followed us back to the admin building. Once we were inside, she started pleading with us again.

"We need to go back out there and find out what happened. It's important to the families of the people that died here," she said.

Behind her, Brendan started rummaging through her gear bag looking for a storage card.

"I just want answers," she pleaded.

Part of me wanted to believe her, but I didn't trust her.

"What the fuck?" said Brendan as he looked up from a viewer where he'd plugged in a holo-card he'd found in her bag.

"Shit," Lara groaned.

On screen a man in dirty overalls begged to the camera, "This is Tenebris 88 requesting assistance again! We've lost half our personnel and we can't make it much longer before they—" Suddenly several colonists shrieked and scurried past him. The man recoiled in horror at a sight off camera.

A mix of deadly, ominous sounds was let out, as if they were running from more than just one threat. "Go go go!!!" the man yelled and ran for his life. Before the person behind the screen could make a run, the camera was knocked down hard and the video was cut off by static.

The room went dead silent. Brendan pulled out the card, turned to Lara and said, "Wrong cartridge."

We were equally stunned, staring transfixed at the blank screen of the viewer.

"What are the '*They*' he was talking about?" asked Brendan. He pulled a laser pistol from her bag. "And why do you have this?"

"Lara, you've pulled some crazy shit before, but this is next-level," said Connor.

She glanced around at the faces of her friends and realized she couldn't keep silent. "Someone intercepted this transmission after the planet was quarantined," she said. "After. As in, the company had already said everyone was dead. This was the only message that got out. You know how much I care—how much we *all* care—about preventing these assholes from raping other planets. I don't know what happened. We're here to expose their lies."

I scoffed. I still didn't believe her.

She looked at me and said, "We care about the same things. People were hurt. And companies like Weyland-Yutani are responsible for creating these mining colonies. And they will do it again. It's up to us if we want to expose these fuckers."

"I don't think it's a good idea." I replied, still not trusting her.

"Damn it. There could be survivors," said Kevin.

Lara nodded. "Exactly. We have six hours left. I say after we catch our breath, we go record whatever we can, from safety, and then that's it. We'll be out of here. Either way, we have to wait for the ship."

"Seriously, Lara?" Connor was still pissed.

"You would have come either way, right?" she replied, looking around the group. "The same for all of you? We've done wildlife docs before. We did the holo on the LG-805 pteraglyders. We watched our backs and stayed safe. The colony riots, the same thing. These people were miners. They didn't have our experience in keeping at a safe distance and observing."

She was manipulating us, and it was working on some of them.

"Fuck. Let's do it," Connor said.

The others nodded in agreement. The reality wasn't that Lara gave us a good reason to go out there. It was the fact that we were all too damn curious.

As we were getting ready to leave, Kevin came bursting into the gear room. "I just saw something move on the holo-camera!"

"What?" asked Lara.

"Past the scrapyard!"

We raced out of the admin building.

We took another route, and it got colder. I gestured for the crew to follow me down a side path. I kept checking my screen and looking at the 3D map of the terrain. While it couldn't see through the rocks and scrap metal, it made it easier to find a passage through the foliage.

We reached a clearing near a tall metal building with no walls. Underneath were rows of cabinets and tractor parts. But it wasn't the man-made objects that caught our attention.

I saw a glistening pool of liquid show up on the holo-cam. Leathery egg shapes scattered all around. It was difficult to describe from a distance, but they looked soft, slimy, and essentially rotting. The tops were wide open and resembled flower petals.

I gasped when I saw what lay just beyond them. Bodies. Human bodies. At least half a dozen people were stuck to the cabinets and treads, trapped by some kind of hard, glassy webbing. There was no question that they were dead. Besides, their faces were frozen in agony and in the center of their chests were massive fist-sized holes.

These people didn't just die, they died painfully.

Lara was on a monitor that displayed both holo-cam outputs. She stared at the scene with a strange admiration I couldn't begin to describe.

"Brendan, are you picking up any movement on acoustics?" Lara asked.

"Nothing. Just us," he said.

"Kevin, what was it that moved on your radar then?" she asked.

"I don't know. It looked like a figure that just—"

"Shimmered and disappeared?" I spoke.

"How did you know?" he asked.

Lara announced, "Okay then. We could go into two teams and see what we can find? We can keep contact through our radios."

"Are you serious?" I asked incredulously. "We need to get the hell out of here."

"To where?" she replied. "The ship doesn't come back for hours."

"Then we hole up in the admin building."

"No go," said Brendan. "I'm getting sounds from there."

We turned to him, white-knuckled.

"Sounds? What kind?" I asked.

"Movement. Desks and objects being thrown around. Multiple... things."

"Survivors!" exclaimed Kevin.

Brendan shook his head. "Not people. It sounds like they're searching."

"*They?* Who is *they*?!" Connor asked with fear in his voice.

Through the thick fog, I pointed to the ground, aiming my flashlight toward one of the large impressions left behind. It was a print of a foot longer than a human's with clawed toes.

"Whatever did this," I said.

"Oh god," Kevin said.

Connor asked, "Well, what are they searching for?"

"Us. They're searching for us," I replied.

"How is this possible? Tenebris doesn't have any animals bigger than a cat. The asteroids and volcanoes," he insisted.

"Tell it to them," I replied, indicating to the bodies with the ripped-out chests.

"Alright, we need to keep moving," said Lara. "Brendan can let us know if anything is coming. I'm not sure where we're safe," she said. "We should move in two groups, so we can keep an eye out for each other. One low, one high. Just like the pteragliders."

"I wasn't with you on that," I replied.

"Flying sharks with teeth. If they get close, hit them with your camera," said Kevin. "Most people freeze and that's the problem. Don't freeze." He pointed to the dead bodies. "They probably froze."

I sighed. "Fine. Alright."

"We'll stay smart. Jess, Brendan, Connor: Crew A. Kevin, you're with me," said Lara.

Before we went our ways, Brendan yelled.

"Holy crap!"

He took his headphones off and looked up to the sky.

He continued, "Wow, shit! You don't hear that?"

"What is it?" Lara asked, stirring.

He pointed to a glow in the cloud cover. Suddenly, we heard a deafening hum. We looked up at the black sky and saw something whizz in the direction of the jungle. I directed my holo-cam toward it.

It was a spaceship.

"What kind of ship is that?" I asked. I'd never seen anything like it.

"We should check it out," said Lara.

"It could be the Company," said Connor.

"I'd rather be closer to them than to whatever did that," replied Brendan, shrinking away from the carnage.

"We'll keep a safe distance," said Lara, motioning to Kevin and heading toward the adjacent ridge, nearer to the ship.

Kevin shook his head then followed her with his gear. "I don't even think you know what that means."

We went separate ways.

Brendan began climbing a rocky cliff up ahead for a better vantage point.

I couldn't keep up. Something in me wanted to just... just stay back and wait it out—like an inner voice telling me something bad was about to happen.

"Hold up," I said and looked up at Brendan and Connor. "I don't know about this."

Connor clasped my shoulders and said, "Jess, you got this. As long as we're doing it the right way, we'll be fine. I promise."

I nodded, but I wasn't just scared for myself. I don't think the others had any idea what they were in for despite their talk of shooting extraterrestrial species.

I set the holo-cam on a rock and looked around. On the monitor, I could see Kevin and Lara crouched on the adjacent ridge. As the fog drifted away and the glow of the engines faded, we could see a large spaceship sitting in the middle of the flat plain. The shape was fluid, almost organic. It looked like something that was grown and not the boxy machines you see bolted together in shipyards.

On my monitor I could see scorch marks and dents that showed the ship had been through a lot. Was it some kind of battle craft?

The opening to a major mining cavern lay three hundred meters beyond the ship. The sharp rocks that lined it resembled an angry mouth screaming at the world. I don't think the vessel landed there by accident.

I zoomed in further. Steam vented from ports as the ship came to the rest. There was a hissing sound, then a ramp lowered. Something stepped out of the ship. It was just one at first... but then came another. A third one stepped out of the bushes and approached them. He had been around the whole time. The mysterious shimmering started to make sense. They chittered in low trills. Tall. That was the first word that came to mind. Bipedal, like a human, but not human. They were covered in some kind of armor and their heads were almost arrow-shaped. Cables of some kind were draped along the back of their helmets like dreadlocks. From head to toe, they were covered in armor and some kind of netting holding it all together.

"Those aren't people," mumbled Brendan.

"No shit," whispered Connor.

I whispered over my radio, "Kevin, do you see that?"

"Unfortunately," he replied.

"Are they androids?" I asked Lara over the radio.

"I have no idea."

I studied their feet. They were ugly, but not the same ones as the print we saw before.

One of the creatures scanned the surrounding ridge, then felt the rocks beneath him. He was a half a head shorter than the tallest one, as was the other. The big one had to be at least eight foot tall. His armor was old and battered. It seemed like he wanted to make use of it until it ripped apart.

There was nothing human about the way they spoke.

I angled the holo-cam, pushing it slightly forward. The tall creatures were focused on the mouth of the cave, not us. Through my monitor, I saw them assembling something. It was a long tube on a tripod. They aimed it at the mouth of the cavern.

Lara whispered, "What are they doing?"

Connor replied, "I don't know… it looks like a rocket launcher."

BOOM! The launcher sent out a shuddering wave, throwing us back. Something shot into the cavern. There was a silence followed by a cloud of yellow smoke pouring from the opening.

It slowly drifted away and the tall creatures took up a position in front of it. They formed a small line and held onto bladed weapons including spears and oddly shaped swords.

"What the hell?" asked Kevin.

"I'm getting a weird reading on that smoke cloud," said Connor. "The chemical has some kind of strange enzyme compound."

"To do what?" asked Kevin.

And then we heard it. Clicking sounds, like fingernails tapping on ceramic, began emanating from the cavern. A few at first, then more and more until it sounded like a crashing wave.

"It sounds like giant bugs," I said aloud.

"Then that was a bug bomb," Brendan whispered into the comm.

The mouth of the cavern somehow grew blacker, and then a swarm of insect-like creatures lunged out of the cave at the hunters. I panned my holo-cam toward it and zoomed in. It was a horrid sight. Hundreds of agile shapes with no facial appearance except devilish metallic teeth crawled and ran toward the creatures with the bladed weapons.

Their heads were opaque shells. Their skeletal structure appeared to be on the outside, with pointy ridges and a long sharp tail then ended in a spear point. What god would create something like this?

As the huge insects emerged, the hunters picked away at them with shoulder-mounted lasers, blasting holes in their oblong skulls which erupted with yellowish liquid that made the ground smoke.

The battle-scarred hunter stood at the forefront using a large metal blade to slit limbs and heads from the bugs, acrobatically moving out of the way after each kill to avoid the spray of blood. The less-experienced hunters focused on using their shoulder cannons to pick off the bugs before they got close.

Some of the bugs seemed disoriented as they came out of the cavern. I wondered if the missile they launched had done something besides just piss them off. It reminded me of how security forces used stun grenades and vomit gas to break up rioters.

Wave after wave of bugs kept coming out of the cavern. The hunters held their ground, hacking and slashing until the bodies were piled so high they had to move to higher ground to avoid leaping attacks from the bugs.

When the old hunter was distracted, trying to protect one of the younger ones, a bug got close to him, and he barely got it by the throat in time. A hideous mouth within a mouth snapped at him. The hunter ignored it and used his blade to slash into the air and sever the end of the sharp tail the bug was about to impale him with. Clearly he'd fought these creatures before and knew their ways.

A younger hunter tried to strike at a trio of monsters and was distracted. A sharp tail stuck through his side, and he fell to the ground. The bugs tried to drag him into the mouth of the cavern, but the older one unleashed a flurry of plasma fire and slashing with his wrist blades, leaving pieces of smoking obsidian bug parts scattered about.

The third hunter dragged the injured one back toward the ship and used his shoulder cannon to pick off bugs from afar.

The older hunter had cleared a wide swath and the bugs, still pouring out of the cave, but in fewer numbers, avoided him.

He resorted to using his shoulder weapon to pick them off. Somehow, I could sense his reluctance even though I had no idea what was under the mask.

The other hunters, now bolder, began moving farther into clusters of bugs and slashed them to the ground.

The bugs were fewer and fewer, and began scrambling off in different directions. I feared they'd come toward us. "We need to get the hell out of here," I said over the radio.

Connor replied, "What are you saying? This is amazing! Tell me you're getting all of this." His riveted eyes were fixed on the hunters.

He moved out from behind the boulder with his holo-cam.

"Connor, stay back!" I shouted, gesturing for him to duck down.

"Just a second. I want to get a little closer."

From the corner of my eye, I saw something approaching us. Brendan went white as he heard it on his sound gear.

I tried calling Connor several times, but he either couldn't hear or was ignoring me.

Brendan and I cowered into the undergrowth, paralyzed with fear. I was praying it didn't see him.

Something moved through the rocks in Connor's direction. I saw the obsidian black carapace of one of the giant bugs as it slithered to where Connor was hiding. Before I could warn him, it leaped forward and wrapped its tail around Connor's neck.

I let out a scream and stood up, watching the massive insect drag him across the ground and toward a small ravine. I started after him, but Brendan grabbed me by the ankle, stopping me.

As the creature was about to pull Connor into the crevice, it stopped suddenly when a metal spear stabbed through its skull and pinned it to the ground. The younger hunter emerged from behind the rocks and pulled his weapon from the bug's skull.

Connor's eyes went large as he glanced up at the giant. I opened my mouth to tell him to stop, but I was too late. A holo shooter to his core, Connor did the last thing he should have done in this situation—he aimed his camera up at the hunter.

A second later, the hunter's shoulder camera pivoted and fired, and there was just a crater where Connor's head had been. The camera must have looked like a weapon.

I let out a yell.

The hunter looked up at me. His shoulder cannon pointed at me. My heart stopped and the blood drained from me.

Then he just walked away like I didn't exist.

I ducked back down. Brendan gazed at me with vacant eyes. Everything happened so quickly.

I looked toward Kevin, whose camera was still recording all of it.

Before I could stop him, he bounded down the ridge toward the hunter with his camera, blind with rage. Lara was frozen in terror. She looked over and saw me. Brendan and I gestured for her to come toward us. She crawled through the undergrowth, dodging rocks while keeping low to avoid any blasts in her direction.

She saw where Kevin was and shouted down to him, "We have to leave!"

He ignored her. That's when I noticed his other hand was holding a pistol, similar to the one from Lara's bag.

Ten meters away from the hunter, Kevin raised it to fire.

"Hey asshole…"

Kevin's chest was a smoking pit before he even finished his sentence. The hunter had pivoted and fired without even bothering to turn around, blasting a hole in his chest with his shoulder cannon.

Hysterical, Lara rummaged through her bag, mumbling to herself, "He took it. He took the pistol. When did he… how…"

I pulled the others away and down the ridge before anyone else decided to do something stupid, guiding us back toward the path that would take us to the landing zone.

Lara was in shock, shaking her head. Brendan wasn't much better off.

"I didn't know," Lara said. "I didn't know."

I shushed them. We had no idea what was still out there.

Once we were a half a kilometer away, I stopped and said, "We need a place to hide until the ship comes."

We scanned the junkyard around us—wrecked spaceships, broken-down vehicles, metal and other auto parts.

Brendan spotted a green hauler. It looked like good camouflage. There were a dozen others just like it. We ran toward it. As we climbed in, Brendan pointed at something on a roof near the main complex. "Look."

I turned with a jerk, scared that maybe it was one of those creatures.

"What?" I asked.

"There was a satellite dish on it when we left. It's not there now."

"You mean it was working?" I asked.

Lara was sitting in the back of the hauler and had her arms around her knees. It was dawning on her.

"The company was tracking everything. They were watching as those… *creatures* killed everyone. They let it happen. Hell, they may have wanted it to happen." After that, we fell into silence for a while.

We stayed in silence, subdued, counting the minutes until the shuttle would be back.

"ETA?" I asked Lara.

"Sixteen minutes," she whispered.

She looked at me with regret. I put my hand on her shoulder. She'd not told us the whole truth, but she'd never meant for this to happen.

"People have to know what happened here," she said, tears filling her eyes.

"They will," I replied.

Lara's eyes narrowed on mine. "I don't care if I survive."

"You will survive. We all will." I cut her short, afraid at the thought of losing another person.

She continued, "They have to know. Promise me."

I didn't know what to make of her. She was a spoiled, manipulative brat who had got half of us killed, but in that moment I also realized she really believed in her cause.

Before I could reply, we heard a *THUMP* on the roof… followed by footsteps, back and forth. We didn't make a sound. There was another *THUMP* and then the sound of gravel as if something heavy landed.

Lara mouthed, "Thirteen minutes."

We waited until it was silent again.

Brendan glanced up from his sound gear. "I can hear our ship coming."

I climbed out of the hauler first, making sure we weren't about to be ambushed. The area was clear. The rest followed, taking quick but careful steps.

We were just a few hundred meters away from the entrance to the landing pad when I saw a shadow on the ground and froze in my tracks. Brendan and Lara trained their lights around and looked back at me.

"You okay?" asked Brendan.

I glared straight ahead. My heart was pounding but I had to take action.

"Set the gear down," I said coldly.

"What do you mean?" Lara snapped.

"Put the fucking gear on the ground."

She sensed my seriousness and did as I said.

We laid our holo-cameras and recording gear at our feet.

A moment later, two hunters shimmered into view.

Lara gasped at the chilling sight.

The old hunter was closest to me. I glanced up at him. He remained motionless except for the shoulder cannon that was aimed at my head. I didn't react. I didn't have to.

"Now, put your hands in the air and walk away slowly," I told Lara and Brendan.

As we started walking, I eyed the old hunter one last time. To a degree, I hoped he could comprehend the disdain I had for what they did to my friends. But what difference would it make? This was their sport. He followed my gaze as we passed them. No reaction. Only silence.

I kept walking, eyes straight ahead. I could hear the sound of crunching gravel as Brendan followed. When we made it past the entrance to the landing field, we heard a loud zap and bang followed by a small explosion. The hunters incinerated our equipment.

The rescue ship was hovering over the landing zone with the hatch open. Heitor had probably seen the alien vessel on his approach and wasn't going to stay to find out who it belonged to. We ran to the craft, weaving through the loading equipment and fuel trucks.

Brendan was first on the ship. Heitor yelled something to us over the thrusters, but I couldn't make out what he was saying. Brendan's face went slack, and I looked back at what he saw.

Lara had been a few meters behind us and she tripped. As she got up, her body shuddered and blood spurted from her chest. Hiding under a cargo truck was the glistening shape of the alien bug that rose out from its hiding place. The menacing figure towered over her as she screamed in senseless agony.

Brendan grabbed me by the collar and pulled me into the ship before I could run to her. The last I saw of Lara was her being dragged into the night. There were flashes of laser fire in the distance and shiny dark things moving in from all sides of the landing zone.

I brushed a tear away. The interrogators gazed at me, their faces emotionless.

Then, the younger man spoke. "That's it?"

I scoffed, "Yeah, that's it. Now, can I go?"

The older man leaned forward. "Ms. Philip, we still have questions about what happened. There are also the legal consequences of violating a planetary quarantine."

"Let me tell it to the judge," I replied.

He smirked. "I wouldn't make plans for that right now."

"I get it," I said. "You don't want anyone knowing what happened down there. Frankly, I don't care. They weren't my friends anyway. You have all our gear. You've scanned me, probed me. All I have is a story I want to put behind me."

"That's a very rational position," said the older man.

What he meant to say was that I was a cold-hearted bitch. And I hoped he believed it, because that was my only chance of getting out of there.

Heaven help me if they found out that I lied about Lara dying before she made it to Jian Station with the holo-cards and the data about what really happened on Tenebris. In that case, Connor and Kevin really would have died in vain, and what happened on that derelict planet would happen again.

Despite the horrific scene I witnessed on Tenebris, after watching how the Company tried to exploit it for their own purposes and then cover it up, I'm not sure if the real terrors we're going to encounter as we spread out across the galaxy are going to be the ones we find, or the ones we bring with us.

NIGHT DOCTORS

BY MAURICE BROADDUS

"It sounds like the flu." Hiding the note of alarm in her voice, Nyota Dorsey jogged ahead a bit. Hitching her pack higher on her shoulder, she waved at her brother to keep up. She grew concerned at the tenor of Miles Byfield's cough. The Weyland-Yutani Corporation promised the best medical care, and she aimed to hold them to their promises.

Their home, New Allensworth, was a sanctuary for those of the African Diaspora and their allies who wanted a fresh start. Nyota simply wanted to be free of the weight of history that shaped their collective story. History always stalked her thoughts.

"Space flu." Miles wrapped himself with his arms like someone desperately trying to keep their heat in.

"The way you keep sticking your face into every strange new plant, you're probably having an allergic reaction to something."

"Space allergies."

"You can't keep sticking the word 'space' in front of stuff now that we're, you know, in space." Nyota punched him lightly on his arm. While he pursued a life in biology, Nyota had become a security specialist, which in New Allensworth were designated griots. Every village had one, the keeper of history and stories. The living memory. Though it was that same history she sought to escape by coming to New Allensworth, the memories lingered deep in her bones. They fell into their sibling rhythms whenever left to themselves. The muscles in her arm twinged with a deep ache, a lingering reminder of her long, suspended animation voyage.

"At least I'm not running around in a hazmat suit."

"It's not a hazmat suit. It's a standard breathing unit." Nyota held her arms as if modeling a new outfit. Hers was a slimmed down version of an exploration suit. She never left her home without suiting up. Nyota flicked her rebreather unit, no longer even noticing its slight hum.

New Allensworth was part of the colonization boom they called the Fifth Wave Migration. A colonization ship, the *Babalu-Aye*, carried just over ten thousand colonists and nearly five thousand embryos, with a half-dozen others scheduled to join them. New Allensworth had come along quite a way and almost felt like home. Inspired by the original city back in California, the Weyland-Yutani Corporation really had stuck to their agreement and left them alone to build the colony the way they wanted. New Allensworth began to feel like a full-on city. Its library and arts center civic complex was its crown jewel. It was an audacious dream.

With his work as a xenobotanist and agriculture specialist, Miles lit up with pride when they passed the garden his work oversaw. He coughed again, the hitch in his throat caught twice like he tried to clear something from deep within his lungs. Spitting off to the side, he met her protective glare. "It sounds worse than it is. You don't have to escort me to MedLab One. We have our own hospital."

"Sweet Sankofa, you're a pain in the ass. Look, Weyland-Yutani offered an opportunity and I chose to accept it. That does not mean that I trust them."

The surrounding mountains were hidden by a mild haze. Behind them, the storehouses and stretch of farmland separated the community from the outskirts where MedLab One stood. Nyota scanned the looming building. The only thing remaining strictly under Weyland-Yutani's purview was MedLab One, with their proprietary tech and oh-so-precious research. Its metal spires were formed from the shell of the original ship which brought them to their planet.

A blond man in a blue lab smock greeted them at the entryway. Male-presenting would be more accurate. He was Weyland-Yutani's resident android. Nothing gave him away in his manner, but his vibe was completely off. No, more precisely, he gave no vibe at all.

"Good morning, Miles Byfield. Specialist Nyota Dorsey. How may I assist you?"

"I'm sick, Chad. Why else would I come here?" Miles asked.

"My name is—"

"You're all Chads to me, Chad." Miles sucked his teeth. Despite barely being in his thirties, he always channeled his inner old man energy. He had a long distrust—remaining just this side of hatred—of androids. He'd read every account of androids accompanying colonists on missions and, to the tune of "you never know if it will be 'the one,'" vowed never to drop his guard around them.

"Why you gotta do Chad like that?" Nyota bowed slightly as greeting. Chad stared at her.

"What's that about?" Miles asked.

"A gesture of respect. I read once that if you bow before shoebill storks, they accept you."

"What you know about storks?"

"I read."

Miles sucked his teeth again. "Well, Chad's not a stork."

Chad watched them both in cool, uncomplicated appraisal, his eyes a blank shade of blue. "What seems to be troubling you?"

"I got some sort of bad cold," Miles said.

"What sort of symptoms are you experiencing?" Chad ushered them down another corridor to an enclosed bay. Moving to a station, he began a preliminary scan.

"Sweating. I'm tired. Hurting all over." Miles raised his fist to his mouth and coughed. "Lots of that. My chest is tight, like I can't take a full breath."

"Low grade fever, fatigue, muscle aches, difficulty breathing." Chad perused the readings with a diffident aplomb.

"That's what I just said, Chad." Miles had no chill.

Nyota paced the perimeter of the room. The austere sterility of the lab was like a cathedral to science. Tall banks of monitors and computers, powerful enough to process an entire continent's infrastructure judging from the size of them. Several complete isolation chambers were embedded into the wall.

"Go ahead and lie down." Chad swept his hand out, presenting a stasis bed.

Miles hopped up on it. "No probes."

"This is a lot of heavy research artillery for our little colony." Nyota continued her discreet scrutiny.

"Your future lies more in the research laboratories, not in the spurious dreams of a colony." The voice echoed from nowhere in particular until a person slowly rose from an unseen lift. Her hair was a level of blond not seen in nature, cut short and swept to the side. Her eyes were an icy blue like frost over a stagnant pond. Her mouth fixed into a perennial purse. Dr. Ann Saenger's hands tapped in impatience within her crossed arms. She stepped through the archway and strode toward Chad with a determination that dared anyone to get in her way. "Hand me the readings."

Her words held the snapping expectation of being immediately obeyed. Though Nyota always felt some sort of way about the Chads, mistrust was too strong a word. However, she felt even more of an unease in the way Dr. Saenger treated him like a servant. That air of superiority, dismissing those beneath her, stirred a long history of memories.

"He's not your servant, Dr. Ann. We don't do slaves around here." Nyota made a point of calling her by her first name. Miss Ann was what black people used to call white women who were arrogant and condescending to them.

The assiduous sneer of the doctor's lips gave way to a wan smile as she touched a finger to her chin, a gesture both condescending and cloying. "No need to be offended on his behalf. His programming precludes such… sensitivities. Isn't that right, um, *Chad*, as you've now been rechristened?"

"Yes, Dr. Saenger." Chad's eyes were expressively blank, as if the idea of offense at human behavior eluded him. He moved with a tentativeness, as if unsure of the delicate nature of the instruments.

Dr. Saenger gave him a stern grimace.

"I've been hearing a lot of reports about similar ailments affecting many of our residents. Wanting to gather information on the scope of this outbreak is why I wanted to accompany Mr. Byfield," Nyota said.

"Yes, his condition appears to be little more than an allergic reaction to native flora. We can treat the progress of this 'cold,' or at least lessen the symptoms. All of the standard precautions were taken prior to disembarkation, yet these scans show you've had the allergen in your system for months. The same infection. It hasn't cleared. Some people have underlying conditions which may require an additional antibiotic." Dr. Saenger gestured, the subtle pressure of expectation exerted by her title and presence.

"What sort of condition?" Nyota asked.

"A genetic predisposition for severe autoimmune disease. You have it, too, Nyota."

Miles rolled up his sleeve. The muscles in Nyota's arm twinged again. History was her hesitation. She could not escape the thoughts of the experiments J. Marion Sims did on black women, and the Tuskegee Syphilis Study on black men. The doctor attended him without further comment, the procedure over before he could begin his next question. Miles nodded with approval. He slid his sleeve back. "You getting checked or nah?" he said to Nyota.

"I'll just listen to the spirit of my ancestors and take my chances with the precautions I'm taking."

"Yes, I'd been warned that you were difficult and exacting with your iatraphobia." Dr. Saenger handed her instruments to Chad who devotedly stashed them away. Chad stationed himself behind her.

"My what?" Nyota asked.

"An intense fear of doctors." Dr. Saenger tapped her chin, this time to indicate Nyota's mask. "You won't even breathe the same air as us."

Something itched at the edges of Nyota's spirit. The way Dr. Saenger tracked their movements, with the severe scrutiny of an escaping patient.

"Look here, space Marcus Garvey," Miles said. "We got our forty acres and a Chad. Why'd you even fight so hard for us to come here if all you're going to do is assume the worst and spit in their face?"

"Whenever the Company cares so much to see about our wellbeing, I get... suspicious."

"Am I good or nah?" Miles scratched at his chest.

"We'd like to keep you for observation to keep a close eye on your symptoms." Dr. Saenger turned her full attention back to Miles. "But you're... good."

"I'm ghost then." Elbowing his sister as they left, Miles stage whispered, "Yeah, but *I'm* the pain in the ass"

New Allensworth was on the planet designated LV-333, in the star system Xamidimura. The Khoikhoi people traditionally called the star and its mate "xami di mura" which translated as the "eyes of the lion." Weyland-Yutani Corporation financed the dream of the colony to the tune of one trillion dollars, for transport and installation. For PR reasons, if Nyota had to guess, to emphasize the diversity aspect of their work. Sensing that such a gesture, expensive though it was, was in vogue. Like her people couldn't see through that. The company's agenda, to exploit them one way or another, never changed. She would leverage any of their resources for the betterment of her people. On *their* terms, not the company's.

Nyota and Miles followed the narrow promontory that wound behind MedLab One. A colonnade of trees surrounded the facilities, the rugged terrain like a barrier to it, with tree branches so thick in places, they interlocked like dead man's fingers. The evening wasn't too cold, barely a noticeable breeze. A furtive movement near a dense copse of trees caught Nyota's attention. Her chest tightened. A dull ache shot through her arm. Something about the image brought to mind images of hidden tunnels along the Underground Railroad, the kind her ancestors used to escape the South.

Hidden by the thick underbrush, a figure emerged. A thick mane of dreadlocks bobbed with his movement. Moonlight briefly reflected from his ill-fitting clothing which seemed to jut at odd angles with an iridescent sheen. Something seemed wrong with his face. Hunched over, creeping low, he sought to gain his bearings and seeming to catch his breath. He searched the night sky, as if for its brightest jewel—the drinking gourd according to her family—to follow its direction. With the muscle memory of someone used to moving through the woods, he disappeared into the trees, but another stealthy movement hinted that he scampered up one of them.

And then… nothing.

Yet Nyota had the unmistakable sensation of being watched. Hunted. Pressing a lone finger to her mouth for them to be silent, she led Miles down behind the cover of bushes. They made their way closer to where the man had emerged. Only the breeze rustled the limbs about her. Craning her neck slowly, she searched the trees for the near-invisible figure camouflaged by the branches. A sigh passed among the trees, signaling a withdrawal.

Chad emerged only a few paces from the tree line. His impassive face scanned the surrounding foliage as he began stalking the woods with a grim determination. The echo of a snarling growl—like a series of crackling, bursting clicks—seemed to emanate from all around them. The sound chilled Nyota. Miles eyes widened in near panic. Her arm wrapped around him and yanked them both to the ground. Chad remained unphased.

With barely a shadow to give him away, the figure dropped from the trees. The android whirled, but too late. That was when she saw the man's face, if she could call it that. It was more a frozen rictus with mandibles and long, hair-like appendages, her mind processed the visage as a beetle with long braids.

A Predator.

She knew about them—all griots had been briefed with stories on them—but hadn't expected to encounter them here. Not in New Allensworth. But here it was, fangs protruding from its resting pissed face.

Palming something, the Predator flicked his wrist and a spear-like weapon telescoped out. He slashed at Chad, the blows finding their intended target, but the android still managed to scramble out from under him. They circled each other warily.

The Predator moved haphazardly, with a staggering gait. His form emaciated, like he was still recovering from a long cryo-sleep. Nyota hadn't had anything to gauge his height before, but the way he towered over Chad, he must've neared eight feet tall. The Predator cocked his head as if he had trouble seeing Chad fully. Taking his measure, he initiated combat with a head butt. Chad barely recoiled. Nyota's stomach lurched. Chad's face plate shifted. He nudged it back into place. She had the sinking suspicion that Chad might have some combat-level augmentations. As she leaned forward for a better look, a twig snapped under her weight.

The Predator glanced in Nyota's direction.

Chad rushed him, delivering a punch that sent him sailing into a tree. The synthetic checked the treeline for whatever distracted the Predator, but Nyota ducked further out of sight. The Predator heaved his spear, a precise throw aimed at Chad's heart. With little effort, the android caught it.

Chad's kick landed squarely in the Predator's gut. Sluggish, as if drugged, the creature could do little more than crumple into a fleshy pile. His lungs drew another breath, clutching his side as if the act of breathing drove needles into his lungs. A succession of stomps landed about his ribs and arms as he desperately protected his face. The rain of android footfalls stopped with his low, surrendering moan.

"We have to set an example for the others. We can't have them thinking in such rebellious ways. There's still so much for us to do," Chad said.

The creature turned and stared in Nyota's direction. With one last blow, Chad rendered him unconscious and unceremoniously started dragging him back to MedLab One. The trees whispered at the wild night's work like silent conspirators.

"What... the entire hell... was that?" Miles asked.

"There's so much that we don't know. Back in the lab, where did Dr. Ann come up from? MedLab One was constructed out of *Babalu-Aye*. We can see it. So what's underneath it?" Nyota scrambled up the slight incline of the hill beside them before lying down. She withdrew a set of scanning binoculars from her pack. Barely discernable channels—grooves along the earth—segmented the vegetation and formed a geometric pattern, like an equilateral triangle. A few remnants rang with familiarity, like the basic elements of construction. Though dirt hid the bulk of the structure, an intricate design was obvious.

"Well, don't keep me in suspense." Miles huddled down next to her.

"I don't know how to interpret what I'm seeing. It's like MedLab One sits on top of another structure. Something… hollow." There was a hierarchy of structures. Each enclosure built separately, perhaps in stages. The highest one almost like a watchtower. "Come on. I want to get a closer look."

Nyota scrambled down the embankment, stopping at a thatched piece of ground near where the Predator had emerged. Dropping to her knees, she groped about it until her fingers found a groove. She peeled back an incised platform, which left a divot in the ground like an empty socket. She slid down the cave shaft's opening, its walls a rough-hewn corridor, setting down on a floor of not quite dirt, more like a quarry of pebbles, reduced to scree.

Miles landed next to her and she shot him a look. "What? I wasn't going to let you explore a long, dark tunnel without backup. That never ends well for us."

Nyota began mapping a grid of the structure. The shafts led to a series of enclosures which formed a complex within the complex. Allowing her eyes to relax, she was better able to see the images on the walls coalesced into a bas relief mural, symbols etched in the stone.

"Almost a sculpture garden. This was once a settlement of some sort." Nyota ran her fingers along the walls. History intruded on her speculations. The structure brought to mind the story of Seneca Village. The land in New York City, from West 82nd to West 89th Street. By 1855, it was an enclave of mostly black people owning most of the property. It became a thriving community, a refuge. But then the city declared eminent domain, acquired the land, and built Central Park over it.

A groan from Miles drew her thoughts back.

"You alright?"

"My head... hurts."

"You don't look good." She pressed her hand to his head. "You're clammy. Maybe you should go back and rest."

"Someone's got to have your back if you on some simple nonsense."

A distant plinking of water droplets echoed from farther down the corridor. The passage opened up into a cavernous room. The walls glistened, its moisture refracting light from an unseen source. The way the shafts were reinforced every ten meters brought to mind the image of ribs protecting vital organs. Except the braces were rigged with failsafe explosives. Miles recoiled, pantomiming a reaction to some smell. Nyota thanked her rebreather for sparing her from whatever assaulted his nostrils. An undulation of movement drew her attention. The shadows pressed in on them from all sides, like a physical thing struggling against it. A series of small objects dotted the floor. As she neared, they reminded her of bulbous, organic egg-like pods. Nyota stepped closer. Something moved inside them.

Whatever it was seemed to enliven at her approach. Enthralled by a curiosity she couldn't explain, she began to reach out to it. An object swam about within the egg, causing it to throb in engorgement, awaiting her touch. Miles stepped between her and it, causing her to halt. He attempted to get a closer look, but the movement within the pod slowed until it stilled completely at his presence. Miles' gaze bounced between her and the pod several times. And then glanced back toward the passage from where they came. Nothing about this felt right. She, too, wondered whether to turn back. But she was no closer to understanding what was going on. She pointed toward the next chamber. Miles swallowed hard and followed.

Several cryopods lined the room, similar but much longer than the kind which transported the citizens of New Allensworth to the planet. The armor of several Predators hung behind them, displayed with the air of mounted trophy heads. Condensation clouded the outside of each face plate. Nyota ran her hand across one to clear the glass. The beaten Predator. Its skin, dark and scaly. Along a deeply mottled countenance was some sort of tribal ornamentation etched into its forehead. A luminescent phosphor green smear streaked the faceplate.

The Predator opened his eyes.

"Sweet Sankofa." Nyota scrambled away from the chamber. "He's still alive."

"What the…" Miles yelled.

"They're less useful dead," Dr. Saenger said from behind them, sounding unsurprised to see them. Chad trailed behind her. "Welcome to MedLab *Two*."

"What are you doing to them?" Nyota asked.

"We've been lucky to have these specimens transported to us for study. We're still mapping the nature and parameters of their physiology."

All about Nyota was the medicalized display of creature parts. Preserved as objects of curiosity, a mausoleum exhibit of exotics. Like a dramatic presentation which argued the inferiority of the aliens' bodies. A collection of skulls. Desiccated limbs. Dissected material. More of the shards of plates that the Predator had cobbled together as armor upon its escape. A disarticulated gulag such that they were not free even in death.

"That's barbaric." Nyota recalled the tortures curious scientists were capable of. Seeing how deep their black skin went; the repeated burning and flaying to investigate. Her fingers trailed along the metal sarcophagus, but she didn't allow Dr. Saenger out of her sight.

"Not every treatment can be considered an unethical medical experiment. Even the word stems from the Latin 'ex' meaning 'out of' and 'periculum' meaning 'a *dangerous* trial.' That's what we do here. Trial studies. To harvest whatever knowledge we can glean and use it for the betterment of—"

"Weyland-Yutani."

"I was going to say 'humanity,' but to-may-to, to-mah-to. Things might be painful or risky, but as long as the effect is more beneficial than harmful, we all reap the rewards. Besides, the Predators are nothing compared to my real prize."

With a gesture, a bay door opened, revealing a creature standing about five meters tall. Its body had the metallic sheen of an armored insect within the foot-thick walls of an ALON cage. Nearly machine-like in construction, the creature's two pairs of arms and appendages—like massive insect legs acting as struts—locked into its containment structure. Rippling scales on its large head protected by what appeared to be a bony extrusion, almost a crown. And oddly human lips. Its external mouth was separately segmented. It rested within a biomechanical throne, made of the same material as her crown, which also supported her. *Her.*

"*Internecivus raptus,* from the Latin meaning 'murderous thief.' I nicknamed this one Queen Hottentot." Dr. Saenger's eyes locked in a medical gaze.

A huge sac extended from the Queen's abdomen, perhaps ten meters in length. The tip of its ovipositor like a prehensile trunk. Beneath it were malformed versions of the pods Nyota saw in the cavernous chamber. A scorched line trailed along the tender underside of the sac, a laser-guided vivisection having been interrupted. The aperture of its ovipositor had been eroded into a series of tears.

"I had to scarify the edges of the opening to attempt repair," Dr. Saenger said.

"That sounds unnecessarily cruel." The Queen's smooth bulbous head turned toward Nyota. She angled her head toward the creature. It might have been her imagination, but the Queen seemed to mirror her movements.

"Not by their standards. It does not feel pain like we do, certainly not enough to justify the trouble and risk attendant to the administration of anesthetics." Dr. Saenger no longer hid the edge of glee in her voice. Tales were told of white physicians, "Night Doctors," who would kidnap, dissect, and perform a variety of experiments on black people. Lost in the rationale all such night doctors gave for how they treated their patients, she continued. "Next I want to introduce radiation to their bodies to measure the amount that lingers in their tissues."

Something hissed off to Nyota's left.

Three cages lined the wall behind her, an array of surgical instruments spread out on a table in front of them just tauntingly out of reach. Creatures stirred within them, a series of parts caught in glimpses that her mind struggled to connect into a whole. Black bodies. A flat ridge of spines. Elongated cylindrical skulls. Hands with sharp claws. A segmented, blade-tipped tail. One turned and edged its face to the clear partition and snapped at Nyota. An inner set of jaws served as its tongue. Smaller versions of this species, they were still much taller than Nyota. But these creatures were hobbled. Plates of their armor missing, sectioned off. Their insectile joints a collection of odd angles and jutting bits.

They'd all been altered, tampered with. Some were missing limbs. Hard light projections of the creatures, what they were supposed to look like if whole, were cast about the room. Each of the test subjects reduced to abominations of what they were supposed to be. A data stream ran alongside the images, including a three-dimensional rendering of a DNA strand revolved about a central console.

"These creatures are pure. Primal, predatory creatures." Dr. Saenger's face beamed, caught up in her beatific vision. "These Xenomorphs exist solely to propagate and eliminate threats to them. Their skin is made up of polarized silicon cells; their blood is akin to acid. They're… *magnificent*."

"I don't understand any of this," Nyota said.

"Ah, it all starts with a simple story. There once was a species some military minds imagined could be used as a biological weapon. For a long time, the evidence of this weapon was studied. One phase of the creature's development, what some people colloquially call their facehugger stage, delivered a version of a pathogen called *Plagiarus Praepotens*. It causes the host DNA to rewrite itself and develop the creature's next stage, the, uh, chestburster. We have been studying the effects of the creature over the course of its gestation."

"This is all about making weapons."

"We're farther along in our research than just militarizing Xenomorphs." Dr. Saenger marveled at the DNA model before swiping along the console to pull up the image of one of the pods. "As a pathogen, this genomic parasite took many forms. Its life cycle was simple enough: waiting for a host to come around, eggs… forcibly implanting itself, not just rewriting the host's DNA to allow it proper growing conditions, but through morphic resonance, allowing a two-way gene transfer as part of its gestation within its host that allowed it to take on some of the physical characteristics of the host. That way, it is genetically pre-programmed for adaptation into whatever environment it finds itself in. A miracle of cross-breeding, hybridization, and engineering. Its final phase is to develop into whatever kind of drone the species needs most by—"

Miles coughed. The raspy bark came on so suddenly, he didn't have time to stifle it with his hand. It turned into a choking gasp. The sheen of sweat had thickened on him. The capillaries in his eyes swelled, the vessels rupturing, leaving his pupils swimming in red. He clutched his chest, struggling to breathe.

"Miles!" Nyota yelled, trying to clear his airway as he thrashed about. She could barely pin him down by his arms.

"You may want to back away for this part." Dr. Saenger skimmed her hand across her table. The pixelated image of Miles enlarged alongside the rotating DNA image, his vitals streaming as data points beside it. His temperature spiked. His heartbeat sped up. "There's a considerable amount of cardiovascular damage at this point."

With his next shuddering convulsion came the wet snap of brittle kindling. Miles' body jerked, seizing into a locked spasm. Red splashed his shirt. Nyota couldn't hear much over the sound of her screams. The material bulged. Something punched through his chest, seeking to escape. The fabric ripped. A bloody, serpentine fetus emerged. Rows of glistening teeth, reared, pausing as if getting its bearings.

Nyota snatched a blade from the table and ran the creature through before it could move. A spray of dull yellow blood splashed on her containment suit. An acid of some sort, it burned through the material. Nyota tore off her glove before the fluid reached her skin.

"No!" Dr. Saenger screamed. She rushed to its side, knocking Nyota out of the way as she cradled the dead newborn. She reached for a tool reminiscent of an awl. Making incisions in its scalp, the doctor pried the skull bones, prizing out the edges into new positions. She added the remains to the nightmare cache of alien parts. "What a waste. There was still perfectly good data to collect. You don't understand what we've accomplished here in New Allensworth. The Xenomorph incubation period is normally somewhere between hours and days. But we've been able to stave off the parasite; halting its development, if not outright rendering them essentially stillborn. They then are broken down and cleared by the body. We were hoping to keep Mr. Byfield under observation. We wanted to study the progression of his particular… infection. To perfect a treatment against xenomorph implantation. Think of it, being able to unleash the Xenomorphs without fear of them infecting us. We're so close…"

"Using the whole colony as lab rats." Nyota stared at her brother. His face frozen in fractal agony, his eyes staring blankly off into the distance. She had no room or time to grieve, as rage began its familiar swell, threatening to overtake her. "You don't even realize the monster this has twisted you into. The blood on your hands."

"There'll be more blood if my work doesn't succeed." Dr. Saenger carried the remains to a nearby tray, Miles a forgotten and discarded package waiting for Chad to clean up and remove. "There are still shortcomings we have to study."

"Why didn't this... *treatment* work on Miles?" Nyota's throat tightened.

"His underlying condition left him immunocompromised in some way. It allowed the pathogen to adapt. It acquires whole clusters of mutations. We need to study this more to prevent the Xenomorph from this kind of adaptation. We've never seen anything capable of such specialized mutations before. But those mutations seem especially receptive against someone of this genomic type."

"I have the same underlying condition." Nyota's voice trailed off. Her condition, her DNA, was valuable to them. A new Henrietta Lacks, whose cell line would be used for decades after her to advance who knew what kinds of abhorrent technologies.

"And the way you've preserved yourself within your suit, against so many conditions of this planet, you are a perfect control subject."

Chad stalked toward her.

Still frozen between grief, terror, and unbelief, Nyota staggered backward. This was the way history too often worked. The circumstances of cruelty not allowing time for her to reel from her loss. She needed a distraction. She needed to draw everyone away from the Predators. Her fingers danced along the console panel. The chambers unlatched.

The Xenomorphs were free. Their sleek, black bodies moved with a jungle cat's speed, ready for the opportunity. They scattered into the shadows. Nyota ducked behind the operating theater. Chad started after her.

"Ignore her! Contain the beasts!" Dr. Saenger yelled. "They are the real threat."

The low lighting created pockets of shadows, illusions of shapes difficult to discern. Nyota doubled back to the previous corridor. Skittering erupted from her left. She jumped at the sound. Scanning for threats, she inched along the passageway. The medical bay echoed with strange chitterings and a dull scrape of nails against the floor. Nyota reached the chamber with the Predators.

Pressing her face to the Predator's chamber, the one she had encountered before, wanting him to take in her face. Her fingers tapped a code into the control, its symbols reflected on the clear partition. The chamber hissed as its cover released. The Predator slowly rose from it. Barely able to stand, he steadied himself against the chamber. Nyota stepped toward him but paused. Not knowing what else to do, Nyota bowed to the Predator. "I'm tired of folks pitting us against one another to support their self-interests."

He turned away from her. She moved to each stasis unit, releasing the rest of his pack. At the same time, he began to don his armor. As the last of his people rose from their chamber, he slid his helmet into place.

A Xenomorph sprang from the darkness. Its mouth open, thin strands of a mucousy saliva dripped from its jaws. Nyota barely had time to raise her hands before a spear stabbed into the creature. It sailed across the room, slamming into the wall behind her. Pinned next to the dissected bits of its brethren as if it had been added to the gruesome collection. The spray from its wound sizzled where it landed.

Nyota glanced over at the Queen. She could feel the creature studying her. Curious, hungering assessment. They were akin to competing animals after a drought who arrive at a watering hole at the same time. There was a conversation in the room only those in the moment could have. An eerie silence settled, each one waiting for another to make the first move.

"On our own, we're all weak, but we all want to be free," Nyota said. "Now's not the time to be focused on fighting one another. Or eating one another. Let's save that until we're out of here."

The Queen struggled against her supports but remained bound by Dr. Saenger's containment. Its thrashing weakened. The Queen was dying. She opened her mouth. A second set of jaws jutted out, snapping several times at her.

The Predator stalked away, probably to deal with the remaining Xenomorphs.

More shapes scuttled about. The sinister scratching of their movement reverberated from all around. Nyota remained near the examination table. She knew that she couldn't outrun them, any of them, not without cover. She'd be ripped apart before she made it halfway across the medical bay. The Xenomorphs didn't seem to understand fear, only the singular instinct to attack. They moved as a pack, testing her defenses and resolve.

Chancing a peek from behind the console where she hid, she saw a Xenomorph creep around the corner, locking its gaze on the distracted Predator. Nyota glanced up. The mounted dissection laser hovered over her. Rising slowly, to avoid drawing attention, she swung the laser around. The

Xenomorph began to close the distance between it and the Predator. She aimed the targeting beam at the creature's thorax. Stroking the keyboard, she blasted it. The creature's carapace ruptured open. It thrashed under the burn of the beam, and then dropped.

Dr. Saenger rushed her. Nyota shoved the woman away from the console. The Company's experiments couldn't be allowed to stand. Nyota pulled up the facility schematics. On the monitor, the chamber of organic pods focused into view. Each one representing an experiment awaiting her people. She opened the security protocols. These weapons couldn't be allowed to fall into anyone's hands. But her hand hovered above the switch. No one gave her the right to make such a decision either. Nyota turned to the Queen.

"All of your young have been taken and experimented on. Not the life you wanted for them. Better for them to end than continue their lives bound, tortured, and enslaved." Many were the stories of members of Nyota's people who were enslaved who chose, as the Igbo did, to walk in unison into the ocean singing "The Water Spirit brought us, the Water Spirit will take us home." Nyota hoped that in some way, the Queen understood.

The Queen's ovipositor released one last egg. Hope for their future. On some level, Nyota perceived an unspoken promise. And nodded.

Nyota activated the failsafes. The chamber of eggs erupted in a series of flames.

"All my work! What have you done?" Dr. Saenger screamed.

Chad returned to the room, his clothes in ruin, scored by dull yellow splatter. The snarl returned. The guttural clicking signaling the nearby presence of the Predator. This time, Chad froze. His head swiveled about, scouring the shadows. From the darkness, the Predator shot what appeared to be some sort of bladed frisbee. It landed in the android's chest. Chad stopped and stared at the weapon lodged in his chest as his fluids sprayed. When he looked back up, the Predator sprung at him. His spear plunged into the synthetic's side, then ripped upward. His head splintered from his chest chassis, the pulpy spray of his internal lubricant splashed about.

"Stop! You're ruining everything!" Dr. Saenger grabbed a surgical blade and charged Nyota. A long tail lowered behind her. The words "Watch out" died on Nyota's lips. With a quick twist, the tail plunged into the doctor. Raising her like a skewered side of beef. The doctor's head lolled to the side as the Queen brought her to eye level with the last of her strength. The creature dashed her against the wall.

As the doctor's body slid to the floor, Nyota turned to the creature. The rest of the Predator's pack slowly closed ranks around her. She locked her eyes onto their leader, unflinching, despite the pounding within her chest. The Predator paused for a heartbeat in careful appraisal.

"We all want to be free." Nyota's voice played back from the Predator's helmet.

The creature took its talon of a finger and etched a mark into her forehead. A trickle of blood issued down her face. The other Predators took note and began to don their gear.

Nyota picked up the Queen's final egg, securing it within a lockbox before stuffing it into her pack. Fulfilling her unspoken promise. Then she turned to the screen. "We're coming for you, Weyland-Yutani, and we're going to bring this whole system down."

SCYLLA AND CHARYBDIS

BY E.C. MYERS

"The bad news is, we're dead in space."

It was a hell of a way to begin a briefing, but it got his crew's attention immediately and Captain Hyeon Bak wasn't one to waste anyone's time, especially when they had no time to waste.

"What's the good news?" asked Blodwen Clarke. The blond communications officer was busily pecking at a terminal, checking on the *Ketumati*'s systems for herself and starting to look as frustrated as Bak felt.

"*We* aren't dead yet," Bak said.

Clarke adjusted her glasses. "That's a pretty low bar for good news."

"What do you mean, 'dead in space'? We are still moving." Kiann Das looked out one of the viewing portholes and wrinkled his brow.

Anika Hassan rolled her eyes. "First of all, you couldn't notice the ship's movement with the naked eye while looking out of a *window*, because of the vast distances in space." She rested a hand on the conference table. "Second of all: we're still moving, but the engines aren't functioning."

"You are sure?" Das ran a hand through his dark, curly hair, which was sticking out comically in all directions and making it that much harder to take him seriously. After two months, three weeks, three days, and seven point five hours in stasis, they all had major bedhead and a certain amount of disorientation. And after just under a month in training beforehand, many of them were already sick of each other, which didn't bode well for a happy community on Babylon.

"I'm chief engineer, so yes, I'm sure," she said.

"Then how are we moving?"

"We're drifting, because of *momentum*," she snapped. "An object in motion stays in motion unless acted upon by an opposing force. Friction. But there's no friction in space."

Only between people, Bak thought.

Hassan sighed. "And even though you're just a fucking *florist*, I feel like you should have a better grasp of the basics of spaceflight before you go on an interstellar mission."

"Hey. Easy," Bak interjected. "We all have an important role here."

"Exactly. I'm a hydroponic specialist." Das sniffed. "Our mission is building a colony. We were supposed to be sleeping through the spaceflight part." He glared at Bak as though it were his fault he wasn't still cozy in his cryotube. "I was having a beautiful dream," Das said.

That was technically Bak's fault. When the *Ketumati*'s computer, gAIa, had abruptly roused him from hypersleep a month too early, it was his decision to wake the rest of his senior crew.

"We all were," Bak said. He'd been dreaming about walking around the Seoul Grand Park Zoo with Amelia on a warm spring day. They had gone together the day before leaving Earth, only the real thing had been less idyllic: it was a cold, drizzly morning, and they'd been having an argument.

You and your partner weren't supposed to go to sleep angry, and it seemed like a particularly bad idea when neither of you would wake up for eight months—to start your lives together on a new planet.

"I notice you're dressed, Captain," Clarke said. The rest of the crew suddenly realized it too: they were still in their sleepwear, but Bak was in uniform. "How long have you been awake?"

"A few days," Bak said.

"Why did you wait so long to wake us?" Hassan asked.

"I hoped I wouldn't have to. But I can't fix this myself. The engines have been disabled. Near as I can tell, it isn't a mechanical problem." Bak let the words hang there for a moment.

"Software?" The pilot, Gunpei Iwata, sat up. He was the silent type, a man of few words who preferred to sit back and let conversations take place around him. Flying was the one thing he did well, and right now, he couldn't do it.

"It's gAIa," Bak said. "Some kind of embedded subroutine. She can't tell me what's wrong or how it happened, only that something *is* wrong. Very, very wrong. And we're locked out of the controls so we can't bring navigation systems back online. Or propulsion."

"Or communications," Clarke said. "A bug?"

"Possibly. But given what's at stake here, I'm betting on sabotage."

He studied the crew's reactions. Das looked even more stressed than he had a moment ago. Clarke betrayed genuine surprise, followed by determination; now that she knew what was wrong, she could try to fix it. Singh looked like he wanted to punch someone. Hassan looked concerned.

"You think one of us did it," Hassan said.

Bak grimaced. "Either this was accomplished before we left, or the saboteur is on board—and awake. But we can sort that out later. If there *is* a later. I've activated a distress beacon, but to be honest, I don't expect anyone to respond out here."

Just then an alarm went off and gAIa's perversely calm voice interrupted: "Another vessel has been detected and is on approach. ETA: ten minutes."

"Looks like somebody heard us," Singh said.

"Thank goodness," Das said.

Clarke shook her head. She pointed at the screen, where a wireframe scan of the other ship was rotating. It was small, most of its bulk comprised of three thrusters port, starboard, and aft. It seemed built for speed, stealth, and short distances. Sharp fins beneath the vessel gave it a distinctly sinister look.

"It's clearly not one of ours," Singh said gravely.

"Pirates?" Das squeaked.

"Worse," Clarke said, examining the record. "The details are scant, but that vessel is flagged as extremely hostile. *'Do not engage. Run. If you cannot run, do not resist.'*"

They sat in silence for a moment.

"What does that mean?" Das asked.

"We're fucked," Hassan said.

Running wasn't an option. The *Ketumati* was locked onto its course, but without gAIa making minute adjustments along the way, they might miss Babylon entirely, and even if they arrived they wouldn't be able to land. Unless nav and propulsion systems came back online, they would float endlessly in space until they ran out of food or power, or collide with something they couldn't avoid. And there was no guarantee they could ride it out in hypersleep until they were rescued and evacuated safely.

But none of that might matter, depending on what happened when their mysterious visitor arrived.

Although the warning in the ship's database said not to resist, the crew couldn't understand why they shouldn't fight back against an enemy.

Bak and Singh, the only two with combat training, handed out laser pistols and showed the others how not to accidentally shoot themselves or one another, though no one liked the idea of handing Das a gun—least of all Das.

"Why don't we wake the security forces? Isn't this their job?" Das asked.

"Not enough time to thaw them," Singh said. "It's up to us."

As the vessel approached, scans showed only a single life sign. It did not answer their hails, but it didn't attack either. Instead, it docked. As security officer, Singh went to meet their visitor at the airlock while the rest of them monitored from the bridge.

Clarke switched on the interior cameras to show Singh standing in front of the open airlock door. They all leaned in close to the monitor to get a better look at the grainy, dark shape standing in front of him.

345

The humanoid creature stood two heads above the burly, six-foot-tall Fijian. Its face was obscured by a smooth mask with two black eyeholes. Dreadlocks cascaded over its shoulders which were covered with scaly armor, like a bug's carapace.

"It's armed and dangerous," Singh whispered. "Blades on its wrists. A spear on its back. It's holding something that looks like a sniper rifle. I don't think it wants to be friends."

"Try talking to it," Bak said.

"Hello! What are your intentions here? Who are you?" Singh said in an exaggeratedly cheerful voice.

Hassan groaned. "We're *so* fucked."

They heard a series of clicking sounds and the creature moved, so fast it was a blur. It lunged toward Singh.

"Shit!" Singh fired three times. Somehow, he missed the creature twice at point blank range, but the third shot hit it in the side. The alien jolted and bellowed. Then it flickered and disappeared. Singh looked around frantically.

"Where'd it go?" Das asked.

"Some kind of cloaking field?" Singh fired again. And again.

They heard his heavy breathing. Another laser blast. Then another. Then Singh's gun went flying out of his hands.

"Fuck!" Singh turned and ran, filling the channel with a string of "fucks."

"Get out of there," Bak said uselessly. He found himself squeezing the armrests of his chair with both hands.

They followed Singh across multiple cameras as he ran through the corridors. They heard a loud *pop*, like a bottle of champagne being opened, followed by the sound of metal pinging off metal.

"What was that?" Bak asked.

"It's shooting at me!" Singh shouted.

"Try to get into a service duct," Clarke said. "It may be too big to follow you."

They heard another *pop*. Singh grunted.

"Are you hit?" Bak peered at the camera. Something stuck out of Singh's left shoulder. The projectile was long with fletching on the end, like an arrow.

Singh lurched forward and fell face-down. He stopped moving.

"Singh?" Bak said, his voice taut. "Do you read?"

The creature reappeared, looming over John Singh's body. It reached down, and lifted him by his head with one hand. The man's body dangled like a rag doll and his comm went dead. Then the enemy looked straight at the camera.

"Hello!" it said in Singh's voice, audible over the security feed. Then it tossed something at the camera and the feed cut out.

Das whimpered.

The rest of the crew were quiet for a long time. Finally, in a soft, trembling voice, Clarke said, "What now, Captain?"

Bak licked his dry lips. He still felt chills from hearing Singh's voice coming from that creature. Did that mean it could understand them? Its vessel was in their database. Someone had logged the warning to run. It stood to reason that some humans had encountered its kind before, and vice versa.

"We can take a stand on the bridge," Bak considered aloud. "Maybe overpower it together. That's the whole reason we're out here, isn't it? 'Stronger together'?"

"Maybe we surrender," Das said. "Like the computer said. 'Do not resist.'"

"Maybe *you* surrender," Hassan said. "We'll wait and see what happens."

"This isn't productive," Bak said.

"We can hide. No one knows the *Ketumati* better than we do," Clarke said.

"It can become *invisible*," Hassan said.

"What are our other options?" Bak asked.

"We have emergency escape vehicles. We should use them," Das said.

"You don't know about inertia, but you're familiar with the EEVs. Why am I not surprised?" Hassan locked eyes with Bak. "I'm going to engineering. If we can't get the *Ketumati* moving, it doesn't matter whether that thing kills us or we die in a life pod. We will have failed in our mission."

Bak nodded.

"If I can get to the interface room and access gAIa's mainframe directly, maybe I can talk some sense into her," Clarke said.

"I'll join you," Iwata said. "If it works, I can pilot the ship from there."

"Okay. Priority one is defending the ship and the fifteen hundred souls on ice in cryo-storage. I'll head down there. Right now they're more vulnerable than any of us."

Everyone looked at Das.

"Das, you head for the EEV," Bak said. "Someone should let the folks back home know what happened if we don't make it. If that thing finds you, hide. If you can't hide—fight."

"Then what?" Das asked.

"Survive. That's an order for everyone. And keep an open channel. Good luck."

"It just entered the hydroponics bay," Das whispered over the open channel.

"What does it want in hydroponics?" Clarke asked.

"I think it followed me."

"Well, what are *you* doing there? Trying to save your plants?"

"He's hiding," Hassan said.

"Which is what he's supposed to do." Bak resisted the urge to head to hydroponics to help Das. Instead, he picked up his pace. If the alien was in hydroponics, he needed to take advantage of the distraction and get to cryo-storage quickly while he could do so without being detected.

The channel went quiet.

"Das, do you read? What's your twenty?" Bak asked.

Das sobbed, whispering a prayer to himself in a low, trembling voice.

They heard the same *pop* as before and then glass shattered.

"Stop! Don't shoot! Please don't shoot!" Das called. "Look, I'm unarmed." Bak heard his weapon clatter to the floor. "I surrender."

Pop. Das cried out and they heard his body thump against the floor.

"Oh no," Clarke said softly.

Das's communicator went offline.

"Shit," Hassan muttered.

Bak cleared his throat. "No telling where it will go next. Watch out for yourselves. And for each other." He continued moving down the corridor.

By tacit agreement, the surviving command crew kept chatter to a minimum, to avoid drawing their enemy's attention.

Bak jumped when he heard a loud *pop* in his ear and pressed himself against a bulkhead, looking for the alien. Then he realized the sound had come from his earpiece.

"Clarke?" Iwata said. "Damn."

"What happened?" Bak asked. He could see cryo-storage from here. It sounded like the alien was still far away, near the computer's interface room. He ran and slapped the panel to open the cryo-storage doors.

"It got her." More shots from the alien. Iwata cursed and Bak heard returning laser fire. "Oh my god. It's huge." Then louder. "I give up! Don't—"

Bak listened to Iwata die as he waited impatiently for the cryo-storage doors to open. "I'm sorry," he said.

"Don't be sorry," Hassan spat. "Make it count. I just reached engineering. That thing must be close by, I heard Iwata's shouts without the comm. I'll try to get systems online while you... What *are* you going to do, Captain?"

Bak looked out at the rows of occupied hypersleep chambers stretching into the distance in the cavernous room. They looked like high-tech coffins in a 135-degree reclining position, their sides bejeweled with flashing status lights. Windows in the upper half emitted a soothing white glow that provided most of the illumination in the dimly lit space.

"I'll keep an eye on our passengers," Bak said.

"And how are they?"

"Sleeping like the dead."

"I kind of envy them," Hassan said.

"Why's that?"

"If we don't make it, they'll never know what hit them."

Wish I could crawl into my own chamber and go back to sleep, he thought. If he was lucky, he would find his way back to that beautiful dream with Amelia, without a care for whatever was happening on the ship.

At the very least he could see his wife in person, one last time. To say good-bye.

He followed gAIa's directions to locate Amelia's capsule among hundreds of identical capsules, identifiable only by a number linked to the computer's passenger manifest.

But when he got there, it was empty.

"Captain." Hassan spoke in his earpiece. Her voice was low and urgent.

Bak spun around in a panic, eyes searching the shadows of cryo-storage. Where was Amelia?

"Captain?" Hassan spoke again.

"Go ahead." He knelt down to peer under the rows of capsules.

"It's in here. Engineering," Hassan said.

"Shit," he said.

"This alien has found each of us, one after one, several times now. It's like it knows where we are."

Bak blinked, forcing himself back into this moment, remembering his rank and purpose here. "What are you suggesting? Is it tracking us with sensors?"

He heard the now familiar *pop* of the alien's weapon and a muffled hiss of air. "Hassan?"

"I turned out the lights in here." She lowered her voice so he could barely hear her. "Figured I would even the playing field, since I can't see it. But it can still see me. I'm thinking it has night-vision goggles or thermal imaging in its helmet. So if we can damage it—"

"We blind it. But that's a big if."

"It's all we've got."

Bak set his jaw. "I'm coming to you."

"Don't be stupid. Sir. You won't get back to me in time. And if this thing does rely on infrared vision, you're in the one place where it might not be able to find you."

Bak nodded. Cryo-storage was the coldest area of the ship. "Good point. But if you're ever going to follow one of my orders, don't forget my last one."

"Survive. Working on it, Captain."

Hassan went silent. Bak muted his comm and spoke to the computer. "Where is Amelia Hamilton, gAIa?" he said aloud.

The computer took a long time to respond. "Unknown."

"That's not good enough," he said. He hurried through the aisles, looking inside each capsule to see if she was there. Amelia could have ended up in a different hypersleep chamber than the one assigned.

Or had the brass discovered her and pulled her out just before takeoff, without him knowing? He couldn't be sure her chamber had still been occupied when they left Earth.

It wasn't long before he heard Hassan again: a string of angry curse words that was abruptly cut short.

Bak breathed in and out, feeling a mixture of sadness, anger, and fear. He hadn't known Hassan and the others long, but they had trained together. They had shared their belief in this mission and the hope for a brighter future that they would build with their own hands on a new world. And just like his hypersleep dream three days earlier, it was all slipping away.

Each of his crewmates' deaths had hit the captain hard, but there were many other lives hanging in the balance. He was surrounded by innocent people who were all counting on him. As much as he wanted to find Amelia, it was up to Bak to stop the alien—or die trying.

It was nearly three hours before the cryo-storage doors opened. Bak thought he saw a faint shimmer in the flashing emergency lights from the corridor and then the doors closed. Seemingly no one had entered, but the hairs on Bak's neck rose and his skin tingled with the sensation that he was being watched.

The alien was in there with him. He ducked down behind a hypersleep chamber in the center row and peeked down the narrow aisle to the entrance. The fact that it had taken the alien such a long time to find him gave credence to Hassan's theory that it was tracking them by body heat, although if it was simply scanning for life signs, the sleeping bodies around him also might have masked Bak's presence for a time. The alien might not even be certain Bak was in here.

He pressed himself closer to the chamber, feeling the cool metal against his skin. He was still the warmest body in this room.

Or was he? He noticed a strange whirling pattern at the far end of his corridor, a mist forming when cold air hit something warmer, and it was vaguely humanoid shaped.

Got you. Bak aimed his laser pistol at the center of the pattern. Then, remembering Hassan's idea, he aimed a little higher; the alien was about a foot and a half taller than Singh had been, judging by the security cameras. He pulled the trigger.

He heard a terrible scream and the creature reappeared as it tumbled backward, its cloak flickering out. Bak had scored a head shot, but not a killing one. A scorch mark on the alien's helmet smoldered just above the right eye, but it didn't seem injured. Only pissed.

This was the first he had seen the hunter up close and in living color. It was huge, towering well above Bak, its body lean and muscular. Its skin was yellowish brown and its dreadlocks were a dingy gray. It had plated forearms and shin guards and its scaly, reptilian body was covered only in tight netting. It swept the room with the short scoped rifle in its right hand.

With all its deadly gear, why had it been limiting itself to such an archaic weapon?

Maybe he should have aimed lower after all, Bak thought, noting the one wound the *Ketumati's* crew had managed to inflict: a gash in its side from Singh's laser pistol. Its armor was still stained with bright green blood. That was going to be his next target.

Bak rose to his feet and stood across from the alien. It aimed the old-style projectile weapon. He dove behind a hypersleep chamber and rolled under the entire row of them to emerge on the left side of the room. He hid behind another chamber, watching the hunter scan the room for him. It spotted him and its weapon fired. Bak ducked and he felt something whiff past his ear. It struck the metal bulkhead behind him and then clattered to the floor.

He turned and located a dent in the wall. *That was close.* He searched around him until he found a wicked looking metal dart the length of his hand, its barbed tip coated in a yellow substance. Poison?

It's doing this for sport, Bak realized. If it just wanted to kill them, it obviously had the technology and weaponry to do that much more quickly and efficiently. Hell, it could have simply fired on their unarmed, disabled ship and wiped them out.

The revelation only made Bak angrier, and more determined to survive. And if he couldn't survive, he was going to take the monster out with him, so the others at least would have a chance to make it.

Another *pop* and the capsule above Bak's head cracked. Coolant spewed from the broken glass around the embedded dart. He heard Hassan's voice echo around the room. *"They'll never know what hit them."*

A chill went through Bak that had nothing to do with the temperature. It had recorded his engineer's words and was taunting him with them. He tried to get eyes on the hunter again, but it was gone. No, not gone—cloaked again. And stalking toward him, based on the barely perceptible shimmering that caught the light from the cryotubes it passed between. The faint mist surrounding it like a wispy aura and the damaged capsule behind him gave Bak an idea on how to take the thing out, or perhaps slow it down a little.

"gAIa, reactivate hypersleep chambers Alpha-001 through 006," he whispered.

"Planning to take another nap, Captain?" gAIa responded.

"Trying to avoid the big sleep," he muttered. "Just do it."

"Working on it."

He crouch-ran over to the chambers he and his senior crew had recently vacated, certain the hunter would see him and pursue. He pretended to stumble and fall, then lay still in at the end of the row, just ten meters from the empty coffins.

"Now, gAIa," Bak muttered.

Through his eyelashes, Bak saw the hunter reappear and

advance cautiously toward him. It suspected a trap. Because this was one.

The hunter was in position, but the chambers were still dark. *Come on, gAIa. What are you waiting for?*

The chamber's lights flickered to life. The alien paused and studied them suspiciously. Bak bolted up and fired his laser blaster, but not at the hunter. Instead, he squeezed off two shots on either side of it, blowing open the hypersleep chambers flanking it. Coolant spewed all over the alien. White frost spread over the hunter's body, freezing it in place. He heard a *pop* and hissing air.

Bak felt a sharp pain in his chest. He looked down and saw a dart protruding from it, inches from his heart. He pulled it out with a scream; the barbed tip was dripped with a viscous mix of the yellow poison and his own blood. It slipped from his hands.

He stared at the hunter, trying to focus through blurring vision. His chest burned and a numbing sensation spread through his body. The ice covering his enemy was already melting—it must have some way of regulating the temperature of its armor.

Bak dropped to the floor, this time for real. As blackness crept over the edges of his vision, he saw someone run out from the shadows and someone calling his name.

Amelia.

———

Hyeon Bak and Amelia Hamilton stand in front of the Siberian tiger cage, searching the dark caves, trees, underbrush. No sign of the large wild cats. They had long been extinct, of course, pushed out and exterminated by people nearly a century ago.

But Seoul Grand Park had cloned them and this was the last place on the planet to see one alive—supposedly.

"Enjoying the honeymoon?" Bak asks Amelia.

"It's not what I always dreamed about." She looks around. "I thought it would involve more sex."

Bak grins. "Save it for Babylon."

Her cheerful expression fades.

"What?" he asks.

"Nothing." She turns away, rubbing the back of her neck.

"Don't do that." He touches her arm lightly. "Married two hours, and we're already keeping secrets from each other?"

She sighs. "You're right. It's just— I appreciate what you're doing for me, but I'm still not sure how I feel about it."

"I didn't marry you as some kind of charity case. I did it—*we* did it—for *us*. Right?"

She nods.

"And you belong on this mission. It's not your fault the higher-ups pitched a tantrum."

The United Americas had just completely pulled out of the InterUnited Space Agency. They were angry that they couldn't have more representation on the Babylon colony and that the IUSA had rejected their choice for the command crew. They claimed the Three World Empire and Union of Progressive People were trying to marginalize the Americas and claim more of the planet's valuable resources for their own nations' benefit.

Truth was, the UA hadn't played well with the other nations for a long time; they'd sat out the War for Korean Independence, leaving the 3WE to come to Korea's aid in fighting the UPP. The Americas weren't interested in being a team player anymore, but they still wanted to be on the team, and the Space Agency was doing everything it could to prevent them from owning a controlling interest in Babylon. Once the UA withdrew, they had unceremoniously dumped every American from their program—except those who were spouses of approved crew and colonists.

"I still think you should be our hydroponic specialist," Bak says. "You're more experienced than Kiann Das. Maybe when we're planetside..."

"So you're saying there are some benefits to sleeping with the captain." Amelia leans in close.

"Aside from the obvious. Yeah." He puts his arms around her shoulders and bends his head to kiss her.

"I hope no one else heard that. Could be bad for your career."

"Screw my career." He'd never wanted to be an officer, let alone captain. But when Korea Aerospace calls you to serve, you answer. And he hadn't been about to turn down a trip to a new world, and a new life with the woman he loves.

Amelia closes her eyes as their lips meet. It gives Bak an electric thrill, just like their first kiss. They'd met each other in interstellar training, and though they'd only known each other for a few months, he had no doubts about spending the rest of his life with her. Good thing, too, because it was a one-way trip to the Babylon colony.

Bak feels eyes watching them. He slowly pulls away from Amelia and looks at the cage from out of the corner of his eye. A tiger is watching them.

"She's beautiful," Amelia breathes.

"She's hungry," Bak says.

As Bak stirred to wakefulness, he felt even worse than he had when coming out of hypersleep. His head pounded, his lips were dry and stuck together, and his mouth was cottony and tasted like sour milk.

He opened his eyes. He was outside, lying in a patch of blue-green grass. He couldn't tell what time of day it was, but there was a sky, cloudless with a yellow tinge to it.

Babylon? How?

He sat up. Three people were huddled nearby, talking in low voices. They didn't notice he was awake, which gave him time to process what he was seeing.

John Singh, Anika Hassan, and Blodwen Clarke. They were alive.

Or he was dead.

"Am I still dreaming?" he muttered. Maybe everything back on the *Ketumati* had been the dream. The alien hunter who had come on board and slaughtered them all.

"Captain Bak!" Hassan leapt up and hurried over. "Are you all right?"

"Depends. Are we dead?"

"Negative, sir."

He drew in a breath. "But I heard you all die."

She shook her head. "Tranquilizers. The intruder hunted us and sedated us and brought us here."

"Why?" Bak asked. He looked around for signs of the rest of the colonists. This might not be the planet they'd intended to land on, but it seemed it could sustain them. "Why track us throughout the ship only to spare our lives?"

Clarke and Singh joined them. Singh held out a hand and pulled him up. Bak tested the strength of his legs, and the gravity. He felt lighter than he had on Earth and on the ship.

That would take some getting used to.

"Where are we?" he asked.

"This is an artificial environment. You can see the seams if you look hard enough, and the horizon is just a projection." Hassan pointed, and now that Bak looked again, knew what to look for, he could indeed see a faint grid pattern surrounding them, delineating the edges of an enclosed space. A cage.

The air was still and smelled nearly sterile. Despite the lush plant life surrounding them, the place didn't feel alive— more like being inside the *Ketumati*'s hydroponics bay. The lighting was flat and dull, and it didn't generate any warmth; it had to come from some hidden source above, not from a nearby sun.

"We aren't approaching anything like this technology on Earth," Hassan went on. "Whoever created this must be incredibly advanced."

"Did that alien create all this for us? Why? Have you seen it since we got here?"

"It isn't very chatty," Clarke said. "It doesn't speak English, but it seems to understand us. It communicates through recordings. I think it calls itself 'Keeper.' It kept playing that word and pointing to itself."

"So it's… peaceful?" Bak said.

Singh snorted. "When it pointed at us, it played the word 'trophy.' We're prisoners, Captain. Whether Keeper killed us on the ship or lets us die a slow death here, it's all the same."

Clarke frowned. "I'd still rather live as long as I can."

"You may change your mind when we find out what it plans to do with us. Hunter trophies are usually dead."

"What about Das?" Bak asked. "Iwata?"

They shook their heads.

"Why choose us and leave them behind? Because they didn't fight back?" Bak wondered.

"So then what? It only wanted us because we were harder to capture?" Hassan said.

Bak shrugged. "And the colonists?"

"Still on the ship as far as we know," Clarke said quietly.

Bak cursed. "It could have saved them too!"

"I wouldn't describe us as 'saved,'" Hassan said. "We don't know what Keeper wants with us. Are we food? Entertainment? It seems to have collected a variety of different lifeforms here, in adjoining... cells."

"And some of them are pretty nasty," Singh said.

"Where is Keeper now?" Bak asked.

"An alarm sounded and it left in a hurry, maybe half an hour ago."

"That could be good for us, if it's distracted," Bak said. "We need to figure out how to escape. Keeper has a ship—maybe we can steal it and get back to the *Ketumati*."

"There's one more thing," Clarke said.

"Of course there is. What?"

"Amelia's here. Though I don't know how."

Bak clenched his hands into fists. So he hadn't imagined seeing her back in cryo-storage, attacking Keeper just before he lost consciousness. And apparently she'd been deemed worthy enough to join them as part of the alien's collection.

"Where is she?"

Hassan jerked her head in a direction. "Over there, on the edge of the cell just past that rock outcrop. She's been studying something in the next cage over."

Bak found his wife standing at a strange demarcation in the terrain: the grassy plains ended in a straight line and on the other side was a barren desert. From the middle of the rocky wasteland rose something Bak had never seen before: a glistening, gray mound covered in whorls and patterns with large dark holes marring its surface. It reminded him of the giant hornet nest he had discovered in his backyard as a kid.

"Hello, love," Amelia greeted him when he approached. "See that?" She pointed into the shadows of one of the entrances but he didn't know what he was supposed to be looking for. He turned to face his wife.

"All I see is a traitor," Bak said.

She sighed. "I have my reasons."

Bak closed his eyes. He'd hoped he was wrong, that she would laugh it off and say, "What are you talking about?"

"I'd love to hear why you sabotaged our ship." He shook his head. "Was it always the plan, or is this some kind of revenge for leaving United Americas on the sidelines?"

She turned to him. "I was supposed to make sure the mission failed and prevent the *Ketumati* from reaching Babylon—so the UA could get there first with their own colony ship." She turned and squinted back at the nearby nest. Bak reached out and his fingertips met resistance: a force field, keeping the two environments, and their occupants, separate. He was relieved. He didn't know why, but whatever was on the other side of the barrier filled him with dread. Or maybe he was just transferring the unease and betrayal he felt from Amelia to what was probably nothing.

"Even if it meant killing yourself along with the rest of us."

"'We all have a role to play.' You were always saying that in training. Always trying to be the peacekeeper, the voice of reason."

"You got close to me because I was the *Ketumati*'s captain. And then when you were barred from the mission, you used me—our marriage—to get aboard anyway."

He waited, expecting her to tell him that it wasn't *just* that. She truly had feelings for him, or she'd come to love him. She regretted what she'd done, had almost changed her mind. He wouldn't have believed her, but he wanted to hear it anyway.

"That's right," she said. "It was just business, dear. Nothing personal."

Nothing personal. That's how she had summed up their relationship, their marriage. He wondered how long she would have carried out the deception if the ship had made it to the colony. Would they have raised children together, and then one day, she would have just disappeared? Or he would have?

The ground shuddered beneath him and he heard the muffled sound of an explosion somewhere in the distance. The gravity shifted for a stomach-dropping moment and something changed in the air. He smelled something pungent and dusty. *Now what?*

"Captain!" Hassan appeared not far off, flanked by Singh and Clarke.

He held up a hand, warning them off. He needed another minute.

"But why?" Bak asked. "Once you left Earth, you didn't owe the UA anything."

She pressed her lips together. "I'm a patriot. But I may have found something even more valuable than the mining opportunities on Babylon." She nodded at the ominous structure across from them, which looked like a blemish on the landscape. "If that's what I think it is, there are people back home who'll send a ship to get me, if they could bring it back as a souvenir."

Bak shook his head. "I still don't see—"

Clarke screamed. At that moment, something leapt out of the sand on the other side of the barrier and flew toward them. It latched onto Amelia's face. She went down. Bak stared at it, trying to understand what was happening.

The creature was pale, segmented, with eight legs and a long tail, like a cross between a spider and scorpion. Amelia struggled, pulling at it with white knuckled fingers, while the tail wrapped firmly around her throat.

The barrier—how did it get past it? Bak reached out, but the forcefield was gone. He saw a large, dark shape unfurl itself in the shadows at the entrance of the cave. Something large, humanoid, with a bulbous head that was shiny like a beetle carapace and a long, segmented tail. It had been watching them. Other, smaller shapes scuttled in the sand toward him.

He backpedaled quickly. Then he turned to see Hassan and the others running to help Amelia.

"No! There's more of them. Go!" He ran toward them. They hesitated.

"Weapons?" he asked.

Singh shook his head grimly.

"What's happening?" Hassan asked.

"I don't know. Those creatures are attacking us and something shut down the forcefields," Bak shouted.

He looked over their shoulders and saw Keeper.

No, this was a different one of its kind: taller, leaner, more muscular. It had shorter, darker dreads. And it wasn't wearing a mask, revealing a grotesque, pinched face with a gaping maw, beady eyes, and four mandibles.

It stared at him and then tossed something which landed, bounced, and rolled in the grass toward them.

"Holy shit," Hassan said.

It was Keeper's head and spine—Bak noticed the burn mark his laser pistol had left on its mask.

"Why would they kill their own?" Clarke asked.

Bak thought about humanity's history of war and how Earth and its colonies were balanced on a knife-edge between peace and war. It often seemed to stem from the same conflict: a fundamental difference in beliefs. Why should Keeper and its people be any different?

Bak watched Amelia, lying still on the ground, the thing on her face pulsing like it was breathing with her.

"Maybe Keeper was a traitor," Bak said.

"What do you mean?" Clarke asked.

"They're clearly hunters. Killers. *We* should be dead, but we're not." He gestured at Keeper's head. "I don't think it was supposed to keep its trophies alive."

"What's *that*?" Singh asked.

Bak followed his gaze. The other alien, a massive, nightmare creature, was slinking its way toward them.

"That is the reason why dangerous game shouldn't be kept in a zoo."

"Captain," Clarke said in a trembling voice. "What do we do?"

The two aliens weren't interested in the humans—for now. On Bak's left, the hunter that had killed Keeper charged the plasma cannon on its shoulder, clicking angrily, mandibles flaring. On his right, the dark monster whipped its tail back and forth and unleashed a soul-rending screech, mouth wide open to reveal sharp teeth. The two titans advanced toward each other.

Bak and his crew were caught between them. The humans would either be killed in the impending battle, or they would have to deal with the victor, which would surely be the deadliest of the combatants. If he had a choice, which would he choose to face?

Neither.

"This is our chance to escape, while they're fighting each other," Bak said. "Run!"

They ran. Bak led Clarke, Hassan, and Singh in the direction from which the hunter had arrived, hoping to find an exit from their cage.

Clarke stumbled. Bak stopped to help her up, glanced behind him. The monster and the hunter were grappling with each other. The hunter twisted and hurled the monster over its shoulder. It landed on its feet and dashed forward again, only to be blasted by the hunter's plasma cannon. But the creature's endoskeleton seemed to protect it from the energy weapon and it kept coming, gnashing its teeth and spitting yellow goo at the hunter.

The hunter went down, clawing at its face which smoked from contact with the acidic venom. And then the monster was on it. It straddled the hunter and clutched it in its claws—opened its mouth and a probe darted out, piercing the hunter's skull.

When the hunter's death spasms ended, the monster dropped its limp body.

Then the creature looked at Bak and gnashed two horrific pairs of teeth.

Bak yanked Clarke to her feet and pulled her along with him. Two more hunters ran past the humans, firing plasma canons at the monster as they closed in on it. How many of them were there?

The monster shrank back on all fours, its head swiveling to look at each of them. And behind it, more black nightmares moved in the shadows, emerging from openings in the massive nest. Two, four, seven... a whole swarm. They shrieked and the air vibrated with terror.

The humans didn't stop running until they stumbled out of the Earthlike environment and found themselves in a long, dim passageway. Its smooth gray walls had been carved from solid rock.

"Where are we?" he asked.

"Subterranean caverns?" Singh mused. Sounds from the battle reverberated all around. "I can't tell if we're beneath a planet, inside a moon, or on a space station."

"Whatever it is, we got in, so there has to be a way out. And there have to be a couple of ships somewhere," Bak said. "We don't stop until we find it and get out of here or..." He left it at that, picked a direction, and they kept moving, urged on by the screams and blasts echoing behind them.

And ahead of them: a pack of four animals that resembled small dinosaurs. Bak held up a hand to halt his team. The lizards' heads swiveled toward them and the two groups considered each other.

The lizards backed up slowly, then turned tail and bolted away. Bak breathed a sigh of relief. Thank goodness not everything down here meant them harm.

"Other trophies?" Singh asked.

"Who knows what Keeper brought back here," Hassan said.

"We shouldn't leave them here," Clarke said.

"We don't even know if we can save ourselves," Bak said. He couldn't even save Amelia. But she'd been beyond saving, once she had made the decision to strand everyone on the ship.

"The more living things there are between us and whoever wins the fight back there, the better," Hassan said.

"Assuming something else just as nasty or worse wasn't freed from its cell too," Singh said.

"All the more reason to keep moving," Bak said.

They pressed on. The sounds of the battle grew more distant, but they kept jumping at sounds and shadows. They passed other doors to cages and entrances to tunnels splitting off to the side, but they stuck to what Bak considered the main passage. It gradually sloped upward, which seemed encouraging.

"I see something! It looks like a shuttle bay!" Clarke started running.

"Clarke! Wait!" Bak called. He and the others ran after her. She was right—the corridor was widening and brightening, and at the end of it: two ships. One of them he recognized as Keeper's, the one that had brought them there. The second was blue with one central rear thruster, four massive cannons, and an alien glyph adorning the front.

"Anyone know how to pilot an alien vessel?" Bak asked.

Hassan put her hands on her hips. "I'm no substitute for Iwata, but one of the many reasons I'm a great chief engineer is not only do I know how to keep a spaceship functioning,

I also know how to operate it. Give me a few minutes to study the controls and I'll get us out of here."

She marched up the gangway of Keeper's ship and disappeared inside. Bak grinned and followed.

Once they recovered the *Kenumati* and restored its systems, they would make the call together: to continue on to Babylon or return home with the sleeping colonists. It had been a mistake to split up on the ship—and he was beginning to wonder if Earth should be spreading out among the stars, leaving small groups of people to face the unknown horrors of space and ultimately die alone.

All things considered, Bak didn't even know if he wanted to be off-world anymore. At least they were familiar with the problems on Earth. At least the enemies there were other humans, and they fought over territory or ideologies, rather than being hunted for sport or killed by savage aliens.

Amelia may have shaken his trust, but Bak believed more than ever that humanity was stronger together. He only hoped her self-imposed fate and the senseless deaths of Iwata and Das would make the UA finally see that too.

ANOTHER MOTHER

BY SCOTT SIGLER

Miriam coughed up blood.

She didn't know if it came from her throat, which had been caught in the noose, or from her lungs.

Every breath brought pain.

She tried to sit up. She could not. Hands and feet bound behind her, she lay on her belly on the forest floor.

When would they release the spider?

Despite her agony, Miriam remembered the training. She turned her head, awkwardly bit a caminus leaf from the branches threaded through her hidey suit. She chewed. It hurt to swallow, but she did it anyway, then bit off another leaf.

Death was coming, but at least she would not become a demon.

How had the demon found them? Miriam had stayed so still, made no sound.

The forest around her had fallen into total silence. No cries of the vindeedee, no croaks from the humped gish, no snorfling sounds from a digging vootervert. Animals knew when to stay quiet, when to stay hidden.

Miriam wished she'd stayed hidden.

When the demons had returned, General Cooper set out to find them and destroy them. Wipe them out, no matter the cost.

That cost? Lives. Rowan's life. Aaron's life.

Miriam's life.

The lightest of thumps, just ahead of her.

She craned her head to look, waited to see the gnarled black body, the backsticks, the toothtongue, but there was no demon.

Just the forest... and a patch of it that shimmered.

A patch in the shape of a tall man...

———

Black curls puffed from the top of the cart's smokestack. Wind rattled the leaves of Ahiliyah Cooper's hidey suit. She prayed to the gods as she held on for dear life.

Creen's contraptions didn't blow up often—not anymore, anyway—but at times, they still did.

She would have rather run, like the old days, but her foot had never healed correctly from wounds inflicted by the Demon Mother. Birthing four children hadn't helped, either.

"Bump coming," Creen said, shouting to be heard over this hiss of steam, turning of gears, and the rattle of iron-bound wooden wheels on hard-packed dirt.

Ahiliyah gripped the wooden handholds. The cart jarred hard enough to rattle her teeth.

Even if she'd been uninjured and in her prime, Creen's invention was more than twice as fast as Ataegina's fastest runners. And while the cart had to periodically be fed wood and water, it never got tired. He was working on a larger version, big enough to carry sixteen spearmyn, with shields, armor, and a week's supplies. When Creen finished it, Ahiliyah would be able to outmaneuver the next Northern invasion with ease.

Soot from the cart's boiler streaked Creen's face, adding deeper lines to his horrific scars. Ahiliyah had known him so long that she often forgot about his scarred face, so bad were they that most people steered clear of him. Creen normally stayed in his labs in Lemeth Hold, but for this search, for these past two weeks, Liyah had needed his mind.

She'd asked. He'd accepted.

Another jaw-jarring bump.

"Riding in this thing is like getting kicked every ten seconds," Ahiliyah said. "How much farther?"

Her hands were starting to hurt from holding on so tight.

"We're close," Creen said. "Or as close as this excuse for a road will get us."

Thousands of people had spent years building this *excuse* of a road, leveling the land where the soil allowed, chipping out paths through the rock where it did not. Roads made it far easier to travel from hold to hold, and over the past decade had increased the efficiency of trade so thoroughly that shortages seemed a thing of the past.

A past that would soon return if she didn't find the new Demon Mother.

The return of the demons had driven a dagger of fear through the collective heart of Ataegina. People were afraid to stay in the fields for the fall harvest. Without that harvest, the Western Holds would be reliant upon crops produced by the holds in the north and east. The hand-pulled carts transporting that food would also be a risk. They'd have to form large caravans, and Ahiliyah estimated a caravan would require at least five modules of spearmyn, enough to form the circular phalanx needed to defend against demon horde attacks.

Five modules meant two hundred and forty spearmyn, for *each shipment*.

More hands out of the fields and rivers, away from the forges and factories.

In the two decades since Brandun had killed the Demon Mother, Ataegina's population had more than doubled. Ahiliyah was not about to let that growth slow.

She'd committed thousands of troops to this search. Creen and Ahiliyah had devised a method to search large chunks of land, then deploy modules along that area's perimeter, slowly narrowing the area where the nest could be.

Eighty-two people had been lost so far, mostly from Pendaran, Hibernia, and Jantal. Everything north of the Pendaran peninsula had been eliminated. Somewhere on that peninsula, either in the small Pendaran mountains or out on the fertile plains, lay a nightmare—the enemy of Ataegina.

The longer it took her to find the lair, the more demons she would have to face when the showdown finally came. Ahiliyah was going to find the new Demon Mother, kill her offspring, and send her back to whatever hell she'd come from.

Today's victims, the ones Ahiliyah and Creen were rushing to see, hadn't been farmers, loggers, or fishermen—they'd been runners. A whole crew. Two missing, one dead, his body reportedly mutilated beyond recognition.

"Up ahead," Creen said.

At the edge of the rutted road, a beacon of hope—a spearmyn module formed into a tight dome bristling with spears. Thanks to shields covered with netting that was stuffed thick with caminus branches, the dome almost looked like a crimson bush.

Creen pulled back a lever. The cart started to slow. He twisted a knob; a hissing jet of steam shot out from the big boiler.

Ahiliyah thought of the runner mantras, one in particular that had saved her more times than she could count: *silence is strength*. This rattling, whistling metal-and-wood cart was anything but silent. Such noise might draw demons, but she and Creen were behind the search line—fast communication between the divisions was worth the risk.

The cart stopped. In one smooth motion, Ahiliyah stepped out onto the road, unslung her bow, drew an arrow from her quiver, and nocked it. The arrowhead was already slimed with poison, the same poison that had delivered people decades ago.

A familiar voice, one near and dear to her heart, bellowed out from the shield formation. The spearmyn dome quickly flowed into four marching ranks—two columns of twelve, to the right and left, holding shields and long spears. Inside of them, two columns of twelve holding either bows or crossbows. A tall man led them, his shield held against his chest, the eye slit of his helmeted head peeking over the shield's top.

Each spearmyn wore a hidey suit, just like the ones Ahiliyah and Creen wore. Hard armor beneath offered some defense against claws, tails, and toothtongues, but only the caminus leaves woven into the netting could protect against burning blood.

Creen fished a hand inside his hidey suit, pulled out the toothtongue he always wore, let it drop against the netting and caminus leaves. He wanted people to see it. He always did. His toothtongue was larger than the three Ahiliyah wore combined, larger than any other on Ataegina. One of a kind— or least it had been until the new demon rising.

"Hail, General Cooper. Hail, Uncle Creen," the module leader said.

Even through the helmet's narrow slits, she saw the boy's eyes, eyes that looked so much like those of Tolio, her husband.

The boy. Only in her heart. Her son was weeks away from turning eighteen. Still growing. While nowhere near the size of his namesake, he cut an imposing figure.

"Hail, Brandun," Ahiliyah said. "Let's make good time, I want to be away from here before night falls."

———

Brandun's module formed a perimeter circle around the corpse.

Ahiliyah, Creen, and Susanna Albrecht, Lemeth Hold's senior runner, stood in the center of the circle. At their feet, Rowan Winden—a ragged nightmare of blood, ripped meat, and broken bone. His leaf-strewn hidey suit had been cut from head to back. His spine had been ripped from his body.

No sign of the spine. Or the head that might still be attached to it.

Even in the worst of the demon fighting, Ahiliyah had never seen the like.

"He was one of my best," Susannah said. "Not strong, but he could run for days, and he was so smart about staying quiet, staying hidden. I can't imagine him making a mistake that would have let a demon find him. But here he is."

The twigs and crimson leaves woven through the netting of Susannah's hidey suit left only her face visible. The hollowness in her eyes—when those in your command die, it is *always* your fault.

Ahiliyah put her left fist against her hidey-suit-covered breastplate.

"He will be missed," she said, because that was what one was supposed to say in times like these. "Any sign of his crewmates?"

"I found Aaron's footprints," Susannah said. "And blood. No one loses that much blood and survives. Another blood trail has to be from Miriam, but I couldn't follow it"—she pointed up, into the forest's sparse canopy—"because it went there."

Creen's scarred face wrinkled in doubt.

"The demons are using the trees? That's new."

Susannah pointed again, this time to a spearhead lying near Rowan's body.

"Demons have burning blood," she said. "Not *that*."

On the tip of Rowan's forearm-length spearhead, a smear of green. *Glowing* green. Ahiliyah had seen demon blood more times than she could count—it was yellow, and dissolved everything other than caminus leaves.

Spearmyn used the long spear, while runners used the short. The butt-spike, two halfstaffs, and the coupler were carried in a holster attached to the runner's pack. The spearhead doubled as a short sword. Runners carried spearheads in a back scabbard, so they still had a weapon if they had to shed the pack for speed.

Creen moved to the spearhead, his huge toothtongue catching the sun filtering through the canopy.

"No acid scoring on the blade," he said. "This blood isn't from a demon."

Memories flared—the ruined ship, Zachariah, the final battle against the Demon Mother.

"If a demon didn't kill Rowan," Ahiliyah said, "what did?"

Creen looked up, his scarred face smiling, eyes blazing with intensity.

"Something new," he said.

He was excited. Two runners missing, one mangled beyond recognition, and Creen was *excited*.

Ahiliyah reached into her hidey suit and pulled out the battered, rolled-up map she and Creen had been using to mark the slowly constricting search pattern.

"If a demon didn't do this," she said, "then I need to know what did. Creen, you have fifteen minutes to get whatever you can from Rowan's body. We need to get back to the cart and spread the word to the other divisions so they can pull their runners back until we know more."

Yeh'kull paused.

It wasn't possible.

She retracted her plasmacaster. She'd been moments from turning on her targeting laser and taking out the human that was clearly the leader, the one holding a nocked bow and standing by the game Yeh'kull had killed earlier.

Yeh'kull wasn't supposed to take trophies at all, but her time on this planet was almost up. The elders would soon arrive, and signal her to bring her scout craft up to the mothership. That day, possibly, the next at the latest, and her time on this planet would be done forever.

She'd been sent to study this continent, to evaluate it as a potential hunting ground. An isolated planet, so primitive when compared to other human worlds. The people here seemed to have no beam weapons, no explosives, no firearms of any kind. They were even less advanced than those on their homeworld had been thousands of years ago, when Yeh'kull's ancestors had been among the Yautja, had been worshiped as gods.

On this planet, humans were equipped only with spears, knives, shields, and armor, all made from a surprisingly decent variant of steel, along with hand-drawn bows and powerful crossbows.

She wasn't supposed to hunt. Her brothers were dead. She was the last of her line. The clan elders constantly sheltered her, protected her. Yeh'kull hated it. She'd never asked for safety—in fact, she'd asked over and over to join real hunts, to risk her life in pursuit of honor just as her brothers had done. She longed to be blooded, an equal in her clan. The elders refused to grant her request, instead saying she had important work to do as an ecologist, sending her on soft missions to survey worlds looking for dangerous fauna that might be suitable for game.

Game she wasn't supposed to hunt herself.

On this, her third such ecological survey, Yeh'kull had come to the conclusion that the elders already knew a significant amount about the planets they sent her to, already knew there wasn't anything she couldn't handle with ease. They knew they were sending her to planets that presented no real danger, no real challenge.

She did her duty, even though she hated it.

No, she wasn't supposed to hunt, at all, but didn't she deserve a souvenir? No one would begrudge her a few human trophies, taken just as her time here expired. With the surprising absence of large fauna here, humans were the biggest game animal she'd yet see.

She'd stalked the scouting party. One of them had fought well. Faster than Yeh'kull had expected, the male had cut her. She'd cached his spine and skull to take with her when the elders came. She'd killed a second scout, but took the third captive.

Part of Yeh'kull's role as ecologist was to learn what she could of local dialects and add that information to the translator's algorithm. The humans here had a previously unknown dialect, one that gave her translator program no end of trouble. That could happen when a human population grew in isolation for a long time, and as yet Yeh'kull had no idea how long these primitive people had been on this world. She had tried to learn what she could from the captive, but the captive had proven weak and useless. Crying, stammering, the captive had repeated one word over and over again—*dee-mon*.

In other human cultures, that was often a word for *ghost*, or *monster*. Considering how primitive this place was, it wasn't surprising that the humans here embraced religious superstition. The scout had thought Yeh'kull was a monster? From the scout's perspective, perhaps that was accurate.

The captive had bled out before Yeh'kull could make further progress, giving her three trophies to take from him. But they'd been so *easy* to collect. Despite the wound, she'd never been in real danger. She'd craved a bigger challenge, one that brought more honor—a challenge like killing a leader and then evading the ninety-six soldiers that had gathered to investigate Yeh'kull's kill.

The female human leader wore the same thick camouflage suit the scouts wore, but there was no mistaking her bearing, nor the way the foot soldiers reacted to her.

Yeh'kull had been so close to shooting the leader, until sunlight had caught the trophy hanging from the little male's neck. A trophy that Yeh'kull could only dream of—the pharyngeal jaw of a Kiande Amedha queen.

It *wasn't possible*.

Dozens of three-human scout patrols in this area. Heavy infantry units backed them up, providing a line behind which the scouts could retreat and rest. Yeh'kull had known the scouts were looking for something specific. She'd assumed it was a rival tribe, or perhaps an invading force.

Dee-mon.

Now Yeh'kull knew what that word meant. It wasn't about her, it was this culture's word for the Kiande Amedha. Yeh'kull now understood why the scouts and the infantry were working together to cover such a large area—they were searching for a nest.

If the elders had known Kiande Amedha were here, they would never have sent Yeh'kull. They would have sent unblooded, to *hunt*, to become *blooded*.

A once-in-a-lifetime chance, a nest, and in it the ultimate prize—a queen. If Yeh'kull made a trophy of her, the elders could never again hold her back, never shelter her from the hunt, from true honor. Yeh'kull would be blooded. She would be an equal, able to choose her own destiny.

The female leader… was she marking a map? A map of the search area?

That would save time, and time wasn't something Yeh'kull had.

A shifting wind washed the boiler smoke into Ahiliyah's face. She hid her mouth and nose in the crook of her arm; her body smelled far worse than the smoke. She'd been managing the search firsthand, hadn't bathed in days.

"Creen, make it go faster," she said, coughing. "It's getting dark."

"No shit, genius."

Creen squinted against the smoke, wiped an eye with the back of his hand. Soot lined the scars on his face.

They were well behind the search line, but both of them had lived through nights alone, out in the open, and neither of them wanted to experience that ever again, no matter how safe things might seem.

"Whatever killed Rowan isn't from here," Creen said, peering through the smoke made by his own invention. "You know that, right?"

Not from here—not from Ataegina.

Most Ataeginians didn't believe Creen's claim that the demons weren't some mystical force of evil, but instead were creatures from another world, carried here by an ancient ship that could fly to the stars. Hundreds, if not thousands, of people had made the trek to Black Smoke Mountain to see the strange shipwreck, yet most of those people believed it wasn't a ship at all, but rather an ancient temple built by followers of some dark religion, a religion hellbent on conjuring demons to destroy Ataegina. Creen's arguments to the contrary fell on deaf ears. How could people believe in beings from another world when most of them didn't even understand the concept of what a "world" was in the first place? Ahiliyah barely understood it herself.

"We have to be careful about this," she said. "Relations with Biseth Hold are already strained, and—"

The cart rocked hard to the left. Ahiliyah grabbed at the wooden frame, trying to adjust, but when the cart rocked back to the right she felt a hard pull at her chest—she flew through the air.

She hit hard, tumbling across the hard-packed road.

Creen's scream, high-pitched and raw.

Ahiliyah scrambled to her hands and knees. Everything spun. She stood, almost fell when her wobbly legs buckled. Her head howled in pain.

The cart had come to a stop. Creen was still inside. No… not inside… he was *above* it. Floating? He grabbed at his throat, hands digging at nothing. Something there, in the smoke, something see-through, like warped glass.

A sparkle, a wash of little flashes.

A huge, helmeted warrior standing in the cart, left arm raised high, hand wrapped around Creen's throat. Clumps of black hair hung from beneath the strange, smooth helmet to rest on wide shoulders.

The warrior was *big*, bigger than any person Ahiliyah had ever seen, as tall as a demon but thicker, far more muscular. Dull armor on its arms and shoulders. It wore a hidey suit of sorts, but the rope was thin and clung tight to its body, more like a net to catch big fish than to hold foliage, and there was no foliage in it at all.

The sound of metal ringing out—two long, jagged, parallel blades extended from a harness on the warrior's left forearm.

With the smooth motion that she'd practiced ten thousand times, Ahiliyah unslung her bow and reached back for an arrow.

Something popped up from the huge warrior's shoulder, turned, pointed at Ahiliyah. The odd motion made her pause. Strange red lights came from the warrior's helmet, lit up the road dust between it and her—something on her chest gleamed, scattering the light.

Ahiliyah looked down, saw a triangle of three red dots playing across her chest. The hidey suit had torn there, netting ripped when the invisible warrior had grabbed her, partially exposing the three toothtongues hanging from her neck. Where the dots of light hit the toothtongues, the clear, rigid demon trophies glowed blood-red.

She looked at the warrior. Eyes hidden behind the helmet, it seemed to stare at the trophies of the demons Ahiliyah had killed in battle.

The thing on the warrior's shoulder twisted to the side. Ahiliyah jumped when a burst of bright light erupted from it—the burst hit a tree, blowing the trunk into a thousand splinters.

The thing on its shoulder pivoted, pointed straight at Ahiliyah.

The red lights moved from her chest to the bow in her hand.

Ahiliyah understood—she tossed the bow aside, shrugged off the quiver and dropped it as well.

The red beams blinked out.

The warrior lowered its arm, set Creen down on the road next to the steam cart.

Humiliating.

These primitive game animals had trophies, trophies that Yeh'kull did not.

The humans were on their knees beneath a tree. Yeh'kull had taken them into the woods. She didn't need a random platoon of heavy infantry coming down the road to complicate things.

She could have crushed these humans with little more than a backhand. Honor would not let her. The little male wore the pharyngeal jaws of a queen. The female leader wore *three* pharyngeal jaws taken from Kiande Amedha soldier-caste.

How had they done it?

They'd driven a steam-powered vehicle. *Steam*. Here, that had to be the pinnacle of technology. Small and weak, with no advanced weapons, these two had somehow killed Kiande Amedha. The humans would have more standing in Yeh'kull's tribe than she did.

How was a question that could come later. The elders would soon arrive. If Yeh'kull was to seize this opportunity, there was one question she needed an answer to *now*.

"*Dee-mon*," she said again, and again pointed to the trophies hanging from the humans' necks, again swept her hand toward the plains to the southwest.

"His voice sounds like a talking fart," the male said. "And he keeps repeating that. What the fuck does it want?"

Yeh'kull's translator program could make out only a few of the male's words. She wished she'd spent more time listening to the humans here, silently studying their dialect as she'd been ordered to do, but it was too late for that now. She paid close attention to his words, thought about them in context, trying to learn as she went.

While the male queen-killer trembled in terror, the female showed no fear.

"I have no idea," it said. "If this warrior killed Aaron, Rowan, and Miriam, why are we still alive?"

"I don't know," the male said. "He must want something from us. Maybe he wanted something from Rowan, too, but Rowan couldn't deliver. We better figure out what he wants, and fast."

Yeh'kull grew frustrated. She'd broken the rules by revealing herself. She'd *had* to—if the elders came and she didn't already have her Kiande Amedha prize, the hunt would go to un-blooded males.

"His armor is so strange," the female said. "Could he be a Northerner?"

The little male looked at the female with an expression that translated into all languages.

"It's not a cocksucking *Northerner*, Liyah. It's from another world."

Yeh'kull's frustration intensified. The humans had dozens of scouts in the field, supported by over a thousand heavy infantry. A definitive search pattern. They had tactical knowledge that Yeh'kull needed. They didn't understand an obvious question, from one hunter to another?

Yeh'kull stepped closer. The male flinched, ducked. The female stared up, defiant, as Yeh'kull reached into the female's camouflage suit, fished around until she felt the paper, pulled it free and dropped it on the ground.

"*Dee-mon.*" Yeh'kull again pointed to the pharyngeal jaws. The female blinked. The defiant look faded.

Its hand went to its necklace of dried jaws. "Creen, I think he wants a toothtongue."

Toothtongue. This dialect's word for trophies?

"*Toooth… tong*," Yeh'kull said, doing her best to imitate the sounds.

The little male stopped shaking. "Rowan didn't have one. None of the runners do. Maybe the warrior asked Rowan for one, and when Rowan couldn't deliver, that was it. If wants a toothtongue, Liyah, *give* him one."

The female hooked a thumb under its necklace, started to lift it.

This game animal was going to *give* the trophy to Yeh'kull?

Humiliation compounded beyond measure.

Yeh'kull roared, roared far too loud, loud enough to draw other humans, but she didn't care.

The little male started trembling again, then stopped. It looked at the map.

"The warrior wants a toothtongue, but it wants to do the killing itself," it said. "The map, Liyah—he wants us to tell it where to hunt."

———

It was getting dark.

Ahiliyah and Creen were on their knees, the huge warrior towering over them, looking down over their shoulders at the map rolled out at the side of the road. Small stones weighed down the corners.

Had this warrior taken Miriam, or had demons done that? Ahiliyah couldn't be sure, not yet. Had the warrior killed Aaron? Had it killed Rowan, mangled his body? That seemed likely, but if so, what had it done with Rowan's spine and head?

The warrior had killed her people, but the warrior's weapons...

The warped glass camouflage, the parallel blades on its wrist, the strange shoulder bow that threw lightning... how many demons could the warrior kill? Enough to get to the Demon Mother? Could it kill the Demon Mother herself?

If so, if Ahiliyah could find a way to help make that happen, then the deaths of Rowan, Aaron, and Miriam wouldn't be for naught. In a roundabout way, those three runners would be responsible for ending the demon uprising, just as Ahiliyah, Creen, and Brandun had been responsible for ending the last one, two decades ago.

Ahiliyah had led thousands into battle. Since taking over command of Ataegina's unified forces, she'd fought four wars—one against the demons, three against the Northerners. She'd won them all, but in war, no victory came without losing soldiers.

She couldn't bring Rowan and the others back. She could, hopefully, find a way to ensure their deaths *mattered*.

She studied the map. The quest to find the new demon lair had been the biggest spearmyn mobilization since the last Northerner invasion. Fifteen divisions, each with five modules, backing up over a hundred runners who were risking their lives every moment they searched the woods, plains, and mountains.

"We've cleared all of this," Ahiliyah said, sweeping her hand in an arc that covered Black Smoke Mountain, the Nine River Delta, Hibernia, Jantal, and everything north and west of those places. "No demon. Here is where our divisions are placed to hem them in."

Hundreds of scrawled Xs marked the previous positions

of the divisions. Initially spread out, the Xs had drawn closer together as the search area tightened, and now lined the base of the Pendaran peninsula.

"She's going to kill us," Creen said. "Once she has what she wants, she'll rip our spines out of our bodies."

"*She*?" Ahiliyah glanced at the huge warrior. "What makes you think it's a woman?"

Even under the threat of a horrible death, Creen found a way to sound annoyed that everyone in existence was dumber than he was, that their collective stupidity tried his patience.

"I take it you didn't notice the odd, less-than-protective design of her chest plate," he said. "She's got *boob armor*, Liyah. No protection for her vital organs, but those boobies are safe and sound."

Liyah saw it then, knew she couldn't *un*-see it. Creen was right. Some of Ataegina's women soldiers—the ones that needed it, anyway—wore armor that made room for breasts. Liyah's own chest plate had been modified for that purpose. The odd thing, though, was the big warrior's armor left her midriff completely exposed, protected only by the thin netting of her strange hidey suit.

Could that be some statement of bravery? Or possibly some religious dictate, in that she had to cover certain body parts, as did the women in Takanta, Biseth, and other holds?

"She'll *mutilate* us, Liyah," Creen said. "We're dead meat." Maybe the warrior would kill them. There was no way to know. And yet, that didn't feel accurate. It didn't feel *right*.

Ahiliyah thought of Rowan's spearhead, lying on the forest floor, glowing green smearing the blade. She thought of the way the warrior's red light had—without words—said *drop the bow*. Rowan had fought the warrior, and he was dead; Ahiliyah and Creen had not, and they lived.

"You're wrong," Ahiliyah said. "The way she keeps looking at our toothtongues... I think she *respects* us, maybe. Like we've done something she hasn't. She's got the map. The search pattern we drew isn't that complicated. She doesn't need us alive to figure it out where to look for the demons. All we can do for her is help her figure the map out faster and..."

Faster. The way the warrior seemed so agitated, so angry that Ahiliyah and Creen couldn't understand what she wanted. Was she in a rush? It was getting dark... maybe the warrior didn't want to be out here when night came and the demons started hunting.

"Besides, it doesn't matter if she kills us," Ahiliyah said. "You saw her lightning thrower. If she wants to kill demons, we help her kill demons."

Creen drew in a ragged breath. He nodded.

"Fuck my face with a furgle," he said, "you're right."

Ahiliyah knew Creen so well, could see his effort to calm down, to put his fear aside. It wasn't the first time he'd had done that. He knew what the greater good was. He would do what needed to be done.

Creen reached out to the map, used the tip of his finger to circle the four marks that denoted the Pendaran mountains.

"I think the demon assholes are here," he said. "Under these peaks. It's a volcanic area. There are tunnels, and it's hot. Demons like heat."

The warrior stood straight. "*Vol-can-ic*."

"I guess now she knows three words," Creen said.

Ahiliyah heard a strange noise, like the chirping of insects, but different. Slowly, she turned her head, needing to see what came next. A rectangular piece of armor on the warrior's left forearm had flipped up, like the lid of a box. She was tapping at the open area with her right pointer finger. Every time she tapped, that insect-not-insect sound.

The warrior flipped the armor back into place, stepped around in front of Ahiliyah and Creen. The warrior reached behind its back, grabbed something that looked like an engraved scepter, but with sharp, arrowhead-like points on each end.

The warrior pressed a button—the scepter expanded, quickly and violently, with the sound of ringing metal.

It was a double-pointed spear.

"This is it," Creen said. "We're dead. I really hate being right all the time."

The warrior dropped the spear on the ground in front of Creen, then turned and walked toward a small clearing in the trees.

Ahiliyah heard something, something like the echoing sound of rolling thunder, growing louder by the second.

"She gave you a weapon," Ahiliyah said. "Pick it up."

Creen shook his head. "Rowan had a weapon. Look what happened to him. I'm not picking up a damn thing."

The thunder drew louder, as loud as a dozen storms all coming together. Ahiliyah felt a slight shift in the air, a bit of wind. Dried leaves leapt and scattered. She shielded her eyes against blowing dirt and grit.

The sound of thunder dropped in half, then to nothing.

In the clearing, Ahiliyah saw something... *lowering*. Something big, like warped glass...

Whatever it was, the warrior walked toward it, then stopped, turned to face Ahiliyah and Creen.

The warrior barked out a guttural sound.

A crackle of white and purple light—just as the warrior had earlier, the warped glass mirage shimmered. In its place, a metal object as big as a sailing ship.

"Told you she wasn't from here," Creen said.

Ahiliyah realized that—for the second time in her life—she was looking at a ship that had come from another world.

A part of the ship object moved, angled down, came to rest against the road. Ahiliyah could see inside the object, saw flashing lights and some kind of mist lit up with a reddish glow.

The warrior made the guttural sound again, then curled its finger inward.

"Pick up that spear," Ahiliyah said. "You're right. It's going hunting... and so are we."

"This can't be real," Ahiliyah said. "The warrior charmed us. This is magic."

A layer of fog oozed around her knees, her feet. Curved walls and ceiling, all glowing the shifting orange and black of a dying campfire. No corners here, this place was all curves.

In an alcove, two human skulls, spines still attached. Flesh stripped, the bone gleaming white. Rowan was one, was the other Aaron or Miriam?

An odd glowing image in the center of the warped room showed a view only gettum bugs and great bats could have, an image of the nighttime ground whipping past far below. It was like looking at the model of Ataegina in the Lemeth Hold council room, only this image was, somehow, made of ghost stuff—it was there, but it wasn't.

Creen's wide smile looked out of place on his scarred

face. Ahiliyah was so used to seeing his scowl that when he showed genuine joy he was almost unrecognizable.

"It's not magic," he said. "We're *flying*. I don't understand it yet, but I will."

Ahiliyah had faced down the warrior and felt no fear, for what fear can one feel after being raped by a spider, after vomiting up a worm, after being bit by the Demon Mother? But this, the flying, the image, the strange room that didn't seem to have edges or corners… it was terrifying.

The warrior stood close by. Glowing symbols appeared in the air around her. The warrior grabbed these symbols, moved them, turned them.

The moving model in the center of the room shifted, became something recognizable: the outline of the Pendaran mountains. The image shifted again—getting *closer*, somehow. Yellow rings made of nothing but lights appeared out of nowhere.

The warrior moved a floating symbol.

The there-not-there mountains grew bigger again, as if Ahiliyah had been in the council room, leaning steadily closer to the model of Ataegina. The glowing rings on the moving map also grew larger.

The rings, three of them, each centered on something small, something… shifting. The rings moved in time with those small things, each ring leaving a red line in its wake, like the path a snake leaves in fresh mud.

Creen reached out a hand to touch the mountain—his hand passed right through it. He pointed to one of the yellow rings.

"Make that bigger," he said.

The helmeted warrior looked at him for a moment.

"*Make it bigger*," Creen said. "Show me that demon asshole."

The warrior moved a glowing image. The yellow ring swelled, enlarged. In the center of the ring, so tiny Ahiliyah could barely make it out, a bit of black, reaching, crawling...

...a demon.

The three red snake-trails spread out, winding down the mountain, but they'd all originated from a single spot—the dark mouth of a tunnel entrance.

———

The lightning lashed again—a blinding flash, a demon bursting apart in a cloud of shiny-black and vomit-yellow. How many spearmyn would it have taken to kill that monster? How many would have died in the process?

So far, the warrior had destroyed at least twenty demons. *Twenty*. The warrior was a god. A god of destruction, of vengeance, sent to deliver the people of Ataegina from the ultimate evil.

Ahiliyah fought back her fear of this place. The darkness. The gnarled, dried black mud that coated the rock. The swelteringly hot air echoing with the hisses and screeches of the demons. It was Black Smoke Mountain all over again. So many Ataeginians had died there, died *horribly*.

Somewhere ahead, there were eggs. Spiders. Demons. A Demon *Mother*.

The Warrior God looked back up the tunnel, at Ahiliyah and Creen. Those lifeless black eyes in the helmet stared. It waved its hand inward.

"This is insane," Creen said. "Liyah, let's get the fuck out of here."

He trembled so badly Ahiliyah wondered how he could keep hold of the big, double-pointed spear.

The Warrior God had given Ahiliyah a weapon as well: a bow made of some unknown metal. It was far lighter than it should have been, far more powerful than it should have been. Ahiliyah could draw the bowstring with almost no effort, yet the arrows flew so fast and so hard they shattered rock.

The Warrior God continued down the rough tunnel, dropping a small tube that glowed white. She'd done that several times since they'd entered. Without that white light, Ahiliyah and Creen wouldn't have been able to see a thing.

"She gave us weapons," Creen whispered. "*Why?* She's killing all the demons. Why are we here? Let's get to the surface. We saw demons leave—what happens when they return and they're behind us? We need to run."

The lightning thrower changed everything. Single-handedly, the Warrior God could end the threat to all Ataeginians. Ahiliyah needed to be there, to *see* that happen.

"The gods put us here for a reason," Ahiliyah said. "Run if you want. I'm seeing this through to the end."

She moved down the tunnel, the nocked bow in her hands.

There was an instant when she thought Creen might head for the surface, but in seconds she heard his footfalls coming down the tunnel behind her.

"Some things never change," he said when he caught up to her. "You always were one intense bitch."

Side by side, the two old friends carefully stepped past the still-twitching parts of the demon and the puddles of sizzling blood.

It happened fast, it happened all at once, and when it did, Ahiliyah Cooper knew the plan of the gods.

The farther they went under the mountain, the more the tunnels branched off, jagged forks winding away into the deepness. There was no way to clear the entire area, nor did the Warrior God appear to be all that interested in doing so. Higher up, she'd taken time to look into the various tunnel branches, to stare into the darkness, possibly looking for hidden demons. The farther down she went, the less time she spent checking the tunnels, the fissures, the cracks, and now she was running past them with barely a glance.

Had Ahiliyah been in command, she would have ordered the Warrior God to slow down, to check those side tunnels, to make sure no enemy was left behind. But Ahiliyah wasn't in command.

The Warrior God's careless tactics caught up with her. She rushed past a fissure, and a moment after she did, two huge demons slid out of the darkness, their shiny heads reflecting the white light of a glowing vial.

In a flash of memory, Ahiliyah recognized them as *protectors*, the big ones that protected a Demon Mother.

Before the Warrior God could turn and throw lightning, the protectors were on her.

"Creen," Ahiliyah said as she drew the bowstring to her ear, felt the bow vibrating with mystical power, "move in."

For reasons Ahiliyah would never know, Creen obeyed her order and moved forward, hunched over a spear that seemed almost as big as he was.

Ahiliyah felt suddenly calm, her fear gone. She'd killed demons before—this was no different. She sighted, waited for a clear shot. A demon rose up to strike; she loosed. The arrow sliced through the demon's long head, taking a chunk of yellow flesh with it to splatter against the tunnel floor. The beast twitched... it was still alive. It turned to look toward Ahiliyah, and hissed—Creen rammed his spear straight through the open mouth.

Burning blood splattered across the tunnel, drops sizzling to gray powder when they hit the caminus leaves woven into Creen's hidey suit.

The dead demon slipped back, sliding off the spearpoint.

The Warrior God stood. It wobbled. The other demon lay at its feet, chest gashed open by the Warrior's parallel blade.

Glowing green blood spurted from the Warrior God's thick shoulder. She clutched the wound, squeezed it, stemming the flow somewhat.

The helmeted head looked at Creen.

"*Dee-mon-ass-hole,*" it said.

Creen laughed, looked at Ahiliyah, a wide grin on his scarred face, a wild look in his eyes.

"*Four* words," he said. "Well, maybe she doesn't get the exact meaning, but her heart's in the right place, and that heart is well protected by boob-armor."

Battle madness. Ahiliyah had seen it before. She'd *felt* it before, in the phalanx against the Northerners, on her raids against the Southern pirates. She'd never seen it in Creen. If he lived, there would be a mental and emotional toll to pay, but better to live and pay a horrible price than die and pay nothing at all.

The Warrior God moved down the tunnel, stumbling more than walking. She didn't need to drop a white light—Ahiliyah and Creen could see well enough by the trail of glowing green blood.

Little Creen, *scarred* Creen, the brilliant inventor that had moved humanity forward more in twenty years than in all the years that came before him, squared his shoulders, rolled out his neck, and trotted down the tunnel.

"Come on, Liyah. There's a Demon Mother to kill."

Ahiliyah nocked another arrow, then followed her friend.

The chamber was smaller than the one at Black Smoke Mountain.

So, too, was the Mother.

The beast was maybe half the size of the one Brandun had killed so many years ago. She was young, perhaps, but still big, much larger than her dead protectors, and that didn't include her egg sac. The Warrior God had come at exactly the right time, to deliver Ataegina from evil before that evil grew large enough to spawn hordes that would slaughter thousands.

Ahiliyah, Creen, and the Warrior God stood at the chamber's opening. The Warrior God had tossed in several white vials, illuminating the chamber, the dozens of huge eggs cemented to the stone floor and the Mother herself, along with the strange, long white tendons that stretched down from the cavern roof to support both the Mother and her bloated egg sac.

And, at the edges of the cavern, barely lit in the dim light, Ataeginians, encased in the wall, held in place by dried mud, looks of horror frozen on their dead faces, and gaping holes in their chests.

No other demons. The Mother's defenders were dead. Had to be, or they would have been here to defend her.

The Demon Mother raised her huge, crested head. The black mouth opened, revealing long, clear teeth that gleamed in the white light.

"Shoot that bitch," Creen said. "Shoot her right in her fucking stupid big head."

The Warrior God did not.

The Demon Mother roared, a sound of hatred that shook Ahiliyah, made her bladder let go in a wash of heat and wet.

The bleeding Warrior God stood taller. She reached up to the lightning-thrower on her shoulder, gripped it, twisted it—it came free. She dropped it, let it clatter against the tunnel floor.

"Liyah, what the fuck is she doing?" Creen shrank back from the opening. "Why doesn't she hit it with lightning and end this?"

Ahiliyah didn't know how she knew the answer, she just knew.

"The Warrior God wants to fight her hand-to-hand," she said. "For... for *honor*."

"For *honor*?" Creen shook his head, shook it hard. "When she could kill it with lightning? That's not honorable, that's just fucking *stupid*."

Maybe it was, but who was he to question a god?

The Warrior God reached to her helmet, pinched her fingers on some unseen ropes, ropes that hissed steam as they were pulled free. She hooked her thumbs under the helmet, pulled it free, tossed it aside.

Fangs. Tusks. Beady eyes beneath a heavy brow. The Warrior God, the killer of monsters, was a monster herself.

"And I thought *I* was ugly," Creen said. "Her face looks like a hairy nut bag. With teeth."

The Warrior God grabbed something hanging from her hip, a disk of some kind with holes in it. She slid the fingers of her left hand through the holes, lifted the disk free. She stretched out her right arm—the parallel blades extended with a sharp, metallic ring.

The Warrior God roared a guttural battle cry even louder than that of the Demon Mother.

The Mother's long, thick back legs extended. She ripped free of egg sac and supporting tendons alike, the gristly tearing sound echoing off the small chamber's gnarled, mud-caked walls. The Mother wobbled for moment, a newborn taking her first steps, then stood solid and firm. She let out a malevolent hiss, as if she was inviting the battle, as if she was saying, *come and face me, if you dare.*

The Warrior God stepped into the chamber.

Ahiliyah drew the bowstring. If the Warrior God failed, Ahiliyah would finish the mission.

"The eggs," Ahiliyah said. "Creen, destroy them."

Creen's battle madness, if that's what it was, broke, sharply and instantly.

"We're doomed," he said.

But despite his fear, he stepped to the nearest egg and jammed his spear through its side.

The Demon Mother howled at the death of her kind but, before she could come at Creen, the Warrior God threw the disk.

The disk sparked and glowed as it sliced the air. The

Demon Mother tilted her massive head away and raised her black hands in an instant, automatic reaction—the disk sliced through a black finger, sending it spinning away in a gout of burning blood.

The Mother's *scream*... half pain, half rage.

The Warrior God rushed toward her, each powerful step leaving a splatter of glowing green on the rough stone floor.

No one loses that much blood and survives...

The Demon Mother's long tail slashed forward, black tailspike driving at the Warrior God's chest. A flash of the double blades knocked the tail aside. The Warrior God drew her arm back, ready to drive those blades into the beast, but the Demon Mother's undamaged hand swung in like a springing trap, sent the Warrior God crashing against the cavern wall with a thickening thud and another splatter of glowing green.

The Warrior God fell to the cavern floor.

The Demon Mother turned her head to look at Creen, who pulled his spear free from yet another ruined egg.

"Liyah," he screamed, "*kill it!*"

Ahiliyah sighted down the shaft. With Creen's poison on the arrowhead blade, she only needed one well-placed shot to end the threat forever.

The Demon Mother turned toward Ahiliyah and Creen.

Ahiliyah hesitated.

"Liyah, *fucking shoot that thing!*"

A huge target, not even fifty paces away. Even in the dim light, it was the kind of shot Ahiliyah could make in her sleep.

Still, she hesitated.

The Demon Mother took a step toward Creen. Then another.

The sparking disk whipped in, sank deep in the Demon Mother's neck.

The black beast screamed again, louder than before, her crested head thrashing in agony.

The Warrior God sprinted and leapt, bladed arm reared back, graceful death arcing through the air. The Demon Mother saw her coming at the last second, tried to react but it was too late—the Warrior God landed on her big crest, her weight driving the Mother down, knocking her over and smashing her head against the rock floor.

The Warrior God jammed the blades through the top of the Demon Mother's black head—it sounded like an axe head thudding into a tree trunk.

The Demon Mother's mouth opened, toothtongue snapping out at nothing once, twice, a third time. Her huge legs kicked. Her clawed hands reached for the Warrior God but the monster's strength was already fading away to nothing.

The Warrior God adjusted her footing and twisted her big shoulders, dragging the deep-sunk parallel blades through the length of the Mother's skull.

Gleaming teeth opened one last time. The toothtongue reached out, slowly, opened, then clacked closed with the faintest *click*. The monster moved no more.

The Warrior God yanked the blades free, tipped her horrible head back, and screamed a victory cry.

Ahiliyah gripped her bow tight as she winced against the burning pain. Eyes closed, she thought of General Bishor, *the Spider*, of his body ravaged by burning blood, and wondered if he was in the heavens looking down at her at this very moment.

"You can look now, you big baby," Creen said. "It's like you've never been burned before or something."

Ahiliyah opened her eyes. Creen was grinning at her. On his forehead, a still-smoldering mark burned into his skin, a mark made from two curved lines. Ahiliyah now bore that same mark.

She looked at the Warrior God, who held the severed demon finger she'd used to mark Creen, Ahiliyah—and herself. The Warrior God had made the same symbol on her black-eyed helmet. She tossed the finger aside, put her helmet back on.

Around her thick neck, on a necklace made from wire, the severed toothtongue of the Demon Mother she'd killed in hand-to-hand combat.

Creen saw Ahiliyah looking at it.

"Mine's bigger," he said.

She snorted. "Size matters, Creen?"

"Always, Liyah. Always."

They were joking. She thought of Rowan, Aaron, and Miriam. Maybe it was a bad thing to joke when they'd been killed by the very warrior Ahiliyah and Creen were apparently bonding with, but when you survive a battle, it's hard to not feel elation knowing you'll see at least one more day.

The Warrior God gestured to her big flying machine.

"I think she's leaving," Ahiliyah said.

During the ascent out of the tunnels, the three demons they'd seen leave had attacked. The Warrior God's lightning thrower made short work of them.

Once back out under the glow of the Three Sisters, the Warrior God had thrown some kind of magic weapon into the tunnel. Moments later, Ahiliyah and Creen had felt the mountain move, had seen the smoke billow out of the tunnel mouth.

"I hope she got them all," Creen said. "If not, we're fucked."

Ahiliyah flexed her grip on the bow, glanced at the double-pointed spear in Creen's hands—literal gifts from the gods.

"We survived before," she said. "We'll survive again."

The Warrior God limped toward the flying machine, leaving a spotty trail of glowing green behind her.

"How about that," Creen said. "I guess you *can* lose that much blood and survive."

———

Yeh'kull had never felt such joy.

It felt odd knowing that she'd blooded two humans, while she had trophies of three others. Not all humans were made the same, it seemed.

The little male. He seemed so fragile, so weak, so *small*, and yet he had an inner strength that he probably wasn't aware of. Every sentient being facing possible death feels fear, the elders said so, but it is the ones who face that fear, who face it and *attack*, that are the true hunters.

Creen—that's what the female leader called him—knew the *kiande* liked the heat. Most of the search area had already been cleared. As soon as he'd said those mountains were volcanic, Yeh'kull had known where her prey would be.

The female leader. Lee-ha was her name. She, too, was a true hunter. Her decisive action and skill with the bow had saved Yeh'kull's life. Yeh'kull wondered what kind of strategist Lee-Ha was. Had Lee-Ha fought battles? Won wars?

Lee-Ha wore her Kiande Amedha toothtongues proudly, as a hunter should.

Creen wore the toothtongue of a *kiande* queen.

And now, so, too, did Yeh'kull.

Her scout craft exited the atmosphere, leaving the planet behind. While she couldn't see her clan's mothership, the signal beacon told her it was there.

Soon, she would face her elders, her new trophy hanging from her neck in the style of the human hunting guides that had helped her.

Yeh'kull was now proven. She was *blooded*.

Never again would she be demeaned as a mere child-maker.

She was, now and forever, a true hunter.

KYŌDAI

BY JONATHAN MABERRY
AND LOUIS OZAWA

1

He was falling.

Falling.

Wind whipping past his face.

Wait…

No.

Not falling.

Fighting.

Bullets missing him by inches, plucking at his hair and sleeve. Dodging and ducking away, dropping a spent magazine, swapping in a new one. Rising, turning, the Sig Sauer P226 in a two-hand shooter's grip, the barrel tracking with his line of sight.

Firing.

Firing.

Falling.

Through the sky.

Blue above.

A vast canopy of green below. A blue river whipsawing through the jungle.

Jungle?

There are no jungles in Tokyo.

The fangs of rock rising above the treetops.

The sound of gunfire still echoing in his ears.

Was this Vietnam? Laos... perhaps even further south? Indonesia...?

If so, how? If not... what the fuck?

Eiji Kawakami realized this was not a dream. He was not dying in that hotel lobby, and he hadn't been killed by those bastards from the Yamaguchi-gumi—the dominant *yakuza* clan in Japan. He was not under a sheet or in a body bag. He was not in an ambulance or dreaming his last dream in an ICU.

All of that belonged to a dream.

Did it?

This, though...

He was falling.

And he was screaming.

2

His mind was a car-crash of twisted thoughts.

Falling...

Where?

How?

And why?

Eiji's hands slapped at his chest and shoulders. Feeling his suit. Feeling the harness straps. He could even feel the Sig Sauer holstered under his jacket.

The straps, though.

"Fuck me…" he cried, but the words were slapped from his mouth by the wind.

I'm going to die.

It was a clear thought. A true thought.

They took me somehow. Flew me out over the forest and kicked me out of the plane.

But the straps.

And suddenly there was a sound, high-pitched. Electronic. Nearly lost in the roar of the rushing wind.

"What…?" he began, but then the chute deployed. It opened fast, caught the wind and nearly jerked his upper body apart as the resistance snapped him out of freefall.

Thank god, he thought over and over, though he believed in no god, no higher power, nothing but good luck and bad. The thought was enough.

And then Eiji hit the canopy of trees.

Luck is a fickle thing.

3

Eiji Kawakami lay in a heap like a discarded marionette.

His feet were above him, on a muddy slope. His shoulders were in the water.

The paralysis of shock wanted to keep him there, and if the sky couldn't kill him, the water wanted its turn. And it tried. It gurgled over his cheek and into his ears, his nostrils, his mouth.

I don't understand, he thought. But it *wasn't* a thought. He said those words aloud and suddenly the water was in his throat, his airway.

Eiji came fully awake, splashing awkwardly in the water, coughing, gasping, stomach churning. He flopped over onto his hands, which vanished into the water up to the elbows, and then vomited a pint of brown creek water into the stream.

For a long time, all he could do was kneel there, hands in the water, knees on the bank, chest heaving.

Then his vision cleared. Slow at first, and as if with a snap, tightening to total clarity.

The stream was narrow and shallow, and the water was warm. Not snow melt. The air was oppressively hot. At least a hundred degrees. Maybe hotter, with humidity so thick it was like he was still breathing in creek water. The straps and lines of the parachute trailed up to where the gray shroud was tangled in a thornbush. It was immediately obvious that the resistance of the bush was the only thing that had kept him from sliding all the way into the water.

Why would they throw me out of a plane but give me a parachute?

He turned his head from side to side as if answers would be posted on signs, but all he saw was more jungle. The plants and trees were not right. The ferns were massive, and there were flowers he had never seen—orchids as big as hubcaps, rhododendrons with bulging pustules all over greasy leaves, a bird-of-paradise with glistening spikes.

This is not right. He kept looking around, trying to find something familiar with which to anchor his attempt to understand. *This isn't Japan.*

He had been to Cambodia once and to Vietnam twice, and neither jungle was as dense as this. Neither place as steamy. And neither was anywhere near Tokyo and that's where he just goddamn was.

Or should have been. Had to be.

Eiji felt for a release on the chute but found no structure he recognized. He had done a little skydiving, and this design was unusual, not at all intuitive. Then his fingers fumbled over something and suddenly the harness dropped away. He slapped it away from him.

It took effort, even courage and some optimism, for Eiji to push out of the water and crawl up the bank. Standing required even more of all three, yet he managed and stood swaying, dripping, chest heaving.

The jungle—or was it a rainforest?—was massive. When he looked up he saw that the sun was above, burning a hot white, but he had no way of knowing if he was seeing it rise or fall. And how was it even up at all? Three minutes ago, according to his watch that was still ticking, it had been just shy of midnight.

Either I'm crazy or the world is broken.

The jungle stubbornly refused to become the lobby of the Shinjuku Granbell Hotel. Or even the ICO or a morgue. It remained a green hell.

Eiji pulled his pistol. It was soaked. He grabbed a section of the chute and wiped the weapon. He released the magazine and tapped it upside down to dislodge any water, and left it drying on the chute while he worked the slide back and forth and dry fired. Eiji then slapped the magazine back in, and did his best to dry the two remaining magazines tucked into his shoulder rig.

Then he paused. The gunfight at the hotel had been fierce. He could still feel the dull ache in his hand from firing. And he damn well remembered going through an entire magazine trying to bring the Utada brothers down. He'd dropped the spent mag and replaced it with a fresh one. And yet… all three magazines were now fully loaded. Fifteen rounds in each. How? And *why* would his captors have reloaded his mags? That made as little sense as giving him a parachute.

There was a dreamlike quality about all of this. Part nightmare, part memory, and for a fleeting moment Eiji had a vision of another man falling through the sky. Another Kawakami. Hanzō, his older brother. Missing for weeks; gone without a trace. Only his car found idling in an alley off Chuo-dori. The police looked, and his own people looked. The Inagawa-Kai had a long reach and deep pockets, and when they wanted to know a thing, the thing became known.

Except when it didn't.

Hanzō had vanished without a trace. Without a cause. There were no outstanding issues with him. His past indiscretions had been dealt with internally and he was in good standing. Had he not been, had Hanzō committed some new sin worth punishment, word would have come down to Eiji. The clan did not hide such things, but rather used them as lessons. Hanzō Kawakami simply vanished.

Eiji looked at the parachute and up at the sky.

Was it possible?

That thought was swept away as a terrible scream tore through the air. A man, shrieking in the most abject terror and pain. Eiji spun, brought the gun up, turning in a slow circle. The cry lingered for a terrible long time, and then a second scream seemed to slice right through it. Different. Not a man's cry. It was harsh and high, like metal grinding on metal, but not a machine. Vital in a way that sent shivers rippling through him.

The second cry hung like a threat, a promise, and then it, too, faded, replaced by a thrashing as someone or something moved through the jungle to his left. Up a slope, beyond massive tree trunks looking like a drunk artist's attempt to paint a dragon tree. Whatever it was... it moved through behind the wall of shrubs that grew in the trees' shadow.

Eiji hesitated. Go look or run? His hammering heart said run. But he had to know, and running from potential answers was safe but stupid.

He began climbing the slope. Hunting for answers. His life was filled with danger, and no matter how tough he had become, or how solidly he constructed a facade of dispassion, Eiji was terrified. There was always fear in the air and in the heart for people like him, and the future was a misty promise. Icy sweat ran down his body inside his clothes.

He went toward the sound of the scream anyway.

4

He saw the cage first. It was the size of a delivery truck.

Eiji approached at a quarter angle, circled the site first and then crouched in the tall reeds for several seconds, going still, taking his own movement out of the moment, allowing the jungle to become what it was without him. He could feel a slight breeze coming from off to his left, and he watched the leaves to see if any of them were moving in opposition to the flow of air.

Yes. On the other side of the small clearing, past the cage, the shrubs were only just now settling back into a natural pattern. Whatever had been here went that way.

Was it the source of the scream, though?

He had his doubts. There was a wet, damaged, terminal quality to the scream. Whoever—and he was sure it was a human throat—had been more than terrified. The pain sewn through the fabric of that scream haunted the air.

The leaves settled and became still, and then moved again more sluggishly and in harmony with the breeze.

Eiji began circling again, taking time to look around and listen. Minutes before, this place had been troubled by the cries and movement; now it felt emptier, as if whoever had been here had taken his energy with him.

That was something he had learned over the years. Trust his senses to gather information, but to allow instinct to play its role. Instinct could not be taught, but it could be refined, and he had put in that work. As had his brother. They'd played strange hunting games as kids, always excelling, always ambushing the other boys. Those games had evolved during thousands of hours in the dojo, and then as enforcers for the Inagawa-kai.

Stillness is an art. Receptivity is its companion.

Then he moved into the clearing, placing his feet very carefully. Looking for twigs, loose stones. Anything. He approached the cage and saw that it was open and empty.

It was constructed not of metal but of some kind of polymer, or at least coated with it. The interior space was big enough for six men if they crouched shoulder-to-shoulder. Or it was big enough for one thing that was larger. An animal? What sense would that make?

What sense would it make to drop me *here?* he mused.

He squatted down and looked at the locking mechanism, which appeared to be melted. Bending close to smell it was a mistake; it stung the inside of his nostrils as if he'd taken a snootful of industrial bleach. He gagged, pawing at his nose with one hand, snorting air through it to try and extinguish the burn. The pain faded quickly, but… lesson learned. Eiji used a twig to touch the lock. A tiny curl of steam rose from the wood but soon faded, as if whatever had burned the lock was oxidizing and evaporating.

He rose and looked around, frowning at yet another mystery. The lock was troubling because those burns were on the inside of the door. Again, how did that make sense? What had they done, trapped a scientist inside with his full kit of chemical samples? That was absurd.

About as absurd as dropping me safely here with a reloaded pistol.

Eiji did not like mysteries. His was an orderly mind. More so than his brother, Hanzō, who was both more emotional and more expressive. Eiji Kawakami tended toward the analytical. Problems had solutions. Nothing impossible ever happened. So what was the solution to this? What were the imperatives here? Where was the sense, the logic?

Behind him was the path to the creek. Ahead of him was the route taken by whatever had broken out of the cage. Close by would be whoever had screamed. Those were logical inferences to draw.

First step: find the source of that scream. See if it could tell him something. A man with a knife in his heart would offer one direction for further assumptions; a man torn apart by a tiger would take matters down a different path.

He backed up and looked at the grass. It was beaten down but not ground underfoot, and some of the stalks were slowly standing up. The angle of compression showed him the direction something had passed. He followed a second trail, one that led from this spot through what looked like a patch of dirt. He moved quickly off and came to a place fifteen yards from the cage, and there they were. Footprints. Shoes with a distinctive tread of the kind favored by PMCs. Okay, but what would a private military contractor be doing here? There were no deals currently ongoing with his clan that involved them. And PMCs operating on Japanese soil wouldn't be wearing that kind of combat footwear; they'd be in civilian clothes.

Eiji followed the footprints, and noted that halfway across the clearing they changed from those of a man walking to the toe-heavy prints of someone running. From the angle of the toes and lack of heel marks, the man was running very damn fast.

Eiji ran in a crouch, gun up and out, moving alongside the trail. He got fifty yards and then jerked to a stop.

The running man lay in the grass.

And he was very damn dead.

5

It was a white man. Tall, judging from the body. There was no head. Not really. Above the neck was part of a chin, most of the lower set of teeth. That was it. The rest of the head was a pulpy mass that glistened as it ran slowly down the trunks of nearby trees.

Something had blown the fellow's head apart.

But how? There had been screams and that other strange noise, but nothing that sounded like an explosion. Nor was the skin that he could see burned. No scorching on the grass, the man's clothes, or the overhanging leaves. And yet, even though there wasn't any of the carbon-scoring most fire would leave, the body was a melted mess. As Eiji studied the corpse, he could see that parts of the teeth were melted.

What the fuck melts teeth?

Eiji shifted over and saw a Heckler & Koch MP5 lying in the grass. The weapon was bent nearly at a right angle and all the plastic and metal around the bend was melted.

Eiji tried to make sense of it. The man had been dressed in non-military camouflage, with a pattern commonly used by PMCs working for private corporations in Syria. Not a jungle pattern. The gear still on the dead man was untouched. He had a combat knife hung handle-down from a chest rig and plenty of ammunition in pouches. A holster for a handgun but no weapon. And the magazines were for a .40. Not a match for his 9mm.

Eiji took the knife and wished the rifle was still usable. It wasn't, so he erased that desire.

Work with what you have, not what you want.

Eiji moved away from the corpse and began following the second trail. The killer's trail? Almost certainly. It was also the path toward potential answers.

The land seemed to rise up, and he realized that he'd been in a valley. He could see some bright patches ahead and thought there was a clearing a half mile away. That would allow him to find the sun and have a chance to orient himself. If not, then he'd go back to the creek and follow it. People tended to live near water. It was a useful Plan B.

The heat was brutal. He wanted to shed his suit jacket, but did not. Weather could turn rough and in any direction, and an extra layer might be useful. It also hid his pistol should he need to holster it. The suit was superbly tailored to conceal.

417

He had gone about halfway toward the clearing when things went to hell.

Straight to hell.

6

It started with a scream.

Screams, really. Two voices. A man and a woman, both bellowing.

In anger. In fear.

Eiji picked up his pace, but he immediately shifted away from the path he'd been following. On the off chance that the screams were a trick, something to lead him—or others—into a trap, then Eiji did not want to play by those rules. He broke right and made maximum use of cover as he ran through the dense jungle.

The foliage thinned quickly and he slowed to a stop at the shadowy edge of a large field. Tall grass waved in the breeze. Eiji saw several things all at once.

About a hundred paces into the field, nearly in his direct line of sight, was a kind of monument made from scraps of metal. Atop it was some kind of exotic helmet, though he couldn't tell which culture it was from. It was long and tapered, suggesting a falcon or other predatory bird. In front of that was something that looked like a sheathed sword.

He saw that at a glance and then completely forgot the monument a second later.

His real attention was drawn by figures moving through the grass as if choreographed for some bizarre and impossible dance. Two of the figures were surely the man and woman whom he'd heard screaming.

The woman was medium height, very blond and very fit, wearing the uniform of the *Jegertroppen*—the Hunter Troop, an all-female special operations unit from Norway. She ran like a gazelle, twisting as she went to fire behind her with a Heckler & Koch MP7. Shell casings arced through the air, the sun gleaming off the brass.

Just ahead and to her left ran a burly black man wearing a bloodstained uniform that Eiji thought might have been from the Niger Delta Avengers, a militant group from that country's troubled Niger Delta region. It was hard to tell, though, because his clothing was in tatters and blood gleamed bright and red on his skin. He, too, fired behind him, burning through a full curved magazine of his Kalashnikov. He ejected the magazine and fished for another, dropped it, almost made the mistake of stopping to pick it up, and instead simply ran.

Something else was running through the grass, too, and it was immediately apparent that it was moving much faster, circling to force them to run directly into it.

It.

That was the word. Nothing else fit. Not in any language. The thing that was setting an ambush for the two people was not human. It was not an animal—not any animal Eiji had ever seen. Not in the waking world. This was something out of nightmares. Out of some drug-infused hellscape. Eiji looked at it along the barrel of his pistol. That gun trembled in his hands. Every part of his body was shivering.

It looked like an insect. Or some kind of bizarre sea creature. It ran on two legs and on four, and had a huge tail that curled over its grotesque body like some kind of scorpion. The body, though, seemed to be entirely encased in a dark chitinous shell that called to mind horseshoe crabs. The shell was segmented in places, smooth in others, and with odd bony-looking protuberances rising from its back.

The head was the worst part—an elongated skull that arched back over its shoulders, and a snarling mouth filled with wicked teeth. No visible eyes, though Eiji could feel himself being *watched*. Or, perhaps, perceived. He wasn't sure how this creature's physiology worked, but it seemed aware of everything.

It passed close to Eiji's hiding place, and for only a moment the creature seemed to slow, its hideous face flicked toward the shadows. Toward him.

As it ran by him, though, Eiji saw that there was something decidedly *in*organic about the monster. There was a device—round, metallic, and glowing with internal light—set into the side of that enormous head. As soon as the creature began to slow, distracted by something closer, it suddenly shrieked and twisted, falling to hands and knees. The implant flared with bright yellow light as the thing crumpled.

Eiji looked from the squirming, shrieking creature to a fourth and even more shocking figure on the field. It, too, was hideous and strange. As if the day wanted to present life in all its malformed combinations, the thing seemed to be both monstrous and human.

It was very tall, at least eight or nine feet, and had a body so packed and corded with muscle that it was almost a caricature. Something from anime rather than real life. It wore armor of such exotic design that Eiji could not even begin to understand what each piece did. It wore a helmet nearly identical to the one on the monument—metallic and tapered like a stylized bird of prey. One hand was clamped around a kind of segmented spear, while the other was outstretched, a taloned thumb pressing on a small electronic device.

When the bigger monster's thumb lifted from the device, the insectoid creature stopped shrieking. It instantly rose up and whipped around, hissing at its tormentor with such deep hatred that it made Eiji want to flee.

The armored creature made a sound that could have been a laugh. It was deep and awful, and then it pressed the device again, sending the smaller monster into fresh paroxysms of agony. It twisted and writhed in the grass as the two humans ran on.

Eiji looked at the man and woman. *They think they're actually safe now,* he thought. *They think they're going to get away.*

As if sharing that same thought, the armored thing released the button. He walked forward and stopped thirty feet away from the insectoid thing. The tortured creature climbed back to its feet, shudders still rippling through it. Then it opened its mouth and snapped at its oppressor. Not with jaws, but with… its *tongue*…?

That's what it seemed like. Something very much like a thick tongue snapped out, but the end opened up to reveal that it was some kind of bizarre second mouth. Though smaller, the teeth were every bit as vicious, and they snapped in the humid air with the sound of a gunshot.

Eiji expected the bigger monster to press the pain device again, but it did not. It merely showed the contraption, holding it up, thumb above the button but not touching it. The smaller creature hissed and snapped, but it did not attack. Instead it retreated a few steps, looking left and right as if expecting help or an exit.

For one horrible moment the creature turned to look directly at Eiji. Although he was deep inside thick shadows, Eiji was positive the thing could see him. Guided by some instinct—perhaps a shred of empathy—Eiji released one hand from his pistol and pointed the barrel up to the sky with the other hand. The barbed tail whipped back and forth, and even though there were no visible eyes to read, it seemed to be somehow evaluating the situation.

The big creature spoke, a guttural tumble of grunts and clicks. No human language, of that Eiji was sure. The smaller monster's tail paused in its thrashing and quivered for a moment, then it turned away. Slowly. With obvious reluctance and a latent defiance that both monsters were aware of.

It understands what that device is. Eiji was as fascinated as he was terrified. *It knows that it has to obey.*

The tall thing pounded the butt of its spear on the ground and growled out another comment in that bizarre language. The smaller monster cut one last brief look into the shadows and then moved off. Following the humans, who were now small dots on the far side of the field. The creature began running on two feet, then it picked up speed and ran much faster on all fours. The armored thing followed.

Eiji stood slowly and watched; and he thought he understood something of what just happened. The big one was a hunter, and the smaller one was being trained—forced—to be its hunting dog.

He remained in the shadows until the four figures had all vanished.

7

Eiji moved out of the shadows. He did it very slowly and very carefully, staying low, moving only at the speed of the breeze so that his passage through the tall grass blended into the natural world. He looked all around, watching for any other kind of movement, but for the moment he believed he was alone.

Inside his chest, his heart was hammering with dangerous intensity.

Those things were not some kind of unknown animals natural to earth. No. They were not *of* the world. It hurt him to accept this truth, and even his logical and pragmatic mind rebelled at the concept. And yet what else could they be? These were not people in costumes, and this wasn't a CGI movie. This was real life and there were monsters in it.

He looked up to try and determine where he might be, or at least get a bead on the directions of east, west, south, and north.

Eiji saw the sky. Moons. Planets. Other worlds.

Alien worlds.

Eiji looked down at the grassy field on which he stood. Alien worlds, including this one. His knees wanted to buckle. His hand wanted to raise the pistol and place the barrel under his chin and blast himself out of this place.

His knees did not bend. His gun hand hung at his side.

"*Damn it to hell,*" he swore softly.

8

Eiji made himself stop looking at the alien sky. That took a lot. It cost him.

He made himself breathe as if things were normal and

this was just another day out in the country. He forced his mind to analyze instead of merely react. There were people being killed.

Was that right? No, he decided, that was imprecise.

There were people being *hunted*. An American ex-Navy SEAL, a Norwegian special operator, and a Nigerian rebel. Why them? What did they have in common?

They're fighters, he thought. *Fighters. High end, very tough.* They were being hunted by… what?

The big one with the spear and the helmet was a hunter of some kind. The other one was its hound. Not willing, though. There was no pack loyalty. The insectoid creature was under coercion; the implant was obviously a pain control device.

Eiji remembered the level of hatred in the "hound's" energy and body language. If it wasn't for that control implant, then it would have gone for the Hunter. That was clear. And maybe that was useful.

The Hunter must have had some tech that was not apparently obvious. Its arms and legs were mostly exposed, unarmored; and the humans had automatic weapons. How did the Hunter protect itself from them? That was high on Eiji's list of things he needed to know. If there was something else, some protection, or—more likely—ultra-sophisticated weaponry that simply outmatched rifles and handguns, then Eiji wanted it for himself.

His roving eyes saw the monument again, and he headed in that direction. There was a helmet there, at least. Maybe that would tell him something useful. He reached it quickly. It had clearly been welded together from scraps of metal, but it was sturdy and even had a sense of stately beauty to it. A tall base topped by a slightly slanted steel slab. The helmet was coated with a light dusting of pollen and bird droppings, as if it had been in the field for some weeks. A gauntlet was placed behind it, with a single wicked and exotic blade extending from it. In front of the helmet, set as if in a place of honor, was, indeed, a katana. It was very old and beautifully made.

Eiji did not touch it, though.

He barely saw it. His eye was drawn to something else. A glass plate was set into the slanted top, framed with strips of metal and riveted into place. Beneath it, displayed for anyone to see, was something bright and colorful. A stylized ancient Japanese warrior on a warhorse. A Sengoku-era samurai and ninja who served the Tokugawa clan. A fierce fighter, unparalleled tactician—a master swordsman who lived a heroic life and died more than four centuries ago.

Hattori Hanzō.

Oni no Hanzō.

Demon Hanzō.

Now Eiji's knees did buckle. His pistol fell from his hand as he sank down onto the grass in front of the monument.

He knew that tattoo. He knew it so well. Just as he knew that the mystery of what had happened to his brother was now solved. The colorful swatch behind the glass had been cut from Hanzō's body. It was skin from his brother's back.

Eiji felt dazed, gutted. Hanzō had come here. Been *taken* here. To this alien jungle world. To this hell.

Had he awakened in freefall, too? *Yes.* Eiji knew it for sure. Just as the three people he saw so far. Prey for predators; animals for hunters. But Hanzō Kawakami had not been run down by hounds or shot in the back as he fled. No way. He'd *fought* one of these Hunters.

Fought.

That opened floodgates of memory inside Eiji. He remembered how his brother and he fought. Not with anger, but with art. Both of them caught up in the art of kendo, clinging to its beauty and discipline when, as boys, their family had fallen apart, casting them adrift.

Hanzō had walked into a kendo dojo one day and taken up the sword. At first Eiji, being so little, would just tag along. Watching. Adoring his older brother. Hanzō learned so quickly, became so skilled. He was the golden boy, the prize student. Even the teachers knew that Hanzō was going to be exceptional. Some people just shine with that light.

Eiji was lost in that memory. Hanzō's kendo was pure. Big, straight. Graceful. Effortless and instinctual.

When Eiji began training, they would spent countless hours, in the dojo and at home, or in fields, fencing. It always amazed Eiji how effective his brother was. You'd see his moves coming. He didn't have a huge range of *waza*—techniques—but it never seemed to matter. Nor did it matter who he fought, or what style they knew. Hanzō's approach was always the same, and more often than not he'd beat whomever he faced. Not with a dazzling display or trickery. Just the opposite. Long and arcing strokes, booming *men*—head strikes. If you weren't strong through the center, he'd break through your weak defense. If the opponent tried to block the *men*, that was fine because Hanzō was the master of the *doh* as well. It would look like he was coming straight down toward the *men*, then at the last second he'd thrust his body diagonally to his right and change the angle of his strike into a beautiful diagonal stroke across the body. Winning. Hanzō always won.

Once the brothers were teenagers, none of the adults at the dojo would practice with them. No grownup wanted to be embarrassed by kids. Instead, the adults would gawk as the brothers would battle it out in endless *keiko*. Soon the Kawakami brothers were the talk of the town, entering Kendo *Shiai* and winning first locally, then provincially, and then finally nationally.

Winning.

Then Eiji was on his feet again, staring at the monument, seeing it again. Seeing it differently.

The helmet and bladed gauntlet. The katana. Were they trophies?

No.

This was something else. A war memorial of some kind. That sword and that gauntlet were matched. They were weapons used in a duel. It was suddenly so obvious. His brother had *fought* whoever wore that helmet and gauntlet.

Had that fight ended in simple defeat, then Eiji knew—on some deep level *knew*—that no such monument would have been erected. That it had been, that it was here, displaying this sword and his brother's tattoos, made a bold and—as Eiji saw it—irrefutable statement that Hanzō had fought a duel.

And won.

Eiji knew his brother and could imagine Hanzō defeating the massively large Hunter. Landing a head strike would be nearly impossible. But after several attempts to land strikes to the head, a feint to a *doh*… a cut to the enemy's waist. Even the best body armor is vulnerable there to allow for movement. In order to pull off that kind of move you have to commit to an all-out attack. That was something Hanzō would have done.

427

It must have been a rare thing for these Hunters to encounter. Not a more powerful opponent, but a smarter and trickier one. Why else would these Hunters erect a monument to mark the event? Maybe even on the spot where it happened.

Eiji felt his mouth change shape, curling into a kind of smile. Not, he was sure, a pleasant one, had anyone been there to see it. It felt predatory. It changed something inside of him, too. Where a moment before there had been terror, deep grief, and hopelessness, now there was a strange joy.

These Hunters can be killed.

Yes, that was true.

They can be fought and killed by an ordinary man.

That, however, was not true.

Hanzō had not *been* ordinary. He was *yakuza*. He was a warrior of the Inagawa-Kai. And Hanzō had known that his younger brother had become the better fighter. Better because Hanzō had *demanded* that. His brother had been more than a training partner—he'd been a ruthless teacher who would have taken it as a personal disgrace for his brother not to excel.

Eiji had. But his path was different. He was colder than his brother. More precise, less given to emotion most of the time. Silent and steady, that's what his *oyuban* had once said.

"Hanzō wa hidesu. Eiji wa kōridesu."

Hanzō is fire. Eiji is ice.

He picked up his gun, checked the barrel was not filled with dirt from having been dropped, and holstered it. He paused, then moistened his finger and drew the *kanji* for a word that meant quite a lot to him. Kyōdai. A simple word with complex meaning. It meant 'siblings,' but also brothers in arms. And more than that, brothers in the yakuza.

Eiji took the katana from the monument, lifting it with both hands and bowing to it, and to his brother's memory. Then he drew the weapon, listening to the subtle ring of the ancient steel. The blade was unsigned but the weight of it was flawless and it had the *feel* of something ancient and precious. Could it be a Masamune blade? It looked like photos of the one that had been in the Tokugawa family for centuries. A sword that historians claimed was that rarest of all things— a perfect blade. Truly flawless.

When the Second World War ended and ownership of swords became illegal in Japan, the head of the Tokugawa family surrendered that sword to the police, and from there it vanished. Had it gone into some American G.I.'s private collection? Hung like a novelty on the wall of some trailer home in Kansas? Or had it been taken by strange hands and returned to the use for which it had been made? Eiji had no way of knowing, and although he tried to resist the fanciful and wishful thinking that this blade—the weapon with which his brother had fought a duel on an alien world—was *that* blade…the belief lingered.

He set the scabbard down and took the sword in both hands. Holding it. Moving it. Wringing his hands together as he performed cuts. Feeling how *alive* it was.

Far off, out of sight and nearly beyond the audible range, came the staccato rattle of automatic gunfire, then a pause… and finally the ghostly echoes of terrible human screams. Eiji knew that the Hunter and his hound had caught up with their prey.

Then he sheathed it and slid the lacquered scabbard through his belt, using the silk wrappings on the scabbard to anchor it in place. He removed his jacket and, after a moment,

429

took off the shoulder holster, which he placed on the monument where the sword had been. He placed his hand over the glass, over the tattoo of Hatori Hanzō. He had no prayers. No words. All he did was touch his brother across the gulf of space, of time, of life and of death.

Then Eiji Kawakami turned away and ran off to follow the monsters.

They were hunters.

So was he.

9

He found the bodies first.

The man, the Nigerian, was easy to identify. From clothes. From skin color. But that was it. The man lay on his chest and his entire back was laid open from rectum to the top of his scalp. It took Eiji a moment to understand the nature of the injury.

His *spine* was missing.

And his skull.

Just… gone. As if torn out of his body.

The sheer muscular strength it must have taken to do that was appalling.

Why? Had the hound been allowed to feed?

He shook his head even as he speculated. No, this wasn't that. If the Hunter wanted his hound to feed there would be no meat left on these bones.

This had been about taking a trophy. Any bloody fool could see that.

Trophies.

He wondered if this would have been his brother's fate if that duel had gone a different way. Hanzō's body desecrated,

430

defiled, and left behind like garbage. Anger tried to well up in Eiji, but he forced it down.

Iye.

No.

This was a time to be the ice man the *oyuban* said he was.

And so he ran on, re-entering the forest. Following the tracks of both Hunter and hound.

The woman's body—what was left of it—was a thousand yards farther on. There had been a hell of a fight. Trees and rocks were melted in the same way as the cage lock had been; the same way the Nigerian's arm had been. Here and there were pieces of black chitinous shell, and wherever they lay the surrounding foliage and dirt was melted.

Acid for blood?

Eiji admired the evolutionary brazenness of that.

There were also splashes of a luminous green substance. The splash patterns were consistent with blood spatter from gunshot wounds.

Was that the Hunter's blood? He rather thought so.

No alien bodies, though. Just the woman's corpse, her skull and spine also gone.

Two kills, two trophies.

No new monuments, he saw, and that amused him. God, how he wished he could have seen the duel between the Hunter and Hanzō. It must have been magnificent.

There was nothing more to learn, and so he moved on, taking each new bit of information and fitting it into place. Expanding what he guessed and what he knew. Like all things in life, there were patterns within the details. The shape and nature of the hunt was not in itself complicated. The Hunters were bigger and stronger, perhaps smarter, but certainly more vicious than humans; but in many ways a hunter was a hunter was a hunter. They went after prey they found to be a challenge—or that challenged what they knew about their own courage—and overcame it the way humans did. They brought superior weapons and high-tech gadgets into the mix, as well as hunting hounds, in order to take trophies from things that were, in almost every practical sense, weaker. Even a big game hunter in Africa tracking a lion still had guides, beaters to drive the animal, and rifles with scopes and bullets that were the refined end-product of hundreds of years of ballistic science. What then were a lion's claws and teeth against that? It was worse when hunters went out to take a buck's head. It wasn't really a hunt. It was slaughter for amusement, and Eiji found it disappointing.

Put two men in a forest armed only with blades. Now *that* was a hunt.

Maybe the monument was there to make these Hunters feel that their sport was truly noble, as measured by the death of one of their own. Stories would be told of that fight, and that would likely spur the next generation of Hunters to bring more sophisticated weapons and tactics to this world.

Maybe that's why they used the acid-blooded creatures as hounds. Upping the game. Eiji smiled. Hubris was every bit as bad as naiveté.

He ran on.

Twilight began closing in and he looked up to see that the sun was not setting but was instead being eclipsed by one of the smaller planets in this world's extended orbit. Or perhaps that planet and this one were moons of the more massive world. It didn't matter, because it was starting to get dark and there were rainclouds brewing on the horizon.

There were two more corpses. People he hadn't seen before. A soldier and someone dressed only in sweatpants and covered with South American prison tattoos. Both dead. Trophies taken from each.

Then he heard something ahead and slowed to a careful, creeping pace. He stopped on the far side of a small waterfall, leaning against the cold rocks and peering through a gap between the flowing water and mossy stone.

Three of the Hunters stood in a group. Each of them was similarly armored, but there were stylistic differences. Horn fixed to their helmets, necklaces of bones and ears and fingers. They each had a hound, and as Eiji watched he could see that the beasts were all writhing on the ground, clearly wrapped in envelopes of pain from their implants, which glowed with hellish light.

The Hunters conversed in their strange language for several minutes, and then two of them released their hounds and sent them running off into the jungle. The two monsters followed and suddenly seemed to vanish. The air around them shimmered and they were gone. Was it heat haze or something else? Eiji could not tell.

The remaining Hunter moved through the clearing, setting up a kind of cooking pot, filling it with water from the brook fed by the waterfall. When the water was boiling, it removed a flask from its belt and poured vile-looking liquid in, then picked up the four spines and skulls and dropped them, one by one, into the pot.

Cleaning the trophies.

The jungle became gradually still and quiet.

And Eiji Kawakami stepped into the clearing and slowly, making sure to scuff the ground with one foot. The Hunter spun around, the massive blade sliding from its gauntlet. On its shoulder was another device that looked like a video camera, but then three red dots appeared on Eiji's chest—a targeting laser, which meant it was a gun.

Eiji stood there. Then he reached up with his left hand and brushed at the dots, as if wiping away meaningless dirt, and laid his right on the handle of the sword. It was deliberate, not just to present a challenge but to make the creature look at the sword. At that very particular sword.

He saw the moment when the Hunter recognized it. The big body stiffened.

He raised the sword, angling it into one of the fading beams of sunlight coming through the trees. Allowing the creature to see it. To understand what it was.

The creature studied him. Then it gave a single nod.

The Hunter removed its helmet. Small tubes fell away, hissing with exotic gasses. The face that was revealed had surely been fashioned in hell. Eiji felt fear. But fear was always there. Only a fool claims to be incapable of fear. But he also felt that familiar coldness filling him.

He slowly drew his sword and pointed its tip at the monster.

He was aware of the tortured hound watching him. The control device was clipped to the Hunter's belt. It could release the monster before Eiji could close the distance and attack.

The Hunter did not.

Eiji looked at the gauntlet without being obvious about it. He wanted that thing. Not as a trophy but because every instinct he possessed told him it was important, that it might hold a key to surviving on this planet.

As if sensing his thoughts, the Hunter raised his gauntlet and extended the blade.

Eiji raised his sword.

The Hunter raised his blade as if in salute. Eiji's mind raced as he picked out and analyzed every detail, clocking the way the ugly blade curved toward the thing's body. The blade's inherent shape suggested odds were high that it would attack in a backhand fashion, likely from left to right. Or possibly a downward across its body from its left to right. Either way, Eiji knew he would have to strike fast and with great precision, with the flesh above the gauntlet as his critical goal.

The Hunter moved, and for all his size he was fast. So fast.

Eiji Kawakami was faster.

And, despite being so much smaller, his katana gave him the reach advantage. He parried and then shifted, into a *gedan-no-kamae* posture, sagging his sword in front of his right knee. Trying to goad the Hunter into striking for the head.

Was it too obvious?

He knew that from that posture he could parry any strikes by moving quickly to the side. Eiji wasn't about to charge forward like his brother. No, he'd wait for the Hunter to charge.

Then Eiji took a deep breath and unleashed a *kiyai*—a fierce warrior's scream. It was a respectable *kiyai*. Not as dropped-in as he'd felt while in his prime competitive days, but it felt good to let out that scream. Damn good.

The Hunter responded with his own challenge—a blood curdling roar that shook the whole world.

Oh shit, thought Eiji. *It's on now.*

But then… nothing. The Hunter seemed content to stand and wait for Eiji to move forward.

Okay, it wants to trick me. It thinks I'll act out of fear.

He almost smiled.

Eiji took a fast forward step, feinting a *morote-suki*—a powerful thrust to the sternum. A provocation to an arrogant fighter. A move that too many fighters thought was desperate. The Hunter pivoted, bringing his wicked blade over and down, trying to smash the katana, to shatter the delicate steel. But Eiji transitioned into a sliding step to evade. The Hunter's weapon tore through the air as Eiji swept his rear leg around to give him a fraction of a second on the creature's blind side. His katana was a silver blur as it flowed into a lateral cut. The ancient sword sheared through the Hunter's back and side, passing through tough muscle and internal organs. If the thing's liver and kidneys were in the same place as a human's, then the katana sheared through them.

The Hunter staggered and howled as drops of luminous green blood flew like strange gemstones through the air. Some of them spattered the face of the tortured hound.

Even wounded like that, the Hunter whirled and slashed with his blade, and it was fast. So goddamn fast.

Eiji went under the attack, checking his own swing, turning the blade, torquing his hips as he delivered a counter-cut that took the Hunter across the right biceps. The angle was imperfect, though, and the edge of his blade hit the thick humerus and slid off. More green blood splashed the floor, and some of it struck Eiji's face. He could taste it in his mouth, but he didn't care. He was moving, using the desperately small moment of advantage to pivot and cut again. This time it was a *yoko men*, a lateral cut to the side of the head. The monster was too tall and the cut took him across the back of the neck instead. The antique sword bit deep, and every ounce of Eiji's strength and speed, his skill and focus, were in that movement.

When such a cut is done perfectly, muscle and bone part as if they are made of smoke.

The hideous head of the Hunter rose into the air. Its eyes were open in an expression of profound surprise. Then the head thumped to the floor and rolled nearly to the feet of the crouching hound.

The big body stood there for a moment, as still as a statue.

Then it canted sideways and crumpled to the floor, where it lay in a widening lake of glowing green.

Eiji stood as still as the Hunter had been.

Then he swept the sword through the air, giving it a wrist snap that shook the blood from the steel. His chest was heaving but his mind had gone to that deep, cold place inside. There was stillness within him that seemed bottomless.

10

Eiji picked up the fallen control device. Aware that the hound was watching him.

He held it out and showed it to the hound.

The creature crouched, hissing, tail whipping. It was furious and savage and there was murder in its eyes. It wanted to kill him. Maybe because that was its nature, or perhaps because he held the hated device that caused such pain. Was this thing capable of feeling humiliation, too? Eiji didn't know, and rather doubted it. Hate seemed to be what fed the animal.

Eiji rather thought this monster mostly wanted to kill more of the big ugly bastards who put things like that implant into the heads of its own kind. That was a guess and it was a gamble.

He looked at the creature. It turned its head toward him and he felt the full weight of its strange perceptions.

Then Eiji turned his hand and let the control device fall.

The hound looked at it on the ground, then it raised its head and gave one of its low, awful hisses. Eiji held up his hand, palm out. Then he stamped down hard on the device. The casing burst apart in a shower of sparks. The dull yellow light inside the implant flickered and went dark.

The hound twitched, shook its head, clawed at the implant.

In that moment of distraction, Eiji flicked out with the sword. A scarf cut—a whipping diagonal angle past the monster's head. The ancient blade sheared through the exposed section of the implant and sent it tumbling to the dirt.

The hound flinched back again.

It stared at the two broken devices. It bent forward to sniff them, hissing again.

Eiji gave a soft grunt and picked up the helmet of the dead Hunter. He showed it to the hound and mimed the same kind of cut that had killed the killer. Then he tossed the helmet away. Into the jungle in the direction the others of its kind had gone.

He looked back at the hound.

This was the moment.

Freed from its control, the creature had three choices. It could run, and he would not stop it.

It might attack, in which case one or both of them were going to die in the next two seconds.

Or...

Eiji pointed with the sword. Toward the helmet. And beyond it.

The hound's head turned to follow the direction of the sword. Its tailed whipped and thrashed. Its inner mouth extended slowly and snapped at the air. Fat beads of drool gathered and fell from its fangs.

Eiji stood there, pointing with his sword. Ready to fight. Ready to die.

The hound moved forward so fast.

And plunged into the tall grass. Following the trail.

It followed the prey. It was not *his* hunting hound. It was not his ally. It could have attacked him, but did not. At least for now. Their shared enemy was more dangerous, and more immediate. Even the animal's limited intelligence was capable of grasping that much. Would the truce last?

Eiji did not think so. Not for a moment. But right now they were both hunting the same enemy. On a world like this... that was enough for now. He stood and watched the ripples of the tall grass as the thing moved off.

Hunting the hunters.

And Eiji Kawakami, a game animal himself, followed this hound into the gathering twilight.

EDITOR BIOGRAPHIES

New York Times bestseller, five-time Bram Stoker Award winner, three-time Scribe Award winner, and Inkpot winner **JONATHAN MABERRY**, creator of *V-WARS* (Netflix) and President of the International Association of Media Tie-In Writers. He's the author of forty novels, many comics (*Black Panther*, *Punisher*, *Captain America*) and is the editor of *Weird Tales Magazine*. Jonathan is also the founder of the Writers Coffeehouse and co-founder of The Liars Club. Find him online at www.jonathanmaberry.com.

Hugo-nominated **BRYAN THOMAS SCHMIDT** is the national bestselling editor of eighteen anthologies including *Predator: If It Bleeds*, *Infinite Stars*, *Monster Hunter Files*, and *Joe Ledger: Unstoppable*, and the author of ten novels and numerous short stories, including the forthcoming *Shortcut*, the *Saga of Davi Rhii* trilogy, and the John Simon thrillers. He was first editor of Andy Weir's international bestseller *The Martian*, and books by *New York Times* bestsellers Angie Fox, Todd McCaffrey, Mike Resnick, Frank Herbert, and many more. His previous works in the Expanded Universe include the story "Drug War", co-written with Holly Roberds for *Predator: If It Bleeds*. His website is www.bryanthomasschmidt.net.

AUTHOR BIOGRAPHIES

DAVID BARNETT is a writer and journalist from the north of England. His latest novel is *The Handover* (Orion Books) and he has written comics for DC including *Books of Magic*, IDW, *Archie* and *2000AD*. He writes on culture for the UK press including the *Guardian*, *Independent* and *Telegraph*. Follow David online at davidmbarnett.com.

ROSHNI "RUSH" BHATIA is a writer-director living in Los Angeles. Growing up in Mumbai, Rush was inspired by filmmakers and writers including James Cameron, Ridley Scott, Richard Matheson, and Rod Serling. Rush has several films currently on the festival circuit, with selections at Leeds International Film Festival and Morbido Film Fest. Her one-minute short film, *Dark Passage,* shot on an iPhone, won the #SixtyScarySeconds competition at Raindance Film Festival and has been singled out for praise by Hollywood heavyweights including *Die Hard* screenwriter Steven E. De Souza. Rush has also been nominated for Best Writer by the Horror Writers Association of America for her short film, *Plasmid*. You can follow Rush at roshnibhatia.com.

MAURICE BROADDUS: An accidental teacher (at the Oaks Academy Middle School), an accidental librarian (the School Library Manager as part of the IndyPL Shared System), and a purposeful community organizer (resident Afrofuturist at the Kheprw Institute), Maurice Broaddus' work has appeared in *Magazine of SF&F*, *Lightspeed Magazine*, *Beneath Ceaseless Skies*, *Asimov's*, and *Uncanny Magazine*, with some of his stories having been collected in *The Voices of Martyrs*. His novels include the urban fantasy trilogy *The Knights of Breton Court*, the steampunk novel *Pimp My Airship*, and the middle grade detective novel series *The Usual Suspects*. As an editor, he's worked on *Dark Faith*, *Fireside Magazine*, and *Apex Magazine*. His gaming work includes writing for the *Marvel Super-Heroes*, *Leverage*, and *Firefly* role-playing games, as well as working as a consultant on *Watch Dogs 2*. Learn more about him at mauricebroaddus.com.

LOUIS OZAWA stars opposite Al Pacino in Jordan Peele's Amazon series *Hunters*, and just wrapped a role in *Pachinko* (Apple) premiering later this year. Other television highlights include *Kidding* opposite Catherine Keener and Jim Carrey (Showtime), the iconic DC Comics character "Hat" in *Supergirl* (CW), *The Man in the High Castle* (Amazon), Robert Rodriguez's *El-Rey* series (Matador), the final season of *True Blood* and the Netflix series *Another Life*. Feature highlights include high-octane roles in *Predators* and *The Bourne Legacy*.

Once a Silicon Valley software engineer, **CURTIS C. CHEN** (陳致宇) now writes stories and runs puzzle games near Portland, Oregon. He's the author of the *Kangaroo* series of funny science fiction spy thrillers and has written for the

Serial Box original shows *Ninth Step Station*, *Machina*, and *Echo Park 2060* (forthcoming). Curtis's short stories have appeared in *Playboy* magazine, *Daily Science Fiction*, *Oregon Reads Aloud*, and elsewhere. His homebrew cat feeding robot was displayed in the "Worlds Beyond Here" exhibit at Seattle's Wing Luke Museum. Visit him online at CurtisCChen.com.

DELILAH S. DAWSON is the *New York Times* bestselling author of *Star Wars: Phasma* and *Galaxy's Edge: Black Spire*, as well as the Blud series, the Hit series, and the Shadow series (written as Lila Bowen), plus comics in the worlds of *Star Wars*, *Firefly*, *The X-Files Case Files*, *Rick and Morty*, *Adventure Time*, and *Labyrinth*. As a survivor of domestic violence and sexual assault, her stories most often focus on women, once victims, who are reclaiming their power. Website: delilahsdawson.com.

SEANAN MCGUIRE (writing as **MIRA GRANT**) is the *New York Times* bestselling author of more than a dozen books, all published within the last five years, which may explain why some people believe that she does not actually sleep. Her work has been translated into several languages, and resulted in her receiving a record five Hugo Award nominations on the 2013 ballot. When not writing, Seanan spends her time reading, watching terrible horror movies and too much television, visiting Disney Parks, and rating haunted corn mazes. You can keep up with Seanan at seananmcguire.com.

SUSANNE L. LAMBDIN is best known for writing the story for the *Star Trek: The Next Generation* episode "Family" (Season 4) and is the author of the *Dead Hearts* series, the *Realm of*

Magic trilogy and *Acropolis 3000: Genesis*. Find her online at susannelambdin.com.

JESS LANDRY is a Bram Stoker Award-winning author and produced screenwriter whose fiction has appeared in numerous anthologies. Her debut collection, *The Mother Wound*, is set for release in 2021, and her screen credits include four Movies of the Week, a sitcom, and her original horror feature, *My Only Sunshine*, which is currently in development, among other projects. Find Jess online at jesslandry.com.

E.C. MYERS was assembled in the U.S. from Korean and German parts and raised by a single mother and the public library in Yonkers, New York. His books include the Andre Norton Award-winning *Fair Coin*, *The Silence of Six*, *RWBY: After the Fall*, and *RWBY: Fairy Tales of Remnant*. His short fiction has appeared in magazines and anthologies such as *A Thousand Beginnings and Endings* and *Mother of Invention*, and he co-writes several series for Serial Box, including *Orphan Black: The Next Chapter* and *Alternis*. E.C. lives with his wife, son, and three doofy pets in Pennsylvania. Find him online at ecmyers.net.

YVONNE NAVARRO is a multi-genre author and artist. She has written numerous media tie-in novels, including *Elektra*, *Species*, *Species II*, *Aliens: Music of the Spears*, *Ultraviolet*, and the first *Hellboy*. Her most recent original tie-in novel was *Supernatural: The Usual Sacrifices*, published by Titan Books on June 27, 2017.

CHRIS RYALL is an award-winning writer/editor. He was most recently the President, Publisher and Chief Creative Officer at IDW Publishing, a publishing house where he spent the better part of the past sixteen years. He is also the comic-book editor of and Executive Producer on *Locke & Key*, currently streaming on Netflix. He is also the Eisner-nominated writer / co-creator of comic series including *Zombies vs Robots*, in development at Sony Pictures; *Groom Lake*; *The Colonized*; *The Hollows*; and more. In 2009, he co-authored a prose book about comics, *Comic Books 101*, and in 2020, formed Syzygy Publishing with artist Ashley Wood, and is currently producing new comic books and television series. Follow Chris online at worldofsyzygy.com.

STEVEN L. SEARS is a writer-producer who has worked on such shows as *Xena: Warrior Princess*, *The A-Team*, and many other hit series. Steven L. Sears' work has been lauded for diversity and inclusiveness, and he has appeared many times to be on panels and as a guest lecturer on the issue of pursuing and enhancing the presentation of diversity in media. From issues of race, sexual orientation, gender identification, and gender equality, his work and core beliefs have always pursued the idea of diversity enriching us all. Website: www. stevenlsears.com.

#1 *New York Times* bestselling author **SCOTT SIGLER** is the creator of nineteen novels, seven novellas, and dozens of short stories. He gives away his stories as weekly, serialized, audiobooks, with over 40 million episodes downloaded. Find Scott at scottsigler.com.